WONDER WO
SUPERM

THE DARK SPELL

WRITTEN BY
BOOK BANK PUBLISHING

BOOK BANK PUBLISHING

Copyright © 2023 Book Bank Publishing rights reserved. No part of this publication may be reproduced, distributed, or transmitted in any form or by any means, including photocopying, recording, or other electronic or mechanical methods, without the prior written permission of the publisher, except in the case of brief quotations embodied in reviews and certain other non-commercial uses permitted by copyright law.
ISBN: 9798858868750
ISBN-13: 979-8858868750

THE DARK SPELL

CONTENTS

CHAPTER 1: THE SPELL
    CHAPTER 2: TEMPTATION
    CHAPTER 3: SPIRITUALLY BOUND
    CHAPTER 4: CONTROL
    CHAPTER 5: GLIMPSE OF OUR FUTURE
    CHAPTER 6: ALL A WOMAN WANT AND NEED IN A MAN
    CHAPTER 7: MOMENTS IN PARADISE
    CHAPTER 8: LOVE'S REVEAL
    CHAPTER 9: LIKE HUSBAND AND WIFE
    CHAPTER 10: TO BE LOVED
    CHAPTER 11: CHERISHED, AND WORSHIPPED
    AUTHOR NOTE

BOOK BANK PUBLISHING

CHAPTER 1: THE SPELL

Oregan: Ecola State Park

Superman was currently facing off against Montari, Lord of an unknown dimension.

With a grunt, Montari lashed out at Superman, but he avoided his attack.

"You're quick, Kryptonian. Though, I am far superior."

Superman shrugged. "We'll see about that."

Montari had powers which allowed him the ability of insanely fast speed, and manifest blades from his hands. But not just any blades, they were full-fledged massive swords that were so powerful that they shook the earth every time they were brandished. With another grunt, Montari made the heavens split, and thunder and lightning crashed around, destroying the ground around him.

Wonder Woman, Shazam, Aquaman, Mera, and Flash were running their own racket fighting Montari's minions. Wonder Woman attacked Montari to help Superman.

"Astounding swordsmanship, Wonder Woman. But there are still imperfections needed to be perfected."

With a swipe of his hand, he narrowly missed the airborne Superman and Wonder Woman.

"I will take the Amazon as my new bride," he smirked. "You are quite the perfect courtesan. With you by my side to conquer many world, I will be even more envied by all!"

Wonder Woman looked at him with disgusted.

"I be damned if I let you touch her!" Superman shouted back over the storm, enraged with his eyes flaming red.

"Oh? Is she yours? All the more worth the taking."

Superman angrily lunged at Montari only to be stabbed in his shoulder. "Ah!"

"Superman!" Wonder Woman yelled.

"I got it! Stay back!" He yelled back using his heat vision to blast Montari in his face then punch him as hard as he could sending him flying into a boulder.

Wonder Woman flew to Superman.

"Kal, are you okay?"

He looked at her and smiled. "Yeah, I will be. It doesn't feel as bad as it looks. Let's finish this."

She nodded slightly.

"Die, Kryptonian!" Montari charged at Superman.

Using her lasso, Wonder Woman yanked Montari toward her and kicking him down back to the ground.

"Something's happening!" Shazam said.

Almost instantly the storm wavered as a portal was opening.

"What the hell is that?!"

Together, Superman and Wonder Woman smashed their fists into Montari's chest, causing him to grunt in pain and float back a few feet.

Green Lantern created a shield around the other leaguers as the minions were being sucked into the portal.

"What about Supes and Wondy?"

"They'll be fine."

"No!" Montari tried to hold on to the boulder to not get sucked into the portal.

"Looks like you're time is up, failed lord," Diana smirked as she and Superman was holding onto her lasso.

"You wench! I will kill the Kryptonian, you will be mine and you will obey!"

"Diana, don't listen to him!" Kal said. "That enough of you! Don't you ever disrespect her again!"

Using his heat vision once again, he blasted Montari into the portal.

"Kal! My lasso! It won't hold much longer!"

He wrapped his arm around her waist. "I'm not letting you go. We'll be okay."

Diana nodded.

THE DARK SPELL

Her lasso loosened, Kal held onto her as tight as he could as they were sucked into the portal and in an instant it was closed.

"It's done?" Arthur questioned.

"Wow...what a mess..." Barry said.

"Where is Clark and Diana?" Mera asked looking around.

Billy flew up to scan the area.

"Yo, Vic? Vic?"

"Vic here."

"We need Big Blue and Wondy's locations."

"...uh...I'm not picking up anything?"

"Dude! I thought you said they would be alright!" Billy said flying down and shoved Hal.

"Hey! Hey! Calm down, kid! They'll be fine...wherever they are."

Location: An Unknown Dark Realm

Diana groaned as she was waking up.

"Oh Gods..." she said feeling a bit nauseous and her head spinning.

She then felt movement beneath her and heard a deep groan.

"Di...Diana...?"

She gasped looking down to see she was on top of Kal. Kal was staring up at her in shock, his body was reacting instantly.

Diana gasped and blushed feeling his apparent erection.

"Oh Kal! I'm so sorry!"

She quickly got off of him as he sat up slowly.

"No, no...you're okay." He cupped her cheek. "Aren't you?" He asked looking into her eyes.

She nodded. "Your arm?"

"Healing slowly but surely." He looked around and saw that they were in a candle lit bedroom. "Where are we?"

"I'm not sure."

The large bedroom doors then opened. An older woman stood with a gracious smile. She had long flowing brown hair and hazel eyes. Though she wear a gown that was practically see through leaving nothing to the imagination.

"Ah, you are now awake. Empress will see you now. Follow me."

"Who are you?" Kal questioned with a frown.

"I am Juri. Please follow me."

Kal and Diana looked at each other, skeptical.

"No need to hesitate any longer, Kal-El, Diana. Empress has been awaiting for your arrival for quite some time."

Kal grabbed Diana's hand as they got up from the bed.

"Stay close to me," he whispered to her.

"I've got your back just as much as you have mine."

Juri smirked. "Cute," she said to herself.

Kal and Diana looked around. The walls covered with weaponry, ancient war paintings, and other abstract otherworldly things.

"Empress has some changes to make with this grand castle to be more pleasing. The previous occupant had such dreaded taste."

The large doors to the throne room opened.

To their surprise, the throne room was quite lavish, fit for an Empress. Large torches lit, all gold walls and floors with a long red velvet carpet that led up to the golden stair case and to her chair. Yet there was still a very dark aura around.

Juri bowed. "Empress Valeria, I present your very special guest, Kal-El of Krypton and Diana of Themyscira."

Valéria stood up from her chair. Auburn color hair, hazel eyes, and pale ivory skin. She wore a black leather bralette set featuring a multi-strapped neckline, spaghetti straps with O-ring accents, a cut-out back band with a hook and eye closure, a high waisted strappy garter belt with O-ring accents, adjustable garters, and a matching panty with cut-out panels and a thong cut back with gloves and thigh highs stiletto boots.

"Welcome, Diana, Kal-El. I am sure you are wondering why you are here."

Neither could utter a word.

"As my lovely confident, Juri, introduced, I am Valéria, once wife of Emperor Claudius."

"Emperor Claudius? You are Valéria Messalina?" Diana questioned.

"Yes, I am. You know of me, Princess of Themyscira?"

"I've been told tales."

"And what have you been told about me?"

THE DARK SPELL

"Lots of men perished of sudden death in a very peculiar way. But not just any men...the rich and powerful. It just so happen to be after sexual intercourse."

Kal looked at Diana surprised. "Wait a minute. Diana, are you saying she's-"

Valéria smiled. "Ah, yes, Kal-El.." Her bat wings, barbed tail and curled horns appeared. "A succubus."

Succubi have plagued men since Ancient Rome. Succubi are not the she-demons to be underestimated, powerful seductresses who loves nothing more than to toy with men, tantalizing them with their words as much as their bodies. They can be domineering and vengeful if they are slighted. Their cruel beauty has led emperors to commit the worst sins, feeding on the souls of these powerful men.

"What do you want from us?!"

"I wanted to finally properly thank you two for your help."

"Thank us...? For our help...?" Diana questioned.

"You see, the spell of my imprisonment was broken some time ago. I needed rejuvenation and shelter. By fate, I stumbled upon this castle. I played the role of the lost maiden waiting for my chance with the lord of this castle." Valéria flew to Kal and Diana. She observed and touched them...slowly...seductively. "I see now. Montari chose well."

A frail man, chained, came from the shadows.

Diana gasped. "Montari?! You drained him?"

"Weeks he planned for his attack on the mortal realm. The more he became motivated by his desires, the more I fed, though that wasn't enough. He had become much too tainted even for my tastes. So now he just serves as my lovely pet."

"And what do you want from us?"

"A deal. One that will benefit us all. I need to feed more but want something more dangerous yet pure. There has been something too powerful in the air, something strong, pure, that I never felt. Something that made me sick and hungry in every way."

Valeria casted a spell creating a magic circle upon the floor. Diana felt something on the back of her neck that sent a chill down her spine and rocked her to her core. She dropped to her knees as her body started to glow, her breathing was heavy and her heart rate escalating.

"Diana!" Kal couldn't move. It was as if his body was paralyzed. "What are you doing?! Stop!"

"Kal..." Diana breathed out slowly. Then let out an involuntary moan shocking herself and Kal.

She didn't know what was happening to her body. She felt flustered. Her skin becoming extremely tender.

"I've never experienced this level of power like the two of you." Valéria caressed Kal's cheek. "Look at her. Isn't she beautiful?"

"Stop! She's-"

"She's awakening her desire. Mental, emotional...even spiritual aphrodisiac effect. All her senses right now are very hypersensitive. All because of you, Kal-El. As both of you are connected."

"Wha-what do you mean?"

Diana sat back on her heels and threw her head back. She bit down on her lip, though, the biting doesn't help and the sensation is getting stronger.

Valeria made Kal sit on his knees in front of Diana.

"Look into her eyes, Kal-El. Don't you see? You both have deep desires that can no longer be restrained. No longer hidden away. Delicious..."

His own body naturally reacting to watching her.

Diana continued on with little breaths and moans, all the while her eyes locked with Kal's. The full force of the orgasm hit her hard. She whimpered before clamping her lips tight together to keep from saying anything further.

Diana doubled over, one hand on her left knee and the other wrapped around her middle, trying hard to keep her body from convulsing as tidal waves of unwanted pleasure ripped through her. A few moans escaped her mouth, despite desperately willing them not to, and to her horror she heard herself mutter his name twice, back to back.

Kal reached for her, touching her shoulder. Diana gasped as his simple touch made her reach an orgasm never seen before.

"Yes! Yes! Yes! Oh the taste of such pleasure of pure passion!"

THE DARK SPELL

As Diana leaned forward, Kal caught her in his arms. Her body was still so sensitive to his touch. She was trembling. Kal took off his cape, placing it gently over her shoulders.

She buried her head into his chest, unable to look him in the eyes, panting.

"Diana..."

He held her tighter as her body came down from its unintended high.

"I think she did overexert herself a bit but that was glorious..."

Kal looked up at Valeria with rage in his red glowing eyes.

"You exploiting her is glorious?!"

"Oh, Kal-El, you innocent man...I've given you...both of you, exactly what you wanted."

"Whatever you did to her. Don't ever do it again."

Valéria smirked. "It's out of my control now."

Kal narrowed his eyes. "What the hell do you mean, it's out of your control?!"

"It seems I have unlocked and activated something so much more extraordinary. Only you two have the control now. It's up to you to find your way."

"Way to what?"

Kal stood up carrying Diana. She had fallen asleep from exhaustion.

"She's in no pain, Kal-El. Only pleasure. Pleasure you gave her. Don't resist."

A portal opened.

"Time to go home, Kal-El. Until next time, which is very very soon."

"We aren't your play things like Montari has become."

"Oh no, of course not. You are much more valuable."

"Stay away from us," Kal warned as he flew through the portal.

Kal had made it through the portal back to Ecola State Park. At the moment, his mind was all over the place and Diana was still asleep.

He didn't want to go anywhere near the League right now, especially with what had just accord. He and Diana needed time for themselves to talk.

He decided the best place for them to be alone was the Fortress of Solitude.

Location: Fortress of Solitude

Kal gently laid Diana down on his bed. It was massive, as if two king sized beds were combined.

"Woof!" Krypto, Kal's alien dire would hound barked.

Kal quickly hoisted the dire wolf up and flew out of the room.

"Hey buddy. You have to be quiet for Diana. She's resting."

Krypto wimpered in worry for Diana.

"She's alright. Just-" He paused as flashes came to his mind. "She's just tired."

Kal got Krypto two frozen steaks, letting him heat it himself and tried to keep himself occupied until Diana woke up.

Sitting in his observatory, Kal all of a sudden winced feeling something burning on the back of his neck.

"What the hell?"

He could hear Diana's voice again in his mind. Moaning and calling out his name. More flashes more distinctive races through his mind.

"No, I...can't..."

He could feel his body once again reacting.

"Listen to her Kal-El."

"Get out of my head!"

"Listen to her heartbeat. The sound of her voice. You want her."

"Stop it. I won't indulge in your sick mind games."

"You want to show her you can be the man to give her the love and pleasure she deserves. That no other can nor ever will give her."

"I...no...this is..."

He leaned back into his chair, doing his best to calm the fire that was raging through his blood. He was already hard. He flung an arm across his face.

"Dammit!" Kal thought to himself, hoping to distract his body with something decidedly unsexy.

Deadlines...Work...Kryptonite...

He took a deep breath finally calming himself down.

"What the hell did she do to us? This isn't how it should be..."

Kal could hear Diana waking up. He quickly flew back to the room to be by her side.

THE DARK SPELL

Diana's eyes fluttered open. She gasped and sat up abruptly not recognizing the figure above her at first.

"Diana? Di...it's okay. It's just me."

"Kal?"

"Yeah...?"

"Where? We're in the fortress?"

"I didn't want to take you to the Tower if there would be any questions and I didn't want to wake you with going to your place. The fortress was the best option."

"How long have I been asleep?"

"About 3 hours maybe."

"Oh..."

There was a moment of awkward silence and tension was heavy between them.

"Diana."

"Kal."

They both called each other's names at the same time only to end up feeling so much more awkward. They tried to take a moment to let the other speak, but it wasn't working out.

"Umm sorry. You go first," Kal said.

"Well..." Diana tried to talk but all of a sudden, couldn't find the words.

"We don't have to talk about it now or just not at all."

"No...I...we have to." Diana sighed. "Kal, I've never been vulnerable with anyone before. Even unwillingly, to show that side of myself...I'm glad that it was you I was with."

"Diana, that's all I want to hear is that you still trust me, feel comfortable with me, and what we experienced won't make things awkward between us."

"Of course I still trust you. There's no questioning that ever. You're my best friend, Kal."

"Best friends...of course..."

"I hope that whatever trick Valéria played won't happen again. We aren't sex toys."

Kal raised his eye brows. "Yeah, that's...that's what she wanted us to be."

Another moment of silence.

"Thank you, Kal, for being so kind. I should go. You need just as much rest." Diana got up from the bed. "Your bed is quite comfortable and very soft."

"Oh...I'm glad you were comfortable..." Kal nervously cleared his throat.

"Woof! Woof!" Krypto barked happily flying toward Diana.

"No! Krypto! Down!"

Diana giggled as Krypto flew into her arms.

"Hello, fluffy boy! How are you?"

Kal shook his head. "Diana, you are only making it worse babying him."

"Oh, Kal, he is adorable. I can't help it."

Diana patted Krypto on his head. "I'm sorry, Krypto, but I have to go now."

Krypto whimpered as if pleading for Diana not to go.

"See, now you've done it. Spoiled him to a point of being a giant puppy."

Diana laughed softly.

Krypto then curdled himself on the bed. Diana smiled patting his head softly again.

"Bye Krypto...Kal."

Kal was a bit hesitant but then grabbed Diana's hand. He pulled her closer into an embrace. Diana tensed up a bit surprised but then relaxed into his embrace, wrapping her arms around his neck. She let out a soft sigh closing her eyes.

The feel of each others body, so warm. Diana was enjoying being held close to him. It was as if the two were in their own little world.

Slowly pulling away, Kal kissed her forehead.

"We'll talk later."

Diana nodded and reached up to place a soft kiss on his cheek.

Kal watched her as she flew off.

Location: Valéria's Castle

Valeria crossed her legs and leaned back sitting on her throne as she sipped wine.

"Are you going to continue to pout? Or thank me for moving things along?"

THE DARK SPELL

Eros, the God of Love, pulled out his gun and pointed it directly in the center of Valeria's forehead.

"You dare play with the emotions of my cousin and the Kryptonian? You do not know of the power of their connection."

"Calm down, loverboy, I know exactly the power it holds. That's why I want it. But I won't be too greedy. This is much too pure...too sacred. However..."

"However, what?" Eros glared.

"They weren't quite ready for their truth to be revealed. I unlocked so much more than intended."

"And? What does that mean, you conniving succubus?!"

"Well...given that I am who I am as a succubus, I unlocked the power with my own, of course, and with mine intertwined..."

"Succubus aphrodisiac effect. You will taint them!"

"No. If they continue to resist, it will be tainted. If they act upon only lust and temptation, it will be tainted. Though, I believe the lovers will find their way. It will be a very pleasurable journey."

Eros sighed. "I warn you now. If this union is destroyed because of your lewd antics, you will have to answer to the Gods."

Valeria smirked. "Relax, Eros. Why don't you stay for just a little while longer with me and the others?"

"I don't think so." Eros quickly disappeared.

Valeria shrugged. "You're lose...my gain."

Location: London, Diana Prince's condominium

It's late. Diana was still so tired, and she needed more sleep. But for some reason or another, she couldn't.

She turned on the shower water, undressed and glance at herself in the mirror. She sighed. She shouldn't think of him nor what occurred.

She sighed again as she stepped into the steaming hot shower. She ran her hands from her breasts down her bare skinned voluptuous figure to her inner thighs and rubbed on them slowly. She then reached out with her right hand and picked up a nearby bottle of body wash and slowly poured out the sweet smelling liquid all over herself. It ran and dripped down every inch of her beautiful sexy body from her head to her toes.

"Gods..." she gasped as she felt the same sensation from before on the back of her neck.

Her body instantly started to react as she said his name.

"Kal...No...I...shouldn't."

She closed her eyes and let out a moan as her body became hypersensitive to the feel of the water.

"Stop...Get out of my head!"

Thoughts of him flooded her mind and a hot flush spread upon her cheeks that made her bite her lip.

"Princess Diana, give in to your desire. Feel his touch. Listen to his voice."

She reveled in the sudden memory of his touch. How he held her so closely, so tight. The feel of his warm strong body so protective.

"Don't resist..."

Diana groaned, teetering on the edge of her climax.

Her heart was pounding and she was breathing hard.

"Say his name."

"I...oh...Gods..."

"Call for him, Diana."

"No...I..." she gasped. "Kal!"

Back at the fortress, Kal was lying in bed. He couldn't help but to revel in the lingering scent of Diana on his pillow. The smell of exotic grapefruit and sea salt.

"KAL!"

His eyes shot open to her voice. "Diana?" He questioned looking around but she wasn't there at all. He sighed and shook his head. "It's all in my mind."

He got up to take a cold shower.

"Say her name."

"Say his name."

Even with the water on the coldest temperature of -55 degrees, it wasn't enough. His hands pressed firmly against the shower wall with the water running down his back. The icily sensation should be numbing him emotionally, waking him mentally, and punishing him physically but it

THE DARK SPELL

wasn't working. He could still hear her voice, smell her scent and feel her soft curvaceous body.

Without a coherent thought, he groaned inwardly even as he stood motionless.

"Diana..."

"Kal-El..."

She could feel wave after wave of wondrous sensual pleasure moving up her spine and explode inside her mind like a thousand tiny fire crackers!

"Ahh!" The alluring naked Goddess cried out.

Diana stood there for a few minutes under the warm spray of the shower coming down from her high.

She then turned off the shower and stepped out through its glass door and wrapped a large soft red towel around herself. She was still dripping wet and all hot and steamy from her shower.

After drying herself off completely, Diana left her towel on the edge of her bed and slip under her sheets still completely naked. She curled her body, holding her pillow close.

Kal laid on his bed with his towel still wrapped around him. She's still there. No matter what he tried to do, he was consumed in the thoughts and feeling of Diana.

Being best friends and colleagues, knowing the risk they'd be taking if they did try to get involved with one another, Kal and Diana really thought they were adept at controlling and ignoring those feelings. They'd managed to do just that for so long now. So impossibly long, much longer than humanly possible, in fact. But then again, they were anything but human. However, no one, not even super powered beings as strong willed as Kal and Diana could fully resist their temptation for one another. It has always lingered, playing at the back of their mind, teasing and taunting and oh so sinfully seductive that no matter how hard they tried to resist, the craving and pure need never failed to overwhelmed them completely.

That familiar burning ache twisted through their veins, blood alight with fire so overpowering and intense that their hands shook uncontrollably, piercing eyes dilated. Never had they felt the craving take hold with such power. They had to gain control back.

Following Day: WatchTower

Kal and Diana sat face to face in the briefing room with the other members. After dodging questions about where they ended up and what happened after they were sucked into the portal.

"We can assure, Montari is no longer a threat," Diana said.

"Great...but how did you guys get out?"

"There was a woman. She didn't give us much detail of who she was but she knew who we were and let us come home," Kal said trying to sound convincing.

Batman narrowed his eyes a bit skeptical.

"Well that was...convenient I guess. Glad you guys are back!" Shazam said.

"Moving on..." Batman said.

Kal and Diana were barely paying attention to what was being said only focused on each other.

It was such a dangerous temptation, and it was a little more than torturing for them. Soon, they'd have to avert their gaze soon, or move away. There was only so much visual stimulation they could take before falling prey to triggering their urges.

Diana could feel the sensation brewing yet again. She crossed her legs and let out a quiet sigh, rubbing her neck. Kal watched her every move. To trace his tongue over the warm skin, feel the heartbeat beneath his lips, to bite down hard and drink her.

Diana caught sight of Kal as his mouth parted almost unwillingly and his tongue darting out to wet his bottom lip. Gods, he was so sexy, sitting there. The muscles in his arm, flexing so deliciously. She can just imagine other muscles flexing under his suit.

After the meeting, Kal and Diana stayed behind.

"Do you have a moment for us to talk, Diana?"

"Yes."

Kal's feet moved before he even realised what he was doing, blinded by the haze of pure undiluted yearning his entire body felt, drawn to the luxurious woman standing on the other side of the table like a moth to flame. He was completely powerless when it came to Diana, his ocean blue eyes now an unearthly shade of electric blue, glinting viciously. Diana can hear his breathing getting heavier.

THE DARK SPELL

"What's wrong, Kal?" Diana asked with a worried look.

Kal lurched to a halt directly in front of her, his gaze hungrily roamed over every single tiny detail of her face. Her beautiful red luscious lips, piercing cerulean blue eyes, her expression so innocent, sweet, sexy and seductive all at once.

This was like going through a drug withdrawal! He needed her, craved her more than the air he was breathing, his skin crawling as the lust and thirst pumped around his system with every beat of his heart. She smelled delicious of a lavender and jasmine soft scent.

With one trembling hand, Kal reached out and smoothed his fingers gently through her long soft raven hair, relishing in the feeling of being wrapped around his fingers. One side of his mouth quirked upwards into a small indulgent smile as he ran his hand down the side of Diana's face, his fingertips ghosting over her soft flesh. A gentle sigh left Diana's lips before she could restrain it.

"When you left from the fortress last night I...I couldn't stop thinking about what happened. Not in a weird...way...but I just..." he sighed. "I'm sorry, Di. I just want to make sure you are okay. That we are okay."

She can hear his breathing getting heavier.

"No need to apologize, Kal. I couldn't stop thinking about it either. That wasn't the kind of experience we could have ever expected. It's going to take some time for both of us to understand and get over this...feeling."

"That's...that's all I wanted to tell you and to know from you. Like I said last night, I don't want things awkward between us."

"It's not and it won't be," she smiled reassuringly. "We have a lot of work to get back to. Maybe it'll help move our minds away from all of this."

"Right...yeah..."

Diana frowned slightly seeing Kal's expression changed to what seemed to be a little disappointment?

"Is there something else bothering you?" She asked.

"Um... no...no."

She cupped his cheek. "Are you sure?"

"Yeah...yeah..."

Diana smiled and kissed his cheek.

Kal sighed and hugged her into his strong warm body.

Diana pushed herself more against him and his arms tightened around her. Her eyes widen a bit in surprise, noticing that she could feel something hard against her. Oh gods, she knew exactly just what it was.

There's that urge again tempting to get her to lose control. They should let go. But for some reason, they couldn't. Not just yet.

Kal let out a very low groan as Diana moved a bit as if intentionally grinding on him. She lifted her head from his shoulder to look at him. His eyes are hooded and his lips parted. He looks so incredibly sexy right now.

Suddenly they both jumped slightly to the sound of someone clearing their throat loudly. They turned their heads to the direction of the door to see Batman.

They pulled away from their embrace, blushing.

"Bruce?" Kal questioned.

"If you two can take a moment from your tryst...need to speak with Clark?"

Diana rolled her eyes and shook her head. "No need for the stand-offish attitude, Bruce."

"Hm."

Diana raised her brow and sighed. She then turned back to Kal.

"We can catch back up later, ok?"

"Ok."

Diana smiled and kissed his cheek again.

Kal couldn't take his eyes off of her as she walked out of the room and he still stared at the door even when it closed.

"Clark? Clark!"

"What? What is it, Bruce?" he asked annoyed.

"You and Diana have been acting odd all day. What happened? Where were you two? I find it very hard to believe you two got back so easily."

Kal sighed. "All that matters is that we are back. Everything else is between me and Diana."

Bruce narrowed his eyes. "What are you hiding, Clark?"

"Nothing, Bruce! Dammit! Would you just drop it?!"

"Not when it could possibly effect the team, No."

"Well it's not. Like I said, it's between me and Diana."

"And what is between you and Diana?"

THE DARK SPELL

Kal gave him an irritated look then sighed. "Bruce, you know how I feel about Diana and you know how complicated it is."

"That's why you shouldn't be crossing the line."

"We haven't. But even if we did, it would be our choice. We are focused on our missions, Bruce. That doesn't mean we can't have a life outside of all of this. I don't know if Diana and I will ever be more than friends. I want to be and I know the risks. I'm willing to take my chances with her."

Bruce was silent.

"It doesn't matter anyway. It would ultimately be of Diana's choice and how she feels."

"You two need to work whatever this is out."

"There's nothing to work out. Diana and I have our priorities." Kal paused for a moment. "Your priority is Gotham. You're needed back now. Something's happening at the docks. Sal Maroni."

Bruce narrowed his eyes again as Kal walked out.

"That's all this is. Playing on our emotions but it can never be anything else," Kal said to himself.

As like last night, home alone, Kal and Diana tried not to give into the effect. The back of their necks burning, their minds racing, their entire bodies reacting to the overwhelming sexual craving.

CHAPTER 2: TEMPTATION

Next Day Afternoon: Boston University

Diana Prince quietly walked into Julia Kapatelis' class for her lecture. She needed the distraction from thinking about Kal.

But no matter how hard she tried listening, her mind drifted off. He was so damn perfect, just for her.

Her cheeks flamed with embarrassment and heat started to radiate from her body from the mere thought of him being so close. He was so godly handsome. He exuded strength, power, and brash attitude but he was still so humbled and kind. She thought about his well-defined chest and biceps and jet black hair that's sometimes messy with his adorable S-curl. Those ocean blue eyes, she loved to get lost in when they are in deep conversation. When he smiled, he smiled with all of his face with crinkles in his eyes and dimples in his cheeks. His deep voice sent shivers down her spine, so assertive yet so gentle and soothing.

When she thought more about all his features, she started to feel the affect again. She felt suddenly so hot and lustful.

She took a deep breath trying to remain calm.

Meanwhile, Daily Planet

Clark Kent was in the break room making himself a cup of coffee when Cat Grant walked in.

She smirked and looked down checking and adjusting her cleavage for Clark to notice. She's had a major crush on Clark ever since they met.

"Well...hello there, Clarkie! Need a little "pick me up", she teased.

"Hi, Cat. Uh...little bit."

She walked closer to him. "Must be a big story."

"It's a bit...personal."

Cat titled her head. "Aww...Clarkie, what's wrong?" She learned closer to him pressing her breasts against his arm. "I can help take some things off your mind."

"Thanks for the offer... but I..."
"You're involved with someone and didn't tell me?"
"I'm not involved with anyone. At least... um...not yet."
"Who is she? Do I know her? Met her before?"
"Well...you've probably heard of her at least."
Cat thought for a moment but no one was coming to mind.
"Just tell me."
"Diana Prince."
"Diana Prince?" she thought again for a moment. "Wait..." she giggled a bit. "You mean the girl that looks like she should be a model or some high class actress instead of an university assistant and ambassador?"

Clark quirked his brow. "Yes...her. Was that a back handed compliment?"

Cat shrugged. "I mean she just doesn't look like an ordinary kind of girl."

"She isn't."

"You aren't ordinary either, Clark..." she said squeezing his arm. "What average male reporter has muscles like this?"

"Sports and growing up on a farm."

"Hmm...what wonders that has done. Let me tell you, Clark, I'm being honest. I think she's out of your league."

"What?!"

"Isn't that what you believe? She needs more than even you? Superman?"

"What?!" Clark's heart dropped. "Cat, I don't know..." He paused looking into her eyes. "Valéria?!"

She smiled. "Hello, Kal-El."

"What the hell are you doing?! Cat doesn't know who I am."

"Relax. She's stuck in the moment of fantasizing about you and believing she is still flirting anyway so she doesn't know any difference."

Clark let out a slight sigh of relief but then frowned.

"I told you to stay away from us."

"Given who I am, I don't do as told. Especially not by a man. If you were anyone else, I would've killed you but like I told you, you and your Amazon interest me and are too much of value."

THE DARK SPELL

"What do you want?"

"You're holding back. That's no good for any of us."

"It's not good for you?"

"Because of our deal, it involves you and Diana."

"We never agreed to any deal!"

"Maybe not by your own will but your desires were unlocked and the deal was made. Resisting triggers my effect." She cupped his cheek. "But it's so much more than that. You feel it, don't you? When you touch the Amazon, you feel the connection. You want more of her."

"Diana is my best friend. I respect her as my partner and colleague. That's all it can be."

Valéria rolled her eyes.

"Poor boy. You've pretended all your child life, now you are trying to pretend your feelings for the Amazon is nothing more. This isn't something you can ignore any longer, Kal-El. How would you feel if another man made her feel what you do? Will you be the man Diana knows you to be or will you continue to cower?"

"I want Diana to be happy and to have everything she deserves and more."

Valéria smiled seeing the truth in his eyes.

"Then it shall be, Kal-El. But remember, if it is to be another man, that is the path you help choose."

"I don't-"

"So like I was saying, Clarkie, you need to show off more of these sexy guns and show the wild side I know you have."

"Cat?"

"Huh...Yes, Clarkie?"

Clark shook his head slightly. "I hear what you're saying. I have to go."

"Wait, where are you going?"

"Need to follow up on a story."

"Oh...well alright. Talk tomorrow, I guess."

Clark nodded slightly. "Yeah...see ya tomorrow."

Clark quickly went back to his desk to pack up his things.

"Why in a rush, Smallville?" Lois Lane asked.

"Probably a date," Jimmy Olsen teased.

"Smallville having a date? Highly doubt that."

Clark didn't say anything, just walked passed them to the elevator.

"I think you hurt his feelings, Lois."

"He's a grown ass man. He'll get over it."

Location: Boston University

"Diana? Diana?"

"Oh? Julia...I'm sorry."

Diana stood up from her desk gathering her papers.

"Are you okay, Diana?"

"Yes, just tired from the pass two days."

"How is Clark?"

Diana paused for a moment as her heart jumped.

"He's fine. What made you ask about him?"

"Well you are spending more time with him."

Diana blushed. "Julia, we are just friends. But I do like his company."

Julia smiled. "It seems to me, he has the potential to be more than a friend."

"I don't know. That's a drastic step that will change so much so fast. And the League-"

"What about the League? It's not their decision, Diana. It's between you and Clark."

"Julia, it's still very complicated."

"Is it? Or are you making it seem so just to justify trying to deny or push your feelings away."

Diana sighed. "I never thought I would be in a situation like this. Coming to man's world, my heart and mind was only set on work."

"Well life takes different turns. Not everything will go the way you believe it should or want. But this I believe can go the way you want it to. Just go for it."

Diana smiled. "Thank you, Julia. It's still going to take some time but...I'll see where things go."

Later: WatchTower

"Max level, Supes," Cyborg said.

Superman had been in the training simulation for hours trying yet again to distract himself.

THE DARK SPELL

There was an immediate hum of resignation as the auto guns powered down, the barrels of which limply touched ground.

"Sorry about that, Vic."

"It's cool. Helped me out a bit, actually. Always looking for what's needed to be upgraded."

"I'll bring in some new tech from the fortress."

"Cool! I'm heading out. See ya!"

"In the mean time, how about we go a couple of rounds, Kal?"

He turned to see Diana at the door. "Hey, Diana."

She smiled. "Hey."

"So sparring?"

"You are a little slow with your reaction timing."

"Really?" He laughed nervously.

"You seem distracted. I told you about that."

He smirked. "I can't deny. I have been distracted."

"About...Valéria?"

Kal was silent.

"I see. Well...it seems we both need the distraction."

They circled each other for a moment, sizing their each other up. Kal watched her closely, his blue gaze predatory as he took in every quiver and twitch of her body. Diana was equally attentive, eyes raking over his muscles, rippling under his suit, a visual testimony to his prowess, watching and waiting for telltale signs that he was about to charge forward.

When she saw his eyes slip down to the swell of her breasts, she struck and launched herself at him.

She watched the fluid swing of his arms to block her attack.

There was something about the way they moved together that fueled the fire between the two of them.

She could hear him panting, his feet moving a bit as he pressed his heels into the ground to keep his balance.

"Are you giving in so easily?" Diana asked with amusement as she took her stance and bent her knees, holding her firsts up in front of her to defend herself.

"Not at all. Going easy is never our thing," Kal smiled slyly.

It happened in a matter of seconds. She ran at him and began swiping her fists at him, hitting into his arm as he moved his arms, blocking her.

Her eyes narrowed as she dipped down and swung her leg across his ankles, making him fall back before he was hopping back onto his feet. He dodged her once more before taking her arm and swinging her over his head, hitting her back on the floor. He looked down at her and grinned. She raised her brow, pushing up at him with a fiery swing.

Kal jumped back easily and landed on his feet.

She took another swing at him. He grabbed her fist in his palm and pushed her back, trying to make her stumble on her feet.

"Better..." she said softly.

They continued their dance, fighting for dominance, retreating then advancing, each step countered by the other. Diana couldn't deny the flush to her cheeks, nor the aching burn deep between her thighs weren't completely from exhilaration of the fight. Whenever they approached each other, bodies wound taut, quivering from exertion, the deep masculine scent of him enveloped her. And each time he retreated she wanted more.

Every so often a grunt escaped his lips, and the sound carried straight through her. Diana loved fighting with him. His usual careful control, so dutifully cultivated to give the air of authority and command, fell away, unleashing something primal, instinctive. Perhaps it was the adrenaline of the fight, or the anticipation of coming together, but the air around them was sexually charged.

Before Diana could track what happened, Kal had spun them, knocking her onto the floor and landing on top of her. She gasped as the hard, solid weight of him settled between her legs, and something even harder ground into her aching heat, sending a jolt of pleasure rippling her and making her body clench in release.

She was breathing just as hard as he was, her chest heaving as he loomed over her. Time seemed to freeze as they stared at each other. His eyes dark, and a few errant curls hung over his forehead as he regarded her, trying to decide, perhaps, if he'd really felt what he thought he'd felt. Taking a gambled that their fight had left him just as wanting as it had her, Diana flexed her thighs enough for him to feel. His member throbbed against her in response.

THE DARK SPELL

As if coming to his senses, Kal eased up off of her. Diana wasn't sure if the rolling of his hips against her aching sex just enough to leave her wanting more was on purpose, but she definitely had to bit her lip to stifle a moan. Kal offered her his hand.

"I guess I am at my best with you" he said, his voice husky, his fingers lingering against hers. "I mean, better concentration."

Diana smiled, the tone of his voice sending more flutters of excitement through her.

"That last move did take me completely off guard," she purred, still high on the afterglow of his body pressed against hers. "You have definitely perfected pinning me down. I can't let just any man on top of me like that."

There was that cocky grin again as his eyes lingered across her form. Diana glanced down, eyeing the very prominent bulge.

"I should go now. Shower."

She dared to look up at him, anticipation coiling hot in her stomach at the look he was giving her, at the way his teeth scrapped over his bottom lip, considering her words. Finally, he nodded.

Her heart pounded turning away from him to walk out of the training room.

Location: Wonder Woman's Quarters

As the time was going by, she became more affected by his presence. That burning sensation on the back of her neck once again. So many fantasies she had in mind as they were sparring. Having him pin her down, tower over her...

"Gods..."

Her body was reacting again becoming ever so hypersensitive to the steaming hot water. She let the water drip down her neck and massage her shoulders, then the length of her arms.

Kal walked down the quarters hall, going to his room. But then as he stood at his door, he turned to the door with Wonder Woman's emblem.

He sighed and smiled to himself walking over to her door.

"Athena's Wisdom," he whispered and the door slid open.

He stepped in. The door closed behind him. He could hear the shower going and she has probably only been in for about 5 minutes so now would be a good time to join her.

Diana was so lost in her thoughts and how good the water felt, she didn't hear the door open and the sound of another's clothing hitting the floor outside the shower door.

She reached for the bottle of body wash only to come up empty handed. She frowned until she felt someone standing behind her and gasped. That sweet scented body wash was being poured down her back and a chuckle sounding right into her ear.

"You didn't mind if I joined in did you?" Kal solicited, his voice so deliciously hoarse.

"What are you-...?"

She froze. Honestly she never knew he would be this bold to literally come into the shower with her naked. While he waited for her answer, he lathered the soap up in his hands forgetting the towel all together and massaging her shoulder blades.

"Oh...Gods..." she let out a soft moan and her eyes fluttered closed.

Diana unable to speak just nodded her head and closed her eyes. She felt her knees grow weak and although she still stood firmly, there was no guarantee it would be for long. Testing her ability even further, Kal moved Diana's long raven hair aside, planting gentle lips on the back of her neck, feathering further kisses down her spine before latching onto the spot just under her ear eagerly, nipping at her flesh. Kal lapped his tongue at her earlobe forcing her to sink back into his chest. He wanted to see her face right now, give him the sweet satisfaction that he was doing right. But she remained silent as he continued to smooth soap down her stomach, waist and hips. Diana shivered pleasantly while Kal continued getting handsy, tilting her head to give him more access.

Tracing her frame as though to memorise, Kal steered his hands over her hips, leisurely up her waist and inched forward to massage her breasts with meticulous care, moving in small circles. She visibly flinched as if a shock went through her, tensing up even more. Fingers fondled her erect nipples, a few pinches here and there to excite her more down below.

"Kal..."

The way his breathing stuttered and grew heavy merely touching her, ignited searing warmth to travel below as Diana slipped a moan.

THE DARK SPELL

Kal growled softly, tracing his mouth down the column of her neck, feeling her rabbiting pulse.

Diana loved the feeling of the hot water cascading down her body and Kal's hands massaging all over her, all thoughts of showering lost in the lusty haze.

His hands still on her soft mounds, kneading each one, pinching the perky nipples earning another moan.

He'd wanted to kiss Diana so many times before, but he just couldn't bring himself to do it, because he knew for a fact that he wouldn't have been able to resist the temptation to throw her down on the nearest available surface and ravish her right there and then. But now what was there to stop him? It was just so enticing... so wickedly tempting...

Just as the thought left his mind, the curvaceous woman turned around to stare directly into his eyes. She has a look of confusion and lust. Diana allowed the water to run off her face and drip off her nose, taking in the sight before her of the handsome man that has twined around her heart. Dropping her gaze onto his chest, she marveled his sculpted body. Such defined structure to his abs. She quickly glanced at his manhood taking in the size. A gifted god in his own right.

Kal allowed her to examine him. However, he was still very nervous to be doing something like this and not letting her be aware of it first. He took in her full rounded breasts, curvaceous figure and the sexiest ass he had ever seen in his life. Waiting for her to meet his eyes again, Kal smoothed his soapy hands down her sides.

Diana trailed back up to stare back in his eyes and the flicker of flames in her eyes making his member jerk. Kal's intense unblinking gaze held her captive just as easily as his hands and pulled her close until the tips of her breasts brushed against his flushed chest.

Making the first act of passion for once, Diana stood up on her tip toes and crashing her lips to meet his slick ones. Her arms formed binds around his neck, weight pushing him back against the tile wall. Kal groaned from the impact. Soft and innocent, his hands slid through her thoroughly soaked hair that seemed to trail a mile down her back and Diana gave into the urge to sift through his wet hair, marveling in how soft it really was.

Kissing wildly between the joined ragged breathing, Diana felt Kal stir against her inner thigh with a coaxing prod. Kal relished the sensation and the quiet little sighs Diana spilled. With his tongue teasing the seam of her mouth, the feel of his talented kisses felt so sinfully pleasant, she ached to touch him, snaking hands up to rest on his soaked chest as the water continued flowing down upon them. Holding the kiss longer than intended, twisting in slow growing passion and listening to his husky groans, Diana finally broke away regaining her function to breathe whilst she held Kal's entranced gaze.

The world beyond them felt non-existent that she had to question whether this was real or merely a figment of a dream Diana hadn't yet woke from. As Kal's hands continued gliding delicately across her skin, leaving a trail of foam over the vast curves of her body, Diana studied Kal again in fascination, heart hammering and breath hitching as he intentionally slowed his movements surrounding her firm breasts and flat stomach. Steamy rivulets rushing down her front while Kal remained concentrated on her frame, unable to pry his eyes away, parted her lips in silent gasps. The realization of how she was further presented so openly to him right here, spurred a forbidden thrill in her.

While Kal kept trying to wash her, Diana ran her fingers down his chest, Diana's hands continued exploration, dancing along the planes of his shoulders to slide down his arms and then ripple amid the muscles of his chest and stomach.

She would never tire of the chance to study him in this way, eyes closed and lips searching within his as her hands followed suit externally down to his hard length and slowly began stroking it lightly.

Kal's teasing stopped as pleasure surged through his body. Diana seeing this, found a rhythm and started stroking continually. Kal closed his eyes and groaned at the feeling. Her hands knew exactly how to make him feel so good.

"Di..." he groaned out panting slightly.

Diana looked up with a smirk of her own. With half lidded eyes, he saw the lust filled gaze she was giving him.

Stars is what he started to see. A sensation that he never felt made hands quiver along her skin, teeth bared and mouth agape. She didn't stop

THE DARK SPELL

moving her hand in a jerking motion. Letting out a small moan of pleasure, Kal felt his manhood harden even more under her hand. For the love of god he was suppose to be washing her, giving her pleasure.

"We shouldn't do this," he breathed out.

"No...we shouldn't," she answer and slightly grind against him.

Kal let out a louder groan and pressed Diana tighter against him. She whimpered quietly into his ear.

"We can't stop."

"We should really not do this."

Their voices were low and so full of pleasure, not sounding very convincing when they try to say that they couldn't do this.

Diana whimpered again at the predatory look in Kal's eyes.

"Tell me we shouldn't do this," he pleads, but Diana hears the exact opposite.

There was no rational thought left in their minds now. Nothing but lust and insatiable thirst for each other clouding their ability to think. They were too far gone now, and there was no turning back. It was much too late to stop this now.

Kal graced Diana with a smile so soft and warm that she wanted to taste it, feeling it flow into her with a tilt of her head in a simple request he willingly granted. He did not disappoint as she felt the press of his lips on hers, the sensual sweep of his tongue flicking over the water there, the slide of his hands to hold her even closer by the small of her back.

Diana moaned unabashedly. Their combined taste was just so addictive. They were gladly getting lost in their kiss for the rest of eternity if they could.

Kal reluctantly tore himself away from her lips and both panted for breath, chests rising and falling rapidly. Hearts beating faster. Diana was shaking uncontrollably, her eyelids flickering over her dilated eyes unbelievably fast as she gasped air, crushing their lips together once again.

This kiss was even better than the first. Sharing it, both savouring it, moaning and panting against each other's lips like their lives literally depended on it.

Kal's fingers were entwined in Diana's hair as he tilted her head whichever way deepened the kiss the most. The two continued to explore one another's mouth and being so into the passion as Kal pushed her into the wall. His hands were now massaging her breasts once again. Diana gasped again and pulled from the kiss panting as kissing down her neck to her chest. He licked and sucked a nipple in his mouth and used his other hand to massage it's twin. Diana arched her back in pleasure.

"Ohh," she moaned out.

Diana brought her hands up to Kal's hair as she laid her head back against the wall behind her and felt Kal circling his tongue around the rock hard nipple before he released it and moved to give the other the same treatment. Diana moaned as Kal kissed back up to her mouth and brought their lips together in a heated kiss.

Finding the sensations stimulating, a trembled sigh passed her lips while Kal appeared almost mesmerised, steady coated hands continuing south around her curved ass indulgently.

Diana tried to hold back but unfortunately it was all in vain with Kal groping her. She moaned out very loudly.

She threw her head back as Kal moved his left hand to her womanhood. His mouth started sucking and kissing all over her neck causing her moans to become louder. He teased her clit with his finger and teasing her entrance with another making pleasure surge through her body.

"I...Ahh!"

She looked up to him then, and her eyes seemed to fill him, and the excitement consumed him with the invitation he found in them. Immediately he shoved his finger into her slick heat with ease, delighting in the panting tone of her breath. Kal looked into her pleading eyes as her insistently high-pitched noises crescendoed.

"Oh please!" she begged, feeling the desperate willingness overwhelm her.

Kal brought their lips back together, kissing her again with more fervor as he began to pump his finger in and out of Diana and could feel her moving her hips with his motion. He added another finger and Diana gasped into his mouth before throwing her head back against the tile behind her. Kal smirked at that and placed his thumb to her clit lightly as he pressed his lips against her neck.

"Mmm. Kal..."

THE DARK SPELL

With an arrogant smile at his name being moaned out and circled his thumb as he continued to pump his fingers into Diana gently, watching her shiver in delight.

Diana brought her head back up and opened her eyes to gaze into the blue eyes in front of her. Kal quickened his motions as he watched Diana bite her lip and screw her eyes closed.

"Oh Gods!" She screamed out.

"Diana..." He breathed quietly.

She whimpered, bucking her hips forward as the friction of his thumb and fingers made her become even wetter than she was.

Diana groaned again and Kal felt her body tense and her walls clenched tightly around his fingers.

"AHH! HAH! HAH! AHH! Kal!" Diana felt strange and could feel her body want more of him. She was breathing heavily.

He continued moving until Diana came down from her high.

Finally, Kal pulled back his fingers as he captured her lips in a passionate kiss.

He then trailed from her lips, to her neck then further, stopping to pay special attention to her breasts once more before continuing his path downwards. Slowly, he kneeled down, kissing her stomach then hooked her right leg over his shoulder. He kissed and licked up her inner thighs, slowly teasing his way close to her center.

Diana gasped as Kal placed a kiss right above where Diana needed him and smirked up at her. Kal leaned forward and ran his tongue lightly to Diana's clit. Diana let out a noise, Kal knew he'd never heard that was so beautiful before.

Her back arched higher and involuntarily closed her eyes. Her head hit the wall hard as it rolled back. One of her hands fumbled in front of her until it found itself tangled in dark locks, holding herself steady. She moaned out his name and tightened her grip on his head pushing it further into her womanhood. Kal chuckled and inserted his tongue into her core making her almost scream in pleasure. He licked all around her folds making her even more wet.

"Kal... Yes... that's..." she started but interrupted herself with a loud moan. "MMMMM!"

Kal showed no restraint with her on this, taking notice how his tongue affected Diana. He trailed his fingers up the inside of Diana's leg to push two of them into her without warning. Diana jumped as she moaned unsteadily, taken by surprise. He looked up at her continued to work his tongue along with his fingers. Diana's hips bucked against his face.

"Kal...I...oh...!,"

He grinned into his work and nipped lightly at her clit hearing her moan again, doubling his efforts with his fingers.

Diana shivered as the throbbing between her legs intensified. Kal felt how Diana was climbing higher, reaching for her release. She was shaking, holding herself upright becoming a harder task. She bit her bottom lip as she moaned, feeling her walls tighten.

Many emotions overflowing her. She then placed her left hand over her mouth and tried to suppress the sound of her hot wet moaning as a flood of ecstasy crashed over her like a title wave. She didn't want anyone in the tower to hear her.

Kal sucked hard and bit lightly and felt Diana come undone. He continued his movements until Diana couldn't think again and stood to press his mouth thirstily to her own. Kal's fingers rubbed over her aching folds, circling her clit gently. He felt the wetness on his fingers, knowing it had not been the shower that had caused it.

"Kal," Diana tried to keep her voice steady, but she could not completely hide the riveting flood of eagerness.

After giving her another moment to come back down from her post-orgasmic haze, Kal pressed his mouth to her neck affectionately.

Leaving the shower, he turned off the shower and grabbed towels drying himself and Diana.

Kal picked her up carrying her to the bed. Diana was absolutely exhausted from her multiple orgasms.

The following moments were serene, peaceful. The pleased look in her eyes and smile were enough to fulfill him forever, he thought, and gently he held her in his arms. She pressed her head against his chest, and together they felt the humming sensation flow through them, becoming one without being in each other—through nothing more than fondness for

THE DARK SPELL

the other. His fingers moved down the curve of her back, and she stroked the back of his neck until they both fell asleep.

The next morning...

Diana had awoken, feeling for Kal to be right next to her. When she felt the side was empty, she slowly sat up.

"Kal?" She questioned looking around.

He was gone.

She sighed laying back down and closed her eyes. She wanted to revel in the memory of the moments when he had touched her, physically, in so many ways, and each one seemed to mean more than lust at the time.

"Well...well...well. Innocent little Princess isn't so innocent after all."

Diana's eyes shot open and she sat up quickly. "Valéria!" She instinctively pulled the sheet up a bit making sure she was completely covered.

Valéria smirked and crawled on top of the bed laying next to her.

"Wasn't last night quite riveting?"

"Was that..was that even real?!"

"Oh yes! Very real. I was surprised the Kryptonian took such a drastic step."

"Why are you here?"

"You know, it was incredibly stimulating seeing you and your lover lying naked in bed."

"You watched us?!"

"Not exactly. Though I, and possibly every other being in my realm heard you. I wanted to thank you both really for the energy that exuded from your very steamy rendezvous."

Diana looked away from her trying not to blush.

"Oh...my, my. Were you hoping for an encore? I was too. He has quite the talent. He knew exactly how to get the right reactions from you. Please you in ways you've dreamed of."

Valéria moves closer to Diana, trailing her hand up Diana's leg. Though, Diana moved away.

"Don't be like that, Princess. He is still all over you. Your body still reacting, still sensitive."

"It shouldn't be like this."

"Oh? Do you truly believe that? Your lover seemed quite conflicted as well when he left."

Diana's heart dropped. She looked back at Valéria and frowned.

"What do you mean?"

"He convinced himself leaving was the right choice. There's something within lingering to make him feel he isn't quite worthy. Or is this pure connection between you two truly a veil of nothing more than infatuation and lust?"

"No...it's..."

"It's not at all complicated if last night was anything to go by." She caressed Diana's cheek. "So what exactly does the Princess want? Would you want another woman experiencing what's only yours to experience with the Kryptonian?"

Diana narrowed her eyes and flung the sheets off her, getting out of bed. Valéria smirked.

"Where are you going?"

"None of your business."

"Be careful, Princess. Be sure when you see him, you maintain your excitement. Although, an encore with an audience would be to my liking."

Diana rolled her eyes. "Leave. I have to get ready for work."

Valéria then appeared in front of Diana, halting her.

"Did I strike a nerve?"

"Leave, now, Valéria. I have no time for your games."

"Listen to me, Diana. You know exactly what I'm capable of. I have my own little toys and yes, I believed you and your lover could've been grand special additions to my collections. However, it seems you two already belong in a certain collection and I have my limitations. There are always ways around that. One wrong move for you, can turn into the right one for me. And it's all fair game."

"What the hell do you-"

With an evil grin, Valéria disappeared.

Diana sighed deeply. Valéria's words replayed in her mind. She never thought she would be in such a predicament. To think that she knew how to control her emotions. In battle, sure, that's more strategic anyway. But the battlefield of love, has it's own rules. There's no logic, no strategy.

THE DARK SPELL

"Damn that succubus!" Diana said aloud in the shower.

All she could think and feel was Kal's hands, lips and tongue all over her.

She started panting, placing her hands on the wall, letting the hot water run down her back.

"Oh...Kal..." she moaned.

CHAPTER 3: SPIRITUALLY BOUND

Location: Daily Planet

Clark Kent was trying to finish typing up his latest report. However, his mind kept drifting thinking about his night with Diana. Holding her. Caressing her smooth sunkissed skin. Without waking her, gently pressing a kiss into her hair and smooth the raven tresses with his fingertips. Breathing in her scent. Hearing her soft breathing and the sound of her heartbeat. The beautiful peaceful look on her face. Her luscious lips seemed to be curved into a smile.

Waking up to her was everything and more. But did he go too far too fast? They've tried so hard for so long to suppress their feelings. Did they end up caught up in the moment only because of the effect?

"Damn," he said under his breath.

"Smallville!" Lois shouted in his ear.

"Hey, CK, you good, man?" Jimmy asked placing his hand on his shoulder.

"What?" Clark said snapping out of his daze.

"Dude, you've been staring at the screen for like 10 minutes. What's up?"

"Oh, I was just-"

"Thinking about his girlfriend," Cat said with a smile.

"Girlfriend?" Lois questioned. "This big oaf loner has a girlfriend?"

Clark sighed. "She's not my girlfriend, Cat."

"Oh, right. It's complicated," she winked.

"You know her, Grant?" Lois asked.

"Wait? So CK does have a girlfriend? Why didn't I know about this before Cat?"

"Well I kind of cornered him into spilling."

"So who is she?"

Cat smiled looking forward. "She...uhh...she's heading this way now."

Clark's own heart dropped as he looked up. Diana Prince was walking towards them with Perry. For a while he had thought his mind was playing tricks on him hearing her heartbeat coming closer.

"No way! Diana Prince?!" Jimmy said adjusting his tie anxiously. "Wow! She's so hot!"

Lois smacked Jimmy in the back of the head. "Shut it, Olsen. This is all just a joke."

"Why must you always be so damn cynical and mean, Lane?!"

"Why must you always be so damn messy and dramatic, Grant?!"

"Kent, you got a...very gorgeous visitor," Perry smiled.

"Hi, Ms. Lane, Mr. Olsen and Ms. Grant."

"Hi..." they all said in unison.

"The way she said Mr. Olsen..." Jimmy swooned.

Lois nudged his arm.

"Thank you, Mr. White. I will be sure to speak with the governor about your concerns."

He nodded slightly. "Olsen, Lane, Grant, get back to work." He ordered as he walked away back to his office.

Clark stood up. "Hey, Diana. I..um-"

"Apologies, Clark, for dropping in but I had to speak with you in person about the foundation with Ms. Messalina."

"Oh, right. We can go into the conference room."

"Hold on..." Lois said raising her brow. "What foundation? And also, how rude, Smallville, to not probably introduce us to your girlfriend."

Clark nervously cleared his thought. Diana looked at her surprised.

"Ms. Prince and I keep things professional and our personal...dealings are just that, Lois. Personal."

"Uh huh."

Clark placed his hand on Diana's lower back guiding her to the conference room.

"And you had the nerve to call me messy," Cat said.

Location: Conference Room

Clark took a deep breath as he locked the door.

"They will probably try to eaves drops," Clark said.

THE DARK SPELL

"This shouldn't be long and I don't think they'll understand what we are talking about if they can hear anything at all."

Clark nodded slightly. "Right..." He cleared his throat. "So what is happened with Valéria?"

"She knows what happened with us last night. She said some things that...I want to know if it's true from you."

"What did she say?"

"She said that you debated on leaving this morning. That you feel the need to question yourself with me. Do you have regrets?"

Clark sighed and moved closer to her taking her hands in his. "Diana...I will never regret what happened last night. But I crossed the line."

"Kal, if that was true, it would've stopped the moment you stepped in that shower with me."

"I don't want Valéria influencing us. I want it to be our choice. I want it to be right."

"Last night was all Valéria's influence? Nothing more than her spell upon us?"

"No. That's not what I'm saying."

"So what are you saying?"

"What we feel for each other, Diana, she wants to take advantage of that. We can't give into what Valéria is doing. I respect you and I care for you so much. We can't be alone. Not like that in the way Valéria wants us too, right now."

"I told you I've never opened myself to anyone like that before. To be so vulnerable. You are the man I trust, Kal. It was unexpected but I know that wasn't Valéria. It was us, letting go of everything." She looked down then looked back up staring into his eyes. "But I understand. It's not for us to truly let go for long. That's why it's so easy for Valéria to play on our emotions and say the things she has said."

As Diana was about to turn to walk out, Clark took her hand.

"But what she's said still isn't true. We need to do this our way."

Clark pulled her to him, he stood chest to chest with her. Their eyes tell a truth they won't verbally admit right now. Clark heard her breathing become heavier, seeing her chest move more clearly. They still just stood there, not saying a word. Diana could feel her body reacting to his. She doesn't want to say anything that would come out too breathless.

Diana knew she should move, but she just can't bring herself to do it. It's as if her body demands a physical connection that her mind will not allow right now.

It's starting again. The burning at the back of their necks. Their pupils dilating, breathing becoming heavier, and their heart rates increasing.

"Diana."

"If it has to be this way so be it. Maybe it is for the best after all."

"Wait a minute. That's not..."

Diana shook her head pressing her finger to his lips sushing him.

"This has happened so fast. We can't and won't risk losing what we have as friends."

Clark took her hand again pulling her closer. He leaned in capturing her lips in a soft kiss.

Reluctantly pulling back, both so torn.

"I should go. We both have work to get to."

Clark and Diana walked out the conference room, going to the elevators. Of course catching the attention of Lois, Jimmy and Cat.

"I'll...uh...I'll see you at the tower," Clark said.

Diana gave him a small smile and kissed his cheek before walking into the elevator.

They kept eye contact until the doors closed. Clark sighed, his heart shattering. And it was that moment he was full of regrets.

Location: Valeria's Castle

"It's been 4 days..."

"Yes, yes... 4 days of all their emotions pent up. Haven't you been watching their every move, Eros?"

"Yes, I have. It's a very fine line of what this seems to continue to lead to."

"The Kryptonian has surprised me quite a bit. The passion in his eyes and voice speaking of Diana. The result could be sensational."

"Has this been some kind of twisted test or game of yours again?"

"Calm down, Love God. It pains me to admit it...but it has been made quite clear my power is no match for the power between Diana and Kal-El.

THE DARK SPELL

The two have made their own rules to the game of love, passion, temptation and desire. They've been in control this whole time without realizing. However, I just gave a bit of a much needed push."

"My faith in the Kryptonian has not wavered. Though, make no mistake if this ends in tragedy and Strife getting the last word."

Valéria smirked and cupped Eros chin. "My offer still stands to join our celebration. Juri surely would love your company."

"I will not take part in your tainted rituals."

Valéria laughed. "So why don't you purify me? Your cousin and her lover has already given me such precious energy. I can't wait for more."

Kal and Diana remained as professional as possible. Partners, in sync on missions, but not going too far with deep personal conversations or even their usual flirtation.

To be honest the limitations and boundaries being set between the two was emotionally breaking them. Kal wanting some bad to take Diana in his arms or the light touches even meant so much. To make Diana smile and laugh. Diana giving Kal a playful seductive look only he knows.

Friday Evening: Boston University

"I got a question?"

"Yes, Mr. Avery."

"I want to know if Aphrodite was actually a man trapping sexy succubus. Goddess of "Love" but from what I've read, it's more about casting spells to bang. I don't believe in that sappy hearts everywhere Cupid. Dude running around with an bow and arrow with an adult diaper?"

The class started snickering.

Diana raised her brow. "I see...First off, Mr. Avery, it would be wise of you to speak appropriately. I do not condone any foul language or references. Do I make myself clear?"

"It was just a joke."

"It seems you have a lot to learn. I expected you to act your age, with professionalism and manners."

"Oohh..." students snickered again and teased.

"It is false to believe Aphrodite is of carnal love only. Her love is much more complexed and pure. She creates the balance with Ares between war and peace or love and hate. She gives birth to the God you believe to be Cupid, however he is known as Eros, from her love of Ares. She is mother of Harmonia, and that, without her, without pure "love", this world would not exist. As for succubi, as you seemed to be thinking of, they ultimately take pride in their ability to please and manipulate men. They are of lust for corruption and control. Feeding off the souls of men."

Diana then looked across the room and toward the back by the door to see Kal standing there with his charming smile she adored.

"The strong feelings and emotions you feel for your significant other should run deep within your souls, creating an ever lasting spiritual connection. A bond that can never be broken." She paused for a moment a smiled. She and Kal locked eyes. "Something so sacred and cherished that has developed from a loving friendship. It's complicated but when you have someone you can trust, is honest, and be vulnerable with, that is the truth of love."

When all the students left out the class, Julia, Diana and Kal remained.

"Good evening, Julia," he said.

"Good evening, Clark. How have you been?" She asked hugging him.

"Been alright."

"You two seem like you need some time alone. I will speak with you some time tomorrow, Diana."

She nodded. "Have a good night, Julia."

When Julia walked out, Diana started sorting her papers and packing everything into her toy bag. Kal just watched her silently.

"Is there something going on with the League, Clark?"

"No, this is a personal visit."

"What is it about?"

"Come with me to the Fortress for dinner."

"Are you asking or telling me? And I thought you said we couldn't be alone."

Within a second, Kal was behind her and wrapped his arms around her waist. Diana's body immediately started reacting sending shivers down her spine, rocking her core.

"Kal."

He held her closer, his body tightly pressed against her back

THE DARK SPELL

"We can't change how we are nor what we have."

"The Fates have other plans than of the Succubus," she commented as she was enjoying being held close to him.

Kal noted she was sounding a bit sad. To Diana's surprise he turned her around and held her even tighter.

"We have other plans of our own."

Diana closed her eyes at the sound of his husky voice whispering in to her ear. He was incredibly confident as he spoke.

"Are you cooking?"

He smiled brushing his lips against the back of her neck. "Of course."

He started kissing her neck and she enjoyed the feeling of his soft lips. She could imagine other places where those lips would feel wonderful. Gods, she could absolutely not control her thoughts when he's around.

Diana finished packing and Kal took her bag carrying it for her as they left the campus and flew off to the fortress.

Location: Fortress of Solitude

"So tonight we are having honey garlic shrimp with wild rice and steamed mixed vegetables."

"Mmmh...can't wait."

Diana leaned over the counter watching him. Kal looked over to her with a smirk as he tossed the shrimp in the skillet, showing off.

"A man of many talents," she giggled.

"Learned a lot from Ma and Pa growing up. I have Ma's cookbook somewhere back at my apartment." He trail off with the trace of a nostalgic smile on his face.

"I'm truly amazed at how you've made the fortress feel so homely."

"It is home away from home in Metropolis and Smallville. This makes me feel closer to my birth parents and Krypton."

"I understand. I'm happy for you, Kal. Proud to know such an honest, confident, honorable man."

"All credit goes to my parents, both biological and adopted." He paused for a moment and looked at her. "I also know this incredibly beautiful, intelligent gentle hearted woman that inspires me to do and be better."

Diana tried not to blush. "I'll have to add that your quite a charmer as well."

Finally, everything was cooked just right, and Kal made their plates.

"Dinner is served!" he announced as I carried the food to the the small dining area.

Diana eyes lit up with excitement again.

"The presentation is amazing, Kal."

"Thanks, Di!"

She smiled back and digs right in. "OH BY THE GODS!" she gushed.

Kal laughed as she blushed.

"You know I grew up eating lamb, venison, and fish. Fruits and vegetables wise olives, tomatoes, grapes, pomegranate, melon and so on. I like trying new things, fascinated by all the different flavors. I really do enjoy your cooking. Thank you."

"Don't mention it," He replied. "I'll cook for you anytime or anything else you would like. I'd do anything for you, you know that, right?"

She smiled. "Yes..."

The rest of the night went perfectly; all throughout dinner, they made light, fun conversation, and Diana laughed at every single one of Kal's jokes!

After dinner, Kal offered to make cheesecake with fresh fig slices on top. The perfect combination of natural sweetness and richness.

Finishing up dessert, Kal took Diana to the fortress planetarium.

"Wow. Your findings are astounding!"

Kal stared at her, mesmerized.

"Diana?"

"Yes, Kal?"

"I wanted to thank you for having dinner with me."

"You didn't give me much of a choice and I can't resist your cooking," she smiled playfully. Then looking at his expression, "did you want to say something else, Kal?"

He moved closer to her and took her hands in his, rubbing his thumbs gently across her knuckles.

"I...I lied."

Diana frowned at him confused. "You lied?"

THE DARK SPELL

He sighed. "I haven't been alright. And things won't get better with the way things are going between us. This trying to stay professional, limit things said and done. I can't do that, Diana."

"Kal..."

"To me, you are perfect and I want to keep showing you that. When we are together, magic happens. Everything we've been through, we've gone through it together. Been each other's support. What happened a few days ago, you were right, that was us finally letting go. Maybe it was pushed more with the effect but that was our moment. I want more of that with you, Diana. I'm grateful to have to have you in my life And I don't want it any other way."

Diana stared at him silently, taking in everything he was saying. Her heart fluttered.

"Diana, what I'm saying is that... I lo-"

Taking him by surprise, she jumped into his arms, wrapping her arms around his neck and kissed him passionately. Kal wrapped his arms around her waist lifting her slightly off the ground. Diana moaned as they kissed, their tongues trying to dominate the other and exploring each others mouths.

After several passion-filled minutes of locking lips, they separated for air.

"I love you, Diana."

She gently pressed her lips against his once more before whispering, "I love you, too, Kal."

"Oh how sweet. Sweet as...honey."

Kal and Diana smiles immediately dropped, seeing Valéria.

"Why are you here? We've had enough trouble from you," Kal said.

"Trouble, Kal-El? I do like to get a bit dirty. However, from what I can see and more so feel, I've done my part as I said and you continue with yours. I'm just here to congratulate you."

"Congratulate?" Diana questioned.

"Your commitment to one other is unwavering. Even when taunted, it only ignited the fire of passion to which can not be contained. Eros warned me."

"Eros? My cousin was involved?"

"Protecting you from afar. But you didn't need it. Quite honestly my spell has had its effect in the most unexpected pure pleasurable sense. If it were not for your divine connection being as powerful as it is, you two would've already became my lust tainted puppets the moment doubt had slithered in."

"We don't need anyone's interference."

Valeria smirked feeling the sexual tension between Kal and Diana building. She casted a spell creating a magic circle upon the floor.

"What are you doing?!" Kal questioned holding Diana tighter as they noticed they couldn't move.

"Let us go! Now!"

Valéria grinned wickedly and disappeared.

"What? No!"

"Oh...my...my...You don't want me to go after all?" Valéria whispered into Diana's ear as she reappeared closely behind her.

"What do you want?"

"Let us go!"

She disappeared, then reappeared behind Kal, dragging her finger down his back. "I won't be here much longer. But there's something very important to be said...to be seen."

Suddenly, Kal and Diana were completely naked.

"Wha-"

"Relax..." she whispered to them both.

Unwillingly, their eyes closed momentarily. There was a moment of silence as they tried to regain their composure.

Their bodies began to glow. A symbol appeared in the center of their chests and a spiritual twine appeared between them, connecting them from each other's symbols.

"Anahata colors mortal life with compassion, love, and beauty. Driven by the principles of transformation and integration, the fourth energy center is said to bridge earthly and spiritual aspirations."

Their bodies began to glow brighter.

"Even more powerful than before."

Opening their eyes, they stared deeply into each other's eyes.

THE DARK SPELL

"There's so much passion but beyond the passion there's a spark in your eyes that has become a flame and the feeling inside is growing larger consuming you both."

"What are you saying Valéria?"

She grinned. "Your hearts will speak for the rest of the night, so then you will have your answer. I bid you both adieu."

As Valéria disappeared, the circle disappeared, and Diana and Kal were fully clothed again.

Diana buried her face in the crook of Kal's neck. Kal closed his eyes, breathing in the exotic scent of her hair. He can hear her heart beat against his, and they're in perfect rhythm together. He smile softly.

"Is she really gone for good?" Kal asked in a whisper.

Diana giggled softly, slightly nodding. "No more interruptions or interferences. I will be sure to speak with Eros soon."

"Diana?"

"Yes, Kal?"

"Stay here with me tonight," he whispered in her ear and gave her butterfly kisses.

She raised her head with an arched brow. "Just tonight?"

Kal smirked. "Every day...and every night."

His hands travelled further down and grabbed her ass. His mouth started to lightly map out the outline of her lips, ghostly hovering over every curve.

He slowly brought his lips closer to hers and waited for them both to meet, he knew if he tempted her enough that she'd come to him. She smirked staring into his eyes. They never broke eye contact as he lifted her up and carried her to the bedroom.

He set her down and they both stood in the centre of the room with their lips just millimetres apart when finally their lips met in frenzy as their eager tongues tried to search for entry of the others mouth. Diana lightly bit Kal's lip and he hummed with approval. She'd never realised how just the hum of a man like Kal-El could turn her on so much. Not separating the kiss Diana slowly pushed Kal towards the bed. As his knees hit the back of the bed, Kal fell back and pulled Diana towards him. She slowly and lightly placed her body over his lap.

They continued kissing as Diana started to slowly grind her hips over him. He smiled into the kiss.

As they separated for a needed yet not wanted air, she threw her head back and Kal moved his lips to her neck to slowly kiss her. He started to leave wet patches around her neck and Diana rocked her body in approval. He made sure to leave his mark he sucks at her neck just below her ear.

He flipped them over and pushed Diana up to the top of the middle of the bed. He started to take her clothes off slowly and began to lick every part of her skin exposed to him. He looked her straight in the eye and moved his mouth back to her before saying "The bra, as nice as it may be... it needs to go!" his skilled hands went to work as he unbuttoned her bra.

Revealing her glorious breasts, he positioned his mouth placing kisses around her erect nipples.

"Ahh! Kal!" She moaned as he sucked on the right one while pinching and tweaking her left nipple.

He looked up at her with his gorgeous eyes. Diana moaned, tugging at his hair. She was loving how he used his teeth, nipping at it. The taste of her breasts was intoxicating. Kal switched breasts and sucked on the left one while pinching and tweaking the right one. Diana moaned and arched her back a bit.

As soon as he released her nipple, Diana reached for the hem of his shirt, eager to see those godly muscles. Kal quickly took off his shirt and tossed it.

Kal then unzips Diana's skirt from the side and slid it off her. He grabbed the waistband of her panties but paused for a moment. He doesn't take them off, but moves a hand to her center, rubbing gently. Diana's hips rose slightly and she sucked in a breath. He kept rubbing her slowly and gently while looking at her closely. It drover her crazy.

He kept looking at her while teasing her.

She gasped, "Kal..."

He nodded slid her panties down her long sexy legs.

Diana, finally free from her clothes, naked in front of Kal who's looking at her with dark lustful eyes and his touch is warmer, almost burning. He stared into her eyes and licked his lips, caressing her thighs.

Diana smiled and flipped him over, straddling him.

THE DARK SPELL

She wanted to give him as much pleasure as he was giving her. Kal had a pretty good idea of what she had in mind as she trailed light kisses down his chest and abs. Diana's hand caressed his member through the pants. She undid his belt buckle and started unzipping his pants; she soon saw his hard, thick member underneath his navy boxer shorts.

She looked up at him and echoed his words back, "The boxers, Kal, as nice as they may be, they need to go."

And with that she slowly started to pull them from his waistline.

He smirked down at her; she looked up, deciding between a bit of banter or desire. The desire in her won a not so fair fight. She licked her lips and placed them around him. The heat and wetness of her mouth sent a shock through Kal's spine. Kal started to moan and placed his hand on her head running his fingers through her hair.

While her tongue gently caressed every bit of Kal's member, Kal was made to forget everything. It worked like magic.

Diana continued to go at a slow pace. Her tongue swirled around the tip till she finally started to take it in her mouth. Her mouth is so wet and warm. Her tongue still gently caressing all over him like a lover's kiss, gentle yet passionate.

"I can't... believe...Di..." he breathlessly said.

Just as he was at the point of no return, Diana smiled seductively. She slowly released him from her mouth and trailed licks and kisses back up to his face.

Kal cupped her chin, being her lips to his and gave her a long, deep kiss. Their tongues tangled with each other, tasting every part of each other's mouths. Kal turned them back over, making Diana giggle.

Kal sat up and massaged Diana's soft legs. His hands got to her feet, which he also massaged.

Diana bit her lip and moaned as he trailed kisses from her ankles up her calves to her inner thighs.

Kal pressed his face into her core. Even his breath worked as a powerful stimulus for Diana. His tongue ran around the area near her entrance. He then kissed Diana's lower lips as he licked around it. Diana gasped as Kal's tongue filled her inside.

"Oh Gods!"

His tongue licked around inside her as he kept her legs from closing.

"Aaaa, aaah! Kal!"

Kal could feel the pulsation of Diana's walls with his tongue. She had just climaxed but he didn't give her a single second to rest, as he continued licking in her.

"Clark!"

Diana tightened her legs around his head and used her hands to press Kal's face more against her.

Kal inserted two of his fingers in her sensitive spot. While fingering her, he sucked her clit.

"Aaaaahhhh! Oh-" she cried out, but before she could yell for him, he licked her into exquisite elation.

Kal licked his way back up her body and gave her a long, deep kiss. Their tongues tangled with each other, tasting every part of each other's mouth that their tongue can reach.

"Mmph...ha..ah.." Diana moaned.

Kal positioned himself at her hot and moist entrance. Diana could feel him teasing her with his tip rubbing her lower lips.

Diana gasped as she felt him enter her, feeling a sharp pain along with the pleasure that flooded her senses.

"K...al..Cl...ar...k..." she groaned, his incredible size being unexpected by her body.

Being sheathed within Diana made Kal lose almost all reasoning. It was pleasure beyond what he had ever received.

"I'm...yours...take me...Kal," she told him.

These words were the key. Kal nodded yes to her request and began to move slowly. Diana moaned more sensually as the pain slowly faded being replaced by only pure unadulterated pleasure. She looked at him who stared back at her, Diana's face soon distorted with bliss from taking the man she loved inside her

"Hah...ahhh..."

Kal penetrated deeper into her. Her walls pulsated around him. After a few gentle thrusts he continued at a more consistent faster pace. His right hand on her right thigh as he thrusted harder into her. A shock ran through her spine.

THE DARK SPELL

"A-aahhh! Mmm!"

Diana's heart felt like it's about to explode, gripping the bed sheets as tight as she could.

"Kal!"

"Diana..."

With each of his thrusts, Diana's breasts bounced up and down. Kal's gaze was taken by the moving mountains, and soon enough he couldn't help but attack them with his mouth.

"Gods! Yes!"

This made Diana's legs shiver. All leading to her having an orgasm.

Kal held on to her hips tightly, moving harder, hitting her sweet spot over and over and over and over again. It was driving her crazy. Diana grabbed his neck and held him tightly, leaving bite marks all over his neck and shoulders.

AH!" she screamed and bit his shoulder.

Kal's hips hit Diana's in a rhythm. Her walls moved in a way that seemed to suck him in. It was surprising how even their involuntary movements were passionate.

Kal continued thrusting in a rhythm. Their gaze never left each other.

"Diana."

"Kal."

Kal kept going faster and faster reaching his limit and soon enough, he did just that, with an explosion of pleasure.

Diana's walls pulsated irregularly due to her currently ongoing climax, which gave Kal an incredible feeling. Both felt the force hit them at once, their bodies trembling with instantaneous orgasms.

Their faces drew closer. Like two magnets, their lips and tongues were attracted to each other. Kal hastened his movements. A heavenly aura was emitted by Diana's body.

"Mhhh!"

"Mmhh!"

Diana used her strength to raise their bodies. She was now sitting on Kal's lap, straddling him. Diana wrapped her hands around Kal's neck and pressed her body against his. She held Kal to her chest as Kal was grabbing her plump ass, groping it vigorously. Diana had such a loving expression on her face that Kal could not hold back.

"Ahh...Kal..." She moaned as he slowly guided her hips up then back down. "Ahh!" She moaned sharply as he slammed her down. "Ahh! Ahh! Ahh!"

His movements hastened, drowning Diana's moans with his kiss.

They both felt something was coming. Their lips separated for a moment only to call out to each other.

"Diana-!"

"Oh, Kal! Ah!"

Diana reached another climax. But Kal didn't stop, neither Diana wanted him to. As if to signal that, Diana raising and lowering herself, they soon synced their movements perfectly. Even the pulsation of Diana's walls and the throbbing of Kal's member were synced.

"Nnaaaahh!"

"Mmm!"

"Aaaaah!"

"Mmmmmmmm!"

They stopped for a second only to catch their breaths, but it was really only for a second.

Diana pushed Kal down to lay on the bed. She then took charge of the movements, riding him at a steady pace. She rolled her hips and also mixed this with her up and down movements. She took full advantage of every possible movement.

Kal placed his hands on her hips, merely touching her. Just feeling her soft skin was enough. Diana was also feeling Kal's muscular chest with her hands.

At some point, Kal also began moving his hips. His thrust naturally perfectly timed with Diana's movements.

Diana's hair covered a bit of her chest, but it failed to completely hide it. Some of her hair even fell on her face, but she merely brushed them aside.

"Di..."

She leaned down and Kal received her with a kiss. They hugged as their tongues danced. Her hips continued to rise and lower in sync with Kal's upward thrusts. Perfect synchronization was the only way to describe them.

THE DARK SPELL

"AHH! Ahh, hah ahh ahh haaahhh! Kal! Kal!" She moaned his name with overflowing passion.

Kal going faster now and thrusting deeper into Diana.

"Yes! Gods! I..."

Diana arched her back from her orgasm.

Before Diana could completely recover, Kal changed his and Diana's positions, turning her around on all fours. Kal positioned himself behind her and pushed himself inside Diana with considerable strength. This time, he didn't even wait a second. He began moving immediately. He wasn't able to help himself now, losing all manner of sanity the moment he had penetrated her.

Diana gripped the sheets, calling out his name repeatedly with such intensity. She loved how he was showing no restraint.

"Yes, Kal! Yes!" She screamed encouraging him.

Kal's hands skimmed up and down her sides then gripped her soft ass. He kept moving faster and harder, hitting against the deepest part of her. He kissed her shoulder while thrusting into her.

Even as he felt like it would explode any second, he had no such thing as a will to stop.

Her walls tightened. It wasn't long before Diana's juices started flowing out, like a broken faucet, as she quickly reached a climax.

Diana raised up, leaning back against Kal's chest. With Kal's hands on her hips, Diana weaved her fingers together with his. She allowed their hands to glide up to her breasts. Kal palmed the soft flesh and Diana's fingers withdrew slightly, resting against his wrist. He groped them and pinched her nipples. In response, Diana could only moan in pleasure.

His hands drew her bodyline, then ran through her stomach going further down, Kal played a bit with her center, slowly driving her towards the edge once again.

"Nnn! Mmhhnnn!"

Once she turned her head his way, Kal kissed her lips. Losing themselves within the kiss, they lost their balance and fell on the bed. Yet they did not stop. Kal continued thrusting with all he had and placed his hands near Diana's intertwining their fingers.

He whispered sweet nothings in her ear. She could only nod and bite the pillow.

Kal sat up a bit for Diana to turn and lay on her back.

He never lost his connection with her, he just simply restarted his movements.

"Ah, aaaah!"

"Mmm!"

Diana reached another climax. Her legs spread open as far as they could. Kal smirked loving her legs high in the air. He slowly glided his hands up and down her soft inner thighs. He saw the rise and lower of her breasts with every breath Diana took in.

That drew Kal closer. In no time, he was already sucking one of her breasts again.

"Aaaaaaahhh!"

Kal didn't stop. Diana's walls pulsated with the same rhythm of her heart.

"Di," he called as Diana looked at him.

"Kal," She called back.

Kal captured her lips in another intimate kiss. Diana put one hand behind his head, forcing the kiss deeper. Her other other hand on his back, pressing their bodies together even more. Lastly, she locked her legs behind his hips.

Kal could feel both their release coming again so, so, so close. He deepened his entry and obliged with a few more thrusts they both came apart together. They'd never experienced something like that; she didn't even know it was possible.

Diana screamed out again due to how fiercely she had climaxed, only experiencing more ecstasy at the feel of Kal's warm release in her. Kal still kept thrusting so that he would pour every last drop.

Slowly coming to a stop, laying still, him still in her, Diana looked up at him. She had such an intense orgasm that she seemed like she was out of breath.

Looking at her gorgeous face, Kal placed light soft kisses all over then gave her a kiss on the lips and said "I love you so much, Diana. I don't need a succubus' spells or tests and not even any of that from your cousin. I've

THE DARK SPELL

held back for so long because I thought it was the right thing to do. I won't do that anymore. I'm going to show my love to you every waking hour."

Diana smiled. "We have so many responsibilities and for the longest time we thought that, that's what our life would revolve around. A life like this, being in love seemed impossible. But together we can have it all. It's not going to be easy but we can make it work for us."

"For us..." Kal repeated kissing her again.

"I'm so happy to be experiencing things like this with you, Kal," she blushed.

He put his hand on her cheek. "Me, too. Happy and grateful."

For the moment now, still being a bit breathless, they could only convey their feelings for each other through sharing a deep passionate kiss.

"Rest a while longer?" He asked with a smirk.

"Oh...heavens no..." Diana giggled.

"Thought so..."

Kal held his body back up, and took Diana's with him. He held her body up and made her sit on his lap. Diana placed her arms around his neck. Embracing each other, Diana's breasts were deeply pressed on Kal's chest.

Diana gasped loving the feel of the man she loved filling her completely, not just physically but emotionally and spiritually.

She voluntarily moved her body up and down and Kal moved his hips at the same time.

Kal began to whisper sweet nothings to her again as he pecked at her lips.

"Yes...yes...yes...Kal," she breathed out.

After a few pecks, it developed into a full-fledged loving kiss. Everything was as it should be. They were together and nothing else mattered.

CHAPTER 4: CONTROL

Location: Fortress of Solitude

Kal and Diana awoken happily in each other arms.

"Good Morning, Diana," he whispered kissing her forehead.

"A good morning it is, Kal," she responded kissing his neck.

"Di...?"

"Yes?"

"Last night..." he grinned.

Diana grinned back as he pulled her to lay completely on top of him. Diana planted a soft kiss to the middle of his chest.

"Last night was everything."

"I love you, Diana. You know that right?"

She laughed softly. "Of course. And I love you, too."

Kal cupped the back her neck, his hand tangling up in her hair pulling her into a passionate kiss. Diana moaned in his mouth as Kal rolled them over.

All of a sudden, their phones started ringing.

They stopped abruptly and looked at each other.

"Damn."

"We were so caught up last night, we didn't turn those off."

"Well we would definitely be late for work if we had've."

Diana smiled and kissed him softly. "Reality calls..."

Hours later, Daily Planet

Clark Kent was trying to concentrate on his latest blog story but his mind kept drifting to his sexy Goddess Diana. It's only been 4 hours but he missed her like she had been away for 4 years.

He picked up his phone needing to call her. His mind and heart racing as the phone was ringing. Maybe she was busy though, meetings at the UN. He should hang up.

No...yes...no...

"Hello, Kal..." he heard her sultry tone.

"Hey, Di. I don't mean to interrupt anything."

"Oh, no. Just the usual. I was actually thinking about you. Glad you called."

"I was wondering if you wanted to have dinner tonight?"

"I would love to..."

"Hmm...? But?"

"One condition."

Clark smirked. "What's that?"

"We go out as Clark Kent and Diana Prince...public date."

"Of course. It wouldn't be any other way. I want to show the the woman I love off to the world."

Diana smiled, her heart fluttering with excitement.

"I should call to make reservations then."

"Ok...I love you, Mr. Kent."

To hear her say those words but not only that, to say it first made him even more prideful.

"I love you, too, Ms. Prince."

Café Pacific

It was very dim, lit by candles and lamps, filled with exotic smells and quiet music playing in the background. Most of the tables are for two. Quite intimate and romantic.

Clark and Diana had managed to secure a corner table, not too secluded to make it look as if they were hiding, but it was perfect for the two of them having their own quiet space.

"This is really nice," Diana smiled.

"Yeah..." Clark was awestruck by her beauty.

"Clark?"

"You're just so incredibly beautiful." He reached over putting his hand on top of hers, sending little electric sparks that spread through them.

"You are such a handsome gentleman."

Clark leaned forward and reached across the table, taking Diana's hand in his. He kissed the back of it.

THE DARK SPELL

"Di, I want you to know, I don't want you to feel rushed or anything. This is us. Finally together as it should've been. I love you. I'm very much in love with you. I'll do any and everything to show you that."

"I do know. That's why you are the only man I know that has my complete trust and heart. I agree, there isn't any rush. We can take our time, keep building together. We maintain control of our relationship. We don't need my cousin, a succubi or whoever else trying to interfere."

Clark smiled proudly rubbed his thumbs gently over his goddess's hand. "Absolutely."

"Hello, apologies for the wait," the waitress said. "I'm Va-Victoria, your waitress for the evening. Would you like to start with our evening special. Our finest wine and appetizers?"

"Ah, sure, why not?" Clark said and Diana slightly nodded.

"Alright, I will be back momentarily," Victoria smiled.

As she turned and was walking away, her innocent smile, turned devious.

"How did you know about this place, Kal?"

"Well... it was actually Cat. She mentioned it a couple of times for me to take you."

"Oh? Me?"

"She figured I had a special lady in mind for the passed few weeks. Was trying to help out. She had only just found out it was you a few days ago, cornering me."

Diana laughed softly. "Well, give her my thanks. It's really beautiful here. I've never had any kind of dinner like this. You know it has always just been charities or banquets. Even if I did go on a date set up by Vanessa, Mera or Dinah, they were disasters."

"I promise, we will go to every restaurant around the world and we can take trips off planet."

"Hmm, yes, would love that, but I would also love your cooking too."

"Anything you want. We can even do some experiments making our own dishes."

"I don't exactly know my way too much around the kitchen."

"We will make our way around together, but it could get a little messy," he smirked.

Diana bit her lip seductively. "We'll enjoy making a mess but we'll clean up just to make another."

"Alright, Mr. and Mrs. Kent..."

Clark and Diana glanced at each other but neither said anything only smiled.

"...finest bottle of wine and appetizers. More time for your choices of the main course?"

Clark quirked his brow and smirked glancing at Diana again. Of course he would rather have her.

"I would like the grilled red snapper and for Mrs. Kent, the risotto."

"Main courses will be out shortly!"

Clark and Diana resumed their flirtatious conversation until the waitress came out with their meal.

With a quick glance, Diana had noticed the waitress had a parculiar look. She seemed quite familiar.

"Di? Di, are you okay?"

"Oh yes... I just had a quick thought. The waitress seems familiar."

"Really?"

"I'm not sure where I've seen her. Maybe the University?"

"Want to ask?"

"Oh no...I may be wrong."

"You sure?"

She nodded slightly.

The rest of the night was filled with soft laughter and pleasantness. The music relaxing, the food delicious, and the company of each other...perfect. The lover's giving each other loving looks when their dessert arrived.

"Hmmm...this was all so heavenly!" Diana said taking her last bite of creme brûlée.

"I'm glad you enjoyed it."

"I hope you know it wasn't just the food I was referring to," Diana responded, winking at him.

She began rubbing her foot against his leg. Clark looked at her with surprise then smirked. He could see it in her eyes and he was sure she could see it in his eyes too.

Ahh...here it comes...

THE DARK SPELL

Diana felt her heart flutter and felt a chill run down her spine and rocked her to her core. Clark's own body was reacting to her. The thought of having each other on this table was so very tempting.

"Kal..." she whispered, licking her lips.

"Mr. and Mrs. Kent will there be anything else?" Victoria asked.

"Just the check, please."

Victoria smiled, taking note at the way Clark and Diana were staring at each other.

"Yes, right away, Sir."

Clark paid the check and they walked arm in arm out the restaurant.

They took a stroll down the quiet street then stopped and stood under an old street lamp. Diana leaned against the brick wall while Clark stood infront of her. She sighed happily. Her body was starting to rage, wanting Clark to...

Yes...touch her. Touch her.

Clark looked at Diana with love and tenderness. He reached out to caress her cheek with the back of his hand.

Diana's breathing was slowly becoming heavy and her heart rate escalating. Her skin becoming extremely tender. Clark moved closer to her, pushing his body against hers.

"Clark..."

"What was it?" He asked softly in her ear. "The food or the drink?"

"First thought...both...but..." she paused, then let out an involuntary moan. She reached up to gently caress his cheek, moving her thumb up and down. She had to maintain. "...the wine...definitely."

Clark captured her lips in a soft kiss. Diana returned the kiss immediately and with enthusiasm. She couldn't can help but make a soft sound as Clark's arms wrap around her waist, and she ran her hands up his back and around his neck. Diana felt a weightlessness to her body that was making her slightly dizzy.

Clark's mouth landed on her neck, and he's thankful her hair is swept up so he has better access. He sucked on her hard, his tongue slipping out every now and then to play on and tease her skin. Diana felt this all the way at her core. It looked like her mouth wanted to form words, but she couldn't get them out. Only quiet yet heavy breathing.

Clark's hands moved all over her maroon satin-covered body. He longed to feel her bare skin but at the same time loved how the satin felt against her. He was pretty sure Diana loved how it felt too as well as the feel of his fingers massaging her everywhere reachable. His mouth moved across her upper chest and ended up tonguing a shoulder.

"It's..." she whispered against his lips. "Gods..."

Clark gave her a slight nod kissing her again. This time much more forceful and held her against him tighter. Diana ground herself against him and brought her hands to either side of his face to steady him as she explored his lips with her teeth. Clark moaned as she bit into his lip and smoothed away the pain with a flick of her tongue. They moaned into each other until they broke apart to breathe. Diana gasped as she was overcome with such pleasure.

Clark's eyes were radiating love, pleasure, and surprise and Diana stared back letting herself bask in the moment.

They both then looked around seeing that no one was paying much attention.

"When I said I wanted to show the world the woman I love, I didn't mean like this," he joked chuckling.

"And when I said a public date, this wasn't what I meant either," Diana smiled blushing, burying her face into his chest.

"Still fun..."

Diana looked up at him and raised her brow. "So now it's fun?"

"We have control, remember?"

Diana kissed him sweetly. "Stay with me tonight."

Clark kissed her forehead and took her hand intertwining their fingers.

Location: Diana's Condominium

Clark shut the door and took off his jacket tossing it on the arm of the sofa. They both kicked off their shoes before going to the bedroom.

They stood staring into each other's eyes for a moment before stepping closer to each other.

Clark kept his intense gaze on Diana as she licked her lips and her eyes wander down the expanse of his chest, his arms, his waist. She stepped forward, her hands caressing the lapel of his shirt and then inching along his shoulders. She traced the lines of his muscles, sternum, and chest.

THE DARK SPELL

Clark breathed in deeply as Diana unbuttoned the first button of his shirt really slowly.

Button after button, his skin comes to view. This is more than arousal or sexual desire, right now. It's the spiritual pleasure of having him, her best friend and the man she loves so close.

Clark closed his eyes for a moment as Diana drove the fabric down his arms. He enjoyed the tingling sensation he felt all over his body when she pressed faintly against him in the process.

His eyes opened once his shirt fell on the ground. Diana kept looking at Clark's chest, down his stomach, the way his v-line disappeared under his pants, she could feel her cheeks getting darker and her breathing heavier.

Control...

Clark's hands come up, cupping Diana's face in most tenderest way possible. The gentleness of his stroke sent butterflies to her stomach and there's a spark along her skin when his thumb stroked her jawline. Diana suppressed the moan rising up her throat, lets her head fall forward instead, his fingers massaging her. He slowly dislodged the bun of her hair, her curls falling down her shoulders, his eyes are drawn to the line of her locks when she straightened.

Diana slowly glided her hands down to his belt, unbuckling it skillfully. She focused this time on the small trail of hair that went from just underneath his belly button and then disappeared under his pants. She desperately wanted to follow that trail so she pulled Clark by the button of his pants, a little rougher than she had intended, which made them both laugh. It's impossible not to graze his flesh when she drags the zipper down. She takes the material in her hands and tugs it down his hips.

As Clark got rid of his pants, Diana's eyes were drawn to the outline of his length in his briefs. She cleared her throat and looked up to meet Clark's gaze, a sexy smile on his lips. Clark reached for her and dragged her dress straps down her shoulders. Diana let her dress drop, pooling at her feet. Clark hummed, dropping to his knees before her, looking up at her again. His eyes gaze her stomach, his lips part, as if he might kiss her there. Diana let her hand brush his hair off of his forehead. She looked at him from above and there's a flutter, low in her belly, that she understood quite well.

He placed a soft kiss to her stomach before he rose to his feet. He pulled back slightly to drink up the sight of his half-naked Goddess, his throat feeling dry when he took a breath. He helped her step out of the puddle of her dress and started to walk backward. He kept her hands in his, his thumb stroked her skin and she smiled.

It's so easy with this man. He doesn't make her uncomfortable, doesn't push her, doesn't rush her, his eyes are so tender.

Diana pushed him gently so he fell to the bed with a thud causing Clark to let out a laugh that caught in his throat as Diana climbed across his body. Right before Diana swung her other leg over him, Clark grabbed her by the hips loving the sight above him. He felt his heart beat out of his chest at the way Diana was looking down at him noticing the quickening pace in her breathing as well. They stared at each other for a while both sharing shy smiles before Clark gently guided Diana over to the other side of him and then pulled the covers over their lower half's.

Diana traced her fingers down Clark's chest, the urge to press her lips against his became overwhelming. Clark wrapped his arm around Diana's hip tighter and pulled her closer. Once Diana looked up at him, Clark leaned down and swept his tongue between Diana's lips as she parted them almost automatically, moaning at the way he tasted.

When they broke apart, Diana rested her head on his chest, her cheek to his heart. Its beating lulled her, his warm embrace soothed her. His strokes are so gentle on her skin. His hand traced the line of her arm, while the other combed through her hair. Her fingers still study his abs, feeling the hard muscles beneath her fingers making Clark's stomach contract when she grazed it.

Clark started to whisper sweet nothings to her, enthralled, his strokes moving higher, along her neck. He's such a good man, a devoted lover.

Location: The Dark Realm: Valaria's Castle

Eros laughed biting an apple. "Did you really think you could trick them again? Disguised as a mortal waitress is child's play."

"It wasn't a trick. More of just a...test. Though, their bodies call for so much more. They have such restraint. Impressive."

"Test of what? They've proven to you their commitment to each other is pure. My cousin has chosen a mate truly worthy of her love. The passion between them, quite unadulterated. Though it is more than physical intimacy they seek with one another as you've seen. Their bond runs deeper."

Valeria quirked her brow.

"We know of their ultimate desire."

"One of which will be easy to obtain. Though, I'm sure, you will create a challenge I'm already in objection to."

"Oh, let's have a little bit more fun, Eros. We have to be sure this sacred flame of love and passion burns for eternity."

CHAPTER 5: GLIMPSE OF OUR FUTURE

Metropolis: Clark Kent's Apartment, Friday Afternoon

Clark, with a navy blue towel wrapped around his waist, had just gotten out of the steaming shower. He sighed and wiped the fog from the mirror. He sensed a presence around him.

"Not you," he said.

"Oh! My...my...Kal-El. Is that any way to say hello?" Valeria smiled, appearing leaning against the wall.

"You shouldn't be here," Kal warned.

Valeria smirked surveying him, studying his massive form from top to bottom. His body was glistening from the shower. From his jet black curled hair, ocean blue eyes, sharp jawline, down to his broad shoulders, muscular chest and chiseled abs. Incredibly muscular arms and legs. Inhaling his masculine musk in the air, she gazed at the line of thin hair disappearing beneath the towel.

"Mmhmm... The Princess really has chosen the perfect specimen of a man. How can this be? There must be something within you? Is Diana truly the only woman you have eyes for?" asked Valeria walking closer to him.

"Of course she is," he said directly meeting her eyes. "She..."

He realized how intense her eyes were. He blinked the rubbed his eyes as his vision start to blur. He tried looking away from her but he couldn't. It was like he was falling into the depths of her alluring brown eyes.

He could hear Diana's voice. "Kal!" She moaned giving into her orgasm. He blinked again quickly evading from looking straight in her eyes.

Valeria grins mischievously as she successfully awakened his desire.

"Turn around, Kal-El," she commanded.

"What?!"

"Look into the mirror."

He sighed deeply and turned to the mirror. He jumped slightly seeing the reflection of Diana. She was dressed in a nude silver sequins double slit maxi dress walking along the shore of Themyscira.

"Oh...so it is true." Valeria smiled and skimmed her finger slowly up and down his spine stops right above where his towel starts.

"The reflection of a man in love is his woman. She's beaming with such pure pride and joy."

"Isn't that how it should be?" he asked mesmerized by the visual of Diana from reflection.

"Yes, it should...and it is. Kal-El, the reason I am here is to say I won't interfere too much for too much longer." She smiled looking at the way his eyes got bigger as he continued to stare at the visual flowing in the mirror.

"You shouldn't be interfering at all." he said trying to shut her down.

Valeria grinned at him. "I can't seem, to help myself. You and Diana give a thrill never known to a being such as I. That burning passion is just too good...too pure...too beautiful. Even Diana's Gods are impressed. It pleases us all. Now I must go. You have things to prepare for. You and Diana visiting your lovely sweet parents."

"Valeria, I'm serious. Don't you dare ruin this."

"Of course not. Relax, Kal-El." She kissed his cheek and whispered in his ear, "I want a glimpse of the future just as you."

Kal looking at the mirror suddenly turned to her. "Wait? What?!"

She giggled and vanished in the air.

Kal looked back into the mirror and saw Diana smiling looking up at the sky. He saw himself flying down to meet her. He took her hand and got down on one knee.

"A glimpse of the future..." he pondered then smiled. "Our future..."

Meanwhile, WatchTower, Wonder Woman's quarters

"Diana? Diana?" Donna called snapping her fingers in her face.

"Oh...? I'm sorry, Donna."

"You've been in a daze all day. What's the deal?"

"Just a lot on my mind."

"Or is it Clark? Aren't you guys staying at his parents for the weekend?"

"Yes, we are," Diana blushed.

"Oh, fun! Meeting the in-laws!"

THE DARK SPELL

Diana gasped. "Donna!"

"What? You and Clark will totally get married one day. It's so obvious. Everyone knows. We are just all waiting for the invitation."

Diana couldn't stop blushing. "We have so much to do. I don't know about settling down now."

"I'm not talking about right this moment. It can be 2 years from now but there will be a wedding."

"Oh, Donna," Diana shook her head then looked up at her. "Maybe..."

"Oooh I knew it!"

KNOCK KNOCK

Donna pressed the sensor for the door to open and smiled.

"Oh...well well... you must have heard us...Clark."

Diana's heart fluttered seeing him. He was so handsome in his denim jeans and white polo shirt that showed off his biceps and pecs.

"Hey Donna, and no I wasn't listening. Should I have been?"

Donna laughed. "No...I mean it wasn't anything bad. And I'm sure you and Diana will talk about it later anyway..."

"Donna..." Diana said with a raised brow

"Oh, yeah...anyway...let me stop rambling. I have work to do, too, and catch up with Richard and Kori. Bye, sis...and bro."

Donna winked at Diana and quickly left.

Clark laughed and closed the door.

"Ms. Prince..." he smirked.

Diana smiled and got up from her desk. She slowly and seductively walked over to him with extra sway in her hips. Clark looked at her up and down. She looked like a treat to him. She wore an olive green cut-out mock neck top that was giving a bit of a cleavage tease that made his mouth-water with tight black cuffed pants and boots.

"Mr. Kent."

She wrapped her arms around his neck and he wrapped his arms around her waist. Diana giggled as he playfully yanked her closer. Her breasts rubbing against his chest.

"How was your day? Besides dealing with that sewer monster earlier this morning," asked Diana playing with his hair.

"I met the deadline but I'm not sure what was going on with Perry. He was just ranting all day."

"Doesn't he do that every day?"

"Yeah, but today wasn't like the others," he sighed giving a peck on her luscious lips.

"Hmm...don't worry. I'm sure he will be fine. Maybe it's stress. It seems every deadline puts so much pressure and stress on you, so it would be even more so with Perry," she assured with a twinkle in her eyes.

"Yeah, you right." He released her hips from his grip and caressed her cheek. "I missed you," he said giving her small peck again on her lips.

"I missed you, too." She teased him back with another quick peck on his lower lip.

"Valeria popped up in my bathroom earlier."

Diana raised her brow. "What is it that she wanted?"

"Well..she said she would be backing off a bit..."

Another peck.

"But?"

Another sweet peck.

"I don't know. She'll be trying something."

"Never mind her. We've proven what we have can not be tainted. They can all try but it's you and me, Kal-El. Together."

"Damn right!"

Diana smiled and kissed him hard. Clark kissed her back harder and lifted her up and sat her on the desk. Their kisses becoming more intense every second. Kal opened her mouth with his tongue and Diana happily accepted him in. He sucked the tip of her tongue, caressing it gently and let her repeat the same. She tasted of Ice macho and he of cinnamon and their mix making it even more delicious. Together their tongues danced a duel slowly. Diana's hands roamed underneath his shirt feeling his rock-hard abs. She gasped as he ran his hands down her back slowly and squeezed the area of her small back. She arched more into him. Clark deepened the kiss, not able to get enough of Diana's delicacy.

It felt like they were on fire and ice at the same time.

Diana wrapped her free leg around his knees pulling him more closer as she playfully bit his lips.

THE DARK SPELL

Clark's hands slowly come forward and to Diana's thighs, and pushed her legs up higher around his waist, rubbing his jeans covered erection against her inner thigh. Leaving her lips with one last bite, he descended down her neck laying open mouth kisses making her moan.

His hands raised up her sides and over her shirt, he stopped when he got to her breasts, cupping them smoothly through her top. Pausing there, he looked at her for a consent. Diana pulled him for kiss as an answer and Kal's hand snaked inside her top through her mock top and palmed her mounds. Diana threw her head back and gave a low moan at what he was doing to her. Clark went back up to Diana's lips. His hands on her breasts and his other hand back to her thighs, moving up slowly driving her crazy. Before he could go any farther, Diana pulled back and smiled, catching her breath.

"We are going to see your parents. I don't think my hair is enough to hide your markings," she teased.

"I didn't leave any...well not yet. But just you wait," he grinned.

"Oh...? You have something planned already?" she asked straightening her shirt.

"I sure do but it's a surprise," he said proudly.

Diana smiled and kissed him sweetly. "Whatever it is, I know I'm going to enjoy it all with my man."

2 hours later: Smallville

As they reached the farm, Diana took a deep breath. A whole new feeling overcame her. She has visited with the Kents plenty of time before but as Clark's best friend. Now being romantically involved is so different.

Clark grabbed her hand raising it to his lips, kissing the back of it and smiled.

Diana smiled back and leaned over giving him a soft kiss.

"I really enjoyed our drive. We should do that more often."

Clark didn't always fly, coming to visit Smallville or having to go certain places even for work. He didn't want to take the chance of being seen. Clark Kent bought himself a pick up truck as a reward to himself after college. A velocity blue metallic f-150 regular cab.

"We can have road trips or even have a little fun in the back on the truck bed."

Diana giggled getting out of the truck.

"Clark! Diana! How good it is to see the two of you!" Martha said as she stood up from her porch chair.

Clark and Diana walked up the porch holding hands.

"How's it going, Son, Diana?" Jonathan asked.

"Hey Ma, Pa!" Clark hugged them.

"Mr. and Mrs. Kent!" Diana smiled.

"Oh Diana, no need to be formal!" Martha said hugging her.

"Yep! Ma and Pa or just Martha and Jon is just fine!" Jonathan said.

Diana beamed and slightly nodded.

"Are you two hungry? Dinner is almost ready."

"Yes! Diana, has been craving some of your homemade biscuits."

"Oh, of course I made plenty! Come on in, so you two can get settled."

Clark smiled at Diana and took her hand intertwining there fingers as the walked into the house.

There was a feeling that washed over them, like a flash of something.

Maybe just maybe...this can be them. A home, marriage and children.

"Clark, just could not stop talking about you on the phone, Diana. All good things of course." Martha said as they went inside the house.

"Really?" Diana grinned and looked at him.

"I've never seen him so happy. Not since he was a boy with Christmas or anytime I make a cake or pie."

"Endless cake right here..." he said under his breath so that only Diana could hear and gave a her ass a squeeze.

Diana's eyes widen and gasped. She was relieved Martha and Jonathan weren't paying attention.

Clark chuckled and winked at her.

"So, Pa, you mentioned needing help with the tractor?"

"Oh no, no you don't. That can be done later. Time for dinner," Martha said.

"Just giving a really quick, Ma. Be right back."

"Clark?"

"Really quick."

"Just 5 minutes, Martha."

"Fine."

THE DARK SPELL

Diana giggled.

Martha shook her head sighed dramatically. "He may be a man of his own now but he is still my baby boy."

"He is such an honorable hard working man, Martha."

"Ah, yes, Clark has always wanted nothing more than to help around any and every where he could. Being Superman was his true calling and really keeps him busy."

"Yes. There are times, Clark could be gone for months off world. I'd miss him so but I know he is doing all he can for the entire galaxy. He has even made quite the impression on the Gods."

"You know the day, Clark's rocket landed in the cornfield, my prayers had been answered for a child but I just didn't expect this special bundle of joy that would be part of changing not just this world but worlds beyond. Of course there was always stories, but to truly know of life beyond this world is amazing."

Diana smiled and nodded.

"Diana?"

"Yes, Martha?"

"It truly bring me such joy and warms my heart to know that my son has found someone that truly makes him happy. Growing up, Clark did have friends but he still seemed to distance himself because of his powers. I can see he is more open to you than he ever has been with anyone else, even with us to some extent. He really does love you. Thank you, Diana."

"Martha, there's no need to thank me. It is you and Jonathan that has taught him so much. He looks up to both of you. He has the power that could rival Zeus but such a humbled man. A pure heart of gold. He is my best friend. He is the one that I fully trust. That I've been able to open up to. That is what I admire about him and what made me fall in love with him. I believe in fate. The Els had the faith he would be guided to a safe place. You and Jonathan took him in and raised him as your own, giving him so much love. That is part of what motivates him."

"That truly makes us proud. I don't want to sound pushy or anything but..." Martha paused for a moment.

Diana tilted her head. "Yes?"

"I don't know if you both have..."

Diana gave a curious smile.

"Would want children of your own?"

Diana's heart skipped a beat and she looked at Martha shocked.

"Oh...I'm sor-"

"No, no..." Diana smiled and blushed. "Yes." She nodded. "I would like to have children...and marriage with Clark. We haven't talked much about it in detail. Right now, we are still taking things a step at a time given our duties but, yes, one day."

"Well that's all I need to know. You two are both still very young, and do have a lot of responsibility so there isn't a rush and it is still your choice but it makes me immensely happy of having hope of having you as my future daughter in law."

Diana smiled proudly. "Thank you, Ma."

Outside

Clark was happily whistling as he looked over the tractor.

"Diana's a very beautiful young woman."

Clark smiled proudly. "She is. She amazing, Pa."

"Hm? So this is long term?"

"I want...I will marry her one day. She's my best friend. She's changed so much for me. I've never felt this free."

"I'm proud to here that, Son. That's all your mother and I have ever wanted for you. The way you look at Diana and talk about her is exactly how I was with your mother and still am. She's the one. Take your time, though."

"I know, Pa. Diana and I are taking things slow still but she is my future. But one question for you, Pa."

"What's that son?"

"Ready for super powered grandkids?"

Jonathan smiled proudly. "Course!"

The next day: Mid-morning...

Clark took Diana to the town Carnival. Lights shined everywhere and the sounds of people having fun echoed in the wind.

Diana wore a mauve pink high-low maxi skirt with a white boho crop top. Clark wore dark blue jeans with a light grey cotton/suede blend v-neck t-shirt.

THE DARK SPELL

"Oh, Kal! This is lovely!"

"I knew you would enjoy it."

"Yes! That was so sweet of you giving that teddy bear to the young girl."

"It was nothing, Di. I mean, I didn't like her crying like that. The guy could've given it to her regardless of the game rules." He sighed. "To be honest, I was so close to punching him, I had to do something."

She reached up and kissed his cheek. "That's why I love you, my super gentleman."

Clark smiled proudly holding Diana's hand tighter.

"Hey, let's get on the Ferris wheel."

"Really?"

"Yeah, we can get a good view of everything from the top."

"But, shouldn't we let others do so? We can fly."

Clark grinned. "Di, come on. You'll see what I mean."

Diana quirked her brow and followed him.

After a wait of about 10 minutes, Clark and Diana were up. The two entered the cart and closed the small door behind them.

When they sat down, Clark enveloped Diana in his arms. His body was slightly turned toward her as the Ferris wheel moved slowly.

"How is this?"

"It's actually quite calming."

"Told you."

Diana laughed softly. "Yes, you did..."

As the Ferris wheel attempted to make its third trip around, the ride came to a sudden stop, with Clark and Diana at its highest point.

Diana waited for the motion of moving again, but nothing is happening. She frowned and looked at Clark.

"Kal, it seems we are stuck."

He shook his head and leaned closer to her and brushed his lips against hers, one of his arms still securely around her shoulders and the other free to roam. The faint sounds of the fair beneath them do nothing to mask the way she was breathing, and when Clark decided to be bold and take her mouth deeper for his own, the soft whimpering sound she made echoes in between the both of them.

They kiss like that for a few minutes. Clark's free hand cupped her shoulder, then traced down her arm until his fingers gently curl around feeling her curves. His tongue swept across hers again as his hand slid around her hip, dangerously close to her ass.

Breathless with a passion for him Diana hardly knew what to do with, Diana try to show him with her kisses that everything he's doing, hell anything he was doing was good. So good.

Without any doubt to fog her actions, every part of her wanted him, and right now the only part she can get to is his mouth, his tongue, the line of his jaw, his throat...

Delicious...

She brushed her lips on his adam's apple.

Clark chuckled low in his throat, inhaling the sweet scent of her. Diana could feel his hand move to cover her derrière now, and his palm was hot, even over the thin cotton fabric of her skirt that's conveniently riding up.

"So sexy..." she unconsciously said aloud.

"Trust me, I've thought the same thing about you," he whispered, pulling her closer so her leg hitched up and over one of his.

"I said that out loud, didn't I?" she asked him, the realization making her blush.

He nodded and grinned at her, his smile infectious and she grinned right back at him, feeling giddy and safe and falling for him all over again so hard, she knew he could hear the way her heart was pounding.

Diana could feel his hand moving again, this time down her bare leg. The soft pads of his fingertips drawing swirls and circles up and down her skin.

He tilted his head down to kiss her again before leaning back.

Diana was amazed at the scene before her: a panting, flustered Kal-El, sighing softly underneath a clear Fall sky. He laughed before opening his eyes again to look at her.

He whispered her name, almost to himself, and nuzzled the tip of her nose with his before sneaking in a kiss punctuated by a bite to her lower lip. The passion surprised her and when she bit back he growls warningly, his long fingers cupping her again, kneading her curves, pulling her impossibly closer to him.

THE DARK SPELL

Diana's hand, the one resting on his chest starts to slowly slip down his stomach and underneath his shirt and he didn't stop her, no, instead he was moaning into her mouth, the sound somewhere in between a chuckle and a groan. Her fingers stop just over his heart and, gods, she can feel it pounding beneath her palm.

"I love you, Diana. I love you so much," he sighed as Diana kissed the spot over his shirt.

His hand moved underneath the flannel over her legs, those long fingers of his inching closer to her white cotton panties.

"I want you," he murmured against the corner of her mouth. His fingers moved again.

He swept his tongue across hers, and his fingers, his strong, long, callous and warm fingers slip beneath her panties and his breath caught to find her so wet, nearly soaked through.

"Diana...," he whispered, slipping a finger inside her.

Diana gasped and moaned, her hand slipping out from underneath his shirt so you could wrap her arms around his neck. He pulled her closer so that she practically in his lap now.

Some part of Diana's brain was still functioning when she asked him, breathless, "Kal...what if...I mean can't people see? I...I...oh gods..."

He slipped another finger into her now and she fell back, his arm supporting her, and as he cradled her, he moved inside of her, gently, deeply, and when she opened her eyes, her vision hazy, he's watching her, biting his lower lip, his eyes heavy with a passion she'd never seen before.

"Nobody can see us," he reassured her, his thumb now circling her bundle of nerves.

"I don't even care if they can," he corrected himself jokingly.

"Kal!" Diana gasped surprised.

Clark's fingers moving faster. Diana pressed her lips together to keep her sighs and moans to a minimum.

Diana needed to taste him again, so she claimed his mouth for her own and he rewarded her by moving those talented fingers faster and faster inside of her.

"Gods," she whispered in between kisses.

She was delirious with passion for this man and she almost felt drunk with love for him.

It's then when his fingers slip out of her and like a fantasy, one she might not admit to having because its so, well, dirty, he locked eyes with her as he slips his own fingers into his mouth, sucks her off his skin like some kind of delicacy.

She watched him, completely frozen, trembling and hot and out of her mind with love for him and his fingers slipping from his mouth, down to her center once more, he kissed her deeply, and sighed, "You taste so much than that funnel cake and cotton candy we had."

"By the Gods, Kal..."

All coherent thought suddenly leaving her as his fingers begin to move inside her again, hitting that one spot that makes her entire body tremble.

He chuckled, the sound low in his throat as he brought her to completion, his mouth marking a spot on her neck as his own. She held a tight grip on the rail trying to maintain the violent shaking of her body.

As she come back down to earth, her body limp in his arms, a thin sheen of perspiration over her skin, he slips out of her again, tasting her one last time on his fingers.

"I've imagined...a lot of things, between you and me, Diana," he confessed. "I want to do it all."

Diana blushed and kissed him. She could taste herself mixed with the rich taste of his own tongue and she sighed lovingly.

He pulled away to kiss the tip of her nose and nuzzled her neck.

"Couple more minutes up here," he whispered against her ear, lazily running his tongue along the outline of her jaw.

"This was your plan all along?"

"Yep!"

"Mmhh...very risky, Mr. Kent."

He laughed, and grinned deviously with a love in his eyes that made her catch her breath.

He gazed at her for a moment, before kissing her softly.

Later: Back at the Kent Farm

THE DARK SPELL

Jonathan and Clark were outside working on the tractor again while Diana was looking through photo albums and family cookbooks with Martha.

"Oh! Clark is so cute!"

"This is when he was about 9. Even that young he was trying to make dinner all by himself for our anniversary. It was one of the most precious moments." Martha thought for a moment. "Ah, Diana, I'll be sure to give you my other recipe book. Just follow step by step. There's even a very special dessert recipe that's perfect for a romantic night."

"Oh..." Diana blushed. "Thank you, Martha. I would like to make you something from Themyscira or maybe you could come to the island with me?"

"Oh, that would be such an honor!"

All of a sudden the phone rang.

"Ah, that must be Anita about the cake I made for her son's birthday. I will be right back."

Diana nodded and continued looking through the albums.

"Hmm...naughty naughty Princess," she heard beside her.

Diana jumped slightly then rolled her eyes. "What are you doing here, Valeria? We knew better than to trust you would let us be."

Valeria smiled crossing her legs. "It's a pleasure to see you as well, Diana. I'm sure you are quite pleased with the little display earlier between you and Kal-El?"

Diana's eyes widen and her heart skipped a beat.

"Quite a public display of affection." Valeria grinned wider mischievously.

"It's our business."

"You just can't help it, can you? That man has such an effect on you that can't be controlled now. But I have to ask..."

"What is that?"

"What will you do once he gets bored? Men love their toys for a while but then something new comes along. You might be an immortal beauty but that doesn't change the ways of a man."

"Kal is no ordinary man. You know that. He loves only me and he is mine. We are committed to one another. I understand that is something you aren't used to dealing with."

"Are you sure?" Valeria smirked.

"I trust him more than anyone else I know."

"Then show him."

"What?"

Valeria smiled wickedly. "Diana, I see the desire in your eyes. He is your, you say? Show him."

Diana didn't quite understand what Valeria was saying especially given the fact that she and Kal had been spending so much time together showing how much they loved each other. What more was there?

Diana sighed and closed her eyes thinking back to earlier. Then suddenly a shiver ran down her spine straight to her core.

"Mine...all mine," she thought. "Every inch of him."

She pondered for a moment longer.

There's nothing wrong with leaving a mark...

"Leave now, Valeria. Martha doesn't need to see you."

"Oh, I understand, Princess. Toodles."

Diana sighed and shook her head trying to get back focused. Then the door opened, Clark and Jonathan walking in. Diana's heart skipped a beat and immediately felt a wave of heat washing through her body seeing Clark shirtless and wearing loose jeans. He has oil smears and dirt on his face and chest. But by the Gods, he was a man that knew how to get down and dirty, knew how to use his hands in more ways than one and it was just so damn sexy seeing him work.

"All done, boys?" Martha asked.

"Yeah. Clark did pretty much all the work with the muffler and spark arrester. I was just giving him company. Thanks, Son."

"It was nothing, Pa." Kal wiped his face with the Jon offered.

Clark leaned over the couch and kissed Diana's cheek. He noticed her skirt was raised a bit. He really couldn't get enough of her sexy legs.

"Clean thoughts, Clark..." he thought to himself. "Ma and Pa here."

But of course, he couldn't help himself, especially not after earlier at the carnival.

THE DARK SPELL

"You okay?" He asked Diana.

She breathed out slowly and nodded with a smile.

"Jonathan, we have to go to Anita's to drop off the cake and go to the market."

"2 minutes, Martha. Let me clean up a bit." He rushed to the bathroom.

"We will be back in about 2 hours max."

"That's fine, Ma. We'll just be here. Maybe take a walk to the lake or just stay in..."

"I'm quite enjoying seeing all your adorable baby photos, Clark."

"Wait...Ma?!"

"Oh, we are past the embarrassing photos. I showed those first."

"Ma!"

Martha and Diana laughed.

"Let us go, can't be late with the birthday cake."

5 minutes after Martha and Jonathan left, Clark kissed Diana's cheek again.

"Alright, Di. It's just us now. What's wrong?"

"Nothing, Darling, really."

"You sure?"

She nodded and gave him a reassuring smile.

"Okay, well I'll go get a shower then we can go out again or stay in."

"Hmmm...we can stay in. Just hurry back so we can...cuddle..."

He laughed. "Cuddle? That's what are we calling it?"

Diana smirked. "Uh-huh... just cuddling..."

5 minutes later...

Clark sighed as he stepped into the steaming hot shower. So many thoughts were running through his mind. But it was something about Diana. He hoped she wasn't having second thoughts about anything. Hope he didn't jinx anything and wasn't rushing anything. He shook his head. No. He shouldn't overthink this.

Suddenly, his whole body then tensed feeling soft lips against the back of his neck.

"Di?"

So caught up in his thoughts, he didn't hear her come in.

She smiled. Her soft breasts brush against his back. She ran her hands slowly down his arms then ran her hands over his abs to his chest. Clark let out a low groan.

"I couldn't stop thinking about it earlier." She stood on her top toes and whispered in his ear. "Then you just had to come in looking so irresistible. Thinking about how hard you work...your hands." Her hand traveled slowly down from his chest, to abs to the V of his abdomen.

"Diana..."

"It's only fair to you, Love, that I return the favor."

She slowly slid her hand down and gently reached the base of his manhood. Gripping there. She stroked him slow, measured movements making him groan. He grew in her hands as she pumped him slow and sensual.

"Valeria made a quick visit here, too," she said kissing the bare skin of his shoulder.

His eyes shot open. "Dammit! Why?"

"She knows about earlier too. But I told her it's our business. Just like right now is."

Her other hand dropped low to massage him.

"Damn...Damn right..." Clark closed his eyes again.

Her hands were doing wonders to him. She never had much of a chance to worship him the way he worshipped her, now making him tremble under her ministrations brought her great pride and satisfaction. He was hard yet his skin was smooth and hot underneath her fingers.

"Clark?" She asked him.

"Yeah, Di?" He reached behind to cup her ass.

"Do you love me?"

He opened his eyes immediately and released her ass. When Diana stopped her stokes, he turned to face her and bore into her eyes. He cupped her face with both hands.

"Diana, of course, I do. Don't ever question that. Don't ever let Valeria or anyone else try to cast doubt on what we have on my love for you. I will always love you."

She smiled. "I don't doubt you, us, nor our love. But to hear you say those words fills my heart even more."

THE DARK SPELL

Clark smiled back and captured her lips in a passionate kiss. Deepening the kiss, their hands again started to roam on each other's wet bodies. Clark's hand settled on her bottom squeezing it hard and Diana gripped him again, slowly stroking up.

Breaking the kiss, their gazes meet, hot and intense.

Diana backed Clark up against the wall, leaning forward, and pressed a soft kiss to his lips, leaning further to kiss his cheek, her tongue flicked out to his ear tracing the shell. Clark caught his breath as her hands started to stroke him again. Diana sucked his earlobe and gently bit his shell again. She dropped a kiss on his nose and opened his mouth with her tongue one more time before working her way down.

Clark was completely at her mercy when Diana sucked softly at the hollow of his throat. She intertwined her free hand with his. And not letting him go, her lips captured his nipple and sucked, teased, circled with her tongue.

Clark bit his lips and trembled at her action. She let his hand go and dipped down to kiss his navel and ran her hands on chiseled abs. He got painfully erect and Diana flicked her tongue tracing his abs to the trail of his curls down below.

Looking at his eyes, Diana ran her fingers once again along the length of him, making him gasp and moan and fluctuate his hips into her touch.

Her tongue flicked out to lick the small drop from the tip, savoring the taste of her lover. She ran her thumb over the slit with just the barest touch of nail, and Clark moaned her name, tangling his fingers in her hair. Diana smiled up at Clark mischievously and kissed his tip again meeting his eyes. She closed her fist around the base of him and takes the swollen throbbing head into her mouth, hollowing her cheeks and sucked hard.

Clark's head thumps back against the wall, but he doesn't break eye contact as Diana swiped her tongue over the crown, licking it like an ice cream cone. Clark was so surprised and so pleased as Diana was swirling her tongue and yet he fought to keep his hips from moving.

That only made her love him more. She slowly lowered her mouth over the length of him. Clark fluttered his eyes to see her release him once from her mouth, running her tongue along his length, and then she slowly took him back in her mouth. Clark's cheeks were flushed and had his teeth buried in his lower lip, trying to hold back the groans that are threatening to escape but he couldn't hold back. The sound Clark made was delicious, somewhere between a moan and a whine.

Relaxing her throat, she took him further until his tip touched the back of her throat. She slowly let him slip out of her mouth until only the tip was between her lip.

Clark's grip on her hair tightened, knuckles rubbing against her scalp. Then she did it again taking him fully each time, faster and faster increasing her pace until he thrust forward and Diana took more of him. Clark said incoherent nothings but his voice was hoarse and ragged, dripping with sex. His fingertips move feather-light over Diana's temples.

Then he's gripping the back of Diana's head, palms snug against her skull, holding her in place. He grunted and repeated the slow forward-thrusting movement.

Diana moaned and swallowed around him, Clark's breathing becoming heavier and more irregular.

"So good, Diana," Clark moaned, fingers flexing against the back of her head.

Diana released him. She was honestly surprised at herself. Experiencing things such as this she never would've thought but with Clark, he brings out something within her she so indescribable. It was truly amazing.

Clark's entire body was tensing up, almost visibly shaking. He looked down at Diana and she looked up at him. Eyes locked, she took his shaft back in her mouth and added her hands to work.

His hips stuttering as he got closer and closer to the edge, and then he's coming. Diana groaned, not spilling a single drop, relishing the taste.

Clark's body went loose and languid, his hands petting Diana's hair softly.

"C'mere," he said.

Diana pulled off and got up from the floor. Clark hauled her in close and kissed her, licking into Diana's mouth and tasting himself on Diana's tongue. Eliciting a low moan from deep within her, his fingers probed everywhere, dancing along her collarbone then caressing her breasts, then lower until they found just the right spot, of her dripping wet womanhood, making her gasp then moan.

THE DARK SPELL

"Yes, Kal... right there... just like that," she moaned as his fingers worked their magic and her back arched against him as she shattered around his fingers.

She wrapped her arms around his neck, letting him hold her weight as she came down from ecstasy.

2.5 hours later...

"Hector sure can talk," Jonathan said as he and Martha walked into the house.

Martha laughed. "He sure was angry about losing that poker game."

"That's something between him and Gavin."

"Aww, look at you two," Martha gushed. "We were gone a little longer than expected."

Clark and Diana were cuddled under the quilt on the sofa watching TV.

"Oh, it's okay, Ma, Diana and I were just...relaxing."

"Well, I'll get dinner started."

"Diana and I were actually going to cook, Ma."

Martha looked surprised. "You sure?"

"Yeah! Yeah! We got it."

Clark and Diana stood up. Clark took Diana's hand as they walked to the kitchen.

Martha and Jonathan looked at each other stunned.

"Our boy really is in love," Jonathan said. "So I guess it's time to expand the house like we always wanted?"

"Yes, it's time," Martha smiled proudly. "It's time."

CHAPTER 6: ALL A WOMAN WANT AND NEED IN A MAN

Sunday 5 p.m. Smallville, Kent Farm

The beautiful evening is calm and free.

Clark, Diana, and the Kents stood on the front porch saying their goodbyes.

"Now, promise it won't take a whole year for you two to come back for a visit," Martha said with a raised brow holding Diana's hand.

Diana smiled and hugged her. "We promise."

Martha patting her back. "Sweet girl. Remember our talk, too?"

Diana pulled away smiling wider. "Of course."

Diana inhaled the delicious smell of homemade sweet potato pies in a box that Martha gave for snacking on the way back to Metropolis. Martha's desserts were her absolute favorite.

"Take care, Champ" Jon patted his son's shoulder as they joined the women in front of the porch.

Clark hugged him around his shoulders. "Sure Pa." And turned to Martha to hug her soft.

"Diana," Jonathan smiled proudly. "Keep my boy on his toes."

"Oh, yes, Jonathan I surely will." Diana hugged Jonathan.

"Well, you two best get going, long drive back to Metropolis." Martha released her son's cheek.

"I appreciate you driving here for sake of our privacy," Jonathan remarked.

"This is actually the best time to take a drive, the view from driving will be spectacular." Clark took Diana's hand.

"I'll call you to let you know we made it back."

When Clark and Diana went to the truck, Clark opened the passenger side door for her.

"Thank you."

He blew out a breath as he helped himself with a look at Diana's long legs before he closed the door, Clark walked around to the driver's side and got in. Clark couldn't stop smiling. Driving in his F-150, with the most gorgeous woman in the universe was a true dream. She was glowing with her hair pulled back in a long ponytail. She was wearing a cherry red off-shoulder top and blue denim skirt.

Diana looked at him, noticing how he was staring, and smiled back. She found him quite irresistible and flaunting his muscular arms wearing a plain white tank and blue jeans.

"Ready?" he checked with her as he starts the engine.

Diana nodded. "I wish the weekend hadn't gone by so fast," she replied biting her lips looking at Martha and Jon's reflection in the mirror.

"We'll be back soon. Ma will be sure of it anyway," he assured.

Clark and Diana waved as he drove off. The Kents waved back until they couldn't see them anymore down the road.

Martha sighed looking at the direction the truck faded in. "I miss them already. Clark is his own man now. Diana has really brought out something within him."

"He found someone that has pushed him to be the man we knew he could be. They are on the same wavelength after all." Jonathan draped his arm across her shoulder and pulled Martha closer to him.

"Indeed they are." Their heads tilt to the side resting against each other, smiling as proud old parents.

Older love that has survived through so many storms is so sacred, so rare...

The drive was quiet and tranquil.

Clark took Diana's hand intertwining their fingers. He raised her hand to his lips kissing the back of it and noticed how her red nail polish complimented her summer tan. Diana smiled and slide her head towards his shoulder holding his hand tighter.

The sun was setting as they continued to somewhere quite unknown.

Diana tilted her head curiously.

"Where are we going?"

Clark grinned, "You'll see..." Changing the gear, his fingertips traced her smooth thighs.

THE DARK SPELL

"Kal..." she whined in mocking anger, a tingling sensation ran through her body.

He grinned boyishly, hearing the change in her voice, and continued his tease.

His hand drifted across her soft skin and found the lace barrier between her legs yet he focused hard on the road as he knew there were dangerous curves ahead.

No longer than 10 minutes later, he drove up to the Flint Hills and stopped in the middle of the road.

He turned off the truck and reached back to get a blanket. He got out to the back of the truck opening the tailgate.

He spread out the blanket on the bed of the truck.

Once the setup is complete, he opened Diana's door with a smile. Diana smiled back and got out.

A light breeze was blowing, and all the blue-violet flowers swayed to the beat of their own song. She was captivated by the vast land of greenery, the Sun was setting, giving it a more alluring feel.

Pure luminous color fighting the silent shadows to the last.

Clark plucked the blue-violet flowers and made a bouquet of them.

"This is beautiful!" She accepted his bouquet with a peck on his lips.

He took her hand and they went to the back of the truck. Clark stepped up first then pulled Diana up with him. He wrapped his arms around her waist and kissed her softly.

They kneeled to lay down. Clark with one hand on the back of his head and the other around Diana. She with her head on his chest and arm around him.

They laid there like that for some time observing the sky changing color from orange candy to raspberry in the blinks of their eyes.

"Di?" Clark overcame the silence.

"Yes, Kal?"

She looked up at him. Clark tilted his head down to capture her soft lips. Diana adjusted herself raising more opening her lips. Their lips stuck like a magnet. Diana tugged him down with a much firmer kiss by sliding her tongue along his bottom lips and Kal made a smothered moan before he took over the kiss, pressing hard against her mouth. They continued their heated make-out session, kissing each other senseless, plundering and exploring each other's mouths with their tongues, until they were both gasping for air.

"You look beautiful."

He drank at the sight before him. The soft light illuminating her skin and the breeze gently dancing through her strands. She is here with him, right now. He kissed her forehead and Diana smiled into his eyes, giving him a quick peck.

They moved closer and turned their heads facing the evening sky.

"I wished I had someone to enjoy this with me. With who could do what I do and see what I see." He kissed her hand, looking deep into the never-ending sky. Somewhere out there where his home planet was supposed to be. "Wish granted. Right here."

Diana's heart fluttered as she blushed. "Kal."

His eyes met her's. His soul pointing at her and with his heart he whispered, "I I love you, Diana."

"I love you, too, Kal. Thank you for bringing me here and sharing this with me." Diana tightened her grip around him.

His eyes hold everything her soul wants.

"I know. My parents love you too. We can... we can have a life like this, too. I don't want to rush anything but-"

He raised his head when Diana sat up. She caressed his cheek and leaned down to kiss him. She kissed deeply like never before, pulled him closer and closer, as they breathe in each other's scent, uniting their soul and let it awaken his heart, shutting up his questioning mind.

Diana was completely on top of him and their tongues danced together twisting and turning. Clark's free hand roamed on her back getting closer and closer until he reached her rear.

Clark pulled away from her kiss asking, "Come live with me." And patted her ass cheeks nicely.

Diana gasped. "Really, Kal?" She felt his naughty hands riding her ass under her skirt.

"Yeah, really! I mean, I know you've been in London for so long..." he said focusing on squeezing her ass cheeks.

THE DARK SPELL

"I'm also mostly in Metropolis nowadays...anyway," she smirked at him to guess her answer.

"So that's a yes?" Clark questioned with a knowing grin.

"Yes, Love! Yes!" She pulled her tongue into his mouth, tasting it, sucking it, drawing it deeper and deeper, their dance continues...

They were intoxicated on the intimacy they shared; both having their mouth paired, losing their breath in each other and eyes half-lidded.

Clark wrapped his arms around her waist as Diana adjusted herself to straddle him properly embracing her core over his bulge.

Between their heated kiss, in one sharp movement, he raised forwards and rubbed himself between the junction of her thighs. Diana shuddered over his hardness

When they parted for long-lost air, a string of saliva connected their lips as they both panted and smiled at each other.

"Clark..." Diana hissed grinding exactly where he needed her. Her hand moved up into his hair, traced around the curves of his ears, and dragged her fingers down his neck across his stomach to his inner thigh, and began to massage the head of his bulge over his jeans.

She raised herself balancing on her legs to shift a little lower settling on his knees. Her eyes slowly getting wider and wider, measuring him from top to bottom, Clark indeed is a well-gifted man. She saw him biting his lip as he tried to hold back a moan.

"I loved you in the shower yesterday. The taste of you..." She looked at his package, her cheeks flushing a sparkling pink. She bit her lip, her palm struggling to enclose all of him. She leaned forward until he could feel the whiffs of her breath on his lips. Clark twitched in response, "I want more of that," she confessed.

She scraped her nails on his jean-enclosed tip and he felt another more intense twitch and tightened in his jeans.

"Diana..." he grunted, his heart pounding, licked his lips, and swallowed thickly. He desired this with her for years and fantasized about it night after night. Pictured it every time in the shower and in the bed stroking his length.

She perched up for Clark to sit up. Clark pulled her close for a clumsy kiss. Diana's hand rushed to remove his tee over his head. Her eyes slid back down over his toned chest and stomach until they finally rested on the jeans that hid the thing she most craved. Reaching to kiss him again, her hand trailing around his side feeling his hard skin. Pulling away from the kiss, she unbuttoned and unzipped his jeans.

Clark dropped his head, "Diana, my love..."

She grinned, her fingers hooked in his waistband. Clark slightly raised for her to pull down his jeans and then boxers. Doing so, a gentle 'hmmm' sounded in her throat. He was freed from his confine and stood in front of her proud and tall. Her hand brushed on him and admired his softness. Like steel enclosed in velvet. Clark gritted his teeth, breathing heavily through his nose.

She dragged his foreskin down, exposing the head to the evening breeze. His purple glistening crown released a salty musk in the air.

She enjoyed the marvelous sensation of sliding her fingers from the base, up to the head of his member, and slid his foreskin up and down. Clark bit back a grunt when she trailed her thumb down the underside, brushing the sensitive area and circling the ridge. The only knowledge Diana has of the male physical body was from books or when she came to man's world and discovered television and the internet. The warmth and musky smell of him enticed her even more. Diana stroked him up and down inch by inch looking for his reaction.

She was quite intrigued by his curve and softness, how he rose and grew in her hand. Every little touch causing him to twitch.

Clark was the first man she has been so sexually connected and open to. She shared an innocent kiss with Steve Trevor, the first man she had ever met before but it was nothing farther than that. At that time, understanding love and what being in a relationship meant was so new to her. She didn't even know what hand-holding between a man and woman meant. It was always Steve wanting to initiate things Diana didn't quite understand just yet. He wanted her to feel more for him, wanting to go farther but her feelings for him never went deeper than just being friends. However, with Clark, she was ready. He understood her feelings and what she wanted. He was patient with her and respected her letting her take her time exploring and appreciating his body. That's what made her love him all the more.

THE DARK SPELL

Pushing him back to lay, she dipped to kneel between his stretched legs and leaned forward towards his throbbing erection. Diana's eyes not once moving from gazing at her lover's eyes, her soft lips caressed his throbbing member like a precious gift. She let the tip of her tongue run up the length of his shaft, one long lick from root to tip. Clark felt a burning sensation everywhere her wet tongue touched.

Flicking her tongue teasingly over the swelling and leaking tip, Diana moaned lightly, her sparkling cerulean blue lust-filled eyes still not once breaking their gaze with Clark's. She relished the way Clark's eyes darkened.

Grazing her teeth over the prominent vein, he groaned lowly bucking his hips slightly into Diana's lips as she laughed lightly before engulfing the tender head into her mouth.

Clark closed his eyes tight at the first contact and Diana could feel the goosebumps rise underneath her hand and heard him groan. He tasted salty like the Pitanga fruit. It was one of her favorites on Themyscira.

Clark melted into her mouth as she sucked him slowly and gently. He took a deep breath and forgot to exhale.

Diana savoring his taste decided to slow down, she released his head with a pop. Clark opened his eyes and felt a shiver run through both of them and they both began to feel the heat of the moment start to course through them. Even though Diana wanted to drag out the teasing, she couldn't deny what she wanted. Her eyes roamed over him once again, loving how sexy he was breathing and sweating at the dawn of moonlight and taking in the fact that he was all hers.

Diana took him in hand and licked him all over. She swirled her tongue around the tip licking his salty essence as he drips. Working down Clark's throbbing length slowly while pressing hard against that one prominent vein, moaning and humming lowly causing pleasuring vibrations down Clark's length straight to his groin.

She dipped lower very slowly, relaxing her throat, and took more of him in her mouth until he was pressed against the back of her throat.

Clark groaned loudly when he was engulfed in the warm, wet heat of her mouth. His hands reached out blindly to grab something and all he got was a fistful of her hair and the blanket. As her mouth started to slide off, he moaned deeply and bucked his hips up in the urge for more.

She pulled up momentarily and focused on the stroking.

His manhood stood upright in her hand bathed in her saliva.

"Diana...." He breathed heavily.

With a small grin on her face, she concentrated on him making long glides from base to head slowly back to back, her grip was firmer at the base and lighter near the head. Clark felt his heartbeat at his manhood pulsating under her fingers, could see it in each throb as she stroked him.

She engulfed the head ever so slowly again, she moved her hand to run her nails along his bare thighs and, then up and down his stomach, making his manhood throb between her lips. He looked up at the dark star-filled sky taking a deep breath. With his heavy breathing and racing heart, a wonderful aching feeling formed at the pit of his stomach taking him over the edge, to a road with no way back. And he was glad for that.

He propped his hand to lift his shoulder and his eyes fell on her, and his gaze was met with her devious cerulean eyes as she slid him off and brushed her tongue over the tip. She massaged him well there until she saw the begging look in his eyes.

Clark dropped his head back against the truck and groaned again. Both of his hands now in her hair, caressing and massaging her scalp, encouraging her to go further.

Diana was loving the reaction she was getting from him. Releasing him from her lips, her slender hand wrapped around the base of his length and squeezed him just hard enough to make him a jerk. He pulsed in her hand, and when she looked back down at his member, leaking out of the tip and dripping with her saliva, electric jolts shot through her veins out of sheer arousal from the sight. She ran her hand over the head, getting her hand slick, and then stroking him slowly. It was a slow but sure movement and she made sure to throw in a few things just to drive him crazier. Her fingers grazed the tip and squeezed him lightly here and there. He began to moan louder and squirm underneath her. Her mouth closed around him, her tongue moving over it in lazy, sensual licks. The whole time her eyes were locked on him and his locked on hers. The connection of their eyes only made Clark more turned on. As she moved her head up and down on him slowly and her hands went back to massaging his inner thigh.

Diana continued her feasting on him, her cheeks hollowed, knowing soon, from the sound of his breathing she would have to stop. The wetness of her mouth on his skin was driving him mad, and he swallowed hard with every breath he took.

With every lusting lick on him and every subtle graze of her teeth against his sensitive skin, his whole body shivered and the muscles in his abdomen tightened. Diana's warm, soft hands moved up and ran over his firm abdomen and outlined his abs with the tip of her finger. She raised him from her mouth and flipped her hair over her shoulder so she had a bit better access to him and his pulsing length that she could never get enough of. Her eyes flicked up to look at him as she continued to smirk. Just the look of ecstasy on his face and the look of his raw and half-naked body writhing in pleasure beneath her turned her on even more.

She flattened her tongue down the length of his shaft licking slowly again and again, and she came to his balls that were hot and heavy. She ran her tongue all over his balls, sucking each of them into her mouth briefly before moving up again and filling him into her mouth, bobbing up and down, moaning as he pressed against the back of her throat.

Clark knew he wouldn't be able to hold it back much longer. He bucked his hips up slightly to meet the movements of her mouth. She took full advantage of this and began taking as much of him in as she could.

His whole body went rigid as the heat in his lower stomach seemed to come rushing through his veins and his orgasm overwhelmed him.

"Diana...!" He groaned loudly as he exploded inside her mouth. He continued to moan her name in an array of dynamics shooting jet after jet of his essence in jerking jabs.

Diana kept her lips tightly closed around him. She gulped from his member's release smiling with her lips closed, she kept her hand on him and stroked slow. Some of his essence dripped from her mouth and rinsed his shaft, overflowed on his legs. Clark groaned again as she licked him clean not wanting to waste a single drop of him.

She smiled satisfied that he softened in such a wonderful ecstasy due to her. Getting him off has equally excited her, she felt drenched through her panties. Seeing her lover breathing heavily and panting, in all his, half-naked afterglow made her desire him more. Not even in her wildest dreams, she could have imagined she would want someone as much as she wanted him.

She looked up as Clark raised. His smile was as tender as it could be and he motioned for her to come closer. She smiled before slowly reaching up to his body, raising her jean skirt, and straddling his muscular legs to meet him with a kiss.

His lips were slow and gentle against hers, thanking her in the way. He kissed her with love and content. However, Diana had other ideas. She nipped at his lower lip lightly and deepened the loving kiss in an attempt to gain entrance. Clark had no other choice but to oblige. He parted his lips slightly and felt her tongue sneak past. Her tongue slid seductively over his, and he could taste himself on her tongue, making him moan into her mouth. But before the kiss could become too deep, Diana broke it off.

"Wow...someone's really eager," he flirted with her teasingly. His grip on her hair loosened and he untangled his fingers from her now messy hair, moving them down to her waist.

Clark heard her sigh deeply as she felt his hardness raising again against her middle. Her eyes went wide realizing the power she has over him.

Clark's raised underneath her feeling how wet she was through her panties.

"Kal-El...I want you," She murmured, her hands running up and down his chest, slowly grinding against him.

"Wait...you mean? Are you sure? I thought we were waiting?"

Diana smiled placing her finger over his lips.

"Kal, we've already waited. We've already proven to ourselves most importantly our love is pure and true. What we share is not determined by anyone else but us. We are in control, remember? I want my man, right here, right now." She rubbed her core fast against him at end of her sentence

Clark nodded slightly. "As long as you are comfortable and ready, Di. One thing, though..."

"What is it?"

"The truck might not be able to take us with our activity."

Diana giggled. "Understood."

THE DARK SPELL

Diana moved off of him and slipped her hands along the sides of her thighs and under her skirt. Clark ran his tongue over his bottom lip as he watched the black lace thong make its journey down those beautiful legs and Diana stepped free from her soaked panties. Clark took a breath and looked at the sight in front of him. All legs in a short skirt. He felt himself hardening like steel once again at the sight.

She playfully tossed her panties to him.

"So...so sexy..." he murmured.

Diana felt herself flush beneath Clark's heated gaze, her breathing quickening as desire pooled in her core. She smirked straddling him once more slowly position herself over him and pressed her lips to his eagerly. Diana could feel the smile on his lips when their mouths met once more. Clark replied immediately, just as eager for Diana's lips as she was for his. Clark moved his hands to grip her hips. Small pecks escalating into so much more as she nipped at his lips playfully, opening up to him and feeling her passion for him build more and more.

Diana grinding her slick center against his member. The feeling teasing them both. Her mouth was open, her lips parted in a small 'o'. Her eyes were wide, searching his own, and he could see his own question reflected there.

Are we really going to do this?

He closed his eyes and when he opened them they were black with lust and resolute, "Ready?"

She nodded, almost imperceptibly, and lowered herself onto him and let out a little gasp as the tip entered her. Slowly she took him, inch by inch. She let out a low moan as she continues moving down and he kept stretching her as she did so. Once he was fully inside her, the pair paused for a moment to enjoy the feeling that they had both longed for.

A short scream escaped her lips, swallowed by warm lips and tongue and teeth. Clark was devouring her, filling her up and pulling her down to sink farther onto him. Diana ripped her mouth away from his, gasping for air as her fingers were knotting in his hair, knuckles white as she groaned, arching into him.

Clark dragged his lips across her cheek, her aroma mixed with the combined scent of their sex smelled like an aphrodite in surrounding cool air. He kissed her cheek and nibbled his way down her neck, humming happily as he sucked on her pulse.

Diana arched her back and bit her lip. She threw her head back with another gasp, feeling him deeply buried inside her. She flooded with wetness, arching her hips into his as her core throbbed with pleasure. Her hand threaded through his hair, holding him against her. Her eyes fluttered rapidly as her breathing increased, desire coursing through her veins, a fire growing between her legs.

After a moment of enjoying the idle feeling, Clark and Diana finally started moving against one another. Diana grasped Clark's shoulders whilst his hands still holding on to her hips. Their movements started slow and paced, causing the truck to rock slightly.

Clark groaned at the way she was grinding and bucking against him, the hoarse sounds escaping her lips as she moaned his name, her fingers pulling on his hair. making a shudder run through him. He looked at her who had her head still thrown back as her eyes squeezed shut in pleasure. He touched her cheek softly, and she moved her head to look at him.

Looking at Clark made Diana want to cry. His eyes held such adoration and love for her that it was almost overwhelming. She knew that she loved him and never wanted this to end between them, and looking into the eyes of her Beloved, she knew that he never wanted this to end either.

Clark slid his arms around Diana's back and she slid her arms around his neck, moving them even closer than they already were.

Diana felt pure ecstasy kissing him passionately. She loved him so much for loving her so fiercely. When she was with him she had everything she always dreamed of. When she was with him she could forget all her troubles and worries. She was free. She could dream and be happy and be taken over the moon by a culmination of marvelous feelings. Feelings that she would never be able to describe.

Their kisses became more eager and demanding. Their tongues dancing frantically, begging for more of each other's taste. Diana pinned him down and ground her hips against his body bracing herself on either side of his head as she leaned over him. She began to roll her hips as she explored him as best as she could, Clark's fingers gripped tightly her thighs and derrière. Diana registered all of the feelings flooding her at once. Her breath came

THE DARK SPELL

out as a soft whimper as she began moving once again, her hips gently rocking and grinding against his and eliciting a deep, rumbling moan from his chest. Clark was lost to everything but the sensation of himself inside of her.

He lifted his hips to meet Diana's, increasing the friction between their bodies every time they moved in opposition and collided together again. They could both hear the slick sound of their joining and smell the heavy scent of sex that hung in the air. The sensations only elevated their lust as they ground against each other furiously, reaching for the completion they both knew they were so close to.

Together, they moved in tune as they were both close to their ends, and she rocked her body into his a little fast and deep as she could. The truck rocked and creaked more but there was the need of reaching her ultimate wave of pleasure making her body respond to an instinct she remembered she only had when she was with him like this. And he was no different than her. Holding her tight and as close as possible, he wrapped his arm around her back and thrust up into her as she grinding against him tightly. It was bliss from down below looking at her face as she clenched around him.

Together, they reached the epitome of pleasure, he pulsed inside her and her walls fluttered around him. Her limbs gave up and her head collapsed on his shoulders.

Her hair spread across his chest and his nose inhaling her scent. They laid that way for what felt like an eternity.

"That was wonderful," Diana whispered, her lips brushing against his neck.

Clark laughed, the sound reverberating through his chest, "Yeah," he agreed breathlessly. "But it's you, Diana. You are wonderful." He drew her tighter into his arms as their lips met in an ardent kiss.

A week later...Boston, mid-day

For the past week, between the Daily Planet, the UN, and heroic duties, Clark and Diana with the help of Julia and Donna, were packing all her things from her condominium to either go to Clark's apartment or at the Embassy in a storage closet.

"Diana, I know you were excited, but you didn't have to buy all this stuff," Donna said.

"Well, just as you said, at the time, I was excited. I plan to sell and donate at least half of this."

"Diana, just be sure you get everything you need and want to keep. I can make space," Clark said kissing her cheek before picking up a few boxes.

"Thank you, Kal."

As Diana was walking back to the kitchen to finish boxing up her dishes, Clark couldn't help but take a pause to watch her. Wearing mauve cheeky velvet dolphin shorts and white V-Neck Form-Fitted Top, he knew it was intentional, leaving almost nothing to the imagination emphasizing her voluptuous hourglass figure. Every time she raised to pick something over, her shorts would rise to give a peek of her ass. And every time she bent, the v cut of her top will dip deep enough to reveal the top half of her breasts generously. The rest of the time, her mounds were jiggling and bouncing as she worked. Keeping Clark's eyes occupied and full.

In her bedroom, Diana dipped in front of Clark to fold her sheet, Clark's jaw almost dropped as he saw her creamy valley popping out jiggling. Her pink areola almost...almost greeted him.

Diana glanced up to see Clark staring. She followed his eyes to see where he was hooked. She looked back down with a smirk. Oh yes...yes, indeed this was on purpose. She pulled her top up covering it with a smirk.

Clark was just as much a tease wearing his gray cotton joggers with the match black and grey sleeveless hoodie. She bit her lip eyeing the slight print of his erection.

"Clark, did you lock the truck again?" Donna asked annoyed.

"Yeah, sorry. But come on, Donna, that's some valuable stuff."

"Yeah, but no one is going to be dumb enough to try to steal it. And if they do, they'll have to answer to us anyway. You have super hearing and could track them down in a millisecond before they can even get 5 feet away from the truck. Now, where did you put the keys?"

"Uh...in my pocket."

"Oh, stop it, you two." Diana walked over to them. "Donna, Kal has the right to be cautious."

Diana reached into his pocket for him. He jumped slightly as Diana purposely rubbed her hand against his erection before getting the keys.

THE DARK SPELL

"Here, Donna, when you get back just put them on the counter. I'll leave the patio open so it'll be easier to see out to the truck."

"Thanks, Sis," Donna said taking the keys.

"Really, Diana?" Clark quirked his brow trying to maintain himself.

She giggled and winked. "I couldn't resist."

She turned to go back to the kitchen with Julia. Clark checked her round ass bouncing as she walked back with extra sway. His delicious cake needed to be unboxed and cherished.

He chuckled and shocked his head. "Taking these down now. Anymore?"

"Kal, don't show off. Take what you have."

He grinned. "Yes, Madam."

Julia laughed. "You two are quite the pair. I haven't seen you this happy in a while, Diana."

Diana blushed. "He makes me immensely happy. I'm in love and with my best friend, Julia. It's something so magical about that."

"With you moving in with him, I assume this is long term?"

"Yes."

"What I mean by long term, dear, is marriage?"

"I know. I know. And the answer is still yes. When the time is right."

Meanwhile, outside...

Clark placed the boxes in the truck.

"Alright, Donna, go ahead."

"Huh? Go ahead and what?" She questioned.

"Now that things are official with me and Diana, you want to grill me as a sibling would do."

Donna stared at him shocked then burst out laughing and hit his arm. "Clark, you supposed to let me do that on my own. Not tell me when to. That way you won't be prepared for what I asked for a genuine answer."

"You know my answers will be genuine anyway. You know how much I love your sister. I want to spend the rest of my life with her."

"Yes, I do. I mean the googly eyes you each other give every 5 seconds tells me way more than I need to know. You've been like a big brother to me for years but of course, I'm still going to be protective of Diana just like she's protective of me."

Clark nodded. "I understand that."

"Can I ask you something, Clark?"

"Course."

"When picking out her ring, could I help?"

Clark smiled wide. "Well, exactly I'm designing it myself."

Donna gasped. "Oh, my GODS! Seriously?! That's so sweet!"

"I'm far from done. I want it to be a surprise. Your input could be a big help."

"Oh yay! This is so exciting!"

"Yeah, I want it to be really special. One of a kind. Perfect...just like Diana."

"Clark, you are so sappy for my sister! It's adorable!"

"Please, don't say anything, Donna. Not even a hint. Don't even think about it when you're close to the lasso and blurt it out."

"Haha!" Donna laughed. "Don't be paranoid, Brother. I'm not going to say anything. I'm excited to see her reaction! Anyway, let's get back before she does suspect something and use the lasso on us and ruin her own surprise."

Clark laughed. "Right, right!"

They raced back up to Diana's condominium.

"Alright, Donna, couple more labels, and the kitchen and living room are all done," Julia said carefully placing the plates in the box. "Clark, Diana has boxes ready in her room."

Clark nodded.

Going into Diana's room, he smirked seeing her bent over taping up a box. Her ass invited him to come closer as it raised up and up, while she continued to work.

He quietly went over to her and smacked her ass before giving a tight squeeze.

Diana gasped and looked back at him with a glare. "Oh, Gods, Kal!"

"Shh...shh..." Clark gently dipped his head to kiss her buns over the cloth and slowly peeled her shorts down a little to softly nip on the small of her back. Diana opened her mouth in awe! She was shocked to see her boy scout marking her ass in broad daylight with her friend and sister in the next room.

THE DARK SPELL

He grabbed her hips and moved her over to lean against her dresser. They locked eyes in the mirror.

Clark rubbed himself against her ass slowly. Diana gasped again feeling his solid erection.

"Kal?"

"They won't...occupied."

Diana's eyes fluttered shut as she let out a low moan pushing back against him. Clark bent over slightly to her ear.

"You started this. You've been a tease all day...and that little pocket stunt trying to get the keys."

Diana raised her brow and smiled. "I told you. I couldn't resist."

"Well neither can I."

Clark had been trying his damnedest to hide his erection. Diana knew that but was purposely making it more and more difficult for him. It was only fair to get some payback for the moment.

He continued rubbing against her and slipped his hand to her front and inside her short. Diana gasped again and grabbed his wrist wanting to stop him.

"Clark..."

He grinned devilishly and kissed her shoulder, up her neck. Diana titled her head back and turned for Clark to capture her lips. He cupped her through her thin panties, damp with her arousal. Hooking his finger into the elastic, he pulled it aside and ran a finger down her slick folds. Diana groaned loudly into his mouth, the vibrations tickling his lips as he slid the first one, and then another finger into her center and began moving them in and out slowly.

Diana bucked her hips hard, the feel of his long fingers stroking her from the inside causing a burning heat to start building in her, the fire getting hotter with each movement. She arched her back wildly, breaking their kiss and a breathy whispered "Clark!" escaped her lips.

She let out a guttural moan in Clark's ear as he began curling his fingers inside of her, making a "come hither" motion with them as he stroked her most sensitive spot. She could feel her orgasm getting closer and she knew it wouldn't be long before she fell completely over the edge.

"Gods..."

Clark smirked and removed his fingers.

Diana turned to face him. Her hand drifted down to his rock solid erection, rubbing his length slowly through his sweats.

"Now who's being the tease? Although, I believe you are still in quite a predicament, Mr. Kent."

"I can manage a little better for now. But I can't wait to get you alone and completely naked."

"Well, you better hurry up with the rest of these boxes." She kissed him softly and tapped him down before moving to the boxes.

"Yes, Madam Prince." he looked down at his erection poking his pants.

Meanwhile...Dark Realm, Valeria's Castle

Eros laughed as he bit into his apple.

"What's amusing?" Valeria questioned sitting on her throne.

"My cousin and her lover have really outdone themselves. The passion continues to run high. They are happy."

"Hmm...yes."

"They've outdone the Succubi Queen," Eros teased.

"Outdone? No. I can never be outdone. What is true love if it is not challenged?"

"A challenge is always fair and needed to strengthen the bond. However, your intentions are not to challenge but to taint. I can see it in your eyes, Valeria. And I am, after all, the God of love, lust and, desire. While Diana and Kal-El are moving forward with their love, it's causing you to step back into your own past."

"I'm not tainting anything. You are just as curious as I. Kal-El has more of his true nature to show once up against those pesky little thoughts in the back of his mind. He is still a man after all."

"Do you still think of him?"

"Of who?"

"Your own lost love? The one you gave your heart to? The one that has caused you to be so bitter and resentful? A succubus falling in love is quite unheard and the Queen ironically is a testament of why it should never be."

"Watch your tongue, Eros."

THE DARK SPELL

"Well do you? Because I'm starting to believe this is why you are tormenting Diana and Kal-El."

"My experience has nothing to do with them."

"Are you sure? Dionysus is her brother after all. He doesn't care for Diana. So if you are trying to get a reaction from him."

"I don't care for that selfish fool! This is for my own pleasure and entertainment. I do as I please, Eros."

"Be careful, Valéria. You've seen the power of Diana and Kal-El's bond." Eros disappeared.

Valeria dug her fingers into the arm of her thrown then crushed it.

"Dionysus...you fool."

Dionysus, a nature god of fruitfulness and vegetation, especially known as a god of wine and ecstasy and a patron of the arts. The son of Zeus and Semele, a daughter of Cadmus, King of Thebes. He had a dual nature; on one hand, he brought joy and divine ecstasy; or he would bring brutal and blinding rage, thus reflecting the dual nature of wine. His unusual birth and upbringing marked him as an outsider.

Valeria and Dionysus met a century ago in England at a Brothel. Gods, demons, and other otherworldly beings disguised as mortals unbeknownst to mere mortals, indulging in orgies, drugs, and the finest of wines.

They caught each other's eye, once alone revealed their true selves. A God and a Succubus. A love that could only lead to chaos.

Back in Boston

Clark placed the last box in the truck. "Alright! All done and ready to go."

When he turned around, Donna and Julia both looked utterly astonished and giggled at him. They could now clearly see his excitement. Diana gasped and blushed, shaking her head slightly. Clark realized his hard erection was noticeable even tucking under his thick hoodie. He cleared his throat and turned around nervously, rubbing the back of his head.

"Keys, please," Donna said trying to hide her laughter.

"Don, you are really like a teen that just got her license," Clark said handing her the keys hiding his embarrassment.

"I don't always get to drive, you know? With the flying and all. And this is too much fun!" She jiggled the keys in front of his eyes and walked towards the driver's seat.

"Just be careful," Clark warned her from behind.

"Yeah, I know I know...Dad!" she said sarcastically. "Julia? Ready to go?"

"Ready," replied Julia.

"Diana, go ahead and go with them. I'll meet you at the Embassy. It's a 30-minute drive, right?"

"What's wrong?" Diana eyed him.

"Nothing. Just need about 15 minutes to take care of something," he said pulling her close.

Diana raised her brow. Clark smirked and pulled her into a passionate kiss. Diana moaned in his mouth as he pulled her tighter against him and felt his erection pressing on her thigh. His hands slid down groping her ass and gave those globes a squeeze over her shorts. Smooching her lips, Clark drew loose circles on her tight ass, her shorts pushed above her cheeks. He thought about their previous rendevous inside and that alone had him stirring in his pants against his thigh. It was impossible even for Superman to walk properly with a steel-hard arousal against one's thigh.

"15 minutes," he said pulling away.

Diana nodded a bit dazed from their heated kiss and watched as he flew off.

"Diana, where is Clark going?"

"He said he had to take care of something. He will meet us at the Embassy."

"Oh ok. Well, let's get going so we won't get stuck in traffic."

On the way to the Embassy, Diana was looking out the window still in her dazing and smiling.

"I haven't asked since you told me although I believe this week, especially today has given me my answer," Julia said.

"Oh? What's that?" Diana asked.

"You are quite excited about this. As I said earlier, I haven't seen you this happy." Julie replied.

THE DARK SPELL

"She's in love! I don't think you've ever been like that with anyone else. You didn't even give anyone else a chance to even ask your name," Donna joined the conversation.

Diana blushed. "Because there's no one else like Kal. He's such the perfect gentleman. So strong, honorable, and respectful. He makes me laugh. He knows all my likes and dislikes. He picks up on the littlest of habits or things said and takes everything into consideration for me. We've been friends for so long, knowing that there was an attraction we tried to suppress and even deny. Everything has changed so fast these past few months but it's all been right. How it's supposed to be," said Diana from her heart.

Donna and Julia awed in unison.

Julia with a smirk, "Yes. There's no one else like Clark. He's such the perfect gentleman," she began to repeat. "...So strong, honorable, and respectful...and Diana, we are your friends. We are so happy for you. But you should also tell us about..." She cut herself off and joined Donna who is chuckling hard along with her. Diana frowned, "About what? I have told everything."

Donna added, "Nope. You hid something from us. But Clark is a gentleman though he tries to hide... I mean tried to...hide it...very hard. Long and hard!" she burst out in laughter before finishing her sentence.

Diana narrowed her eyes and stared at Donna, "Donna, stop it."

Donna and Julia continue their steak of laughter, "Relax, Sister. I knew you two would do something alone in your room. But you should have warned us about his...size."

Diana smiled innocently. "His shoe size?"

Julia's smile broadened wickedly as she gestured with her hand.

"Warned you about Clark's—Oh..." Diana's cheeks turned red as she tried to form words.

"Have you seen it yet?" Donna asked cheekily.

Diana nodded her head and picked up something from her bag. It was her new Ipad pro, she set it across in front of them and slid her hand down an inch from the top and took an A2 pencil from the utensil box "...imagine like 12-16 of these," as she wrapped her fingers around in the air.

Both Julia and Donna looked at the Ipad and pencil back to back speechlessly.

They arrived at the Embassy. When Donna drove around to the back entrance, they were all shocked to see Clark already waiting there.

"He's already here?"

"Well, he is Superman after all."

Getting out of the truck and as she was walking towards him, Diana noticed the print of his erection disappeared. She was more curious than ever now, wanting to know what was he up to or what he had done. She would get her chance to find out later.

As Julia and Donna were putting the extra boxes in the storage, Clark and Diana were putting the boxes for Clark's apartment into her magical mirror from Themyscira. It was convenient for any and everything she needed to move from place to place for travel.

"This is amazing, Di."

She smiled. "There are lots more amazing things I have yet to show you."

"There's a lot of amazing things I have yet to show you as well," Clark smirked.

"We will get to it all in time." Diana blushed getting his innuendo.

Clark pulled her into an embrace. Diana sighed lovingly.

All of a sudden, they both felt a vibration in Clark's pocket.

Clark sighed annoyed, getting his phone out of his pocket.

"Oh, it's Perry."

"Go ahead and answer."

He gave her a slight nod before answering. "Hello, Mr. White?"

"Kent, where are you?"

"Uh... I'm with my girlfriend. She's moving in with me."

Diana's heart fluttered, hearing him call her his girlfriend so proud confident.

"Ah, I remember those days with the Mrs...Congratulations."

"Thank you, Sir."

"Well, Kent, I'm sorry for interrupting but we have a situation and deadline.."

THE DARK SPELL

"Don't worry, Mr. White. I'm almost done. I'll be in the office in an hour."

"I knew I could count on you, Kent."

Hanging up, Clark gave Diana a sympathetic smile. Diana shook her head and kissed him softly.

"My sexy super reporter is needed. Go, Love. I can handle the rest and then Donna and I will take Julia home. Afterward, she's going to the market with me in Metropolis."

"The market?"

"I'm cooking tonight."

"Really? I thought you didn't cook?"

"Not often but I know my way a little bit. At least with what I'll be making. Also the few lessons you and Martha have taught me."

"Can't wait."

Diana kissed him again.

"I'll see you later at home."

Clark smiled proudly. "Yeah...our home."

Location: Metropolis Market

After taking Julia back home and the moving truck back to the rental place, Donna and Diana flew to Metropolis to the market in disguise. From stepping into the store and going from aisle to aisle, admittedly Diana felt a little nervous.

"Where are you, Diana?"

She frowned looking up at Donna. "What do you mean? I'm right here."

"You've been staring at the avocado for like 5 minutes."

Diana sighed and rolled her eyes. "Don't exaggerate. I'm just thinking."

"Of? Wait. Nevermind. I know. Are you second-guessing domestic life with Clark?"

"What? Oh no! No. I want this with Kal more than anything. I am a little nervous because it is a drastic change but I'm excited."

"Seriously, Sis, I'm happy for you and Clark. Let's make tonight fun for the both of you! Make it sexy!"

An hour and a half later...

While Donna flew to Titans Tower, Diana took a taxi to the apartment building. She couldn't stop smiling carrying her bags up the stairs.

"Woah...here let us help with that."

Diana turned to see two men. Both slightly shorter and smaller build than Clark but seemed to be around the same age as she and Clark.

"Oh, no, I've got it. Thank you, though."

Diana was just about to turn back.

"Uh..so you live here? Haven't seen you around before? I'm Jackson, by the way."

Jackson seemed as if he was a fashionisto, wearing a turtleneck and black check chinos who loved staring at himself in the mirror using massive amounts of hair gel.

"I'm Warren. And you are?"

Warren was a bit more casual with his fringe cut hair wearing just jeans and a graphic T-shirt.

"I'm Diana. I just moved in..."

"Oh," they both said in unison with smirks.

"...with my boyfriend..." she added.

Their shoulders dropped. "Oh."

"I'm sure you've seen him before."

Jackson shrugged. "We only know the guy from apartment 27."

"Oh yeah! Tall dude with the glasses," Warren stated.

"Calvin...? Carl? Carleton?"

Diana rolled her eyes. "Clark."

Warren and Jackson looked at her shocked.

"That's your boyfriend?!"

Diana smiled proudly. "Yes, he is. Now, I have to go. It was nice meeting you two."

She walked away going up the last flight of stairs.

"Damn!"

"Bro! She's so hot!"

"How the hell did the glasses guy get that?!"

"We gotta talk. Like ASAP."

Diana rolled her eyes and shook her head hearing them talking.

THE DARK SPELL

When she got to the door, she felt butterflies. She opened the door.

"Clark?" She called walking in and closed the door.

Suddenly, she felt strong arms around her waist and warm lips against hers.

"Welcome home, Diana," he said pulling away.

"Oh a welcome home, indeed!"

Diana surveyed him. He was just in his boxers.

"I'll take that and unpack it for you."

"No, no, I got it, Kal. I don't want you peeking. And you have to get back to work."

"Oh ok." He kissed the tip of her nose.

"I'll just set these down, get a quick shower. Oh! and I already met two neighbors."

"Really? Who?"

"Jackson and Warren."

"Oh, those two. They were trying to flirt right?"

"Yes," she laughed going into the kitchen to put the bags on the counter.

"I knew it. Didn't think it would be the first day though." Clark sat back down on the sofa picking up his laptop. "I forgot to tell you about the back entrance."

"It's okay, Kal. I told them you were my boyfriend. I don't think they will be a problem."

"I just want you to be comfortable, Di." he smiled warmly looking at her.

"I am. I really enjoyed shopping at the market."

"I'm glad. I know it's a drastic change from your condo to this smaller apartment."

Diana leaned over the back of the sofa and ran her hands down Clark's chest. She kissed the side of his neck.

"Beloved, I adore this. You know materialistic things I don't care for. My luxury is having you and your love."

Clark tilted his head back to look at her and smiled, "I love you, Di."

"I love you, too, Kal."

She leaned down and kissed him.

"I'll be right back."

Diana went to the bedroom, she saw everything neatly put away. They both had plenty of room in the closet. Diana laughed to herself seeing how Clark even organized her undergarments in the drawer.

She smiled wider going into the bathroom. He had the towels already laid out for her.

She turned on the shower and wrapped her hair in a messy bun. She took her clothes off and tossed them into the hamper.

She let out a relieved sigh, stepping into the shower. The steaming hot water cascading down her body. She had never felt this relaxed. She closed her eyes for a moment. She could see so clearly building their own family together. 2 children a boy and a girl...maybe more down the line. Living out their older years together. It's a dream she never thought would be, let alone a dream she would have at all if it weren't for Kal.

A God and a Goddess in love. They share a bond of purity. Selflessness. A God and Goddess in love. A power so far beyond belief.

Diana turned the shower faucet off. She dried off and wrapped the pink towel around her body, walking out of the bathroom, to the living room, she still kept her hair up in the messy bun.

"Feel better?" Clark asked reading over his report.

"Oh, much! I'm so happy we got everything all moved and I love how you already organized everything."

"Course, Di..." he paused looking at her standing in a towel dripping from a fresh shower.

Diana walked over to him and gave him a quick peck on the cheek.

"Dinner will be ready soon."

"You sure you don't need any help?" Clark's eye lingered on the spot where the towel is knotted.

"I'm sure, Beloved." She couldn't help but smirk as she picked up a sexy black thigh-length deep v-neck satin robe with 3/4 sleeves and a satin tie belt, She knew Clark would love it.

Clark glanced up from his laptop to see Diana drop her towel to the floor and draped her robe around and he noticed she had nothing underneath.

She was already starting her teasing.

THE DARK SPELL

Diana took her towel back into the bedroom then came back, heading to the kitchen. She started humming unpacking everything. She worked her way through the kitchen getting herself familiar with where everything was. She was determined to do this not in the domestic sense but for herself. For so long, even living on her own, it didn't exactly feel like home. This was the start of it all.

She started off by cutting up everything for the Greek salad: tomatoes, cucumber, red onion, kalamata olives, Italian flat-leaf parsley, and avocado. Because the ingredients are sturdy, Greek salad is great for making ahead of time before serving. It also tastes good the longer the flavors mingle.

Once the salad was done, she placed it in the refrigerator then started on the mashed potatoes. The recipe for garlic mashed red potatoes was given to her by Martha. As she was following step by step she could hear Martha's voice. Everything was going so smoothly. She was quite proud.

While the potatoes simmered, she was just about to start on the steak and lobster.

"I'm all done with my report, Di."

"That's wonderful, Love, and I'm-" Diana glanced up with a smile then did a double-take, about to drop her bowl of butter. "Oh, by the Gods, Kal!" She gasped.

Even with placing it on the counter, she was so focused on him, she sat it still too close to the edge and almost dropped it again.

He stood there completely naked, grinning. His manhood proud and at full attention.

"Kal? What?" asked Diana as she couldn't turn away.

"Don't think I have forgotten about your pocket stunt earlier. That was torture of Junior here." Clark pointed at his sex. He was hot, heavy, and very responsive to Diana's gaze.

Diana stared at him for a moment longer then burst out laughing thinking about her conversation with Julia and Donna.

"Oh? You, think it's still funny, hm?" He walked over to her and grabbed her by her hips hoisting her up to sit on the counter.

"Kal, I'm in the middle of cooking. I don't want anything to mess up."

"Don't worry. We have a little time." His erection rubbed on her thigh.

"You are relentless."

"You started it." He tickled her through the robe.

"Well I'm sorry, Kal...and Junior..." She couldn't help but giggle. "You're just too irresistible."

She grabbed his erection wrapping her hand around his girth slowly pumping him up and down licking her lips in anticipation. Diana now knew his manhood by touch like the back of her hand. Her fingers found the places that brought him the most pleasure, resulting in him throwing his head back. Feeling his shaft rapidly grow hard and push her fingers apart. She wanted to jump off the counter and taste him but before she could get any further he pulled her into a deep kiss.

Diana felt his aggressiveness as the kiss lasted for minutes. It was an intense, passionate kiss with no room for breath. His tongue pressing deep into her mouth. Diana immediately gave in to her own desire and kissing him back. As he slid his hand to her waist she moaned slightly wanting him to go further. He knew she would not deny him his want. He kissed her as if there was no tomorrow. He was craving and he wanted her so badly.

"Kal," she breathed when they finished.

His hands were eager to work her curvaceous body loosening her robe. Her lovely frame came into his sight. Her perky breasts revealed themselves as she pushed robes from her shoulder. He traced his large hands on her curve and felt her body tense. His eyes lingered on her breast and he can see her pink nipple already hardened. He heard her gasp as his palms traced both her breasts. He kissed her lips one last time before working down her neck kissing her collarbone working down to her breasts. He bowed his head and buried his face on her cleavage. He licked around her succulent areola before licking her nipple and biting down hard.

Diana squealed as she felt his teeth sinking into her ripe flesh. "You're tempting to skip dinner."

"Nothing wrong with an Amazonian appetizer. Though, you are my main course, too. And dessert," he answered, his mouth already tracing her bosom, his hands squeezing on her backside.

He smirked and carried on working down her stomach, circling her belly button, before kissing and suckling the insides of her thighs.

"Kal-El." She grounded.

"Yes, Diana," he teased.

THE DARK SPELL

"I... AHH!"

He blew air onto her vulva making her twitch. Her bottom lips looked like a fresh rose in dew. It is the most beautiful image he has ever seen, glistening in her arousal. He slightly traced her petal with one digit. His nose moves too close to catch her scent. He stops his ministrations and looks directly into her eyes. Diana swallowed thickly as she lost all her sense except his long finger at the corner of her sex. Clark slowly dragged the tip of his finger on her folds. Diana arched her back as an involuntary reaction and his thumb finally brushes just where she wants him. Her entire body trembles violently as he strokes her folds. Clark slowly pushed the tip of his finger inside her. She tensed, shuddering with pleasure as his fingers slide into her core, curling and pressing behind her pelvis, and his thumb strokes gently. Diana bit her lip as his fingers continued to tease her. Clark drags his finger back to taste her in his mouth. Exquisite! The sweet dew on the pristine rose. He sucked his finger deep in cherishing her taste.

Diana lost all thought and composure when she felt his tongue this time lick through her helplessly wet folds. His tongue was hot and wet. Diana bucked against his tongue. His hands clamped around her thighs to hold her in place as he continued his assault; sliding his tongue along her folds and then pressing inside her. He lapped her up, her taste and smell divine but yet feral and so addictive. He soon moved to her swollen clit, first licking then suckling, biting, and flicking over and over again. Her hips were rocking back and forth as he increased his tempo.

Her whole body was on alert to his touch. She needed more she needed him inside her. She needed him covering her body filling her up. He slid 2 of his long fingers into her and began pumping them quickly. Diana was moaning and squealing from the amazing feeling he was causing her to feel. He was licking and thrusting faster and faster, bringing her to the brink of her orgasm.

"Oh, gods! CLARK!" she screamed out as she came hard and he licked her clean.

She was panting heavily as she was coming down from her high.

Clark leaned up and kissed her mouth while caressing her hips.

"I take it you enjoyed that?" His chin was glistening and he smirked against her lips.

"Hmm...I did. My man of many talents." She gave an appreciative kiss on his lips for his hard work.

"You know, I'm curious to know how you took care of your predicament with Junior earlier? And so fast."

"I'm Superman," he said with a cocky smile.

"Kal." She raised her brow making him laugh.

"Alright...alright...Well... I had a space cold air shower and meditated."

Diana tilted her head giving him a questionable look.

He smiled wider. Her confused expression was so cute.

"What's the coldest planet in this sector's solar system?"

"Neptune."

"So I took a flight to Neptune, clothes off, letting the cold air cool my body and just relaxed a bit with meditation. I mean I thought about you the whole time still but it was more like a spiritual release knowing I'll have you later."

"Hmm...I like that. I want to go with you next time."

"Di..." he laughed. "The point was to go alone to get turned off not more turned on."

Diana giggled. "Or you know, we just need to find time for those instances where I take care of Junior myself. But the thought of you meditating naked in space is really something..."

"We can think of somewhere else to go for sure."

Diana leaned forward and kissed him. "I'm almost done here. After dinner, you're all mine."

"And you're mine." Clark kissed her once more before helping her off the counter. "Since you don't want my help, I'll just watch you."

"Naked?" She asked draping her robe back.

"If you want me to. I'll be more motivated for you."

"Or my distraction." she tied the belt.

"I'll be a bit of both."

Clark watched Diana as she continued cooking. He couldn't help but smile at her, knowing that cooking wasn't her forte but she was determined, was doing damn good, and looked so damn sexy.

THE DARK SPELL

Diana was feeling even more confident with him watching even showed off a little bit. She bent over when opening the oven giving him a view of her succulent cakes he loved so much.

"Everything smells good, Di. I'm hoping it tastes just as good, too."

"It will."

"Don't just say that, Kal. I want your honest opinion. If you even thinking about lying, I'm already prepared to get the lasso."

"You know I'll be completely honest, Di. But you were going to have me tied up in the lasso anyway."

Diana laughed. "I have been thinking about it probably way more than I should."

"Maybe it's time we give it a try."

Diana looked back at him with a smirk. "Oh, Mr. Kent, you are just daring me to do all the things I've fantasized to do with you."

"Miss Prince, we both know all those things we've both fantasized about. We have plenty of time to play it all out."

Diana bit her lip and took a deep breath as her thoughts fleeted for a moment.

As she made their plates, she concentrated to make them perfect as a work of art.

"Dinner is ready, Love." Diana smiled. "Are you going to eat naked too?"

"Yep!"

As Diana sat their plates down, Clark pulled out her chair.

Diana shook her head. "Sit."

Clark sat down and stared up at her with an anxious look. Diana was of course well aware he wasn't just hungry for food.

"Will Junior be hanging free all day or was this just my welcome home gift."

"Well it was your welcome home gift and payback for your stunt but this is actually quite comfortable. If you like, he will be like this for you every day... or you want him otherwise locked?"

Diana smiled innocently, slowly untied her robe, and let it fall to the floor. She leaned down towards him.

"This is better, My love. Easy access."

Clark smirked as she straddled him on the chair. They both let out a quiet gasp as the tip of his sex sunk into her. He was huge and she was so tight. Clark leaned forward pressing his lips to hers. Diana let the tiniest of moans barely audible as sparks were sent throughout her body as she could feel his warm lips on hers. Clark slowly and teasingly slid his slick tongue into Diana's warm wet mouth, entangling his tongue with hers.

"Let's have dinner before it turns cold."

She twisted with him inside her to take the plate from the table. His hardness twisted in her, stretching her. Both writhed in pleasure from the moment.

Both panting, she dipped a little lower on his hardness and Clark looked at the plate with a proud smile.

He leaned forward, kissing her, tongue sweeping across her lip. "Looks amazing, Di." He groped her ass tightly and gave it a smack.

Diana whined, grinding down on him.

Diana cuts the incredibly tender steak and raised the fork to Clark's mouth. Clark opened his mouth and let the fork pass and closed his full lips around it. Diana removed the empty fork slipping away from his closed lips and his tongue made an appearance licking his bottom lips.

Diana wet her lips and swallowed hard watching him swallow the food.

"Damn..." he took a deep breath. he cupped her ass cheeks and drew her down for a kiss.

Diana tasted the steak from his mouth; soft and juicy. She twisted the fork on the plate, raised it with the steak, and dipped it into her mouth. She made pouty lips dragging the empty fork out "This is so good!" and rolled her hips.

Clark growled deep in his throat and pulled her for a kiss. Diana pulled back and smiled at him, her eyes lit with a mischievous gleam. "Patience, Clark. Haven't your parents taught you not to play with your food?"

Clark rubbed her thighs on both sides and mocked, "My dinner is playing with me." He kissed her shoulder and bent down to kiss the side of her neck. Her scent surrounded him and she was panting for air each time he moved.

THE DARK SPELL

Diana laughed feeding him more and as he devoured it, she dragged one finger down his chest and flatten her palm against his abs, and stopped right before where they are connected.

"I'm glad you like it, Kal. I give credit to your mother, however. Following her recipe. I would like to cook more actually." She drew circles with her hand around his navel.

Clark took her hand in his, brought it to his lips, and kissed his "chef". Diana dragged her finger over his lips. She pushed her finger inside his mouth and he sucked on it with his cheeks flushed. Diana shrieked involuntarily at his moment. She heard her heart pounding and core dripping.

Clark took her fork to feed her. She nibbled at the meat without breaking his eye contact. Blood rushed to his core and he felt stretching inside her as they hummed half-drowsy.

As she was chewing, he nipped at the curve of her neck. He was hungry for her.

Clark slid deeper when he slammed his hips against her making her body shake. "Too Hot?" he asked.

Diana tipped her head forward against his shoulder as she felt he is throbbing inside the core.

He raised teasingly and she arched her back. Clark's hand tightened on her ass as she felt him stir.

Diana heard him take a deep breath.

"We can take turns and cook together. It'll be more fun together," he said.

Tightening his grip on her ass, Clark pulled her down a little further. Diana sank her teeth into her lower lip and held back a whimper.

Between feeding each other, Diana took the opportunity to place soft kisses all over his neck and shoulders sucking on his pulse.

"We'll risk burning the food being each other's distraction then." Diana jerked a little causing him to stifle a grunt.

Clark laughed. "No. I'll behave for the moment. Though, I think our next thing will be making dessert. I'll make sure to have you covered in icing, powdered sugar, or whipped cream." Clark reached down between them, his fingers touching Diana's magical button of flesh, making her whimper and wriggle her hips.

Diana quivered. "So you really thought of everything with me moving in?"

"Sort of..." he trailed off picking up speed as he stroked her.

She could feel him twitching each time he moved her against him. She was teasing him as much as he was teasing her.

Diana yelped and scrabbled at his lap, her thighs closing around him for a moment before she relaxed and took more of him.

Clark set both hands on her hips rocking against her in a slow rhythm and he felt her inner muscles flutter around his erection.

His hands roamed her body and he sucked on her nipples until they were red and swollen.

"Oh...Gods...Kal-El..." Both hands moved to her ass lifting her up and down.

Releasing her nipples, Clark leaned up and his tongue brushed her lower lip. Diana flung her arms around his neck and held on rocking along with him, a soft moan breaking out of her. Clark kissed her until she shuddered for breath, then lowered her back to his erection.

His sex pushed halfway and pulsated again inside her stretching out, which sent shivers right to Diana's core.

Finally, both finished with dinner and had sex dripping all over. Clark held her tighter and stood up, sitting her on the table. "Time for dessert." Finally, he pulled back from her.

Diana leaned back on the table as Clark got on top of it with her. He slid his hands around her back and bent over. His lips touched hers, his tongue slipping across her lips. Diana immediately opened her mouth inviting him in and they locked. Their embrace began with one of his hands touching her back, the other cupping her ass, pulling her into his crotch. Diana moaned in his mouth feeling his manhood press against her. The world fell away as they kissed. A warmth boiled inside Diana and bled down to her nether region. Heating it like a hot spring.

The table creaked but they didn't care. For quite a while their tongues danced with one another. Diana let out a soft whimper as Clark ground his sex against hers, rubbing the tip against her, up and down, each slide

THE DARK SPELL

pushing her folds farther apart then thrust into her with just his tip. He pulled him away for a moment breathing roughly leaving her lips burning.

"Teasing again?" Diana questioned with a seductive smile.

Clark planted a confident smirk on his face seeing the beautiful flustered Goddess beneath him. He pinned her to the table and pushed into her.

Diana gasped, "Clark."

He pulled back and gently eased into her again and again until he filled her fully.

Diana whimpered. Clark watched her face. After the long foreplay they had with dinner, now she had him, all of him, inside her.

He continued grinding against her making the table move.

Diana shrieked, writhing underneath him.

The room filled with the wet, slick sounds of him moving inside her and creaking of the table more until suddenly the table gave way.

"Ah..it was an old table anyway. Things need to get broken into now. I can make things more sturdy to handle us."

Clark stood up pulling Diana with him and hoisted her over his shoulder. Diana giggled.

"Oh, Kal. What has-" she gasped abruptly and jumped slightly when he smacked her ass.

"Kal!"

Within a millisecond he was in the bedroom and playfully threw Diana down on the bed and she bounced slightly.

"Oh..." She sat up on her elbows.

Clark took a moment, taking her curvaceous naked body in with a hungry look on his face. His pupils delighted, eyes turning of heated red.

He clambered on top of her, their faces inches apart and his erection pressing against her sex. His hand slipped behind her head, sliding through her hair.

"What has gotten into you, Mr. Kent?"

"Di, I've been waiting all day to have you," he breathed and then kissed her again attacking her mouth viciously.

Diana groaned in triumph, knotting her fingers into his hair. They kissed passionately; sometimes Clark would bite her bottom lip, or lightly suck it into his mouth; this drove Diana crazy.

Diana opened her mouth slightly to let Clark venture in and play with her tongue with his. She had never been touched this way by a man before, but she loved every second with Clark, and he kissed her with just the right about of passion and gentleness, it made her feel so loved.

At the height of their kiss, Clark pulled his face away to catch his breath while he raised up and stared at the breathless blushing Goddess with her luscious lips coated in his saliva sent sensations right to his groin.

He raised her legs up then spread them apart wide open before him. Clark shook his head and smiled, his eyes turning redder by the second.

"You are just so damn gorgeous."

Diana blushed as she struggled to find the words to tell Clark that he was all she wanted at this moment in time.

Clark slid his hands down her body. It was like a waterfall in the Amazon, pouring over Diana's body, tracing her curves and her body with a perfect firm gentleness she had never felt before. Diana's mind clouded with pleasure. Her mouth hung agape, her body arching into her lover's touches.

"You don't know how much I just wanted to take you, right then and there earlier. You in those shorts and top."

Clark cupped her ample breasts. Lips curving into a devilish smirk as he pinched her nipples harshly, laughing at the delicious moan Diana made. He began pressing teasing, open-mouthed kisses on her inner thighs. Her body trembled in response.

He leaned up a bit more and gave both of her breasts firm squeezes before he started to lick her nipple the soft skin hardened immediately under his moist tongue.

"Mmm," she moaned loudly as she arched her back from the shock of the sudden contact.

Diana shut her eyes tightly and bit the bottom of her soft lips. Clark, satisfied with her reaction tentatively licked one nipple in a circular motion and teased the other with his hand. Diana's nipples felt like they were on

THE DARK SPELL

fire. The more he teased her, she felt like she needed more. She wanted Clark to touch her more. It was completely exhilarating for her.

"Cl-ark" she panted freeing her bottom lip from her teeth "t-touch me more..." she shouted in between pants with her face flushed.

He smirked at the woman below him. He slowly let his finger trail down off her breast, through her flat stomach, and over to her womanhood.

She was dripping wet and begging for attention. Diana buckled her hips and shivered as his finger finally made it to the place that is yearning for his touch. Clark's warm finger slowly penetrated and he let his long thick finger slide happily into her slick entrance.

A loud moan escaped Diana's lips as he slipped in a second finger. She tried to close her legs but they just end up hitting Clark's strong hips. Clark slowly moved his fingers in and out and lifted his head to watch her expression. He quickened the pace and Diana arched her back and let out loud gasps for air.

Hearing her begging words and feeling her spreading gates of moistness against his hand, he became even more aroused, his gift, laden with the precious cargo that she longed for, rising and bouncing in the confluence of her and his waves of desire. His two fingers rhythmically dove into her warm soft depths and he suckled her nipple to their tempo. Her hips raised higher with each thrusting of his fingers, each sucking of her nipple, as she pulled his fingers in deeper, all the way up to his hand. He felt her clamping on his fingers, gasping, quivering, and moaning.

"Oh, love, I'm . . . mm . . .Oh!" she said "Oh! Oh! Ah-h!" she shrieked and became fixed against his hand, waves of contractions stimulating through his hand, rippling up his arm, surging down his body, and pumping his manhood tighter, longer, and hotter.

A long moment later, he felt her relaxing around his fingers, her hips slowly lowering, and curled his fingers upward against her G-spot. He slowly massaged.

Suddenly, she trembled, stiffened, and thrust one long hard time against his hand.

"Clark!" she screamed loudly the pleasure was almost too much for her.

But this wasn't enough for him. He needed more of her, craved her, and he unlatched from her nipple, quickly removed his fingers, and in a trembling frenzy whirled around, wrapped his arms around her rear, and buried his face in her center feeling its heat. His lips were firmly embedded in her soft pink petals and start to slowly lick it lewdly, thrusting his tongue in deep and lapping in her juice.

"I just can't get enough of you, Diana. Sweet sweet divine taste."

He rose up, sitting on his heels, and yank her closer, raising her legs up and over his shoulders. He lifted her ass up more, helping her to rest her hips on his shoulders, with her head and shoulders still lying on the bed. Diana closed her feet together on his back and her eyes rolled back when she felt his tongue dive deeper into her core.

The scent and taste of her sex were almost enough to take him to the edge, but he managed to fight it back. Diana gasped and dug her hands in the bedsheets with her knuckles growing white from the force of her fists.

"Clark!" She screamed once more she couldn't take this much longer. "Oh Gods!" she huffed.

He didn't give her quite enough time to recover, switching their positions. He pulled her up and around so that she sitting on his face. With his hands placed firmly right where her legs and her ass met he started licking her core. Very slowly, but not for long, he then started kissing and licking harder, inserting his tongue getting her more turned on.

Diana raised and turned around facing his erection which is dripping in her coating. "Beloved, I need my Kryptonian dessert now."

She began sensing that he would give her multiple climaxes before he finally exploded with one of his own.

He stopped abruptly however as Diana gently took his length in her hand. She became so fixated on the phallus looming gigantically in front of her that she memorized every ridge and vein of it, from the bulbous head to the thick shaft to his balls were also a source of fascination, large and loose and seeming to tighten or quiver at times.

She had begun at his tip slowly licking. She licked around the head several times before engulfing him with her mouth. It was impressive, feeling Clark fill her mouth until it hit the back of her throat.

THE DARK SPELL

Clark regained his composure and resumed licking Diana's silky thighs, marveling that anything could be so soft and smooth. When he reached her labia he combined licking with sucking and nibbling. He could feel her react on his manhood. A loud moan came from him as he finally began directly stimulating her clit.

His energy was tireless, and he was already gaining a sense of exactly when an orgasm was coming upon her, and when it did, he let up a bit in his ministrations to let her enjoy her paroxysm to the fullest. Then he resumed, intent on coaxing yet another climax out of her.

Diana alternated between long hard sucking and soft gently licking. As she did that, he started moaning, giving her encouragement to suck harder and faster. He responded by inserting his tongue into her as deeply as he could, savoring her. His fingers, wet with her juices, ran up and down her dripping lips, pausing occasionally to make small circles in places.

Um-mm," she hummed, and he felt her clamping and contracting on his tongue.

Both were moaning into each other and moving their hips. Moving her head up and down on him with one hand fondling him and the other moving in unison with her mouth, she began sucking even harder.

The pleasure was coursing through every fiber of their bodies as each one ground their hips into the other's eager mouth.

His slowly probing finger and his tongue were too much for her and she lifted her head up from his member. Her orgasm began and her hips ground against his mouth harder.

Clark increased the speed of his tongue until it was moving faster than a Hummingbird's wing. She was beginning to make all kinds of noises, like as if she was talking with her mouth full, and then her legs started to tremble.

They both were thrusting and writhing and then trembling as if they were sharing a synchronized seizure in this position.

Clark maintained his rhythm he managed to keep contact with her while she was smothering him in her ecstasy. Still connected in all of these ways, his pumping slowing, her thrusting and clamping relaxing, her mouth holding him inside it, and his tongue slipping back into his mouth, swallowing her essence and began returning to reality.

Diana rose up slowly from Clark's face letting him slide down from under her. He sat up with a smile. His eyes still fiery red. Diana couldn't help but smile back at him, run her tongue around her lips. Their eyes locked for just a moment. Then he grabbed her by her waist pulling her close. Their lips were together, sharing one of those long delicious open-mouthed kisses that they loved, one that went on and on and on. His hand stroked her hair and feathered down her back as their tongues softly played. Her body felt wonderful on him; her breasts against his chest, their sex rubbing sensually against each other's. He held her tight, totally lost in her, loving the intimacy.

When the kiss broke, she ran her tongue slowly around his lips and then said, "Please, Beloved."

Clark nodded and laid her down. He lay over her and leaned forward to kiss her. As he did, he pressed himself into her temple. Clark pulled back from their kiss, both breathless and moaning in pleasure as her tight wetness close around him. Diana gripped his muscular arms and they flex under her hands.

His healthy member felt like a cloud of existence, filling her up from her entrance to the back wall of her silk tunnel. Stars form before her eyes as he filled her fully. He expanded into her like waves crashing into every nook possible. Her wet womanhood enveloped him perfectly and he wanted nothing more than for every thrust to continue without a halt.

Clark grabbed Diana by the sides of her head and laid his body weight on top of her. They locked stares as Clark withdrew slightly then pushed back slowly into her. Each gentle thrust felt like a large arrow pressing into her warm target. Each powerful hip press brought Clark's body weight through Diana's body, slightly pushing her up and into the pillows and the bed's headboard.

He buried his face in her neck as he pressed all the way in, groaning. With every thrust, he goes deeper causing Diana to open her lips and moan loudly.

He bit her earlobe and groaned in her ear. She felt his hot breath in her ear. It tickled her in the most sensual way, sending chills all through her body.

"Kal," she moaned.

THE DARK SPELL

Blissful sensations continued to rise. This was going to be something special, something unexpectedly wonderful.

They didn't need to find a rhythm, their bodies are already in sync with each other. They started off slow and gentle, the chemistry between them igniting in the air. Diana's hands found his shoulders, nails raking his flesh.

As Clark's hard shaft slowly massaged Diana's walls, he kissed her face, licked her smooth neck, and nibbled on her cute chin. Clark craned her head back by her hair with his hand as he thrust deep into her. This exposed her creamy neck for Clark to suck and bite as his powerful length parted her existence into half. She had placed her hands on his head and neck, clinging on to him dearly; she revels in feeling her skin against his. As they move into one another, the lovers looked at each other eye to eye.

He thrusts into her harder and deeper with each stroke, feeling her orgasm starting to build, Diana tried to catch her breath screaming. Her eyes struggled to stay open and locked with his but so easily they become half-lidded by rapturous, libidinous, wanton euphoria. Her hands still gripped his biceps, his muscles flexing and relaxing beneath her hands.

Clark plowed into her, making sure his rhythm played in tune with her immediate needs. He needed to speed up, slow down, push harder, and move around inside her at the right moments to help her achieve what she so desperately wanted. Clark maneuvered his piercing sword in such a way as to hit Diana's special spot.

Diana loved the tickle in her clit as she moved her body in rhythm with his enjoying the contact. She loved his groans, and how he could not get enough of her face, neck, and ears while he pumped between her thighs.

"Oh god, yes!"

Diana began to orgasm, and her beautiful haven began to hug and pulse around his thick manhood. Her tight tunnel attempted to forcefully pull his hard member in with each maddening muscled grip. Her soft legs close like grips around his warm body. Clark continued to piston pump Diana through her own marvelous orgasm.

Her body took everything he had to give and gave back more with gentle rolls of her hips or arches of her back. Her fingernails were raking the skin on his back, fueling him to continue his lovemaking, enjoying every sensation her body was giving his.

Her body glistened with sexual desire. There was nothing like watching the skillful dance of a woman on the verge of an orgasm. Her body shuddered like an earthquake before collapsing and melting into the bed. The world seemed to melt into a pool of pure pleasure. She continued to coo for minutes after her initial orgasm.

Clark's throbbing flesh still moved like a piston in her slickness. As his body flushed, he heard her moans become tiny yelps and he could hold back no longer. Thrusting deep, he felt his member pulse and he growled at the sweet release. They kept going, locked together in this dance of passion. They held one another tight, savoring the wonderful sensations, their lips together in a passionate caress.

Diana then let out another deep throaty moan as a small orgasm turned into a big one. "Oh!" she cried out. Her nails dug deeply into Clark's shoulder as another unexpected orgasm tore through her body. Every thrust sent her to the moon and every kiss brought me back to earth. He kept thrusting with so much need and determination and raw lust, driving deeper than she thought possible.

Her back arched, being sent over the edge once again into the abyss of pleasure and climax with orgiastic abandon, screaming Clark's name so loud it echoes for several seconds in his cavernous room.

"Clark! Clark! CLARK!"

She held onto him tighter, closing her eyes as something within her snapped beyond control.

"AH!" She screamed louder than ever before.

She opened her eyes, feeling this enormous amount of power illuminated from her body.

She gasped. "Kal?"

He looked up at her, her eyes were glowing with lightning blue. Though, she looked worried. He took her right and with a smile intertwining their fingers.

Diana's god powers had been unintentionally activated.

"It's okay. Focus it all on me," he whispered to her and placed soft kisses all over her face.

THE DARK SPELL

Diana nodded slowly, tightening her hold on his hand. She then pulled him for a deep kiss, their tongues dancing and duels each other. Both moaned in the kiss as the two tasted each other.

Clark's thrusts intensify to the point it became as intense as a jackhammer.

Diana's moans get louder again as Clark became bolder and going deeper, hitting her g-spot.

They broke their kiss some minutes later when the pleasure just intensified even more and they needed air.

"Ahhh! Clark!" Diana screamed out when they broke their kiss; Clark thrust into her steadily, hard and deep, too high levels, already sending the two of them to this Nirvana feeling.

Clark could not hold out from the coming release as the pressure built and he couldn't contain anymore. Clark's deep grunts and Diana's shrilling moans filled the room with this ecstatic duet from each thrust Clark made.

The dams now give way and it all comes gushing out.

"Diana!"

"Clark!"

They groaned and screamed as they spill their honey to one another. At the moment of their climax, both of them held each other tightly from the spasms of their incredible release. Clark could hear Diana's heart beating at a rapid rate. Diana embraced him tightly, not wanting to let him go. She again seized his lips for another kiss. Their tongues dance in their love routine, their lips locked very tight.

Clark wrapped his arms around her, rolling over on his back for Diana to lay completely on top of him and straddle his hips. Words cannot effectively describe the feeling of sinking into her dripping wet, hot as fire womanhood. He could feel her muscles inside massaging him, trying to pull him in even more.

Slowly Diana lifted up about halfway and then back down, grinding her hips a bit. Clark, moving his hips in time with her, began a slow pace that began building speed. She then goes to his neck, inhaling the masculine and hard scent of his being.

Clark held her tight with his arms around her, his hands going anywhere they want. He enjoyed the immense ecstasy Diana was giving him; now it's his turn to moan. Diana was pleased to hear him like this. She kept up the pace, giving him nothing short of a pleasure. Once more the intensity builds up and they orgasm again.

"Di!"

"Ahh Clark! Yes!"

Clark pulled her down and suppressed their screams by a deep kiss; Diana gladly responded by locking her lips to him. They thrust into each other with sheer zeal until their low regions exploded from the ecstasy. Their juices had come to soak their hips while their screams were suppressed by their deep kiss.

Clark then sat up, Diana goes along as she now straddles his lap. Clark took a moment to look at Diana's lovely glowing figure. The moon's light glistens on her naked form, making her look even more stunningly gorgeous.

Diana writhed and moaned in pleasure as she clings on him tight. Clark's right hand took hold of her left hand while his free hand goes around her body to touch her and holding her as tight as he could while doing this. Diana put her right hand on his neck and her legs secure themselves around his waist, holding them tight like before. Clark rammed upward into her wet and hot core.

He leaned forward to her neck to kiss it, with Diana moaning his name clearly, and then he goes up to kiss her. Their tongues clashed again making Diana moan loud within his mouth. Minutes later he parted his lips from her, now going focus on hammering in her, thumping at her g-spot every time.

"Oh, Gods! CLARK!" she screamed out again.

The pleasure was so intense, her body and eyes glowing brighter.

Clark loved the view of Diana being like this; her face showed intense enjoyment and her writhing in pleasure while holding him. They felt nothing but the hot pleasure that is engulfing them. Clark grunted and moaned along with Diana's moans and screams that fill up his room.

The atmosphere intense and the smell of arousal dancing all through the air. They were both reaching the peak of their pleasures and move in time with each other, both of them wanting the other to feel as pleasured as themselves.

THE DARK SPELL

Now the pleasure has reached sky-high. Clark's thrusts become extreme. Diana threw her head back, pressing and rubbing her body harder on him. She now felt the pressure rising and is almost to her edge. She was close to her euphoric release and enjoying every second as the inevitable explosion drew closer fast.

And then it happened as her walls clenched around his length. They held onto each other's hand impossibly tighter. Diana's legs constrict around Clark's muscled torso as her body shivered uncontrollably.

With eyes closed and teeth clenched, Clark tilted his head to the ceiling and grunted loudly. Diana could feel his massive member pumping hot liquid into her like a fireman's hose. Each convulsion of his member is felt by her sensitive walls, as he dumps more and more white honey inside her flower. In rhythmic waves, their bodies again let loose a momentary eruption of their essences, spilling it all into one another.

"DIANA!"

"CLARK!"

Clark let out another loud groan muffled only by her scream as they rode the sensations together. Their chests heaving up and down. Pheromones and testosterone flowing through the air.

Their love for each other was overwhelming, feeling every molecule of their inner being vibrating outward to a warm, soft, afterglow, basking in true love.

Valeria's castle

"This...can't...be..."

Valeria fell from her throne, gasping for air. She felt pressure and tightness in her chest.

"Mistress! Mistress!" Juri gasped frantically.

Valeria screamed as she felt a burning sensation all over her body. Her heart beating rapidly.

"It's...them..."

"Who?!"

Her back arched. She could see nothing but flashes of Diana and Kal-El as they made love.

"So...much...power."

Her body began to convulse. Her eyes fluttered shut.

"Dionysus! Dionysus! DIONYSUS!" she screamed out.

A God and a Goddess fell in love. A love so otherworldly powerful, reveling in unadulterated truths.

CHAPTER 7: MOMENTS IN PARADISE

Clark and Diana's Apartment

Rubbing the sleep out of his eyes, Clark slowly opened his striking blue eyes.

The first thing he saw was the familiar bright red digits of his alarm clock on his nightstand. It said that it was 8:24 AM.

He hadn't expected to sleep this much and till this late... well, it was late for him. But the warm feeling of her body pressed against his own was something so amazing. The soft, light snoring and mumbling sound from her pouty lips was such a soft, lovely melody to him and he found it adorable. The way his Goddess would cling to him at night, holding him tight, made him realize there was no other way he would want to wake up. There was no other person he would rather have cuddling into the side of his body either.

Clark felt the soft curls tickle his neck as Diana shifted, pulling her closer to him and snuggling deeper into his neck. A part of her face was covered by her long, silky smooth raven hair. He slowly raised his hand to push it out of her face. Clark's heart fluttered when her lips pressed against his skin. The Amazon's curvaceous body was covering him almost completely. Diana had one leg thrown over Clark's legs, an arm wrapped around him, and her head was resting on his shoulder. Clark looked once again at his beloved Goddess, loving the way the sheets shaped around her figure. He couldn't help but notice how every curve of her fit against his body perfectly. She completed him like a missing piece of a puzzle. It gave him a strong feeling of euphoria.

Diana made a soft sound somewhere between a hum and a moan as she started to wake from her slumber. Clark looked down at Diana as he brought his free hand to the tangled raven curls and slowly ran his fingers through them. Diana hummed again and pulled Clark closer to her. Clark smiled slightly and bent his head down to drop a kiss atop Diana's head, slowly taking in the scent of her hair. It was a subtle and sweet smell that Clark had grown used to smelling everywhere. In his bed was certainly his favorite place to smell it, though.

His mind drifted to all the intimacy and passion they shared last night - wild night! Wild, wild night! He thought. It was wild, unpredictable, beautiful, and sensual. The way he sank deep inside her, their alignment, their entwinement, their coupled warmth, and the way their soaking flesh connected like forever.

When he felt a soft kiss being pressed to his neck, he knew Diana was awake. Warm cerulean blue eyes soon opened and then Diana leaned her head up so she could press her lips to Clark's. There was something about the feeling of Diana's full lips against his that made his heart make an odd flip-flop as they kissed. It was soft and sweet; lips brushed together slowly and tongues tenderly stroked and circled each other. Clark brought his hand to Diana's cheek and his fingers brushed her soft skin as they ended their kiss with a few lingering pecks.

"Good Morning, Beloved," she said groggily and yawned.

"Morning, Beautiful," he replied with a smile and captured her lips again.

How could she be so beautifully sexy and adorable at the same time? Clark wondered.

Diana moaned feeling his thick, hard member pressing against her leg. She reached a hand down between their bodies and wrapped her hand around its impressive size to stroke her lover's length. Clark moaned against her lips as she peeled his foreskin down and ran her hand up and down his length. She could feel him twitch under her touch.

"Good Morning, Junior," she giggled softly.

"Hmm...so you do realize you were having an inappropriate dream." His voice was husky.

"Was I?" She laughed, her cheeks flushing.

"It was about me," he smirked, his eyes dancing around her face.

"Hmm, maybe." She looked away unwilling to give him the satisfaction, freeing her hand from his phallus.

THE DARK SPELL

"It was totally about me. You were calling out so profusely." He exaggerated. "Clark! Kal! Clark! Take me harder!" He mumbled jokingly into her ear.

"Ok, alright!" She blushed, hiding her face in his neck.

His morning scent peeked her desire and she nipped his neck as an instinct.

"Diana..." he obscenely sounded shortly.

She could feel the vibrations of a chuckle through his chest, and she smiled, lifting her head to meet his lust-filled stare.

"I'm pretty sure I said that all night too anyway." her eyes blushing.

"True. Yes, you did." He kissed her slowly, nibbling on her pouting bottom lip, then pulled back.

His hands slid down over her bare curves to her voluptuous cakes he loved so much giving a gentle squeeze.

"You know, this just feels so different. We've stayed the night together but living together now brings a whole new feeling I enjoy."

"I love you," he whispered his lips once again find their way to hers.

Diana tried to mutter it back, but it came out as a garbled, happy moan. Of course, that only encouraged him more to grope her ass tighter.

Location: Mount Olympus

Eros looked down into the scrying pool with a satisfied smile.

"Up to no good as always, Cupid?" Strife asked.

"Call me that again and a bullet will be going through your skull." threatened the Cupid

"Oooh...someone's on edge. Who is it? The Succubus again?" Strife backed up.

"Our friend, Valeria, seems to still harbor feelings for Dionysus." Eros replied.

"I'm still trying to understand how could that be. A Succubus in love?" Strife laughed.

"Be it a mortal, god, demon, or any other creatures, Strife, love happens," said Cupid.

"That is impossible. Gods and Demons do not revel in such tedious things. It's inconceivable. Dionysus is his father's son." Strife smirked. "Just as Diana is her father's daughter and the daughter of the slut Queen of the Amazons."

Eros frowned. "What are you saying?"

"Do you truly believe she loves that alien? It is in her nature to have such a being bow at her feet."

"Strife, you know nothing. You are just as bitter as your Mother."

"Careful Eros, my Mother is your Queen."

"Your empty threats are nothing. Just as I warned the Succubus, Diana and Kal-El are not to be meddled with. Both of you will regret it."

Strife smiled deviously. "I like my odds, Eros. A little discourse to fuel the passion."

Back with Clark and Diana

Clark licked his lips and smiled at Diana as she sat up, facing away from him. Clark had never known anyone else who could look so beautiful in the morning - though, he was very biased when it came to the topic. In his opinion, and well actually it was a fact, there was nobody more beautiful than the woman that was in the bed with him. It was a natural beauty that had nothing to do with makeup or clothes, those he was sure Diana could really go without at all times, it was all about the beauty that radiated from inside the Amazonian Goddess.

Clark sat up and went behind Diana's body, wrapping his arms around her as he pressed a kiss on her shoulder. Diana smiled one of those ridiculously sweet smiles at him and then placed her hands over Clark's. Clark kissed her shoulder again and then moved his lips to her neck and placed an open-mouthed kiss there. He moved his lips all the way to Diana's ear and for a moment he just let his breath wash over her as he replayed the past few months of pure bliss in his mind. He was more than grateful to finally reach a place in his life where everything was working for him and he could see nothing other than happiness in his life. He had Diana to thank for most of it, he was sure.

Clark sucked her ear into his mouth and lightly bit on it, knowing very well that it was one of her weaknesses.

"Mmm," Diana hummed and Clark smirked against her ear. "Darling, we have a briefing to get to," she barely got out before a deep moan slipped out.

THE DARK SPELL

Clark gave her ear one last nip, wanting to awaken the beast he knew he could make come out within seconds.

"There's no rush," he whispered into her ear in that silky tone that he knew Diana loved.

"No... no...no, rush but staying in bed and missing the briefing is so tempting."

She pulled back so they could share another quick kiss. Diana hummed into the kiss and then pulled back to look into the deep pools of blue that were shining brightly as the sun made contact with them.

"Have I ever told you how handsome you are?" Diana licked her lips as her eyes gleamed.

Diana's lips pressed a kiss to his once again. Clark's heart sped up and Diana melted against his chest as their lips molded and their tongues searched.

However, it ended too soon, and Diana found herself following Clark's lips as he pulled away.

"I love you," he rushed out in a breath.

"I know," she responded cockily, which earned her a playful nip on her lip, making her giggle. "I love you, too," she smiled softly and closed the space between their mouths once again.

2 hours later - WatchTower: Briefing Room

Their eyes lock from across the table, only seeing the very souls of the other as they battle their innermost carnal urges. They had long sense-tuned out what was being said by Batman and Cyborg.

Diana could feel butterflies flying around in her stomach. Her eyes fierce and confident, never blinking, her gaze never wavering. Clark returned with equal fervor, his eyes boring into hers. And he gets it.

He smiled and she smiled back, tentatively. It was as though they were constantly undressing each other with their eyes. The way that they watched each other, the way that they caught each other's eye just right when nobody else was looking or had noticed this. No one had said anything - yet.

The heat from his gaze smoldered into her, filling her with a steady throb that she couldn't ignore. His eyes sank into her so deeply, it was as though they were a part of her and she relished in them.

The flutter of her eyelids would send shockwaves through his entire body, making him putty in her hands. And then, when Diana thought she could take no more, the dip of his stare down her body gave her no doubts as to his intentions. It made her squirm, and yearn for more, even while she glanced about to make sure no one else was watching.

Diana in her uniform that managed to show even more skin, thanks to her breastplate and star-spangled bottom. She looked scrumptious to him.

And he in his Kryptonian tights flashing his chest muscles and godly thighs...

Yes, it was eye-sex and they couldn't get enough of it.

"Superman? Are you listening?" Batman asked irritated.

"What? Uh..."

Suddenly, the WatchTower alert went off.

The monitor screen showed a large man in vintage medieval leather armor with a sword in hand. His face was severely burned with only one eye.

"What the hell is that?!" Shazam questioned.

"Looks like a demon from Tartarus," Wonder Woman said standing up.

Superman stood up as well. "Diana and I will handle this."

"Oh, sure, you two will go to be all flirty and smoochy!" Shazam teased.

"No, we're not!" Superman and Wonder Woman retorted in unison.

Batman narrowed his eyes and sighed turning around.

Clark and Diana glanced at each other blushing as they flew off out of the briefing room.

"Taking bets now on the what level of the weird flirty stuff?" asked Shazam.

"It's not even a bet, kid," Green Lantern said.

Location: Bossier City, Louisiana

"Hear me, Mortals! I am Xanathe! You all will now have the honor of becoming valued sacrifices! Come forth!" Xanathe inhaled deeply and grinned devilishly.

Superman and Wonder Woman came flying down in between Xanathe and civilians.

THE DARK SPELL

"Ah, not one but two Gods, have come to challenge me. It shall be an honorable death!" Xanathe declared and raised the sword.

"The honor of death will be all yours demon!" Wonder Woman rushed in with the first strike.

Xanathe flew miles away with the strike.

Adjusting his vision back from the impact, "Ah, Princess. It's so delicious to finally be in your presence. The daughter of Zeus. Why don't we rule this world together?"

"That sure as hell will never happen!" Superman said as he punched him sending him flying into an unoccupied building.

The building collapsed and exploded with Xanathe inside.

"Kal, I have this. Make sure everyone else is away and safe." Diana noticed the civilians running away from buildings and cars to take cover.

"Di..." he stopped in mid-air before shooting a laser from his red eyes.

Xanathe collapsed again on its feet.

She said reassuringly. "I have this. Go."

He quickly flew off to the bystanders still running to safety.

"Alright. It's just you and me, demon," said Diana cracking her knuckles and clenching her fists tight.

Xanathe mocked in return "Ha! Come to me, Princess..." Suggestively licking his lips.

Diana smirked and launched at him.

The battle began.

She did not hesitate nor relent her strikes. She dodged most of them only getting hit once in her arm but that did not stop her from attacking.

"Yes! Yes! Princess! Now, this is a fight! A true opponent!" He laughed amused relaxing his attacking stance.

Diana jumped over him and kicked him in his back knocking him across the street.

"Ha! It would be quite an adventure in my bed with you." He wiped the blood on the corner of his mouth.

Diana looked at him disgusted and dashed forward. Just as she was about to punch him. Xanathe grabbed her arm twisting it behind her. He inhaled the scent of her hair.

"Ah... you smell of divine power. Though a pity! You are uncleaned! The smell of that vile creature is all over you. The creature runs through your veins. Though, I guess I will have you both," he said sniffing in her hair.

"I don't think so!" Diana yelled back.

Diana slammed her head back on his forehead. He let go of her arm being knocked away. Diana wrapped her lasso around him yanking him back to her, kicking him in the head. She then flew up with him and slammed him to the ground.

Xanathe tried to stand but Diana placed her foot on his back and sword to his neck.

"Stay down," she warned.

"You are...you are exquisite, Princess," catching his breath

"Diana!" Superman called.

"I'm alright."

"I can see that."

Xanathe was flattened to the surface, Diana with her foot still on his back and sword to the back of his neck.

"Princess..." Xanathe chuckled. "You and your creature have passed this round, it seems. I'll take my leave." The surface sucked him in and he vanished like smoke.

"Wait a minute?! What?!" Clark questioned.

"He's gone!"

"What did he mean passed this round?" Clark wondered.

"I don't appreciate him calling you creature." She frowned putting her sword back in its sheath.

"He called me what?" He smiled and shrugged. "I am yours, Di. Don't worry about it. Let's get some of this cleaned up and there are some kids that want to meet you." He pointed to the kids at the end of the block. He had created a shield with their school bus covering them.

Location: Valéria's Castle

"My Queen... My Empress..." Xanathe bowed. "Everything went as you expected. Princess Diana and her lover, Kal-El fought valiantly. She is the fighter and he, the protector. Their smell..."

"What of it?"

THE DARK SPELL

"It has intertwined. A disguise as one or the other can easily be detected."

"I see. Well, that goes that little plan. I was looking forward to playing the role of Diana. It would've brought me so much pleasure to seduce the Kryptonian. To know first hand what makes him so entranced by the Demi-Goddess and to have a taste of him myself. Though, it wouldn't be any fun if neither could play along. I guess I will try my efforts with something else."

"It has been an honor to serve you, Empress."

"Thank you, Xanathe. That will be all for now."

"Ah, Valéria, you haven't changed one bit."

Valéria raised her brow. "Strife? Oh, what a surprise. You certainly have changed."

"You like the look? As the time change, you know."

"Yes...yes...and what brings you here, Goddess of Discord? The last time I've seen you was in Milan or Guatemala? What was that? At least a century ago. Quite a revelry we got ourselves in."

"As I recall, it was you and Dionysus."

Valéria rolled her eyes.

"Oh, right. Apologies, Valéria. I wasn't aware that was still such a touchy subject. I shall make it up to you. That is why I am here anyway. I spoke with Eros about my dear sister, Diana and her pet lover, Kal-El."

Valéria smirked.

"Hoping for a Minajatwa?" Strife asked.

"Ah, yes...yes...that was the initial plan. Your sister and her lover exudes such power, so much passionate. I wanted it all to myself. To be the Succubi Queen I once was. But to my surprise, they have evolved into something more. The purity of their love and devotion has changed my perspective."

Strife sighed dramatically. "Yes, it seems we've all became victims of this love affair. Protected under the Gods and Fates." Strife smiled deviously. "But it's not to say we can't have a little fun. Add a little more fire."

"Hmm...?" Valéria stood up from her throne quite intrigued. "Do tell."

"I'm sure you have a servant or two to spare. Let's continue this little chat over a glass of Romanée Conti."

Back at the WatchTower: Monitor Room

Clark took Diana's hand. "I'll meet you in the shower. I just need a minute with Bruce."

"Okay." Diana kissed his cheek. "Don't be too long."

"I won't." Clark smiled proudly watching Diana walk away.

When she turned the corner, he flew off quickly to the monitoring room.

"Alright, Bruce. Let's make this quick," he said folding his arms.

"You two are...happy." Batman still in the monitor chair checking the fire in Vietnam through the radar. Flash and Impulse were on it.

"We are." Clark nodded his head agreeing.

"Just make sure your focus isn't swayed." Bruce watched the fire being put out one place to another at a rapid pace by the speedsters.

"Careful, Bruce. Your crossing the line of hypocrisy. I never questioned your relationship with Selina so why question mine with Diana? We know what our responsibilities are but for far too long we've put so much ahead instead of our happiness."

"I understand that. I'm just thinking of-" Batman paused abruptly knowing him well. Clark is smart enough to catch his mind.

"The team? What's between me and Diana is just that...between me and Diana. That's it," Clark said ending the argument.

Bruce sighed. "Clark, I am happy for both of you."

"You have a funny way of showing it," Clark followed immediately.

"I'm serious. I am. We just don't need anything compromised. You two are in the public eye. It's a risk. A weakness to exploit. I've already told you, if anything goes wrong, especially with Diana. Can you make the right choice?" he turned back to stare directly into his eyes.

"We seem to be in the same boat with the women we love, Bruce. It's a risk I'm willing to take. Whatever sacrifices Diana and I have to face, we will make the right choice and get through it together. As I said, it's me and her. That's it. So are you done? Is that all?"

"That's all."

"Later, Bruce." Clark left out taking a deep breath.

Location: Wonder Woman's Quarters

Clark smiled hearing Diana's voice as the door slid open. She was already in the shower, singing a beautiful melody. As his suit degenerated

THE DARK SPELL

he walked into the bathroom. He was now completely naked and he could see the wavy outline silhouette of his girlfriend's body through the glazing marbled glass sliding door of the shower. He stops just before entering to take a moment to just look at her... to really look at her.

Diana rolled her head back and let the hot water pour over her chest and neck, then turn to wet her hair and back. Steam boiled over the top of the shower and enveloped the room. The gathering steam distorts the view but does not obscure it completely. He entered quickly and secure the door behind him to retain the heat.

She must have heard the door close because he saw her head turn ever so slightly with a smile to acknowledge the clicking of the latch, and indication she knew of his presence.

"Sorry, it took longer than I expected."

"It's okay, Love. Work before pleasure."

Clark sensed a change in the room. The air became charged with an almost palpable sexual energy. He waited and watched for her next move. Her demeanor had changed. Where once she was standing still and letting the water cascade over her, now her hands have begun to dance over her body. This was no simple lathering as part of her daily routine. No... this was deliberate. This was salacious. As she turned her back to him and ran her hands down over her hips, bending ever so slightly to accentuate the swell of her perfectly round backside.

Clark felt a stirring in him, a thirst only she can slake began. His heart rate increased and beat hard in his chest. He watched as her hands traced distinct tracks over her body. Her hands cupped her breasts. She pinched one nipple between her finger and thumb and compressed delicately. She bit her lip, all too aware of what she was doing to him. He watched as one of her hands descend from her breast, sliding down her abdomen and beyond.

His heart was pounding now, and he felt it lower than his chest. The tick-ticking of his pulse was now evident in his rapidly growing erection. His face was flushed. In all his years, he had not known a lust greater than that which he had now for her.

Diana smiled to herself and bit her lip again as the fingertip from her middle finger traced a line straight down her stomach and to her center. She enjoyed seeing how hot she made Clark. She pressed a finger between her lower lips and drag slowly vertically, sliding easily due to her excitement and she shuddered as she grazes the nub of her clit. She uttered the coup-de-grace to this temptatious game and let out an unstifled moan knowing full well that Clark wouldn't be able to take any more.

He heard the audible release of her desire and he stepped closer to her, wrapping his arms around her and kissed her shoulder.

"You are so damn sexy," he whispered in her ear.

Her eyes fluttered closed and she let out a soft moan as his hands ran slowly up and down her sides. He then cupped her breasts, cupping them and giving a gentle squeeze.

"Love, what's wrong?" Diana asked snaking on his chest.

"Nothing," he said in a muted tone.

Diana slowly turned around to face him. "I can feel it in your hands. Now I can see it all over your face. What was said?"

He sighed. "Let's talk about it after our shower."

"Kal...?"

He smiled reassuringly and cupped her face bringing up into a passionate kiss. Their tongues swirl together. He held her close and kissed her harder pressing her against the side of the shower as the hot water rained down upon them. Diana could feel his erection pressed against her stomach and this increased the heat of her own lust.

They kissed deeply, with the warm water falling upon them. The fire in that kiss was hotter than anything that could have come out of the water heater and in an instant they knew that this shower would be like nothing they had had in quite some time.

As the kissing continued, Clark started letting his hands explore her body getting slick as the water ran down her sexy curvaceous body. Moving across her back they quickly found their way to her voluptuous ass and pulled her closer to him. In doing this, her amazing breasts pressed against his chest and he could feel her hardening nipples pressed into him. Feeling this, kissing and being with this goddess, Clark knew it wouldn't be long before his body began to show her just how turned on she was making him.

But he wanted more of this woman, and without pause one hand slipped between her legs and he felt how wet she was, and not from the water, this was the hot sticky liquid that only comes when a woman is

THE DARK SPELL

getting aroused. Moaning through the kiss, he knew she enjoyed his touch and wanted more.

Her hands were doing the same, running her nails up and down his back and giving him that shiver that only a sexy woman can do. As his hand started exploring her center, he felt her hand as it made a bee-line for his manhood. Slowly at first, she began to stroke his manhood. She broke the kiss for a brief moment and stepped away to admire the object that she made stand at full attention, smiling at him all the while with so much unspoken passion and wanting.

Clark took this moment too, once again admiring her body, her smile, and her utter sexuality. But she was insatiable as her hand reached down again and wrapped around his member as they breathed into each other's mouths. Diana could feel him quiver and smile at her touch. She slowly started to stroke him, squeezing at the base and pulling up the length.

Clark kissed and bit her neck and moan as she dragged his foreskin down and slid her thumb over the tip. Diana could feel his moan originate deep within him and resonated through to her throat where his lips were.

Clark bent his neck to her breasts, surrounding a nipple with his mouth, taking her between his teeth and suckling gently. His teeth apply pressure and dug his bite to the peak. Diana's hand stroked up and down his member faster now as she felt it throbbing in her hand. She pulled his mouth back to hers and stood on her tip-toes, parting her legs slightly. She bit his lip as she rubbed the head of his length between her wet nether lips. Clark sucked air in through his teeth, barely restraining his overwhelming desire for her. Diana had been leaning into him and they were now two steps from the wall of the shower. Clark pressed one hand to her hip as the other cupped the back of her head, his fingers wound into her wet hair. Clark then pushed her back slightly to create some space between them and they both look down to watch as Diana jerked his member. Clark glanced up as Diana licked her lips hungrily.

Watching the water run over Diana's breasts. He picked up the body wash, squirting some onto the washcloth, and smiled.

"Time to get clean."

"Only to get dirty again at the same time."

He answered with a mischievous smile.

He switched places with her, moving her out of the water stream, and went to work lathering soap all over her body.

Diana closed her eyes, enjoying the feeling of Clark's hands on her body.

"Your hands feel so nice..." she told him.

He started at her neck and making his way down, not letting any surface go untouched, paying extra attention to her breasts and womanhood. As he cleaned her, he lightly ran a finger over her slit, feeling the wetness that wasn't just from the water.

Next, he put a pile of shampoo in his hands to massage it into her scalp. "Oh by the Gods...Kal-El..."

Clark pushed her up against the shower wall and kissed her deeply. It was like heaven to feel his fingers on her scalp, his mouth connecting with hers, his body pushing up against hers in a soft restraining way.

Thinking that he had used enough soap for the two of them, she pulled Clark out from the water, turned around, and started rubbing her soapy ass over his length. Once she felt him starting to move with the motion of her hips in enjoyment, she turned around and began to run her hands over her breasts and then used the soap to clean the rest of Clark's body. She pushed him lightly back under the water and joined him there in an embrace, allowing the water to run over them both, clearing the soap and shampoo away.

Clark's hands began to roam over her breasts, lightly at first, rolling the nipples in between his fingers, pinching occasionally to change the sensations. As she began to squirm a little in pleasure, he bent over and took one of her nipples in his mouth, sucking vigorously, and increased the pressure and tempo on the other nipple. When she began to moan softly, he switched the attention between the two nipples, continuing until her moans became louder and he knew she was thoroughly aroused.

Clark looked into Diana's eyes and said, "you are so incredible. I can't get enough of you."

The steaming hot water was hitting both of them, and combined with their bodies being so close together, they were both red and hot.

THE DARK SPELL

Clark turned her around, his manhood now pressed up against her firm ass. He reached down and began to tease her clit gently, all while kissing and sucking on her neck up to her ear.

"Gods..." she moaned, pressing her ass against him. "Beloved you are such a tease..." she whined.

"It's just something about your reaction," he told her, kissing right behind her ear.

She moaned in response, and he kept rubbing her clit. She gripped his wrist as he kept going at it. Her voice has grown hoarser and aroused, slipping two fingers into her wet center.

"Oh..." she moaned, her head tilting back. "You spoil me, touching me like this," she told him.

"My beautiful Goddess deserves to be spoiled. Every chance I get," he confidently told her.

"Oh, will you?" she teased.

"Promise."

He began to rub her g-spot, using the ever so famous "come here" motion.

She loved it, obviously, and moaned loudly.

Using his free hand, he reached up and cupped her large breast, groping it all while his manhood was pressed up against her ass. She began to grind against it as well.

"You're so... gifted...beloved," she said, biting her lower lip.

"Super in all ways but this is a gift for you," he teased back.

"Mmhh...I'm so in love with my incredibly sexy gift."

Clark smirked and began to pinch and tease her nipples, and she pressed back against him even harder.

She gripped his wrist tighter, her nails digging into his skin.

"Clark..." she moaned

"Diana..." he moaned back.

She slowly turned to face him, and he kissed her deeply.

All the while, she pressed down against his hand now, letting him rub her g-spot even easier now. Her moans were getting louder. He pinched her nipple hard, and she moaned excitedly into his mouth.

Clark fell back against the wall, taking her with him, and her moans were becoming more like whines now, pleading him not to stop.

And he doesn't.

Her body begins to quiver, and she was practically sucking on his tongue. Using his thumb, Clark began to tease and rub her clit as he fingers her, all while not taking his other hand off of her breast.

With one last push into him, her moans became louder, only muffled because his tongue was in her mouth, and he felt her body start to shake and rely more on him holding her up rather than her own legs.

Finally, she broke the kiss, and leaned into him, relying on him to make sure she didn't fall. Her breathing was heavy, and she didn't speak, only moaned and panted.

He smiled, kissing her.

Then he turned her around and bent her over. He admires how sexy she looked, her body dripping wet, flushed from the heat of the water. His eyes traced her hourglass figure and focused right on her perfect round ass. He rubbed the tip of his length against the entrance of her.

He slowly pushed the head of his member inside of her.

"Oh!" she exclaimed in excitement. "Yes, Beloved!"

He laughed, grabbing her hips as he pushed more inside of her.

Instead of moaning, she lightly squealed in delight, making his member twitch in excitement.

As he pushed farther into her, she yelped out in response but started to giggle.

"God...you fill me up in so many ways!" she said, her hands against the wall.

He continued groping her ass, her breathing getting heavy again.

Clark spread her cheeks apart, pressing them together, and then finally, giving her a firm, hard smack across the ass.

"Hey!" she said.

"I had to," he said, spanking her again.

She laughed and moaned out in response.

"Gods, this feels so incredibly naughty..."

"That's the fun of it, though?" he replied, slowly beginning to move back and forth.

THE DARK SPELL

She grunted and gritted her teeth, but quickly began to moan, her knuckles clenched against the tile wall of the shower.

He began to up the speed of his thrusts. He grabbed onto her hips and slid out to where he was barely inside, and then pushed back inside of her as deep as he could go, savoring the feeling of her tightness gripping onto him all the while.

"Oh! Gods..." he heard her whisper.

He pushed deeper inside her for emphasis.

"Oh! Gods!" she moaned louder.

He slapped her ass hard, watching it bounce.

"Yes, Clark! Yes!" she screamed out.

He smirked. "Louder, Diana," he told her, spanking her ass one last time.

He felt her quiver once he said that.

He began to pump in and out of her much faster now, the sounds of their bodies slapping together echoing through the bathroom. He grabbed a fistful of her raven hair with one hand and gripped her perfect ass with the other.

She had gotten even tighter, each thrust felt like a warm hug trying to stop him from leaving. Her moans had gotten wilder, with her only being able to say his name.

She reached back and grabbed her ass cheek, pulling it back while she looked over her shoulder at him, biting her lip.

"You are so good, Beloved!" she told him.

"You, Diana. It's you."

"Mm!" she squealed.

"Everything about you, I can't resist," he admitted in between his groans.

"I...know," she responded with a smug smile.

He laughed.

"You're a wild woman, you know that Diana?" he teased.

She giggled. "I'm well aware of that now because of you. So what are you going to do about it?" she asked as if he wasn't already inside of her.

"This," he answer.

He pulled out of her, turning her around in the process, and grabbed her ass, lifting her as she wrapped her legs around him instinctively.

"Mm, I like this," she smiled seductively, looking deep into his eyes.

Clark with a cocky smile back, slid into her, holding her up the entire time. While he does that, she doesn't stop looking him in the eyes once. As he slid in, she opened her mouth, only closing it to bite her lip once he got all the way inside of her.

Clark leaned forward and kissed her, slowly sliding his member in and out of her.

To their surprise, the water was still as hot as it was when first stepping in.

As he was sliding in and out of her, she dug her fingernails into his back, moaning into his mouth at the same time.

As he gripped her ass tighter, Diana moaned, throwing her head back and closed her eyes.

She grabbed onto him tighter. Clark felt her warm and soft breasts pressed up against him. Clark couldn't tell what was warmer, Diana or the water, but he doesn't want to get out of either one.

He hits to thrust faster.

"Oh! Oh! Oh! Ah, Clark!" she screamed, which quickly transformed into moans of pleasure.

She dug her nails into his back again, this time enough to hurt a little. Her moans were turning hoarse and rapid in his ear, and she was even tighter than before.

He started to thrust even faster, and her moans got louder in response. Thank the Gods, the WatchTower Quarters were soundproof though that didn't stop slight shudders.

"Yes, Beloved! Gods, yes!"

"God, Diana," he moaned out, tilting his head back.

She wrapped her legs around him even tighter as he was practically slamming in and out of her. He kept slamming into her again and again. Her moans were getting more erratic, and her body was starting to shake again.

He knew what was coming.

THE DARK SPELL

"Love..." she whimpered. "I- take me...more...more," she said in a begging tone.

That alone was what made him feel like he was close to the edge.

He pushed her upper body back down and held her hips as he picked up the pace again. Her nails dug into him once again, and he gripped her ass firmly, holding her steady. Their moans both getting louder, with hers turning into screams and squeals of pleasure. Watching her body convulse with pleasure and hearing her moans, it did not take him long.

"Beloved...pleaseeeee..."

And with that, he came with her. Hard. Shooting rope after rope inside of her, filling her up. All the while, she was wrapped around him so tight as if she was going to break him, screaming his name and saying things he could barely understand.

And with that, Diana came down from orgasm she leaned her upper body forward against his, feeling his breath in her neck. His mouth biting her ear lightly before telling her how much he loved making love to her... feeling her on him... around him.

After holding each other for what felt like forever, Clark let her down gently, though still held her with her legs shaky.

After a couple of minutes of silence, they begin to clean off again. Admittedly, with plenty of groping while doing so.

Diana turned the faucet off as Clark got their towels with the last of the hot water being used. Stepping out of the shower, they playfully dried each other off.

Clark wrapped the blue towel around his waist then wrapped Diana's marron towel around her body.

Walking out of the bathroom, Clark sat on the edge of the bed, pulling Diana down to straddle him.

Diana wrapped her arms around his neck to kiss him softly.

"I don't want to ever take another shower without you. I know that's impossible. But it just feels so wonderful."

"I know. Having me get you all clean and dirty at the same time," he teased, pinching her firm ass through the towel.

Diana giggled.

"Now, will you tell me?"

He sighed. "I really don't want to, Di."

"Clark...just tell me."

"Okay...okay..." he sighed again. "Bruce is just acting like his paranoid self. He said he is happy for us but still didn't stop him from questioning whether or not you and I can handle our relationship being public, responsibilities, and priorities. How will it affect the rest of the League? I honestly think it was mostly projecting how his relationship with Selina has been. I told him what's between you and I is just that."

"Darling, of course, there will be questions about us. But you're absolutely right, it's between you and me. We've already gone through so much together, Clark. We can make it through anything. No matter what, even when it seems like we're at a breaking point which I don't think we ever will be, you and I are bound to each other."

"Not to take away from the seriousness but by bound...is there a double meaning that you hinting at wanting to tie me up?"

Diana laughed. "Hmm...maybe."

"I knew it," he grinned and kissed her neck. "But seriously now, Di. I just...as you said...we've gone through so much. This is our happiness. We are building our future together."

"It's not easy, Beloved. It never will be. But our bond is stronger."

"I love you, Diana." He placed kisses all over her face.

Diana smiled as he did so responding, "I love you, too, Clark."

Clark then descended her neck and his hands glide up her thighs under the towel to grope her rear.

"Mmh...how about we go to my home island this weekend?" she asked.

"Will your mother be okay with me staying? Your sisters?"

"How many times have you accompanied me?"

"That was different. We are dating now."

"No difference to me. You are still the man I introduced my mother to as my best friend. Still, the man my mother knew I would eventually become romantically involved with. In her own way, she adores and trusts you. The majority of my sisters do as well. It's fine."

Clark grinned. "This weekend it is then. And we need a getaway anyway."

4 days later: Themyscira Library Temple

THE DARK SPELL

"Queen Hippolyta?" Torra, the Amazonian Guard bowed.

Hippolyta looked up from her book. "Yes?"

"Princess Diana has arrived."

Hippolyta smiled and stood up. But seeing the expression on Torra's face, her smile quickly dropped.

"And?" She questioned.

"She has brought her...companion. The Kryptonian."

"Ah...I see." Hippolyta sighed in amusement and shook her head.

She knew the moment Diana had introduced kal-El to her 5 years ago, he would be the one her daughter would give her heart to. No matter how much Diana tried to deny, she knew it was only a matter of time.

Kal-El has shown his honor, respect, and loyalty to Diana, but she will still protect her daughter as her mother.

"Have a feast prepared" she instructed.

"Yes, Queen Hippolyta," Torra bowed again.

Queen's Royal Palace

Clark looked around nervously making Diana giggle.

"Clark, calm down."

"I am calm."

"Terrible liar," she teased.

"Di, your mom is going to walk through the door and when we tell her we're together she's going to have my neck."

Diana laughed and latched onto his arm. "Stop it. No, she will be happy for us. I told you, you've been here with me more than enough times and every time I'm sure my mother has taken note of how close we are. She won't be surprised at all."

"I can only hope-"

"Diana, Kal-El. What a lovely surprise."

They both turned and smiled.

Clark bowed. "Your highness."

"Don't be so formal, Kal-El," she said sternly with a raised brow.

"Oh... Uh... yes... yes ma'am."

Diana giggled. "Hello, Mother." She embraced her. "I've missed you so much."

"I've missed you, too, Dear." Hippolyta pulled away slightly and cupped Diana's face with both hands. "You are glowing. Is there something you want to tell me?" She asked with a raised brow letting go of Diana's face.

Diana smiled and blushed. "It's nothing like that. But..." Diana looked at Clark and reach out for his hand.

He grabbed her hand and intertwined his fingers with hers.

"Ah, I see..." Hippolyta turned her back to them. "I can't say I'm surprised. However..." she quickly turned back to them, sword in hand pointing it directly at Clark's adam's apple.

Diana gasped. "Mother! Put the sword down now!"

He gulped. "Told you..."

"Fret not, Kal-El...for now at least. This is only a warning. Hurt my daughter and I will have your head."

"Yes ma'am, your highness. Understood."

"Mother..."

Hippolyta placed her sword back into its sheath. Clark sighed of relief.

"You two go ahead and freshen up, a feast will be prepared for the both of you."

Diana guided Clark to one of the hot springs areas

"Here, you will be alone."

"You aren't staying with me?"

Diana smirked. "No, my Love. We'll get distracted."

Clark gave her a look of disappointment. "But I like bathing you."

Diana giggled and kissed him sweetly. "It's just for now. Relax a bit. You'll have me all to yourself later."

"Fine...Fine," Clark slapped her ass as she was walking away making her squeal.

Clark chuckled and looked around. It was certainly such a majestic atmosphere. He took off his clothes and stepped into the hot water with a sigh. He leaned back against the wall and closed his eyes, relaxing.

All he could think about was was Diana.

After 20 minutes Clark got out of a hot bath. The room he was offered is built around an open-air courtyard. It has pebbles, timber, and clay bricks. The room was sturdy and comfortable. It has a big klismos bed by the window confronting the ocean. No electricity or WiFi as such. The

THE DARK SPELL

room is coated with white limestone in the wall and dyed indigo blue on the roof and pillars. Diana was sent to her room which he predicts in the palace to freshen up but still, his room is not that bad. Its simplicity and refinement captured Clark's heart.

He steps to a three-legged round table that has his clothes neatly folded. He is presumed to wear their traditional outfit for the feast. It is two pieces of clothing. Themyscira clothes were mainly based on necessity, function, materials, and protection rather than identity. Thus, clothes were quite simple, draped, loose-fitting, and free-flowing. Clothes were homemade and cut to various lengths added with ornamental clasps or pins, a belt, or a girdle.

The first piece of clothing was a loincloth. He ties it around to cover his genitals. The next piece was the tunic. He draped and fastened it as chitoniskos. His strong physique looks spectacular in that short gown. His right shoulder is free to expose until his heavy chest and tunic edges bear his athletic thighs.

He joined his escort Artemis outside. She welcomed him in Ancient Greek. Clark returned the salute. Guard Women standing behind Artemis giggled at the glimpse of Clark in a chiton and the way it revealed his muscular frame. He was quite on par with their Greek God statues.

Artemis acquainted him, "Κύριος, our highness is waiting for you."

He met Diana in the hallway. She was wearing a knee-length white toga draped by her right shoulder. Diana appreciated his frame and their eyes roamed over each other's assets.

"Ah! umm..." They both turned around to see Queen Hippolyta looking at them, "Shall we?" the Queen asked.

Diana and Clark followed Hippolyta quietly to the temple where the feast was held. When they entered the temple, the fellow Amazon sisters were already gathered, sitting at long large tables filled with food and loudly socializing.

Their attention was immediately brought to Clark. He noticed the stares and whispers. Some welcoming, some questioning.

"The Princess's mate."

"He is not of man's world, you know."

"Diana chose to be with a pale imitation of a God?"

"Clark?"

He snapped out of focusing on them and looked at Diana.

"Don't do that. You are here with me not only because I want you to but you should be as my love."

Clark smiled and leaned over kissing her cheek. "Thank you, Diana."

While Diana and Clark sat down, Hippolyta still stood and raised her goblet.

"Tonight we celebrate my daughter's return home as well as our guest, Kal-El. Kal-El has shown his loyalty and worthy of our trust, fighting alongside Diana to protect this island many times. Let the feast begin!"

They spent hours of eating, talking, and laughing. Diana was proud to see the man she loves be accepted by her mother and sisters.

Later that night... Amazon living Quarters

"Tomorrow morning Clark and I will be taking a stroll to the science complex."

"I'm sure it will be to your liking and quite fascinating for you, Kal-El. Quite on par with Kryptonian science and technology."

"I look forward to seeing and studying it all...if allowed, Hippolyta."

"Of course."

"Thank you," he smiled.

Hippolyta gave a slight nod. "Good night, Diana, Kal-El."

"Good night," Diana and Clark said in unison.

When Hippolyta walked away, Diana took Clark's hand, pulling him into her room.

"Woah?! Di?"

"Come here and look at this with me."

Diana walked over to her balcony and sighed leaning over it. Clark wrapped her arms around her waist from behind and kissed her shoulder.

"I used to stare up at the moon for hours hoping and wishing for the day I would be able to leave and explore the outside world. I just knew there was something more for me," Diana started to explain. "I have been guided into the right path. I wouldn't want this any other way to be with you. You are my best friend, Clark. The man I love, the man...the one I trust the most."

Clark kissed her shoulder again and trailed up her neck.

THE DARK SPELL

"Thank you, Diana, for opening up and sharing this with me."

She turned in his arms to face him and caressed his cheek.

"I love you, Diana," he said as he captured her lips in a passionate kiss.

He lifted her and Diana instinctively wrapped her legs around his waist.

Catching his lips again, she slid her hands up to his neck, letting him curl over her. His tongue swept through her mouth, and his teeth nipped across her jaw, his breath panting over her collarbones.

Clark floated over to the bed and gently laid her down on the edge of the Handcrafted and pleated royal 5.4" ft tall bed with her legs hanging in the air.

He slowly stripped her from her toga continuing their make-out session.

When he cupped her sex with one hand her hands clutched the sheet.

His erection through his chiton rocked into her thighs and she widened her legs to give him better access. She gasped as he slid through her folds and circled her clit, threw her head back as his other hand palm her breast.

Her eyes shot open feeling his lips latched onto her neck.

She moaned as he worked her closer and closer, rubbing himself against her as his fingers tweaked her breast and rubbed her clit. She had to lean heavily on the bed when he slipped one finger inside of her.

He raised her to face him, she quickly caught his lips and kissed him until he moaned. Clark released her lips and kneeled on the floor. His hands rubbed her inner thighs, encouraging her to open wider.

"Lay back," he whispered.

She frowned, her sisters or mother might hear them.

Swallowing, she allowed him to push her down on the bed. Once she was resting on her elbows, he tugged her hips to the edge and started pressing kisses to the inside of one knee. He met her eyes as his mouth trailed higher and higher.

"Oh, Clark," She felt her cheeks flame red. "Are you sure? Mother and Sisters...?"

"I'm very sure. I mean I think I'm in the clear. I hope I am." He smiled and placed another kiss an inch above her knee. "Can you hold your screams?"

She let her head fall back, cupping her hands over her face. "Yes," she mumbled. "Um, I guess...yes."

"Tell me, Princess, being that this is your bedroom...did you ever think of this happening?"

She dropped her hands and tilted her head to gape at him as his lips moved closer to her core. "What?"

"Diana, Princess of Themyscira," he murmured against her skin. "You told me growing up, you read books about love. The entanglements of lovers."

He wrapped his arms under her thighs, curving his hands over her knees and staring up at her face.

"Oh." She cleared her throat. "Well, yes."

He dipped his head to kiss her hipbone, and the muscles in her stomach jumped.

"So did you dream of this?"

She blinked at him as he watched her, letting his tongue swipe across the skin he just kissed.

"Yes! I mean...not exactly this. Of course, it's different. But this is...you are so much better! Oh!"

He pressed his lips directly on her core. Her legs instinctively tried to close, but he held her open. She grabbed the sheets tightly, taking a shuddering breath. She squeaked as his tongue slid into her folds, gliding through her most private of places and dragging up to her clit. A moan escaped her, and her back arched off the bed.

His breath was hot on her cunt and he spilled a drop of saliva on her core without breaking his eye contact with her. He flicked his tongue over her clit, swirling and licking as she keened.

Diana was squirming when he continuously lapped at her, slurping up all the drops that drizzled from her lips, reveling in the sweetness of her taste.

Her thighs fought against his hands and she reached above her head and held onto the sheets, screwing her eyes shut "Clark!" She yelped as his

THE DARK SPELL

tongue flattened against her sex, moving towards her entrance. "Don't stop, Darling."

He moaned as he dipped inside, and she whimpered when he did it again, and again. She was pulsing against his mouth and he stiffened his tongue feeling her heat clamp around it. Her hips began rocking against his mouth, and her fingers raked down her face, reaching down to cup her breasts.

"Just like that, Diana." He licked up to her clit. "Touch yourself..." Not letting her get away as he continued to lavish her with swirls and licks, backing off just enough every time she got too close to the edge.

Her lips parted as he kissed and sucked at her. And then his finger pressed against her entrance, and her toes curled as he slid inside. His lips never left her clit, sending her scrabbling at her chest.

He pulled away momentarily, "You taste better than the fruits from the feast!" he said licking his lips.

His tongue found her core again, and she jerked up on her elbows when he circled her clit. His finger began pumping into her, slow and steady.

Diana rolled her eyes back, and she strained upright to bury her fingers in his hair. He moaned into her cunt before she collapsed.

His lips locked around her clit and sucked as he added a second finger inside of her.

She shattered with a scream, clamping down around his fingers and holding his face to her core as her hips rutted against his mouth. She felt like she'd never stop coming, her orgasm tearing its way out of her as Clark refused to relent on her clit. His fingers curled inside of her, and she jerked up, holding on for dear life as he rubbed at her.

"Clark..." she tugged his hair tightly until his lips released her.

His eyes were dark and on fire, and she whined as he slowly withdrew his fingers.

"I am sure they heard us," He laughed and kissed her thigh before rising from his knees.

"You seem very relaxed about it?"

"I'm trying to be. But if your mother comes in hear with something sharp in her hand, I'm flying out from the balcony."

Diana laughed and shifted to face him, "Honestly, it's fine Kal. I don't mind, really of them hearing." She kissed his lips, wrapping her hands around his waist. Her nipples tightened against his chest, and her belly swooped at the feel of him stiff and warm on her stomach. "I've heard things before so it's nothing."

"But you're their Princess."

She smiled into his chest and reached the end of his chiton, sliding her other hand down to cup him through loincloth. He blew out a sharp exhale, dropping his head on her shoulder and moving his hands to her hips.

She quickly lifted his chiton, untied and dragged down his loincloth. The sight of him sent a rush of heat through her core as she began stroking him pressing her forehead against his chest.

"Well...You're here with me after all. It should be expected. Now it's your turn, Kal-El."

Clark reached his hand down and drew his chiton off in one fast action. He stood there bare in front of her and Diana's eye roamed all over his naked self before she reached down to grab him again in her hands. She peeled him open and his erection jumped again, and a drop of pearly liquid escaped from his purple head, rolling into her fingers.

He groaned and mumbled something into her hair. With the hand still stroking him, she staggered backward on the bed on all four and swept her hair off to one shoulder, and leaned forward to feather kisses down his happy trail to the patch of dark curly hair right above his pubic bone.

He was rock hard and standing at full attention, jumping slightly in anticipation of her mouth. She continued to massage him lightly in a teasing manner dropping kisses on his pubic bone.

Clark looked at her in awe and she raised an eyebrow at him as she licked her lips.

Diana reached out to wrap her other hand to play with the head of his member, running her thumb over the bead of moisture that appeared there around his length before humming in appreciation. She squeezed his shaft tightly in her fists. He closed his eyes and groaned in satisfaction, getting lost in the moment of being enveloped completely by her. Before he could respond, she leaned forward and kissed the seam, her hot breath blowing

THE DARK SPELL

over him. Clark stood there no longer able to form coherent sentences. Diana circled his tip with her wet tongue, then kissed her way down his shaft, her mouth and hands moving in tandem. He fisted his hands into her silky hair, needing something to grip onto as he grits his teeth and watched her.

She poked her tongue out and licked the underside of his member, flattening it out to give him slow, wide strokes that had him crossing his eyes in delight. She continued with slicking up and down the length, those seductive eyes smoldering with want for him.

Her free hand moved down and cupped his balls. She fondled them gently with her palms before tasting her way down and sneaking one into her mouth. She hummed as she licked the sensitive skin, her mouth creating a buzzing vibration.

He bit down on his lip hard, suppressing the groan that wanted to break free as she worked him over. Clark wondered how it was she was always able to continually bring him the most pleasure he'd ever experienced.

He watched intently as she worked the other one into her mouth and continued to lick at them for a few seconds before moving back up. She gave him a mischievous smile.

"Don't hold back," she whispered and he could only nod his head.

She opened her mouth wide and closed them around his thickness, swallowing as much of the length down as she could fit. He hissed out a breath and rolled his head back, his hips automatically pumping up to greet her mouth as he tried not to explode at the sensations she was creating inside of him.

"Just like that," he panted in encouragement as his hips moved in rhythm with her. He wanted to prolong the moment, but her mouth was too hot and too wet and the slurping noises she made had him clenching his teeth tightly together.

Her eager mouth was tugging on his skin hungrily as she sucked him down her throat. He opened his eyes and saw her ass waved in the air seductively and he can see her dripping core in the reflection of the mirror in front of him as she bobbed her head in and out.

"Diana," he grunted out. "This is so good," massaging her scalp. He knew he was close now. He could feel his whole body tingling, the tremors rumbling like waves. His heart was palpitating and his breaths started coming out in panting quivers.

Clark moved his hands up into her hair, pushing them that had fallen around her face back and fisting them in a ponytail with one hand. He wanted to look at her beautiful face as she took him over the edge.

The visual she made with him inside her mouth was another one he wanted to be seared into his memory.

She was really bobbing now, her swollen lips wrapped tightly around him and he could feel his member pulsating. It was flushed red, the veins popping and he watched as it disappeared again and again into her mouth with every pass she made. Hallowing her cheeks, she swallowed him down even further. He hit the back of her throat and before he knew it, his climax detonated like a bomb, a fury of an explosion that rocked his whole body and he shoved the crook of his elbow against his mouth as he let out a torturous groan.

Clark could feel the fluctuations of his seed spilling forth and her mouth devouring it all with every pull. She continued to suck him and he rode it until he absolutely could not take another second and finally pushed back from her.

Diana released him with a pop as she sat back on her knees, panting heavily. She reached up, primly wiped her smirking lips with her fingers.

Diana stood up and Clark wrapped his arms around her yanking her closer. She giggled and wrapped her arms around his neck. Clark's hands trailed down to her ass groping and lifting her. Diana immediately wrapped her legs around his waist. Clark then kneeled on the bed, moving up the middle and layer Diana on her back still on top of her.

He kissed her softly then trailed her neck, down her chest, and licked between the valley of her breasts.

"Mmmhhm...Beloved, you are so good to me," she moaned.

Clark laid his head against her breasts, soft like pillows.

"I love you, Di."

"I love you, too."

Clark and Diana fell asleep in each other's embrace tired.

THE DARK SPELL

3 more hours had passed...

Clark awoke to Diana with her back facing him snuggled against his chest. He craned his neck to kiss the back of her neck. In response, she let out a soft moan.

He grinned knowing she could feel his hardness against her soft ass.

Without any hesitation, he slowly burrowed his arousal between her plump asscheeks.

"Mmh...Kal..." Diana whispered sleepily.

She reached back and grabbed his hip and started rubbing her plush bottom on his throbbing length harshly. His leaking tip left a smear of wetness on the naked swell of her ass. Clark sucked in a sharp breath from the sudden stimulation and she smirked.

He nipped her neck punishingly.

"Raise your leg," he ordered with a growl and her right knee goes up obediently.

Clark gripped her inner thigh and adjusted his hips before pushing. His bulbous tip wedged between her slippery lips, pressing the tip to her opening.

"Oh Gods," she uttered breathily.

Her heart pounded with excitement.

"Now we can't be too..." she gasped. "Gods!"

"Hn..."

Diana's loud cry of pleasure is muffled by his heavy hand over her mouth.

"Shhh," he hushed her. "You were just about to say we can't be too loud now," he teased.

"Why must you tease me in such predicaments?" She asked through the pleasurable haze.

"Because you are just so damn sexy with how you react in such predicaments. So now try to stay as quiet as possible."

Clark plowed into her without mercy. His furious thrusts into her jostle her whole body.

Soon, the force of his thrusts turned Diana almost completely on her stomach.

"Shhh..." Clark grunted like a beast in heat as he pistons, in and out, in and out. His hips made wet smacking noises when they hit her soft ass.

Diana bit her lip trying not to cry out.

"Clark!" She gasped gripping her pillow.

"Di," he rasped, switching from long strokes to deep jabs and grinding.

His hand wandered up and cupped her breast, rubbing the underside.

"Darling, I can't..." Diana whined, grabbing at his hand to stop him. "You tease..."

Clark chuckled and kissed her neck. "Right."

He rolled her nipple between his fingers making her moan.

When they were both ready to climax, Diana reached back and grasped his thigh as she raised her leg up just a little bit more. Clark pushed in deeper and that was all they both needed. Clark enjoyed how the velvet heat of her inner walls convulsed wetly on his throbbing hardness only for a moment before his own release hits. He leaned over her, resting his head between her shoulder blades, and groaning loudly with his release.

Diana smiled and cuddled back into Clark. He locked his arms around her.

For a while, they lay there in their post-orgasmic haze, the only sound in the room was their panting before Clark pulled out of Diana and rolled her over so she was facing him. He smiled at her boring into her beautiful eyes. Diana leaned up and kissed him softly.

Early the next morning...

"Wow, Di! This really is amazing! It's better than the Fortress!"

Clark looked around in awe at everything Diana had in her private science lab.

"I told you Themysciran technology is on par with Kryptonian technology. I want to share all of this, Clark. What if we combine it all to be something world-changing in the best of ways."

"I know what you mean, Di. I wish we could but some of the Kryptonian tech is just way too dangerous. We don't need any of this getting into the wrong hands."

"I know," Diana sighed looking down.

"Hey..." he cupped her chin making her look up at him. "We'll just take it to step by step, ok? There's so much we can and will do together."

THE DARK SPELL

"Having our own experiments?" Diana grinned.

Clark chuckled. "Lots and lots of experiments."

"Are we still talking about scientific experiments?"

"Yeah....yeah we can definitely go with that," he kissed the tip of her nose.

After a while, Diana and Clark took a stroll to the stables.

"I used to wake up at Dawn and come here before Mother. I would ride out to the cliff to watch the sunrise." Diana beamed. "I love riding horses!"

Clark grinned cheekily. "Oh yeah, I know first hand how you like to ride."

Diana gasped. "Clark!"

Clark groped her ass making her squeal and giggle. He pulled her into a kiss. Diana moaned in his mouth, wrapping her arms around his neck.

"You are so enticing. As much as I want to go back to the temple, I have more to show and tell you."

"I know. I know. I just can't help myself. It's like your glowing even more than usual being here at home."

Diana smiled blushing. "You know the feeling of being home with your parents, that's how I feel with my mother and sisters. I had so many adventures of my own growing up!"

"Yeah, this does remind me of the farm. You know, it is something special that you and I grew up pretty much learning the value of nature's beauty. Having those adventures in the forest or woods. Becoming friendly with the animals."

"That's part of what I love about us. We have so much in common yet different in aspects, little details. Compliments so well."

Clark smiled. "Fitting like a puzzle," he said as he captured her lips again.

Diana and Clark left the stables walking along to the forest and cliffs.

"I used to run through here being chased by my sisters. I hid for hours while they were looking for me. Only Dessa and Umara knew where to find me. I wanted to just explore so many things on my own without hovering over my shoulder."

Clark was amazed as they continued walking through the forest.

"It's really beautiful, Diana."

"I love when we fly. But it's still something to be this close to all the unique plants and animals. This is another part of what made me long to leave to have my own journey. I knew there was more unique life to learn about." She smiled. "Like you..."

Clark chuckled. "Me? Nah. I'm-"

"A man from beyond the stars who uses his gifts for the greater good. Not a mortal yet not a god. Though both in your own right within your heart."

"Di..." he pondered for a moment. "Well, when you put it that way..."

Diana smirked. "My man is no ordinary man and I love you." She started levitating up pulling his arm. "A swim, Beloved?"

"Yeah, okay!"

Diana and Clark flew down to the shore.

"Oh wait, Di. We don't have a change of clothes?"

She looked at him over her shoulder and grinned. She reached back untying her dress.

She let her dress fall to her feet.

"Clothes off, Clark!" she said with a laugh before she started running out to the water.

"Hey! Wait, Di!" he shouted and laughed along with her, quickly taking off his close and ran after her.

Clark was in the sea and by her side in seconds. He felt perfectly happy as he heard her giggles disappear under a wave. He watched and waited for her to appear again and once she did she swam over to him and trod in the water, her hair wet and rivulets of salt waterer running down her face and dropping off her chin onto her breasts popping out. Clark let his eyes follow it down her body in crystal clear water, across her flat stomach, and to her center. Clark had an urge to follow that path with his tongue; maybe making a few detours on the way. He'll definitely get to that later. His eyes roamed up her body again. His hunger, passion, and want could be read in them clearly. As his gaze reached her breasts he sucked in a breath, his fingers itched to reach out, to touch them and his tongue flickered across his lips wanting to taste them. The hunger started to consume him.

He raised his gaze to her neck, her perfect smooth neck, he wanted to kiss it, lick it, bite her just a little. His whole body throbbed with need and

THE DARK SPELL

all that need was for the woman in front of him. Clark's eyes finally reached Diana's and her eyes widened as soon as she saw the look in his.

Diana pushed him away playfully and swam ahead at her orderly speed. Clark followed her. Thunder started to crack and Diana paused to observe the dark sky.

There were dark and puffy clouds overhead, and they would not shift because there is no trace of the storm. However, more clouds began to form and waiting to rain.

Diana hovered in the water watching Clark reaching behind and his gaze wanders down her body. She could feel the heat radiating off him and a throb started between her legs. She wanted to slide her hand down and ease it and she wanted to do it in front of him in the pristine clear water. She wanted him to watch her as she pleased herself and see him lose control, her nipples hardened at the thought of Clark grabbing her and taking her hard and passionate. Diana wanted to feel him pulsing inside of her. She watched his gaze as it focused the top of her breast bobbing on the water, his jaw going loose as he took her in then up to her neck, she had to force herself not to move, not to bear any more of it.

She had to bite her tongue to stop herself from screaming 'take me' the way her body screamed for him. Her body wanted his touch. All of a sudden he looked into her eyes and her own widened in surprise because the power, the want, and the need in them were all for her. She was amazed and her need matched his. They stared at each other neither one moving; everything around them disappeared and it was just the two of them.

And it started to drizzle.

"It's raining. Should we go?" Clark questioned looking up.

"Unexpected I know but this time of year it does. It's okay, though. It's more fun for us."

Diana smiled in the rain as she saw the waves coming towards them. She dived back and swam a little bit then as one hit her, Diana smiled to herself as she watched Clark dive into the water again, then coming back up a moment later, running his fingers through his jet black hair. Clark's hair always looked too damned good when it was wet and she had every intention to make sure he was dunked beneath the waves a few times.

They halted swimming and enjoyed the new rain as it came down heavily.

She held her breath and turned around facing the sky to float like a log in the rain. Clark shortly catching her, notices her meditative stance. Clark copied her action but in the opposite way.

Clark and Diana floated like yin and yang in the rain. The rain kept pouring hard on them and they both anchored facing each other.

Diana turned away and glanced over her shoulder at him, scooping up a handful of water and throwing it back at him. Clark started laughing, dodging the water narrowly.

"No! Clark! No, don't!" She laughed as he picked her up. She squealed and grabbed his wrist refusing to let go. "Don't you dare!" She begged him trying not to laugh. She blinked at him knowing when he had that grin on his face he was up to something.

"You look good with your hair like that."

Clark shook his head, shaking the water from his hair. "Oh, you like the wet look?"

Diana rolled her eyes playfully at his smug expression, "Don't get cocky, Mr. Kent." She reached up and brushed a wet lock of hair off of his forehead, biting down on her bottom lip as she looked up at him. "But I can't deny how sexy of a man you are."

"You, Diana, look very sexy all wet."

The pounding of her blood rang in his ears, the smell of her arousal overtook his senses so he pulled her to him and kissed her hard. The rain running down their faces added to an amazing sensation. Their mouths seemed to be punishing each other. This hunger had to be satisfied and there was no stopping them. They were going to touch and taste every inch of the other.

Clark flashed a devilish grin and Diana narrowed her eyes knowing exactly what he was going to do.

"Clar-"

He dipped her sideways into the water, going in with her when her leg caught the back of his knee and he toppled.

Water splashed and limbs flailed as they fought beneath the waves to get out of the water first. Diana came up clinging to his back, arms curled

THE DARK SPELL

around his chest and legs curled around his hips. She laughed and panted as she tried to catch her breath, her chin resting on his shoulder and her hair clinging to her shoulders and his neck.

Clark reached his arm around behind her, his fingers playing over her bareback. "You are on the wrong side of me."

"I'm comfortable here," Diana retorted, clinging to him a little tighter when she felt his weight starting to shift backward. "For goodness sake!" She gasped out as he dropped her backward into the ocean, causing her to lose grip of him.

Clark surfaced again, his hand scrubbing over his face, wiping the water away. "Diana?" He questioned as he looked around in the softly rolling waves and didn't see her anywhere. "Di?" He could hear her heartbeat.

And then he gasped when her hand made contact to his manhood. She came up out of the water in front of him with a grin on her face. Her free hand brushed her wet hair off of her face, while her other hand palmed him.

"Are you going to play nicely now, Clark?" she asked sliding her fingers up to the head and slid his foreskin up and down the glans before gently dragging it back.

Clark narrowed his eyes, inhaling sharply, "no..."

Diana smirked, fluttering her lashes, her fingers wrapping around him, and slowly started to stroke him.

Clark's gaze fell to her lips and within a second his lips were pressed against hers. His fingers curled around her waist, the tips of his fingers rubbing tiny patterns against her skin as he pulled her closer. His left hand cupped her womanhood, caressing her slick lower lips.

Diana moaned in his mouth, fingers gripped a fistful of his jet black, wet, hair – tugging sharply on it and continued stroking him as she kissed him back. This was what she wanted - the fight of their lips to gain dominance in the kiss, the taste of saltwater clinging to his lips as he kissed her hard enough to leave her lips bruised tomorrow.

Releasing their lips the two of them laid their foreheads against one another with their eyes closed as she worked her hand over his length, causing low, growling groans to rise up from deep within his chest.

He slipped two fingers inside of her quite suddenly and began to slowly and softly push them in and out gently. She clenched, already feeling the wetness pool between her legs. mutually, the two of them moved in sync. He stiffened in her stoke like steel and she flowed like a river in his fingers with wetness.

"Clark," she breathed, eyes fluttering closed, her walls tightening against him.

Cold rain ran down their bodies. "This feels amazing..." he whispered, his voice going hoarse from the incredible movement that she was making with her hand.

"Look at me, Diana." She opened her eyes and gazed up at him to see pure pleasure pulsed through him. Touching each other intimately for a long moment, Clark and Diana trembled together. The friction they were creating for each other adds soothing contrast to the cold rain pouring down at them. The rain had ignited their passion more.

Clark reached and grabbed her bottom hauling her up to his body. All the while their mouths never left each other. Diana wrapped her long, lean legs around his waist and he moved closer to the shore. He lowered her to the ground. Diana laid down, letting her body be caressed by the clear rain and Clark sat back on his heels as his eyes raked down her body he knew there was no stopping now. He couldn't, he didn't want to.

Crashing waves blanketed them with a regular rhythm; soft white sand everywhere washed off from their bodies as the rain pouring down.

He slowly climbed over her and covered her soft body with his own, kissing her face, soft, gentle kisses. His mouth went back to hers and their tongues dueled with each other, her hands coming up and wrapping around his neck as kissed his way across to her ear where he nibbled, sucked, and blew on it. Diana's whole body shuddered the need and want to course through her.

"More, Clark... Please." Her voice begged softly, and a masculine chuckle was made in her ear. "Oh gods," she muttered and raised her body against his.

Clark kissed down to her neck, he licked and sucked at her there pulling the skin into her mouth and sucking hard. He saw the redness of the skin and grinned, He carried on down until he reached her breasts where he

THE DARK SPELL

took one into his mouth, rolling his tongue around it and sucking until the nub became hard. Clark's remaining hand took the other breast and rolled it between his thumb and finger.

He reached between her legs again and running a finger through her slit. She was already wet and swollen for him, and he went even harder as he viewed her, making her thighs shake with anticipation.

Diana groaned arching up trying to get more, the feeling of his mouth her body calling out for him, for the connection, to finally be one with him.

With his hard body laying over her soft supple one again, Diana wrapped her legs around his waist, and with one strong push he was inside of her and they both groaned in unison, loving the feeling of being whole and complete. Clark pulled out so just the tip of him was still inside of her and then with a firm push he was deep inside, he did it again and again but so slowly that Diana dug her heels into his bottom wanting more, wanting harder, faster and deeper. She couldn't form the words. Clark's pace picked up he couldn't hold back anymore and he pounded into her. It was a struggle to hold back, he was moving so fast and hard she felt him all the way through her being and her body screamed for his touch.

Clark seemed to be in control enough to lean back up to her and kiss her. He pushed his tongue into her mouth, exploring every inch. He moved his hips so fast and she moaned into his mouth before her hands were on his shoulders, fingernails clinging to his skin. He ran his hands down her soft sides until he reached her hips. Diana groaned again when he tightened his hold there so that she stayed in place as his hips flexed, sinking further and further deep inside of her.

Love and rain came in full force.

"Oh gods, yes!" she screamed.

Clark couldn't stop. He broke their kiss thrusting harder and faster continuously pumping his hips roughly into hers.

Diana arched her body, her head fell back leaving her neck exposed, Clark leaned for he felt his body tightening, he could feel her muscles clench around his shaft, he opened his mouth wide and bit into her neck.

His teeth marked her skin red. A sweet smile spread on his lips when he saw the mark of his love imprinted on her skin like love notes written in the flesh.

He palmed her breasts and squeezed lightly, she groaned into him and rocked her hips upwards. She was matching his thrust for thrust.

Clark teased her nipple with his teeth before sucking it deep in his mouth and swirling the tight bud with his tongue. She let out a cry and raised a hand to the back of his head, threading her fingers through his wet hair.

"Clark!" she screamed in pleasure, he released her nipple with a pop and looked up at her. The sea and poring water made their bodies wet and slimy. He used his hands to pin her down above her head and flexed his hips at a new angle, hitting her clit with every thrust, and Diana back arched off the shore.

The rain drowned out her moans of pleasure and he grounded his pelvis into her, rubbing against her clit harder, the pressure building higher and higher. He picked up speed, doubled his efforts.

with a few more harsh thrusts, suddenly he growled and leaned back on his heels. His posture gave her a chance to stare at his naked self breathing and panting, her eyes dropped to his thick and still hardness.

Clark flipped her over on the sand onto her stomach. His hands caressed her smooth and curved rear.

He squeezed her buns hard in his palms with rainwater dripping all over her curve and washing away the sand.

His hands reached beneath her hips and pulled up her body until she was on her knees with her ass in the air. Clark ran a finger through her folds and she arched into his touch with a moan, the roughness of his fingers causing a wonderful sensation along her slit. She was rewarded with a slap on her left cheek. The slight stinging pain sent more wetness between her thighs. Clark ran his fingers up her folds and circled her clit repeatedly.

She needed more of him, she moved her body to try to catch his fingers on her clit. He slapped her other cheek. "You like that, my beautiful Goddess?" he asked her with a small chuckle.

"Yes," she replied. without wasting a second, he thrust into her again with one swift motion. She dug the sand in her hands at the intrusion. In this position, the fullness was almost too much to handle. Then he started to move again.

"Oh, love..."

THE DARK SPELL

His hands were now on her hips, guiding her forward and back against him, his rhythm picking up the pace until his sacks were slapping against her clit with each thrust. He was in complete control of their rhythm and the movement of her hips, but she loved the feel of his legs against her thighs, as he pulled and pushed her hips against his.

"Oh, Rao... so good..." he murmured between thrusts as he picked up the primal pace. They made love in the pouring rain like how rain is mixing with the ocean; never ceasing.

Clark slapped her right cheek and she moaned, digging the sand tighter in her fists. She was so close. "Keep going-" she panted. "I'm so close beloved, please-"

He picked up his rhythm, they were like a fire burning in the rain. She felt him pushing roughly inside of her and he hit that sweet spot that she needed, making her scream out in pleasure as her head went back and he fisted her hair for grip.

They both screamed as their orgasms ripped through their bodies.

He had no idea how much time they spent like this, just holding her tight as they came down from their highs and caught their breaths lost in the waves of extreme bliss washing over him.

The rain ceased as they emptied into each other. Clark turned her back to face and they whispered into each other's ears, gently placing soft kisses on the other's face. They finally stared into each other's eyes. A smile lit Diana's face and he soon followed.

His hands moved expertly to the full, supple roundness of her breasts, massaging them gently and rubbing her nipples between his thumb and forefinger.

She rolled him around and moved her legs on either side to straddle him and right away she could feel him at her core, pressing at the wet opening.

His hand reached between them, then slid the head back and forth and she could hear the wetness as he coated himself. Her thighs here trembling and she could feel herself pulsing wildly every time he brushed up against her sensitive spot.

She positioned herself, then moved her hand to rub his chest, he kept his eyes fixed to where they were pressed lightly together. She slowly lowered herself down his shaft, felt him splitting her open again as she slid him deeper inside.

She started to ride him at a slow and steady pace and he lay his hands on her hips, sort of guiding them. As she rode him faster and harder, he tightened his grip on her hips and she moaned louder every time she trusted down onto him. Thrusting down on him harder and harder she felt herself reaching her climax and moaned his name and he did the same.

It felt so good. The waves from the ocean and the bodies meeting on the shore. The grip that he had on her and the force that she rode him with.

As her hips pounded against his, her walls starting to clench around him as the head of his member hit that spot deep inside of her that begged to be touched. "That's it, love, right there..."

Clark snuck a hand between them and his fingers found her clit as she rode him, running the pad of his thumb in small circles around it.

"Keep doing that, Beloved..." She panted, feeling like she was on the edge of something. "Yes..." Her eyes closed and her head fell back.

A few more thrusts and she felt him spill his hot seed inside of her, making her moan even louder as she came too.

They both collapsed and Diana laid on top of Clark as the small waves continued rolling in on top of them. She cupped his face kissing him passionately

"Ahem....Princess....?"

Diana looked up surprised.

"Baila?!"

Baila frowned slightly. "The Queen would like a word."

"Oh, alright. Clark and I wi-"

"...Alone."

"Oh...well I need a moment to get clothed, Baila," Diana raised her brow.

Baila scuffed and rolled her eyes turning around and started to walk away. "The Queen is in the Palace."

"Thank you." Diana got up from Clark and picked up her dress. "You should get dressed, too, Clark."

Clark watched as Diana was putting back on her dress.

He chuckled. "It's still a few of your sisters that still really don't like me."

THE DARK SPELL

"Don't worry, Love. They'll come around eventually."

"Really hope so. Especially because I want to mar-....." he quickly paused catching his words. "Uh...here I'll tie that for you."

Diana smiled and turned her back towards him as he reached to tie her dress.

"What were you going to say you wanted to do?"

"Oh...uh...I wanted to...I just want your mother and sisters to know that I'm going to take care of their Princess."

Diana turned around wrapping her arms around his neck and kissed him.

"I believe more than anything, they see I'm well taken care of and very happy." She gave him another peck. "I'll be back soon. Just relax. You can go back to my room if you want?"

"I'll stay here for a while. Watch the waves...think about you."

"When I get back we can take a tour around the culture complex and the coliseum."

One more peck before Diana flew off to the Palace.

Location: Royal Palace

Diana flew down being greeted by two guards, Yasha and Imani.

"Good evening, Diana," they said in unison and bowed.

"Yasha, Imani, good evening."

They opened the large doors.

When Diana walked in, she suddenly became nervous. What would Hippolyta want to speak to her alone about?

"Mother?"

"Diana." Hippolyta raised her brow immediately noticing a mark on Diana's neck. "I see you and Kal-El are enjoying yourselves."

Diana gasped and quickly placed her hand on her neck. She bit her lip trying to hold in her laugh and blushed.

"What is it you wanted to speak to me about, Mother?"

"Will you be baring Kal-El's children?" She asked bluntly.

Diana's heart skipped a beat and she felt butterflies.

"I..." Diana sighed. "I don't think that will be any time soon. We have responsibilities and bringing a child into this world right now isn't ideal. Right now, Kal and I are just enjoying each other."

"Do you want to?"

"I...do, Mother. I love him. I'm in love with him. There's no other man like him. He's my best friend and I trust him."

"I can see it in your eyes and the way you look at him."

"He has shown you how worthy he is time and time again."

"Yes, he has. It is still quite surprising actually."

"What is?"

"A man that wields such power is a man of humbling honor and respect."

Diana smiled. "His adoptive parents are incredibly sweet. I would like to bring them here. And his biological parents were warriors and scientists." Diana beamed. "His world is just as fascinating as ours."

Hippolyta caressed Diana's cheek. "You aren't that child I tried to protect from the outside world anymore. As much as it pained me, you made your decision to leave home in search of another life and your true purpose. You've met a man that has your heart and you have his. Though, I will not hesitate to behead him if he disappoints."

"Mother, no!" Diana laughed. "Kal is well aware of your no hesitation with sharp objects."

"Good. As he should be." Hippolyta smirked.

Clark sighed happily as he walked along the shore.

"Ah...so more cliche dabbling meeting the extended in-laws."

Clark quickly turned around with a frown. "Valeria?! The hell are you doing here?"

"I couldn't resist as you already know. I had to check up with my Lovers."

"Diana and I are not your lovers."

"Oh, don't be selfish, Kal-El. You and Diana have an abundance of love that can be shared more than a million times over."

"It's between us."

"Hm...sure. So tell me...How do you feel as a man about being second?"

"Second? What do you mean second?"

"Steven Trevor is the first man Diana had met and been here on this island."

"So what?"

THE DARK SPELL

"The first man Diana had ever laid eyes upon. The first man accepted on this island. It was fate that had Diana see him first. He still has quite the infatuation with her, you know? Why is that? Has Diana given him hope?"

"What are you trying to do?"

"You feel special, don't you? You said it yourself some of the Amazons still aren't accepting of you. Why is that?"

"The Amazons aren't accepting of most men for reasons. I respect that. But I vowed to show them all that they can trust me."

Valéria laughed. "You are not a man of earth. Not a god. You are nothing to them. A guard dog for their precious Princess, perhaps?"

"Stop it! You said you would no longer interfere."

"Kal-El, this is more of just showing the truth. Isn't that what you two are all about? What of the mortals you protect? What will they say of the union between these two brings they see as Gods? You want them to love you yet they will only fear you."

"I know our truth. We don't need anyone like you trying to cast doubt or whatever on what we have. There's no fear. Diana and I being together has nothing to do with our responsibilities. Leave us alone, Valéria. Diana and I are together now and no one else matters!"

"If ever another man catches Diana's eye?"

"Diana isn't like that. Other men can look at her all they want but Diana is with me. She has entrusted only me with her heart. Even still, as long as Diana is happy, that is what matters to me."

"Your devotion to Diana is quite admirable." Valéria looked off then smirked. "Though the temptation is always near."

"What?"

She disappeared without another word.

Clark shook his head and sighed.

"Dammit."

Clark walked a few more feet until he got to the larger rocks and leaned against one closing his eyes for a moment.

His eyes then suddenly shot open hearing breathing.

"Who's there? If that's yo-"

Clark paused as the Amazon stepped from behind the rock.

She was about the same height as Diana.

"Hello, Kal-El of Krypton. I am Maite."

Short chestnut color hair and green eyes.

"Oh, um...hi...Maite."

"Did you think I was the Princess?"

"Yes, I did. I'm waiting for her to get back."

"Well...how about I keep you company?" She smiled seductively and stepped closer.

Clark quirked his brow noticing she was staring him up and down. "No, I'm sure it won't take much longer. I should just get back to Diana's room."

"Hmm...I see why the Princess chose you as a mate. You are much more man than expected."

"Um...I don't think this is appro-"

Maite stepped even closer. "I'm sure the Princess won't mind. That's why she brought you here after all. Enjoy Paradise."

Clark frowned and stepped back. "I'm sorry, Maite, but I came here to spend time with Diana, getting to know how she grew up. I have no interest in anything other than that...or anyone else for that matter."

Maite smirked. "You dare deny an Amazon?"

"Yes." Clark backed farther away. "I think I should go."

As he was about to fly off, Maite grabbed his tunic, tearing his sleeve.

"Hey, there was no need for that!"

"Clark? Maite?!"

Maite gasped. "Princess Diana! Queen Hippolyta! Princess, you bring this horrible man here. He can not be trusted!"

"Wait a minute! What? You were coming on to me!"

"This man is like every other!" She looked at Diana. "Princess, you would put your sisters in danger for the personal selfish pleasure of a man?! A man with his own selfish tendencies?!"

"Enough, Maite!" Hippolyta yelled.

"My Queen?" Maite questioned.

"That's enough trouble from you, Maite. You've had your own little fun. You disrespect your Queen being untruthful?"

"He does not suppose to be here!"

"How dare you raise your voice?! You will be reprimanded."

THE DARK SPELL

"Please, your Highness...I don't mean to cause any trouble. I understand my presence makes things a bit uncomfortable. So reactions may be extra-"

"Kal-El, you are our honored guest and shall be treated as such. Maite, come with me back to the palace." Hippolyta ordered.

"Yes...my Queen."

Maite walked slowly behind Hippolyta with her head down.

Diana walked over to Clark and latched onto his arm.

Clark sighed. "Diana, I'm so sorry. I was just waiting for you. She came on to me talking about you."

"I know, Clark. Maite and I haven't seen eye to eye since I was 12. What else happened?"

"Before this.... Valeria showed up."

"She what?!"

"Yeah...I told her to leave us alone. She said before she wouldn't interfere."

"What did she say?"

"She...she brought up Steve. He was the first man here. Wanted to know if I would get jealous if you wanted to be with someone else. She also brought up the public reception of our relationship."

"Clark, you already know my feelings in regards to Steve and any other man. Steve was the first man on this island but that was only because of the plane crash. Fates answering my prayer for a way to man's world. I wasn't looking for any kind of romance. My priority was on my mission and my desire to explore the world. But then I met you. You are the one that had my heart right at that moment, Clark. You are the only man I trust to give all of myself to. I love you, Clark. You are mine." She pulled his arm. "Come on. I changed my mind about the tour. That can be tomorrow. There's something else I want to do."

"Where we are going, that's what the bag is for?" He questioned.

She smiled and nodded as they flew off.

Diana and Clark flew to one of the smaller islands.

"This is Bloomadour island. The name means the blooming of love. This is Aphrodite's temple. My Amazon sisters come here to pray to Aphrodite also for a...pleasured experience."

Walking into the temple, Diana held up a torch. "Will you?"

Clark smiled, using his heat vision to light the torch. Diana walked over to light the other torches that were spread around the temple. Clark looked around the now-lit temple.

It was an ancient bathhouse where small built tubs were put along the north and east side adjacent to the swimming pool of mineral-rich hot spring water. The pool had a decorative mosaic floor depicting an Amazon driver and chariot pulled by four horses, and a dolphin below.

At one corner, there was a large 5 inches tall and 25 inches wide glossy black pebble-like stone bed. Clark let his hand caress the stone bed and wondered how smooth it was for a stone. It was carved in edges smoothly and chiseled in a way to add comfort and it was warm and firm in the center but as soft as a feather bed. Must be some kind of a magic stone Clark thought to himself.

Diana opened her bag and pulled out towels and several bottles containing massage oil. She spread a very large towel over the stone bed and the other kept folded as a pillow.

"Clothes off now, Clark."

Clark quickly undressed his remaining cloth clinging to his frame.

Diana took a purple potion and walked to the spring. She dropped few droplets from the potion and the musk from the hot spring smelled like Aphrodite in the surrounding air.

Diana eyed his naked frame, his body reacting to the potion. Diana lit aromatic candles around the edge of the bed. She decorated the bed with flower petals all without breaking eye contact with him. Clark can feel his rush in his lower stomach.

Diana bit her lip and smirked, deciding to give him a little seductive show. She turned around and reached behind and untied her dress letting fall into a puddle at her feet. She bends over so he could see her soft ass and part her legs so he could see her dripping wet womanhood and her rosebud. she heard him give a soft little groan. His thoughts were submerged beneath a deluge of erotic images. Full pouting lips; eyes gleaming with lust; ripe, round voluptuous breasts with perky erect nipples; glistening pink lower lips—all calling out to him, hungry for him.

THE DARK SPELL

The bath was steaming up with the essence of Aphrodite released in the air.

She moved to the hot spring and stepped inside the pool slowly and seductively swaying her hips. And then he heard a small splash and realized that she had got into the water hiding her delicious body from his view. She came swimming into view with the water reaching her chin, she dipped in and out cleaning her completely.

Clark was frozen just standing there and feasted at the sight in front of him.

Diana in a hot stream washing her body sensually and calling him in the eyes to join her.

Clark climbed down the spring, "Oh! It is hot as lava, Diana." Clark started as he finally submerged himself and she walked over seductively to kiss him hard, her tongue tracing his lips and thrusting deep in his mouth.

Diana dragged the water from steam and washed his pectorals and dragged her hand on his abs and washed him thoroughly everywhere and completely.

Pausing the kiss, she gave him a smirk and continued to wash herself, dipping them back into the stream and wetting their hair.

The smell of Aphrodite was hitting his senses. He slid further into Diana, holding her firmly against him, she groaned, placing her mouth gently against his, savoring the taste of his warm, soft lips. He curled his hands around her back even tighter, pulling her closer to him.

He lifted her and climbed out of the bath dripping from steam. Diana took a towel and dried them both fast and step back. She loved the cocky grin that was on his face.

"Full body massage, Di?"

"Yes, Beloved, but I will be the one giving the massage."

"You sure?"

"Lay down on the stone, Love," she gestured.

Obediently, Clark laid down on the stone on his stomach with his head on the folded towel.

Suddenly, a warm weight settled on Clark's back as Diana climbed on top of him and straddled his back.

"Now, my Love just relax," Diana explained confidently.

Snapping the lid open, she poured the warm liquid onto his shoulders and he sighed as she rubbed it into his skin. Diana started expertly working Clark's neck and shoulder muscles, kneading them with her deft slender fingers. The fragrant aroma of the massage oil tickled his nostrils. Clark sighed happily, amazed at how good it felt. His body started to relax and unwind more. Diana also massaged his scalp, ears, and the sides of his face. He pushed his forehead into the towel to stretch the back of his neck and as she rubbed the tension from his neck and shoulders.

"The oil is called Aphrodite's tears. With its divinity, you will be able to feel the soothing of any tension."

Diana poured more oil onto his back and danced along his spine with her thumbs. She pushed her hands up either side of his spine and then across his shoulders, spreading a pleasant little buzz in her wake. Diana loved the way his skin glistened with the coating of oil. With long, gentle strokes, she pressed down with her palms and slid them out to Clark's sides, smoothing out the flesh beneath them. A nice feeling of warmth permeated through the muscles of his back.

"Damn, Diana. This feels incredible," he said in a low tone.

"I know, Beloved. You've never had a massage like this."

"Never had a massage at all."

"Really?!"

"The joys of having invulnerable skin. But I'm lucky enough now to have an incredibly talented sexy Goddess. To be able to feel your touch. To touch you. No holding back...yeah." He let out a satisfied groan.

Diana smiled and bent down low, sniffed the back of Clark's neck, and murmured contently. Clark felt the wetness of her sex where it rubbed against the small of his back.

"Well, Darling, you deserve a relaxing massage for all the things you do," Diana whispered in his ear.

Diana drizzled oil along his arms and massaged them slowly, working her way to his hands, where she rubbed each individual finger before concentrating on his palms. More oil was then poured along with the dip in his spine and she smoothed it into his skin, kneading his back and sides with more long, firm strokes. She shuffled down the table and began working on his feet; pushing her thumbs into his insteps using a circular

THE DARK SPELL

motion, before repeating this action over his heels and around his ankles. She used her knuckles along with his brawny calves and the backs of his thighs, releasing the tension from his muscles to leave him feeling lax and stress-free.

"Have I ever told you how much I love your buns of steel," she giggled.

Clark lifted his head slightly with a quirked brow. "Really, Di?"

She laughed softly. "The buns of steel and junior are my weaknesses."

The oil rolled down over his cheeks and she kneaded them soft. His manhood twitched with anticipation of what was to follow.

He suddenly felt Diana climb on his back again and spread her naked body flat on top of his. Her arms went around him, her thighs squeezed against his sides and she squashed her soft breasts against his back. Clark's mouth gaped open and he released a little sigh. The pleasant tingle of skin-to-skin contact was all around him. He felt a pleasant buzz wherever she came into contact with him, a luxurious tingle which left the rest of his skin hungering to experience the same pleasure.

Ripples of pleasure ran out across his skin from where her nipples pressed against his flesh. Her skin felt so good against him—warm and smooth like silk. Her heat and lust enfolded him. He soaked in it, drew it in through his skin in a form of osmosis. Diana murmured. She held him tighter. The flow of pleasure increased. Clark felt trailers of fire race through his blood vessels. He moaned as he felt the heat settle in his balls. They felt bloated, overripe, and the desire to plunge his member into a soft, snug cavern of Diana and relieve the pressure growing overwhelming and shouldering aside other thoughts.

She grabbed his arms with hers, stretching them forward, and started gyrating her body along with Clark's naked frame, giving him a full contact massage. Diana's womanhood was rubbing against his firm smooth buttocks.

Clark felt his member hardening more.

Diana swapped rubbing her legs between his: she would have her left leg between Clark's spread legs and then her right. Her aroused womanhood would alternately rub up and down the back of Clark's legs. She was so wet that she was sure she was leaving a trail on Clark's oily skin. She was holding onto Clark's shoulders as she slid up and down his back.

She changed her grip to his head as her breasts caressed the back of Clark's neck. She knew he was enjoying feeling her soft breasts sliding on his back. He let out a deep, hoarse moan as she wriggled bosoms around.

All too quickly, however, it was over and Diana slid from Clark's back. She sat next to him.

"Turn over, Love."

Without any hesitation, Clark turned and laid on his back, with his hands behind his head. Clark's fully erect member sprung up and was waving from side to side.

Diana smirked. "Hmm, Junior seems very very happy."

Diana turned the bottle over and spread around more of the oil on the front of Clark's glorious godly body. Diana poured it over his chest, his abdomen, over his length, and his legs. Clark gasped lowly when Oil hits him. He was loving the feeling of the warm oil running over his skin. Diana put down the bottle and massage the oil into him. She started with his chest, her hands moving in circles as she could feel his muscles twitching under her hands. She moved down to his abs and hears his intake of breath as she moves down lower but she skipped over his manhood at the moment and gave a good rub down to the top of his thighs, legs, and feet.

Diana loved the scent of the oil and how her hands can glide over his body. She moved back up and cupped his balls in her hand lightly squeezing them before she took his hard length in her hand and slick oil up and down it.

She looked down and loved the way his skin was so shiny and hard his manhood was jutted out from his body glistening.

Diana then climbed on top of his legs. She deliberately moved up his legs and allowed her womanhood to slide over his rock-hard member. His member poking between her legs. She carefully moved up and down so as not to let him penetrate her. Diana sat astride his thighs as he gazed lustfully up at her glistening body. Her whole front was covered with a light sheen of oil.

Her breathing had quickened as Clark reached up and caressed her breasts and she continued to stroke his length with her womanhood.

THE DARK SPELL

She grabbed his manhood, pulled it down, and inserted it between her outer nether lips, sliding them up and down along the full length of his member.

Clark groaned softly. He knew that a little more of this treatment would cause him to have an explosion. Diana must have sensed it too since she quickly ceased her sexy gyrations. Clark started to get up but she pushed his chest down, indicating that she was not finished yet.

Diana poured some more oil on Clark's torso and spread it around his chest and stomach, slowly caressing his well-defined 8-pack and his sculpted oblique muscles. Diana started sliding her body up and down his torso, with her breasts moving from his face to his stomach and down farther.

Her dripping sex leaving a trail of its wetness over his torso and Clark can smell her sweetness mixing with the intoxicating smell of the oil.

After a couple of minutes, Diana raised and moved to sit on his legs and grabbed his member with both her hands. She squeezed it between her palms and started slowly massaging his love muscle, moving her palms vertically upwards with slight rotating motions.

Clark was now breathing heavily, his chest steadily rising and falling. Diana's delicate persistent fingers continued to perform a complicated dance along the full length of Clark's member, playing it like a piano, feeling out all the veins and ridges on his throbbing love muscle.

"Darling," she said as she momentarily stopped her ministrations and looked Clark straight in the eye. She smiled with a mischievous gleam in her eye.

Diana liked the power she had over him.

She then leaned over and took the tip and ran it right under her right breast, Clark was watching her catching his breath with the barely-there sensation. And then Diana moved, achingly slow, leaving a trail of his pre-essence, until its right against her nipple. Then she rolled it over her nipple before gently pressing the tip to dip on her areola. His hips jerked against his breasts and she lets out a laugh.

She repeated the same manipulaion on her left breast until his head kissed the hard nipple there while their eyes still pierce into each other. When the head rubbed the underside of her breasts again he couldn't muffle his groan. His hips jerk up again instinctively, and she pulled her breasts back just a little. and runs it along her parted breasts.

They both were panting heavily and Diana squeezed her oily breasts completely around Clark's rigid member. He didn't need any further instruction, he started rocking his hips back and forth, sliding his hard length in her generous cleavage. She was moving them slowly up and down, gradually increasing the pressure. Clark's breathing got even harder.

"Di...Ah-a-a," Clark moaned softly.

Clark's mind was whirring with wonder and excitement. He had never imagined he would be in this moment with this gorgeous Goddess manipulating and stimulating him in such an erotic and sensual way.

His thoughts were interrupted by Diana leaning over his member, sticking out her wet tongue, and flicking its tip along the surface of Clark's glistening crown.

"Oh, good God!" Clark shouted as his pelvis jerked.

He looked down with heavy-lidded eyes. Diana could see Clark looking at his length sliding in and out of her cleavage. Diana leaned forward and took the head of his erect member into her mouth. Clark grunted loudly as Diana started suckling on his head, running her wet soft tongue all along the surface.

Releasing him from her nestle, She took him in hand and started running her tongue along the full length of his thick manhood. Clark was moaning and panting louder.

"Diana!" he groaned.

He lifted his head and looked at Diana as she was energetically sucked him. With the head of his manhood in her cute mouth, Diana looked at him confidently and smiled at him with a mischievous twinkle in her cerulean eyes. Clark grinned back and reached forward to caress Diana's long, loose raven curls.

She concentrated on his manhood again and in a quick decisive move deep-throated almost the entire length of him.

That was way too much for poor Clark. His chest arched, his body convulsed and he started shooting volleys and volleys of hot essence in Diana's mouth.

THE DARK SPELL

Clark finally stopped twitching and his eruption subsided. Diana lapped the rest of the seminal liquid from his member and her palm. She leaned forward and suckled the sensitive head of his member gently, swishing her tongue to clean off the remaining nectar. She then lifted her face and grinned at Clark again wiping her lips with back of her hand.

Clark sat up, leaned forward, and took Diana's smiling face in his hands, and kissed her tenderly, chewing on her soft luscious lips with his own. They both opened their mouths and felt the tips of each other's tongues, wiggling them lightly. The two lovers alternated suckling on each other's tongues and slowly exploring the insides of their lover's mouth. Clark savored the sweet delicate taste of Diana's velvety lingua, also tasting the remnants of himself in her mouth and on her lips.

"You didn't really think I was going to let you give me a massage without giving you one in return, did you?"

"I knew it was a matter of time..."

Feeling more assertive, Clark smirked and swung Diana's body on the table on her back, pushing her hands above her head. He then attacked her tender firm breasts, sucking on her nipples and lathering them with saliva. Diana giggled and squealed approvingly. After what seemed like an endless assault on her tender peaks, he released her nipple with a pop. Clark then started vigorously licking her entire curvaceous soft body, from the neck down, reveling in the delicious taste of her sun-kissed creamy skin, lapping on it like fresh honey, savoring the sweet raw taste slightly spiced with the oil.

Diana giggled, laughed, and thrashed her body, and grabbed Clark's head, caressing his ears. Clark laved her smooth flat stomach, feeling the lean muscles under the satin skin and marveling how strong her body felt. He bypassed her core and concentrated on bathing her strong limber legs with his tongue. He then sat on his knees and tongue-worshipped each of Diana's dainty delicate feet, licking the arches and the pads of her soles and suckling on each of her toes like on sweet candy.

As Clark was savoring Diana's tasty toes of her left foot, Diana moved her right foot up his body and started stroking his chest, pecs, and stomach with the soles of her feet, wiggling her fingers to provide extra massaging motion. Clark sat back enjoying the unusual sensation. Diana then moved her foot lower rubbing his length with her sole.

"Ah, kinky!" Clark exclaimed approvingly.

Diana laughed and proceeded to rub his manhood with her agile toes, stroking the length of his shaft.

"Wow," Clark thought to himself.

Clark sensed that he was getting hard again when Diana stopped her sexy footy ministrations.

"Turn around, Di."

Diana turned to lay on her stomach. Clark poured the oil all over her back and ass, his hands soon following the same path. His hands part her ass cheeks as he drips oil in her ass and she felt his thumb running over and over it in circles. She felt him lay down on her, his body sliding over and over hers. His length rubbing between her ass cheeks and the tip of it is entering her. It felt so erotic and so naughty.

"Oh, Gods, Kal-El..."

Diana ground up against him and Clark reached to tease her womanhood, feeling her slick with oil and drenched with her creamy juices.

He kissed a trail down her back to her ass, playfully biting her ass cheeks making her squeal. He took great care to pour a drops of oil on her puckered hole. Diana had never felt anything like it, she writhed in pleasure when his tongue snaked its way between her cheeks.

"Clark!"

Clark kept the momentum circling repeatedly her rosebuds. She could feel the tension building in her body. The massage clark is giving her had her moaning unlike any other she had experienced thus far with Clark.

Clark thrusted his tongue repeatedly following it with a motion carefully licking an ice cream cone to ensure not a drop spill. Diana screamed, her body going rigid and shuddering with the force of her orgasm. Clark continued until she was completely limp, and stopped panting.

"Needed to get a bite of my cake. Come here and let me get a taste." He gently kissed and nuzzled her cheeks, while rubbing her back as the quivering subsided.

THE DARK SPELL

"Oh...you know you are too greedy for just a taste," she raised her brow and smirked.

"You got me," he grinned boyishly. "Now come here."

As Clark laid on his back, Diana shifted her position until she was crouched above his face and facing his feet.

Clark got an extreme close-up view of the lips of her womanhood. They tugged at him with a primal urge and his manhood twitched as the image of slipping it between those cushioned lips entered his thoughts.

Diana bent down to caress his erection with her hand. Her labia twitched, gaping hungrily to reveal a glistening red tunnel. Clark shivered, massaging it gently.

Diana sat down, smothering his face in the soft luscious curvy flesh of her ass he just feasted. He felt the moist folds of her sex rub against his nose and mouth. Her warm juices dribbled onto and between his lips. Each drip set off firecrackers of sensation across his nerve-endings. Her fluids heightened the sensitivity of whatever skin they came into contact with. Clark's lips and tongue fizzed with pleasure. Diana laughed and wiggled her body on top of his face as Clark did what came naturally, and stabbed his tongue between her nether lips. She squealed as he dived in. He lapped at the entrance of her canal, drinking up her nectar, and probed with his stiffened tongue. Then he moved up to her clit, and gave it a long, slow, broad-tongued lap. She whimpered and her toes curled from his touch.

Clark tongued her feverishly, making her twitch and moan. Diana rode his face hard, smearing it with her wetness.

The scent was like a fine wine—the taste was smooth, warm, pleasant; something to crave. Tendrils of perfume twined up his nostrils and wrapped his mind up in soft cotton wool. He felt like he was floating up in the clouds.

The next time Diana raised her ass, Clark was eager to inhale more of her sweet smell. He felt it rush down through his body like a head of steam. The pressure built up beneath his manhood and it swelled up even harder throbbing with need.

"Mmm...yes," Diana purred.

She folded her body down on him until her breasts were resting on his midriff. Long, skillful fingers touched, prodded, and flicked his erection.

Clark's sigh of pleasure was cut off smothered in the descending folds of Diana's sex. A soft hand wrapped around the base of his manhood. Soft, full lips kissed the tip. Just a light peck for the first, second, and third touch. For the fourth, the lips remained there, pressed against the swollen head of his member. They slowly sucked, drawing the tip into her mouth.

Clark groaned into her smothering core. His body twitched.

Diana pursed her lips and blew on the tip of him. Her warm lips enclosed the head of him and gave another teasing suck. Her warm breath flowed over and teased the throbbing head with maddening swirls. Diana dipped her head forward and took another teasing suck, going deeper this time, letting the head rest on her moist, fleshy tongue. One hand pumped the base of his length while the fingers of the other fondled and toyed with his balls.

Clark writhed and squirmed beneath her, battered by waves of sensation crashing through his body. He was helpless as she used her fingers and mouth to play him like a virtuoso musician.

Clark buried his head between her thighs again and he knew exactly how to use his mouth on her, within moments she began to convulse atop him and wail in orgasm, she quickly raised up arching her back. Her breathing quickened.

Her cries grew louder, and higher in pitch. She writhed even more energetically. Every bit of it drove Clark to even more enthusiastic efforts. Soon enough, her every breath was a gasp, expelled in a cry of pleasure. Clark dug his fingers into their thighs, holding her down against his mouth, and kept licking.

"Oh, Gods, YES!"

Diana screamed, squealed, lurched, and reached back pulling his hair as the throes of her orgasm took complete control of her body. Clark reveled in how hard she was coming, and did his best to prolong it.

She remained atop him — gasping and wheezing for breath — for quite some time. Clark absently stroked her back, feeling her chest heave, until her breathing began to slow.

Eventually, she shivered, letting out a quavering moan and shifted positions, sliding off him, and flopped onto her back. Clark smiled as he listened to her moan and watched her caressing her breasts with one hand, and her glistening womanhood with the other. He was lost in the moment.

He loved to see her flushed face and chest, her hard nipples, the look of bliss on her face. He took the oil bottle and emptied it all along her body, and then he knelt between her legs laying down on top of her, and rubbed this sex against hers teasingly. He grabbed the sides of her face and kissed her deeply as he moved his body around on her, until they were both even more soaked in oil and incredibly slippery. She started matching his movements, and ran her legs up and down his thighs, his ass, his lower back, while she tried to grasp his slippery back and pull him even closer.

However, suddenly, Clark pulled back and sat up. He spread her legs wide and gripped her ankles in her hands.

He drew her knees up over her shoulders.

"Oh, Goodness, Clark."

He smirked as he kneeled between her legs and raised her compact bottom and buried his face in her stretched-out core, once again inhaling the intoxicating sexy smell. Clark then went to work on her in earnest. He explored with his hungry lips all the folds and crevices of her womanhood, lapping up her delicious juices.

Diana moaned, said something in Greek, and started caressing Clark's head, hair, ears, and cheeks with her hands. She was also gently rocking her curved back providing a light rolling back and forth motion to her body.

As Clark was feasting on Diana's delectable womanhood, he used his lips to suckle on Diana's clit, teasing it with his tongue and gently biting it from time to time, eliciting louder moans and squeals from her. He alternated attacks on her clit, stabbing his tongue deep into her opening, flicking the tip of his tongue up and down inside, and making quick tongue-fucking in and out motions. Clark saw she was starting to contract faster and he realized that she was closed to the edge. He stuck two fingers of his right hand deep into her, suckled hard on her push-button with his lips, and bit it hard with his front teeth.

"Aaah!" Diana screamed loudly in a pitched voice, and exploded in Clark's waiting mouth, flooding it with her love nectar.

Clark lapped up everything like a man dying of thirst.

"Yes, my Love! Oh, Gods, you're so good!"

As Diana slowly came down from her high and her breathing started to slow, they again switched positions. Clark laying on his back with his hands gripping her hips firmly. Diana now straddling his hips firmly, sitting upright.

She lowered her body and they both tensed as her weight press lightly against the swollen head of his length. Her labia, those thick fleshy lips, parted around him and he felt the wet folds of her inner sex against the head of his member. His hips twitched seceding from the rest of his body. They jerked and flexed of their own accord.

Clark reached forward and began caressing Diana's breasts and slender stomach with his powerful hands. Diana grabbed his palms with hers and locked her fingers with his. She raised and lowered her body, rhythmically impaling her flaming womanhood on his rigid shaft. Diana laughed, low and sultry. She had all the control. She rode his upward thrusts with languid ease. She kept the head of his length pressed against her moist folds, but didn't permit him to go any deeper. She wiggled on top of him, teasing him as she ran his sex along the dripping groove of her sex.

Diana's fiery cerulean blue eyes were locked on Clark's ocean blue ones. She started gyrating her pelvis forcefully, making them both moan loudly. Diana grabbed the fingers of Clark's tight hand and stuck them in her mouth, suckling hard.

"Oh, Rao, Diana!" he exclaimed, feeling his body overwhelmed with lust for this fierce Amazon Goddess.

She leaned backwards, bracing her hands on his thighs. She pressed her hips downwards. Clark watched her plump labia swell out and engulf him. He let out a soft groan as he felt the muscular walls of her core contract around the tip of his manhood. Diana closed her eyes. Her cheeks were tinged with red.

"Mmm," she purred.

Clark's head also fell back and another involuntary groan of pleasure escaped him. He felt her juices. Warm and wet, they bathed him and dribbled down his shaft. Just as with his tongue and lips from when she'd sat on his face, her juices magnified the sensitivity of his skin. The warm folds of her sex swept across his world, sucking him and coating his skin in more of her body's secretions.

THE DARK SPELL

Diana looked down and met his gaze. Her eyes gleamed and she smiled. She started to sink down farther on him, slowly taking him inside her, inch by exquisite inch, hugging the length of his shaft. Sinking as far down on him as she could, she convulsed. Her walls undulated up and down Clark's erection. Inside her, his manhood was deluged in thick, warm fluids that sank into his skin and sent his nerve endings wild with pleasure.

"Diana..."

Calm and perfectly poised, Diana moved her hips up and down. Her full breasts bobbed with her movements, but the rest of her body was still and composed. The stone rocked and swayed beneath them and Diana incorporated that into her undulations movements, timing each downward thrust to match the rising crest of each wave.

Clark just stared at her. Her face was beautiful and radiant.

All his thoughts were being crowded out. The only thing left was the sinuous motion of her hips as she smoothly engulfed his cock within her silken sheath again and again.

Diana came down hard, pushing Clark's erection all the way up inside her. He was pressed against that soft cushion and came away with a nice tingling sensation and desire to bury himself even deeper into her. Soft, hot, moist flesh ballooned around the fleshy head of him and engulfed him absorbing him almost in a tight muscular grip.

Diana gave a sharp intake of breath. She paused. She contracted hard around Clark's shaft, trapping him in a tight, fleshy vice. Her eyes widened.

"Oh...Clark...Clark...!" She gasped. "Clark!"

Diana's head dropped forwards. Her lovely supple lips pouted in a cute little 'o' as a short sigh of pleasure slipped from her mouth. Her cheeks blushed deep red. Her womanhood pulsed again and a whiplash of breath-taking pleasure thrummed through Clark. His spine arched backward, pressing his shoulders back against the stone.

Diana lifted her head up and gave a loud cry.

"Mmm," Diana murmured.

She relaxed again and sank back down on Clark, letting his trapped erection be drawn up deeper into the smothering flesh of her womanhood. The muscular walls undulated and sucked, sending another blast of ecstasy rushing through Clark's body.

Diana looked at him with eyes full of fiery passion. She sang words in Grecian tongue. They sounded like the sweetest, purest notes, with angelic harmonies.

The liquid interior of Diana's womanhood slithered and tugged at him. She had full control. Clark felt she could make him come at any time, but instead, her motions were slow and practiced. She teased him with silken tugs that left him always just short of a threshold that kept rising a little each time.

She wriggled her hips, rubbing more of her juices into Clark's throbbing length. He couldn't move. The slightest motion and his over-aroused member would rub up against her walls, incapacitating him with a burst of intense pleasure. She had him completely helpless and she knew it.

After a couple of minutes of grunt-filled copulation, Diana shouted something else in Greek and Kryptonian as she re-enveloped Clark in her tight love canal.

Clark grabbed Diana's ass and the small of her back and started moving her body up and down, fucking her on his straining member. Diana clung to Clark closer, pressing her slick satin breasts against his heaving muscular chest. They both moaned and panted noisily.

Clark then leaned forward and planted a hungry wet kiss on Diana's mouth, his tongue fighting an intense duel with Diana's. As Clark came up for air, he planted kisses down her neck then buried his face in her breasts. He caressed the firm pillows, feeling the pliant flesh underneath the silky skin, and suckled on each of her nipples, chewing them lightly with his lips. Diana continued stroking his hair, neck, and shoulders.

Pure sensation overwhelmed Clark with Diana's motions only short, controlled thrusts of her hips. Clark heard liquid sounds as the thick, soft walls of her sex crawled over his erection. Her lust had engulfed him whole. Clark gasped through gritted teeth. His hips bucked upwards.

Clark maneuvered Diana on the stone, laying her on her back, and her legs hooked over his shoulders. He raised his hips, supporting his weight on his forearms, and started slamming into Diana like a jack-rabbit. She emitted a high-pitched scream and pulled Clark's face for a ravenous kiss.

THE DARK SPELL

He felt her moist tongue forcefully enter his mouth and he started suckling on it like sweet candy.

Diana moaned, reached between their bodies with her hand, and started rubbing her clit furiously. Clark increased the speed and the urgency of his thrusts, burrowing deeper and faster in her core as if trying to reach her womb. One orgasm merged with the next as Diana abandoned control of her body to these unconscious reflexes.

Supporting herself with her hands on Clark's knees. She continued impaling herself on him, also rocking her hips backward and forward. Clark reached out with his right hand and started rubbing her clit, while caressing her stomach with his left hand. Diana's moans got louder, and she screamed something a mix of Greek and Kryptonian. Clark had no idea what that was but it sounded good!

She shifted position and leaned forward for a hungry kiss, grabbing Clark's neck. He returned the kiss and embraced Diana's nimble torso, caressing the sides of her breasts. Diana screamed again and suddenly made a 180-degree turn, with Clark now on his back, still embedded in her flaming womanhood. Clark thought that he saw stars but continued pummeling her. Diana threw her head back, with her right hand on Clark's chest and with her left hand working her push-button furiously. Clark knew that they were both about to explode at any moment.

She pulsed. A warm, thick fluid poured into her fleshy cavity and submerged Clark's trapped member. Diana closed her eyes and murmured. Her walls slowly undulated, stirring the fluid around his erection and massaging it into his flesh. Clark gasped. His hips twitched. His member surged and strained, eager to burrow deeper inside her. Diana leaned down over him and crushed her soft lips against his. She caressed the side of his face with her nails. Fires raged in the depths of their eyes.

His body convulsed. Her sex continued to throb around him. Her full breasts rested on his chest. Her skin felt so hot against his. A raging furnace.

The tide of pleasure rose up and claimed the last of Clark's thoughts. It was wonderful, the most natural thing in the world. He felt only the contentment of absolute release. His body sang with pleasure as if he wanted this to continue forever and ever.

With a loud grunt, Clark started spewing streams and streams of hot essence deep inside Diana. He felt her pelvis contact wildly, and with a loud scream, Diana exploded again too, her love juices flooding between their copulating bodies. His member throbbed, again and again, each time depositing another hot, sticky load into the Amazon's smothering grip. The ejaculation kept going, way past the point it should have ended as Clark pumped jets, streams, rivers of essence into Diana's greedy sex. The soft walls kept stroking and stroking, coaxing more and more juice from his straining manhood.

Diana relaxed around him. Clark went from feeling as though his manhood had been trapped in a vice to feeling as though it was sunk in luxuriously soft putty. A gasp slipped from his open mouth as more warm fluids swirled around his member. Diana's walls stroked against him in pleasant undulations. It didn't matter that their sexual organs were sealed together. She didn't need to move; the internal motions of her womanhood were friction enough. The flesh stroked and stroked up his shaft and teased the end with moist kisses.

Diana's hands caressed Clark's back and neck with tenderness, as she nibbled on his ear and his adam's apple. She lifted her head and Clark kissed all over her face softly before capturing her lips in a passionate kiss. Diana caressed his face, smiling at him.

They could feel each other's hearts racing as their deep breathing whistled in and out of their heaving chests. His member remained buried deep inside her.

"That was glorious," Diana panted.

"That was sensational," responded Clark with a huge grin. "I think we should have these kinds of deep tissue massages more often. The oil was nice. My beautiful Goddess all sexy and slippery."

Diana giggled. "Oh of course! Especially after a long battle, days away on out world missions, or Daily Planet, UN and University work. I'll get a few bottles of oil to take back home."

"Hmmm...?"

"What is it?"

"I think...how about we go to the Fortress instead?"

THE DARK SPELL

"The Fortress, the apartment, the Tower...anywhere we can have our time alone is fine with me, Love."

"I meant for...safety reasons..."

"Oh?"

"We made not just the temple shake but the entire island."

Diana gasped then burst out laughing.

"Mmhmm...we can't help ourselves in the throes of passion." Diana kissed him again. "I love you, Kal-El."

"I love you, too, Diana."

"Kal, Beloved..." Diana cupped his face staring deeply into his eyes. "It's only you." She said sternly. "No one will ever take away what we have. No one else will have my heart like you do. We tried holding back the love we have for one another but we couldn't. Yes, because of the meddling of a succubus it came about in a way we didn't intend but we are together now. Reveling in our unadulterated love."

Clark smiled proudly and cupped Diana's face. "You are so gorgeous. I'm so grateful for you, Diana. I don't know what I did to deserve you bu-"

"Being the most honorable, respectable, honest man, knowing all the right things to do and say."

"Diana, I promise you, I'm going to do my damnedest to keep that gorgeous smile on your face."

"I know, Love. I know," she said kissing him passionately.

Early the next morning....

Clark woke up looking to his right side where his beautiful Diana was still sleeping. He smiled at the peaceful, happy expression on her face. Clark turned over on his side and propped his head in his hand. He gently brushed strands of hair out of her face and leaned overlaying soft kisses all over her face then a gentle kiss on her lips.

She moved slightly. "Love..." she mumbled.

Clark smiled and kissed her lips softly again before easing out of bed.

He walked over to the balcony and leaned over it. Themyscira was truly breathtaking. The sun was beaming ever so brightly, the cool breeze felt so good. Clark inhaled deeply taking in the fresh air.

Looking down, he saw Queen Hippolyta on her horse, taking her morning stroll on the beach.

He quickly got dressed and flew down from the balcony.

"Good morning, Queen Hippolyta," he smiled flying down to her.

She looked up. "Good Morning, Kal-El." She frowned and tilted her head. "My daughter?"

"She's still asleep. I wanted take this opportunity to speak with you alone. I have something very important to say and ask."

"Oh? Well, go on."

Clark took a breath and nodded slightly. "I wanted to thank you for welcoming me. Regardless of being with Diana, you had every right to still refuse me being here. The other Amazons have every right to feel how they feel about me. I don't want to cause any kind of rift. I love Diana. I'm very much in love with her. I want to prove that I can be trusted by all of you. I know that Diana and all of you can protect yourselves as the greatest of warriors. But I feel it is my duty to protect the home of the woman I love."

"Well Kal-El, I must admit that upon your first introduction a few years ago, I was quite skeptical of you. As a mother, my daughter's well-being is my priority. I'm sure Diana has told you of our history with the outside world of man. I myself have encountered powerful men, like you." Hippolyta raised her brow. "You can understand where the skepticism comes from?"

"Yes ma'am, I do. And like I said, I understand. It's why I'm grateful to be here like this. When I first met Diana, she too felt skeptical. That I would be just like the men she'd heard of. I made that my personal mission to show her my truth. That she can trust and open up to me. We've always known that our feelings were deeper but we set a boundary putting our responsibilities first. We developed our friendship and it was inevitable to take the next step to something more." Clark paused and took a deep breath. "Queen Hippolyta, what I'm trying to say is that I want what Diana and I have to continue to evolve and take further steps. We don't want to rush things. I don't want Diana feeling pressured. When the time is right and we're both ready, I ask for your blessing, Queen Hippolyta, to have your daughter's hand in marriage?"

Hippolyta raised her brow. "You want my daughter to bare your children? To cook and clean and be submissive to you? Conform to man's world domestication."

THE DARK SPELL

Clark's heart immediately skipped a beat. He shook his head. "No! No! Your highness, no. That never crossed my mind. Well except for children..." He paused seeing her expression. "But only if Diana wants to. I would be the one honored to be the father of Diana's children." He ran his hand through his hair nervously and sighed. "Your highness, I mean I know that the views of the Amazons are different than man's world when it comes to things like this...and I don't expect us doing things in a traditional sense. I just want to make Diana happy. Whatever she wants and needs, how she wants, I'll do my damndest to provide."

Hippolyta smirked. "You are a brave man, Kal-El. A man of truth, honor, loyalty, and respect. My daughter is quite fond of you and she speaks highly of you. You've shown your worth and I give you my trust. However..."

Hippolyta took out her sword pointing the tip to Clark's adam's apple.

Clark jumped slightly, raising his hands in defense and gulped. "Dammit, not again," he thought to himself.

"Do not disappoint me and make me regret my decision, Kal-El."

"Yes- I mean no...no ma'am. You won't regret a thing."

"As you said, when the time is right, you shall have my daughter's hand."

When she placed her sword back in its sheath, Clark sighed of relief and smiled proudly. "Thank you, Queen Hippolyta," he bowed.

CHAPTER 8: LOVE'S REVEAL

Location: Themyscira, Diana's chambers

Diana moaned and reached over feeling for Kal. Her eyes fluttered open and focusing she saw the bedside was empty.

"Beloved?" she called softly.

No answer.

She sat up with a groan. "By Gods, Kal. You wear me out more than fighting Gods or monsters and demons from the depths of Tartarus." She looked around and still no sign of him, not even on the balcony. "Kal?! Oh, no, Mother!"

Diana quickly got out of bed and got herself dressed. She tried to calm herself down but so many thoughts were racing through her mind. She knew Hippolyta wouldn't do anything to him nor let any of the other Amazons do anything either. So where was he? Where did he go? What if he left on his own? But he wouldn't leave without saying anything unless it was an emergency. But he still would've told her, left a note or...

"Damn," she said to herself.

She hurried out of her room and to find Hippolyta and Kal.

Turning the corner she bumped into an Amazon Guard.

"Oh...Eiza, I'm sorry." said the Princess.

"No, no, Princess, that was my fault."

Diana smiled. "Eiza, it was my fault. I can take the blame for my faults, you know?"

Eiza slightly nodded. "Are you okay, Princess?"

"I'm just looking for Mother and Kal-El."

"Oh, I believe the Queen and Kal-El were at the Amphitheater but quite possible now in the Palace?" informed Eiza with a small smirk.

"Oh okay. Thank you."

Eiza bowed.

Diana quickly went to the Royal Palace.

"Good morning, Princess," Roe and Asha said in unison.

"Good morning. Are my mother and Kal here?"

"Ah, yes!" Roe said with a smile and opened the door for her.

Diana smiled. "Thank you." Diana walked in with a sigh. Her heart racing "Mother? Kal?"

Diana heard Hippolyta laughing from her private study.

"Mother?" Diana froze at the sight in front of her.

She saw Kal and Hippolyta sitting at the table with stacks of books.

"Oh, Diana! Good Morning, my Dear!" Hippolyta stood up from her chair with her arms open.

Though, a bit hesitant with her mother's unusual over joyous greeting, Diana smiled and embraced Hippolyta. "Good morning, Mother."

Hippolyta raised her brow at the scent of Kal all over her daughter, obviousness of sex oozing from her with how she was glowing. If it was any other man, Hippolyta would be disgusted and ready to castrate him. But she saw the love between her daughter and Kal-El. Kal-El being a man of honor, respect, loyalty and honesty. How happy her daughter was.

"I take it you slept well?" She parted the strands of hair that bunched before Diana's face.

"Yes, I did," Diana smiled awkwardly and glanced over at Kal.

Kal cleared his throat and stood up smiling at her.

"Morning, Di."

Diana walked over to him and embraced him.

"You okay?" he asked in a whisper.

"I was a little worried," she whispered back in such the quietest tone only Kal could hear with his super hearing.

He shook his head slightly and kissed her forehead. "Nothing to worry about."

"So what was it you two were talking about?" Diana asked with a raised brow turning back to Hippolyta then looking at Kal again.

"Oh...uh...well..." Kal stuttered a bit.

"I was just telling Kal-El about the time you were attempting to 'defend' us from Karna when we were trying to be at peace for the moment. And you bit her wanting to challenge her to a fight..." said her mother, exactly knowing her reactions.

THE DARK SPELL

"No, Mother! I was 6. And I heard Mala say she couldn't be trusted," Diana gasped interpreting.

Kal chuckled and kissed her cheek. "I imagined you were a cute ball of fire, Diana."

"Not funny." She pushed him away.

"There was also the time you were in the forest when I told you not to and you went too close to the forbidden area and you touched the water. Your hands were like you dipped them in green paint for 2 weeks." Hippolyta continued to pull her daughter's leg.

"Oh, Gods! Mother! Stop! No more. Please!" Diana's face turned pink.

"Di, it is cute hearing stories of you as a little girl." Kal joined with Hippolyta.

"Do not encourage her." Diana shot fireballs from her eyes directing it to Kal.

Hippolyta smiled. "Well, I have a few things to take care of. You two go ahead and go about the day."

"Oh, did you need any help, Mother?" Diana asked her mother.

"No, my dear. Go on," said the Queen, simply.

Diana hugged her mother tightly. "Thank you, Mother."

"Hmm...for?" she asked staring straight into her daughter's eye.

"Acceptance." A small hint of tear showed up in her iris.

"Ah," Hippolyta smiled. "He didn't give much of a choice. Quite the respectable young man." She turned her head pointing at Kal.

Kal beamed proudly. "Thank you, Hippolyta."

Hippolyta nodded slightly and walked out the door as a proud mother and Queen.

Diana, walked over and latched onto Kal's arm and reached up to kiss his cheek.

"I know just where to go first," she said as they walked out of the library.

As Diana and Kal took their stroll down to the shore, they were greeted by the Amazons.

"Good Morning, Princess, Kal-El."

"Diana, Kryptonian."

"Princess. Kal-El."

Diana smiled and happily greeted her sisters along with Kal.

"See? I told you they'll come around, Love. Just need a little more time. They're not used to a man like you. But do you like being here?"

"I understand, Di. I'm glad they are coming around because it would break my heart not being worthy of their Princess in their eyes." He kissed her temple. "Of course I like being here. I'm with my gorgeous Goddess' family."

Diana sighed lovingly and titled her head on his shoulder as they continued walking. "That's exactly why you are worthy. Is that what you and Mother were really talking about?"

Kal was caught off guard laughing nervously. "Yeah...."

She raised her brow. "Don't make me get the lasso. What else happened?"

"No, no. No need for that," he smirked. "But seriously, Di..." He stopped walking and sighed. "Okay. Well, I woke up and you were obviously still asleep. I went to look out on your balcony and saw Hippolyta down here with her horse."

"Oh, her usual morning stroll."

"I had to take that opportunity to speak with her alone because I wanted her to know how serious I am about you. Nothing else happened besides her having her sword to my neck as a warning."

Diana gasped. "Kal!"

He laughed. "It's okay. As I said, it was just a warning. I agreed, keeping my word. That's the deal."

Diana jumped into his arms, cupping his face with both hands, and kissed him passionately.

Her soft breasts brushed his broad chest as their tongues interlaced.

"I love you, my beloved Kryptonian," she said and continued to suck on his tongue.

"Oh damn, Princess."

He let her feed on his tongue and she giggled knowing that the source of the hint of saltiness on his tongue is her from last night. "I'll be calling you so much more soon enough."

They went to their room, bathed, and dressed appropriately to stroll around the rest of Themyscira.

Diana looked up at him smiling.

THE DARK SPELL

Kal glanced at her. "What is it, Di? You still haven't told me where we are going?"

"To a secret place of mine."

Kal and Diana flew over a few of the big shore rocks.

"There is a cave just right over there. If I wasn't at the cliffs, in the forest, or the shore, I was here. No one knew where I was for a long time. That was until my mother followed me once."

"You were a bad girl, Diana. I like it," Kal wiggled his eyebrows.

Diana laughed. "No, I wasn't. I was adventurous. As much as I loved learning and training, I didn't want all my days consumed with that. I wanted to explore."

"I get that. When I started learning how to control my powers I did the same. Needed to go to remote places."

They both landed on a desolate island with tropical trees. It was so dense, sunlight couldn't penetrate.

Kal lit up the torch with his heat vision as they walked into the cave.

When he looked at her, he was struck by the vision of beauty she envisioned. The firelight lit up her skin, making it glow. The flames flickered, sending silhouettes of her form dancing against the cave wall. He was mesmerized.

"Wow! No matter where you are Di, you're breathtaking."

She blushed.

He looked around the cave and touched the walls. "These carvings...?" He touched the wall. "You did this."

"Yes. I used to bring books that I had to study. In mathematics, sciences, and most literature, I would create things of my own and teach myself. Even a few of my dreams I drew it all out here telling the story."

"This is amazing, Di!" He looked around completely in awe.

"Thank you, Love."

Diana touched the wall as well and glided her hand over her carvings then to a space that is left empty.

"You left a space?"

"I didn't know what to put here, even visiting home like we are now. I just don't know yet."

Diana then looked down and sighed.

Kal clasped her chin to look deeply into her eyes. "What's wrong?"

"I was really worried, Kal. Waking up with you not next to me. I didn't know what happened. Having you here makes me so happy. I don't ever want to have to choose between the man I love and my sisters. So to see you with Mother talking and laughing together, I haven't seen her like that in such a long time. I know that you are a very, very, special man." She almost leaned completely on him, sandwiching him between her and the cave's wall.

Kal felt her heartbeat, the truth in her words. But her jasmine scented hair teased his nostrils and sent a shiver to his groin.

"I'm sorry, Di. I just really had to take that moment," he explained ignoring his activated erection.

Diana can feel him poking her in the navel through their togas.

"I was looking forward to waking up next to you," she whispered in his ear pressing herself more to him, "I didn't even get to properly say good morning..." her arm from his chest dropped down there, "Hello, Junior!" she said wrapping her hand around him.

Kal jerked in her hand and tried to focus when she kissed him on his neck.

Kal chuckled controlling his pleasure. "Sweetheart! You can have your time with junior when we get back to your room later."

Diana's fingernails scrape the outsides of his thighs on the way down. She pouted. "Later?"

Kal laughed and wrapped his arms around her waist.

"Yes, later because you know once we get started we won't stop for hours."

"True..." she sighed. "I'll be anticipating the rest of the day until I get you completely alone."

Diana felt a tenseness in her stomach and a warmness flood between her legs. The hot flush of desire.

"It will be worth the wait. I promise."

Kal embraced her, grabbing that voluptuous ass of hers and kissing her forehead; Diana wrapped her arms around his neck. She tipped her chin upward and opened her lips so that he could kiss her. Their kiss was full of wonder and exploration. Kal's lips opened and Diana immediately probed

THE DARK SPELL

gently over his teeth with her tongue. Kal returned this inquiry with an expedition of his own. The teeth that made up her perfect smile even felt wonderful on his tongue. Their tongues engaged in playful fencing and she sucked his tongue deep into her mouth. Kal had one hand still groping her rear, his other entangled within her hair.

"I can't get enough of you, Kal-El."

"Feeling's mutual," he smirked.

He peered into her eyes a moment before ravishing her again.

"Di...I love you," Kal whispered in gasps between kisses.

Kal raised her right leg to wrap around his waist, rubbing his arousal against her.

"I love you, too, Kal," she gasped and released his lips slowly.

Kal tried to bring his lips back to hers again, but Diana laughed slightly and ducked away, teasing him. Now he did whine and she laughed outright, reaching to give him a brief kiss.

Kal laughed and looked back to stare at the empty space on the wall. He then looked at Diana and took her hand intertwining their fingers.

"I think I know what to put in that spot."

"What's that, Love?" she asked, looking up at him.

"Us."

"Hmmm? What did you have in mind?"

Kal smiled and Diana tilted her head curiously.

Looking back at the wall, he used his laser vision ever so gently starting to carve into the wall. Diana was amazed watching him, like an artist creating his finest piece of art.

Once finished he smiled proudly.

"Uh-huh, perfect!"

Diana gasped. "Darling, that's lovely!"

He carved them holding each other hand combining within a heart.

"Oh.... Wait..."

He carved their Superman and Wonder Woman emblems within the heart as well.

"Now, it's perfect." He turned to her, pushing a lock of her raven hair behind her ear and the corners of his mouth turned up in that tentative smile she loved so much.

Diana reached a hand up to run her thumb across his cheek and sighed as he turned his face to kiss her palm.

"I love you," she whispered.

"I love you too," he said.

Diana reached up to kiss him. Kal opened to her slowly as her tongue sought out his goodness again.

Location: Valeria's Castle

Valeria and Strife lay naked upon Valeria's enormous bed with 6 incubus servants.

"Well...I may have to come to visit more often for this little conquest," said Strife

"It is quite a joy for chaotic pleasure and intimate pleasure," Valeria stated.

"I'm more inclined to chaotic pleasure though this will do from time to time. Dionysus was such a fool. However, I would say all males, god, and mortals are fools," smirked Strife.

Valeria moaned as an incubus kissed her neck. "Mmh... yes. They are fools, so easily tainted. Though, there is one I can't seem to have my way with just yet."

"The Kryptonian, Diana's lover?" asked Strife

"Yes. His passion for her is much too strong. And she...for being the daughter of Zeus and an Amazon, her heart is only open to him."

"She might be the daughter of Zeus and part of those wench Amazons...though, she is...different. And he...is not from this world or Gods or mortals. Though, he can rival even Zeus in power. There is a uniqueness to Diana and Kal-El."

"So what are we to do with them?" Valeria asked moving closer to Strife.

"The mortal world is not so kind to them at times. The selfish creatures are afraid of such a union. Diana and Kal have not yet let those they protect know of their personal endeavors together. I believe it's time for them to know."

Valeria smiled and trailed her hand on Strife's side.

"Oh, the mortals' involvement will be quite entertaining."

Location: Themyscira: Culture Complex

THE DARK SPELL

The Culture Complex was where the Amazons would gather for various entertainment activities, ceremonies, arts, music, songs, and stories.

Kal watched in amazement as Diana was sitting with one of her sisters, Yemi, playing harps.

To see Diana's elegant fingers glide and pull the strings creating such a heavenly melody, he was enchanted by her.

The other Amazons and Kal clapped once they stopped.

Diana smiled and embraced Yemi, "Thank you, Yemi, for letting me join you."

"Of course, Princess! I remember those days when you were younger and we used to play. I'm glad we had this time."

"Me, too."

Kal smiled. He was happy and grateful to be with Diana getting to know more about her Amazonian life and culture but also that Diana was home. He could sense every once in a while she felt homesick and to see her so relaxed and enjoying being at home warmed his heart.

"Kal?"

"Yeah, Di?"

She smiled and took his hand intertwining their fingers.

"Let's go."

As they walked along, heading to the coliseum, Diana told him more stories of when she was younger.

"I trained a lot and I competed in the games. I want to show that I could be just like the others. I didn't want to be treated as just the Queen's daughter...the Princess."

Diana sighed as they walked through the coliseum.

"The last time I was here, I was competing to be the representative of Themyscira accompanying Steve back to man's world," she sighed. "My mother wouldn't let me but my with stubbornness, I did anyway using a disguise. I won and my mother had no choice but to keep her word. But I...I saw the conflict in her eyes, she didn't know whether to be proud of me because I didn't give up on my choice and belief, winning the contest or disappointed and hurt because I went against her."

"Your mother is very proud of you, Diana."

"Now? Yes. Though, I still had to prove to her that following my own heart and mind was the right choice."

"She just wanted to protect you. I understand that. The talk we had. I'm glad we did. We both want you to be happy, Diana but do any and everything to protect you. You are much too precious to both of us."

"My mother and my Love getting along...yes, that makes me very happy."

"Hey...Di?"

"Yes, Kal?

"Come back home more often, okay? I know it's difficult with our responsibilities but I see it in your eyes how much you miss home and the way you were with your sisters and mother. They all miss you. Whether I'm with you or not, either way, you are covered. Don't worry about anything else."

Tears started to well up in Diana's eyes as she wrapped her arms around him, embracing him tightly.

She buried her face in his chest.

"Thank you," he heard her mumble.

He smiled and wrapped his arms even tighter around her, kissing the crown of her head.

A few hours later... Themyscira shore

It was time for Diana and Kal to take their leave back to man's world.

While Diana was distracted talking to some of her sisters, Kal and Hippolyta were off to the side continuing their discussion from earlier.

Hippolyta took his hand and placed something in it. Kal looked down. It was a small tanzanite gemstone.

"This is no ordinary stone, Kal-El. It's a communicator. The first time Diana left, I...communication was cut off for a while. I never gave it to her. We use these for when other fellow Amazons traveled to man's worlds. Since we have been planning to do it, it is the best way for us to keep in contact. All you have to say is "Queen Hippolyta". Remember, do not let Diana know or see it. She will know."

Kal nodded. "Thank you, Your Highness. Thank you for everything. Diana means so much to me. I love her. I keep my word and do all I can for her." He looked back at Diana with a proud smile. "This surprise will be one to remember for all time."

Kal slipped the stone into his pocket as he and Hippolyta walked back over to Diana and the others.

"Kryptonian, while some of us still have our reservation. You have proven yourself worthy of our Princess to be her mate," Artemis said.

"Our guards however are not down, nor weak. Dare take advantage of our kindness and dishonor Princess Diana, my spear will be so far up y-"

"Okay, Nova..." Diana stopped her. "He gets it."

Kal chuckled nervously, rubbing the back of his head. "As I've told the Queen, you all have my word."

"Mother..." Diana hugged Hippolyta. "I love you and I'm sorry for... "

Hippolyta shook her head and smiled reassuringly. She caressed Diana's cheek.

"My dear daughter, you are well on your journey. I can not hold you back from that. I just ask and pray for your well-being. Kal-El has made his promise and holds him to that." Hippolyta embraced her daughter again. "You will always be my little moon and stars." Hippolyta smiled, pulling back and cupped her daughter's face. "Be safe." She looked at Kal.

Without a word from her, he already knew and he nodded.

Diana looked at Kal with a smile and took his hand.

"You ready?" He asked.

She nodded.

As they flew off, they turned to wave and Diana stayed turned flying backward until she could no longer see her home island.

Kal glanced over to look at her, seeing the sadness all over her face.

"Di, we can go back. You want to stay for another day or so?"

Diana shook her head slowly and gave him a reassuring smile.

"This was just so good for us."

"But I know we have to get back to reality. It is a feeling of homesickness already just as it did with leaving Smallville. It's just so peaceful getting away from the chaos but..." Diana smiled and wrapped her arms around his neck. "My peace is with you. You are my peace."

Kal smiled and took her sweet face with his hands, kissing her warm luscious soft lips. As their tongues engaged in a sensual dual, Kal nibbled on her lips gently making her moan so ever softly. Kal then moved his hands down to her waist pulling her closer, pressing their bodies together more.

"Superman, this is Cyborg. This is an emergency. Superman?" He heard.

He broke their kiss. "Yeah, Vic. Superman, here."

"Sorry for interrupting your vacation, man."

"We were just heading back actually."

"There's an emergency at the Tower. The system has crashed. Batman, Flash, Lantern, and I have tried everything we can but even going so far externally not sure what's causing this. It seems I'm completely blocked."

"We're on our way. Superman out." He paused pondering. "Hm?"

"Beloved, what's wrong?"

"Some kind of system breach in the Tower. We have to be careful. We don't need anything confidential being corrupted or worse ending up in the hands of someone else."

"Right. Okay. Let's go."

Location: Justice League WatchTower

Outside of the Tower, Superman did a full scan and found nothing out of the ordinary.

"Everything seems fine. No wires damaged."

Welcome, Superman.

Welcome, Wonder Woman.

"Recognition still works fine."

"Maybe it was just Files?"

"Vic was saying it's the entire system. But I'm not understanding how when Bruce's tech. combined with my Kryptonian tech, and Vic, nothing should be able to be corrupted."

Kal and Diana walked into the central hub. Diana gasped seeing Victor on the ground unconscious.

"Hey, Vic! Vic!"

"Victor!"

Kal and Diana helped him up to sit in a chair.

"Victor?!"

THE DARK SPELL

"Ah, man..." He focused on seeing Kal and Diana. "Glad you're both here. Whatever is happening took a bit of a toll on my circuits. Need to recoup me."

"Go ahead, Victor, Kal, and I have this. Did you need my help getting to your quarters?"

"I think I have enough power to do so." He stood up.

"Are you sure?"

"Yeah."

"We will give you an update if there's any change."

"Thanks, Diana."

Diana slightly smiled and nodded.

As Vic walked out, Kal sat down in front of the enormous monitor using his super-speed going through the database.

"Kal, does the reactor core need to be checked?" asked Diana.

"No, it's definitely something going on within the system here. It's like the system put itself in a lockdown recovery mode."

"I know you scanned everything and didn't see anyone. The only way in is flying in from space or the teleporter but just in case I'll go check around and check the cameras. We also need to check security footage for the past 48 or 72 hours." Diana prepared for a round on the aisle.

Kal looked up at her with a smile and nodded. "Just be careful, Di."

"If an intruder has been here, they are the ones that should be careful," she smiled back. "My overprotective lover...you will be listening to me the whole time anyway. So there's nothing to worry about." She kissed his cheek and flew out of the hub.

Kal smirked and shook his head turning back to the monitor he frowned. "What the hell is going on?"

"Clark? Clark, it's Bruce," he heard from the intercom.

"Yeah, I'm here checking out the Tower with Diana," he reported back.

"I'm in Gotham following a lead on Hugo Strange. I'll be ba-"

"No need, Bruce. Diana and I can handle whatever is going on with the system. I'll contact you when it's all figured out," he interrupted him to assure everything is in control.

"Fine. Batman out."

The intercom buzzed off.

Kal sighed and sat back for a moment then sat up quickly.

"What? Seriously, Billy, a damn video game on the database. Bruce with this security and surveillance. Cyborg's tech updates. Ah...let's see configurations for Kryptonian tech updates."

Configurations estimated time: 10 minutes

"Kal, I'm heading back now. I've flown through every section twice. Everything seems fine. If there was anyone I would've run into them by now," Diana reported.

"Well, I just finished a very deep internal look into the database. Billy uploaded a video game."

Diana laughed softly. "He is still a child so it's not all that shocking."

"It's probably part of the problem but I have my doubts that's the sole reason with what's going on," Kal responded. "It would be embarrassing for the entire WatchTower to be corrupted because of a simple video game. I'm updating the system, maybe that's what it needed and was blocked somehow. I'm guessing our tech combination isn't as seamless as we thought. But that's only the first step of maybe getting this back on track. We may have to go to the Fortress to check out the computer and my dad's old journals just in case. But I'm sure that's fine. But still, I have to reset everything from the start which is going to burn my brain..."

"Relax, Superman."

"Yeah! What makes you think I am not relaxed..." Superman stopped talking when his eyes narrowed to the door.

The door opened with a hiss and Diana walked back into the hub with her hands on her hips. "Do you know how sexy it is when you talk like this?" She walked seductively swaying her hips towards him. "I can hear the tension in your voice and now..." she stood in front of him and then sat in his lap. "I can see it all over your face and in your eyes."

She bent to peck on his lips.

"Fixing a Supercomputer system is not easy, Di. I have to code trillions of cryptic data again which might take another hour after the configuration is complete"

"Oh! It's okay. Those fingers of yours are faster than hyper loop." She cupped his cheek and kissed him softly. "You are such a talented man in so

THE DARK SPELL

many ways but you need to be relaxed. Billy is just a child. So don't be angry with him."

Kal groaned. "Di..."

"And I know you can multitask..." she giggled against his lips, "...if you are relaxed..." She slowly took his index finger and kissed the tip.

"I have a computer to fix, Di." He melted in the wetness of her mouth.

Diana took his finger in her mouth and rubbed her hand on his thighs. Kal tried hard to resume his eyes to fix the malfunction.

8 more minutes for configuration

Diana dropped his finger and whispered, "Shame...we have a very short time. But I exactly know what you need." She kissed him hard.

Diana could feel the flush in his cheeks and the tension in his brow. She twisted and squeezed on his lips with her wild kiss and they both feel it nearly impossible to keep silent.

Diana broke their kiss and licked her lips. "Suit off. Keep the cape."

"Di?" He was thrown back at her advance.

"Now, Kal."

As his suit slowly degenerated Diana pressed a kiss against his shoulder before resting her head against him.

Her fingers wander down between them until she finds him, already pressed hard against her thigh, and Diana felt his pulse. She slid her hand slowly down. His head drops and Kal buried his face against her shoulder as he gave a groan and his hips bear down against her hand, body curling in against hers.

She raised and adjusted herself in front of him.

'Now, Relax", she said, kissing him and her fingers running down his neck. She nips across his collarbones and-

"Oh! Beautiful, I will," he said as Diana kissed down his torso, nipping at him, running her fingers across his skin.

She giggled and reached his hip with her mouth. She slipped her body between his legs, running her hand up to his thigh while her tongue follows the v of his pelvis, Kal Instinctively gripped her shoulder as he twitched eagerly

Finally, she took hold of his manhood, stroking slowly.

"Well, Hello Junior!" She kept moving slowly.

"Really, Di? Right now?" He breathed in through his teeth in the process he almost knocked her off balance.

"We're alone. We can have a little fun." feeling him smooth and warm in her palm but as hard as marble in her grip.

Kal wove his fingers into her as he leaned forward and captured her lips. She adjusts her grip and strokes downward once and looked down at him. He is thick and hard, branching out from dark curls, as thick as her wrist, eagerly waiting for her mouth.

Her jaw inched forward toward him and as Diana was just about to take him into her mouth, the emergency alert went off.

"No." Kal lulled his head back and sighed dramatically.

"What?" Diana said standing up.

"Kal stood up with his suit regenerating. "I was getting prepared for a different kind of call." He reached to slap Diana's ass.

She squealed and laughed. "You'll be getting it once we get back, Love. So hurry, hurry. Race you!"

Diana flew off before him. Kal raised his brow and smirked, flying off after her.

Location: Downtown Metropolis

"Easy picking...hehehe..." Rudolph "Rudy" Jones, known as Parasite, laughed as he picked up an officer shooting at him.

"No! No! Ahhhh!" The officer screamed as he felt like he was being electrocuted and drained of energy, drained of life.

Parasite had the ability to temporarily absorb the life energy, superpowers, and knowledge of their victim.

Parasite threw the officer's now lifeless body on top of his car.

"Who's next?!"

"I'm next!" Wonder Woman yelled and kicked him in the face.

"Wonder Woman be careful!" Superman warned.

"I know! Get everyone else to safety. I have this!"

"Wond-"

"I've got this."

Taking a breath, Superman nodded. "Be careful, please."

Wonder Woman winked and flew off grabbing a light pole hitting Parasite in the face, having him flying down the street.

THE DARK SPELL

"Oh...feisty..."

Wonder Woman launched at him again and swung at him again with the pole.

"MOMMY! DADDY!" she heard a loud scream mid-swing.

She looked around and saw a little girl hiding under a car. Though it was dangerously close to the building Parasite hit causing large amounts of debris to fall. She gasped and was just about to hit Parasite when she was backhanded.

"Snack size. Then you, Wonder Woman, the main course!"

Wonder Woman caught herself in mid-air and flew off fast trying to get to the girl before Parasite.

"MOMMY!" The girl screamed again and cried harder seeing Parasite racing toward her. "DADDY! DADDY, HELP ME!"

Suddenly the car she was under was being lifted up and thrown hitting Parasite.

She gasped and looked back. "Superman!"

Wonder Woman swooped her up.

"Wonder Woman!"

"We got you. There is no need to worry, little one," Wonder Woman smiled reassuringly. "Superman, take her."

"What? I'm going to handle Parasite."

"No. I will."

"No way!"

"Ka-...Superman, I have to. I know what to do. He wants power, I'll give it to him."

"Wonder Woman, that's too dangerous even for you."

"Once absorbing one's power. He absorbs weaknesses as well."

"You don't ha-" he paused. "No! No! I'm not letting you do that!"

Wonder Woman took off her gauntlets. Her eyes started to glow with lightning blue.

She smiled. "I'll be alright."

"Wonder Woman, no."

"Get the little one to her parents, Superman."

"Wonder Woman..."

She flew off back to Parasite.

"Wonder Woman is cool! She'll beat the bad guy!"

"Yeah..."Superman sighed. "She's amazing." He said under his breath. "Let's get you to your Mother."

"Rudolph, this ends now!"

"Ah, come and get me, Wonder Woman." He took a deep breath in. "So much power! Give it to me!"

Wonder Woman flew faster punching him.

"Hahaha! You foolish woman! You are just making me stronger."

Wonder Woman smirked and lassoed him.

"You are blinded by resentment. Do you think power will help you fill your void? It won't. You aren't as in control as you think you are. It is nothing more than greed controlling you. I'll show you what real power is and I'm more than sure you can't handle it."

Clouds began to roll in.

"Oh no..." Superman flew faster. "Do you see your mom?"

The young girl squinted. "No."

"Don't worry we'll fi-"

"Have you seen my daughter?! Long sandy red hair, white ribbon, a unicorn on her shirt, jean shorts?" He heard. "Melanie? Melanie, where are you, honey!?"

"I think I've found her."

Superman flew down to the frantic woman.

Melanie gasped. "Mommy!"

She turned. "Melanie!" She cried and held out her arms.

Melanie jumped out of Superman's arms into her Mother's.

"Oh, Honey! I'm so glad you're safe!"

"Nicole! Melanie!"

"Daddy!"

"Bernard!"

Bernard held his wife and daughter in his arms tightly.

"Thank you, Superman. We are forever grateful."

Superman smiled and shook his head slightly. "It's my job, Sir and it was Wonder Woman who saved your daughter."

BOOM! KRRAACCKK!

Thunder and lightning

THE DARK SPELL

Superman quickly flew off.

"Please...please don't, Diana."

Wonder Woman's body slammed parasite into an abandoned high-rise building. The building immediately began collapsing.

"I won't die, you stupid broad. But you...it's over!"

"You've taken 3 lives today without any remorse. I should end you just as you did them but that would make me no better than you. We're not at that point yet. But keep trying me and we will be," Wonder Woman warned. "No one else dies today."

Wonder Woman's lasso started to glow brighter as well as her body and eyes of lightning blue.

Another loud roar of thunder and cracking of lightning. A large bolt struck Wonder Woman and went through the lasso to Parasite.

"Power! So much power! So...much.... Aaahhhhhh!" He screamed in pain. "What are you doing?!"

"You wanted power, right? Take it!"

Another loud boom of an explosion and a flash of light. The aftershock knocked Superman back. The building completely fell.

"Wonder Woman!" Superman yelled out as the light faded. "Wonder Woman!" He flew to the building and started picking up large pieces of debris. "Wonder Woman answer me, please!"

"I'm over here, Superman."

He turned to see Wonder Woman leaning against a piece of the building still standing with scratches and bruises all over her.

"Wonder Woman!" He flew to her but stopped a bit hesitant. "Where is Parasite?"

"Under here somewhere. Unconscious or dead."

"We have to get him out."

"No! Let's get out of here. Let the authorities handle the rest."

"What? No. We need to get Parasite to A.R.G.U.S. ourselves or risk him getting energy from someone."

"As I said, he is dead. Leave him."

Superman looked into her eyes. "Where is your lasso?"

"What?"

"Your gauntlets and lasso are missing."

Wonder Woman sighed irritated. "I'm too tired for this, Babe. Just help me find the damn thing and let's go."

As she turned to walk away, Superman noticed something was very wrong.

"Come on, Babe. Don't you want to go so we can be alone?"

"Babe?" He questioned himself.

The sound of her heartbeat, the way she talks, the way she walks.

"Wonder Woman?"

"Oh my God! You are annoying! What is it now, Su-"

Superman hit her with a beam. She flew into a wall. He flew after her and watched as she fell to the ground.

She coughed and spit up blood. She wiped the corner of her mouth.

"What was that for?!" she yelled.

"Where is she?!"

"What are you talking about?!"

"I won't ask again," Superman warned.

"Wow, Boy Scout. You aren't the dumb flying brick with heart eyes for the broad I thought you were," Parasite smirked turning back to himself. "Don't know. Don't care."

Superman's eyes turned fiery red.

"I'll tell you this..." he started coughing up blood. "The dame is a god damn powerhouse. My insides feel like they're burned to a crisp."

"Now you are about to deal with me."

"He has had enough, Superman." Wonder Woman said flying above them. Her eyes still glowed with lightning blue. "Right, Rudolph?"

"Shit." Parasite coughed up more blood. "Look, the men are talking now. You've proven your girl power thing. It's one on one with your boyfriend now. Or just get me to the damn ER!"

Wonder Woman quirked her brow and cracked her knuckles. "Didn't we just have a conversation about being rude?"

"Shit."

Wonder Woman lassoed Parasite again and flew up with him.

"No...please..."

"You brought this on yourself. Being so angry...You need a long nap."

She then swung him over and flew straight down to the ground.

THE DARK SPELL

Parasite hit the ground creating a small crater. He gasped with the wind being knocked out of him and coughed up more blood.

"You...damn...broad..."

He fell unconscious.

Superman shook his head. "Didn't learn a thing."

He looked up and saw Wonder Woman's eyes turn back normal, though she seemed weak and started to fall. He flew up and caught her.

"Hey. Hey, Di. I got you."

She groaned. "Remind me not to ever do that again. It really drains me."

He chuckled. "I would but you're going to do it anyway. But I'll be here after to catch you, take you home, and take care of you, giving you a full body massage."

She reached up and caressed his cheek. "You are the sweetest. How did you know Parasite was trying to impersonate me?"

"He may have tried to look like you, but there are little details only I know. You are just too special to impersonate, Di. Also, I've never heard you call me let alone say 'babe'."

Diana smiled. "You are my Beloved, my Love, my Darling, my Sexy Spaceman, and Sun."

"That's better." He held her tighter and kissed her softly. "Di, you really did scare me a bit, though. I know it's a choice we have to make but I was worried. Especially dealing with Parasite draining your power, not knowing how that would've affected you."

"I know, Kal. But I had faith. Although, yes, it was draining, I was going to be alright. I am alright." She gave him a quick peck. "What about the little girl?"

"Safe with her parents."

"Thank the Gods."

"Let's get Parasite to A.R.G.U.S, then we can get back to the Tower. I have something in mind for you later."

30 minutes later...Washington D.C. A.R.G.U.S.

Colonel Steve Trevor huffed as he stood out with his group of soldiers.

"Superman and Wonder Woman will be arriving with inmate 70594632 in less than 2 minutes, Sir."

"Yeah, I know. Make sure all are on stand-by. Containment is ready."

"Sir, Waller wants to speak with you after Superman and Wonder Woman leaves the inmate."

"Of course she does."

"They've arrived."

"Ready to fire if an inmate gets out of control."

Steve looked up and his focus was immediately on Wonder Woman.

Parasite was tied in a tarp and Wonder Woman's lasso was still unconscious.

"Wonder Woman," Steve smiled.

"Colonel Trevor. We don't know how long Parasite will be incapacitated."

"We should get him to containment now," Superman said.

"You can handle it, Superman. I need to speak with Wonder Woman for a minute."

"Can this wait, Colonel?"

"No."

Wonder Woman looked at Superman.

"Go ahead. It's fine. This guy is out like a light."

"Fall back, team," Steve said as started to walk closer to Wonder Woman.

He glanced at Superman as he flew off with Parasite inside the building.

He looked back and waited until the doors closed then sighed, looking at Diana.

"How are you, Diana?"

"I'm fine." She frowned, confused. "Steve, is that really what you wanted to ask me?"

"No." He sighed again. "Diana, we haven't talked in a long while."

"What do you mean? We talk every other day or so about the League and A.R.G.U.S dealings."

"I mean really talk. Personal talk, Diana."

"There's nothing personal to talk about."

"What happened to us? One minute I'm showing you the White House and we're having dinner with officials. People see us together and

THE DARK SPELL

believe in us to be together but then, it all just stopped after you joined the Justice League."

"Do you believe going to the White House, having dinner with officials, and being showcased as something I was not was flattering? We were never together in that way, Steve. I've told you my feelings have always been that you were my friend. Of course, I cared and loved you as such but it's never gone any farther than that."

"It can be, Diana. Just give us a chance."

"I'm not that young naive girl anymore who doesn't understand relationships and my feelings. I understand and know how I feel. I know who I love, in love with, and want to be with."

"What? You...It's him, isn't it?"

Diana remained silent immediately hearing the anger and disappointment in his voice.

"I knew it! You've slept with him, haven't you? What is it? The powers? The God complex?! The dude is running around in some tight blue onesie and a red blanket. Is that what you want? I thought you were different, Diana. Ever since you joined the all high and mighty Justice League you've become unrecognizable to me. Shallow isn't you. You-"

Diana slapped him. "I said I'm not that naive girl anymore. The intimacy of my relationship with Kal is none of your business! You will not talk to me in such a condescending, belittling manner. You can't control me, Steve. I'm not some doll you can mold into what you want or tell me how I should be!"

"I'm trying to get through to you because you are making the biggest mistake!"

"A mistake? What makes me happy is a mistake? Because it's not you?" Diana shook her head in disbelief. "This was not what I came here for. This is not the conversation I want to have and shouldn't be having period. I can't believe you, Steve!" Diana was about to walk past him.

"Diana, no! We're not done!" He grabbed her arm.

She looked down and looked back up at him with narrow eyes. "It would be best to let go of me right now."

"You need to listen to me."

"No! I'm not listening to your demands! You listen to me! I'm with Kal because I am truly deeply in love with him. I love him because he respects me and treats me as the woman I am instead of some kind of possession. He actually listens and he puts what I want and needs first. I am myself with him."

"Diana, I know you! He isn't right for you! I know what you need and want."

"What do you know is right for me, Steve?! It's what you want and needs. You are only thinking about yourself! You want me to make you look good in the eyes of the public of your team! I will not be some trophy for any man!"

"Really? You are for him. Oh wait... he isn't a man. He is some alien from a whole different planet far away from here!"

Diana slapped him again. "Don't you dare disrespect the home he lost! Because he is not from man's world, he is not a man? What about me? Because I'm not from a man's world, I'm an Amazon and Olympian, that makes me not a woman? Is that what you see, Steve?"

"That's not what I meant."

"Whatever you meant, it doesn't matter because it's all wrong anyway. You crashed on my home island and my mother and sisters could've killed you but they didn't. Kal could've been captured to be used as a test subject or weapon if his parents didn't take him in but they did and raised him to be the kind humbled man he is!"

"You talk about fate. The day I saw you, that was fate. I didn't die because my angel saved me. You are my angel, Diana."

"No, Steve. I'm sorry but I'm not."

"Diana, don't do this! He isn't worth it!"

"He is worth it! He has proven to me, my mother, and my sisters that he can truly be trusted. That he truly loves me and he makes me happy. Happier than I've ever been before. Steve, what kind of life or fantasy do you think this is to force someone to feel something they do not? I hope that you will find true happiness and love with someone else."

Steve shook his head. "You don't know what real love is because you never grew up with it. You said it yourself, the Amazons never cared for men. They are hellbent on thinking all men are bad. But power is accepted. You are no better than them. This is a mistake and you will see."

"Hey, what the hell is going on?!" Kal questioned flying to them. He looked at Diana. He can see the anger, irritation, and sadness in her eyes. "Are you serious with this?"

"Let's go, Kal," Diana said, grabbing his hand.

"Wait, Di. I have to say this."

"I don't want to hear from you."

"You are going to listen to me, dammit. You are so caught up in having soldiers following your orders, we aren't them. We both love Diana and we want her to be happy. That's what matters most to both of us. Be happy for her."

"You're only saying that because she is with you."

"No, I'm saying it, because it's true. It's Diana's choice. I'm just grateful to have her in my life regardless. Your problem is not even trying to understand her like you claim you do. Do you want her to be someone she isn't? Want her to do things she isn't comfortable with? You're being selfish. I'm far from perfect but I'm doing my best for her. She is the priority. I may not be from this planet but I had my Ma and Pa showing me how a relationship, a partnership is supposed to be and my biological parents had just as much of a partnership. Diana and I have connected in ways no one will ever understand and we for damn sure don't expect anyone to."

"When she breaks up with you and kicks your ass to the curb I'll understand I guess."

"I see. Trying to have a civilized mature conversation isn't happening. You can think whatever you want but nothing will stop us from being together."

"Careful, Superman," Steve mocked. "Sounds like a threat to a government agent. Federal offensive. You'll be sharing a cell with inmate 70594632."

"Alright. We're done." Kal held Diana's hand tighter. "We can go now."

Kal and Diana flew off heading back to the WatchTower. Their flight was quiet. Diana could tell Kal was just in as much deep thought as she was.

Location: Valeria's Castle

Valeria and Strife were watching from the scrying pool.

"Oh...the drama has intensified!" Strife laughed. "She is her father's daughter. Men fall for her and she breaks their weak hearts."

Valeria sighed. "Love...Love is such a complicated and challenging thing. It can be quite ugly. And devastating."

"Quite chaotic and toxic. Though, Diana and Kal-El are too sickeningly pure." Strife looked disgusted.

"Yes, well that's part of where our fun comes in. That mortal is only one of many who oppose this union. How will they handle the pressure of those pathetic ungrateful mortals they've sworn to protect and sacrifice their lives for?"

"They are nothing more than guard dogs for the mortals." Strife grinned mischievously. "Well, it seems as though it's almost time. They will see truly how much time they've wasted. They don't belong with them. And we have the perfect picture capturing the two lovers for the many mortals to see."

"Oh yes...everything will go perfectly. Diana and Kal-El will become mine to bring Dionysus to his knees and bow down before me after all these years."

20 minutes later...WatchTower
"Welcome Superman."
"Welcome Wonder Woman."
"Hey Di, I'll go check the main computer then I'll be right with you."
She nodded. "Okay."
Kal pulled her close and kissed her forehead then her lips ever so softly.
"Kal?"
He pulled her into another kiss though this time deepening it.
"Be right with you."
Diana's heart fluttered.

She'd made clear her feelings but why was it so hard for Steve to accept and understand? She'd never thought she would see such a side of him. Every day Diana realizes that although the world has changed, there are still those set in old ways. There are still those who will project their selfishness to guilt trip for others to bow down to their wants. Why should she feel guilty for who she loves and wants to be with?

There's no selfishness in her happiness and being with the man that is equally happy with her.

THE DARK SPELL

"Athena's Wisdom."

Diana stepped into her quarters and sighed walking towards the bed. She sat on the edge and hugged herself. His cruel words replayed in her mind.

"How could he say that?" Diana questioned out loud.

"Di?"

She looked up to see Kal at the door. He came in, the door sliding back closed.

"I finished the programming and I think the system is back up and normal again. Still not sure what caused the breach but Vic can probably handle that better now."

Diana stood up and embraced him.

"Diana..."

She held him tighter. Kal sighed, kissing the crown of her head, and embraced her back even tighter.

"I know you heard everything. I'm so sorry."

"What do you have to apologize for?"

"What Steve said and insinuated was wrong. I never knew he would say such things."

"He was angry, Diana. Sometimes people say things out of anger they don't mean."

"How can that be?" She asked, looking up at him. "Even out of anger, it was something he's thought about."

"Well...yeah...maybe..." he sighed. "I don't know. It's over now. I meant what I said about you being happy, Diana. Whether you want to be with me or not, all that matters is your happiness. You don't know how worried I was when you were fighting Parasite. For you to use your God-power like that. I'm just glad you are okay. You are here with me."

Diana nodded. "Kal, I do want to be with you. That's all I want. There's nothing selfish or wrong about us and our love. I love you."

"That's right and I love you, too, Starshine," he beamed.

Diana smiled brightly as her heart fluttered again. She felt her face heat, loving when Kal would call her by sweet little nicknames.

"How about we finish what we were starting earlier?"

"Oh yes."

Kal smiled and captured her lips in a very deep kiss. They stood there for a moment. Hands running up and down each other's bodies. Tongues viciously circled each other. Deep and passionate. They both moaned into each other's mouths. Whenever he'd slide his tongue into her mouth, her whole body would relax and she'd feel a pleasant warmth forming between her legs.

His hands moved to her hips, lifting her, and Diana wrapped her legs around his waist as he laid her down on the bed. He pushed her up the middle then sat up smiling.

He took off her boots, throwing them behind him making Diana laugh.

He kissed and licked his way up her legs, kissing her inner thighs.

"Oh, Kal..."

When he got to her center, he didn't even bother slipping off the blue leather bottom of her uniform. He bunched them up and pulled her boy shorts down her legs. He rolled the shorts into a ball in his palm and inhaled it like some kind of aroma. Undoubtedly it smelled like her. He kissed the piece of cloth and threw it over his shoulder. Diana rubbed her thighs together in response. His finger feather touched her inner thighs and split her legs apart, he could see the sweet nectar already beginning to ooze out of her. He continued rubbing her inner thighs and he inhaled her thick aroma in his lungs as much as possible.

His hot breath made her twitch in response, she murmured, "Kal.."

He bunched the skirt up and kissed the skin in his expanse. He marked her thighs back to back with his skillful mouth, first kissing it deeply, biting the same spot hardly, and followed by gently licking the area as he marched up and up until he has near her core.

He deeply inhaled her aroma again and locked her legs over her shoulder.

His tongue snuck out and licked her smooth and puffy labia. Diana jerked at the first contact.

"Sweetheart, relax," he looked in her eyes and gave her one long, full lick, parting her lips into what looked like the most beautiful flower he had ever seen.

"I thought I..." she trailed off with a moan.

THE DARK SPELL

He pulled her more to his face by her hips and buried his head between her legs. She tasted like pure honey. So sweet and pungent and very wet. His tongue lapped up and down both sides of her labia and up and over the top of her hood. His tongue darted into her opening, in and out, in and out, then from bottom to top.

"I told you...I'm taking care of you..." he said raising off her, a glistening strand of saliva clinging between her lips and his lips.

"Oh...Ah...!"

Diana reached down, her thighs shaking, clit throbbing, and gripped his hair, pulling him against her without shame. Kal sucked, nibbled, slurped.

It felt so good, it was like she was melting in his mouth. Each movement of his tongue made her thighs shake. He began a pattern of swirling his tongue around her clit, pushing it, and then sucking.

"Ah!" She wasn't going to last long. She could feel him breathing heavily against her womanhood, his chin pressed tightly against her entrance as he licked and licked. She finally completely tensed up before shaking violently, her thighs pressing to his cheeks, her toes curling and he licked her through it.

Kal turned them upside down and all of a sudden, Diana found herself sitting upright with Kal now below her. He had planted her womanhood square on his face, effectively pinning him to the bed.

"Ride my face, Diana," he said boldly.

Diana looked down at him, with a seductive smirk, her eyes were half-closed. "Is this what you had in mind, naughty man?" She cooed, lowering her sweet honey box to his lips and he tongued her swollen, open flower.

"Mmhmm..." was all he could manage as he swallowed a big gulp of her juices. He continued to alternate tonguing her opening and flicking his tongue back and forth across her clit, as the aftermath of her first orgasm ran down his neck.

Slowly, with long, wet strokes as he softly nuzzled her clit with his nose. He goes more and more firmly and at the end of each stroke, gives a sweet circle with his tongue on her clit.

Diana grabbed his head with her hands, yanking it forward, and started to grind her womanhood in his face, working her hips and thrusting, wining, bucking, and grinding.

Kal responded readily, sucking deep into her, greedily, licking and sucking and slurping. He drove his tongue like a shaft into her, giving her the tonguing of her life. He drew back a little and sucked long and deep on her clit until she started to arch her back and push it hard at him. Kal returned to the tonguing and sucked deeply, calling for her juices.

As he plunged his tongue back inside, she rode herself to another orgasm on his tongue and rubbed her clit against his nose.

As he licked her wet slit up and down, in rhythm with her softly undulating hips, he felt her hips pressing down, consuming his tongue even more. He was trying to take as much of her delicious juice into his mouth as possible.

Her thick thighs tightened around his head. Kal was in heaven. He hungrily licked and sucked her womanhood. He felt her body jump as he sucked. She ground her center on his face as he sucked and licked harder. He grabbed her thighs and pulled her impossibly closer, smothering his face. Her body started to buck as she breathed heavily.

Kal rose higher to the occasion and responded to her grinds and thrusts with both lips and tongue. The harder Diana pushed the more vigorously he responded. From somewhere deep inside of her, Diana felt a pressure building like never before. Every nerve was tingling and she was losing control over her body as if some smoldering volcano within her was rapidly coming to life.

Little moans were escaping her lips every time his tongue came in contact with her hotspots. His tongue flicked and swirled around her clit, assaulting her with pressure variations and motions.

"You're so good to me! Yes!"

Diana tried holding it back making the moment last as long as she could as this Niagara-like force built up within her, ready to explode. She knew she had passed the point of no return with no ability to control what would happen next.

She was panting and rocking her hips over him, moans of sweet torment were coming from her lips as she went completely still before spasming over him from her orgasm. She screamed as she exploded a raging river into his mouth. He responded in a flash almost in anticipation of her body's demands. His mouth spread wide and pressed tight over her slit and his hands grabbed her as holding her tight to his willing face. Her climax came pouring out, ready to be lapped up by him.

"Oh, Beloved! Oh, Gods!"

He loved hearing her moans and screams, loved her taste, loved everything about this. The way she would stiffen and quiver, a quiet, tender moan of pleasure emanating from her each time he lightly passed along the side of her clit with his tongue, her soft reactions slowly giving way to a loud, frantic cadence of shorter and shorter bursts until her breath caught as if she were dying. He knew to go extra slow and gently lick right over the hood of her clit with a flat tongue as she began to orgasm, which would assuredly drive her over the edge into pure ecstasy. It seems to be coming from deeper inside her. It builds slowly but relentlessly, filling her whole body with a fierce, engulfing pleasure.

Kal was locked into the most beautiful task he had ever been given the privilege of completing. He loved bringing her to orgasms with his tongue. Nothing turns him on more than that moment when her climax is all-consuming and her need for release removes all rational and petty thoughts from her mind.

She continued thrusting her pelvis up and down into his face for her own pleasure and needs, and it was a pure delight to him. Diana repeated this motion a couple of times as she moaned softly and the juices began to flow onto his face, all over his lips and cheeks. As he reached her clitoris for the umpteenth time, he gently sucked it into his mouth and swirled his tongue around it. She gasped and maneuvered his tongue into her soaking slit by raising her torso, wiggling her hips side to side, driving his tongue deep into her delicious womanhood, just in time to trigger her mouth filling spasm.

Diana must have done this several times but she lost count as her entire body and mind were engulfed by a tidal wave after a tidal wave of pleasure.

She so deserved this attention. She had the power of a Queen as she took out her raw carnal desires on him. Her hips would slow down, grinding in a circular motion every once in a while, then back to business, then pause, commanding him to suck her clit as she drove his head into the mattress, then start again humping his face. This drove her over the edge and he felt her body tense up as she grabbed his hair tighter.

"Oh yes!" she breathed, "Oh, Love, keep going..."

Kal licked harder and her movements became more frenzied.

"Oh please, don't stop!"

With Diana bouncing slightly up and down on his tongue, he sucked directly on her clit and she started screaming.

A few deep breaths and, "OH GODS!" Later, she gushed all over his face as she fell down on him. Her thrusts got slower and slower as the orgasm echoed throughout her entire body. Once she stopped shaking, she sat there for a good minute letting him continue to lick her gently. Her orgasm subsided and she rolled off. Kal was covered in her lust and she was trying to catch her breath. Kal sat up and watched her breathe. Her chest rising and falling and with one deep breath she sat up on her elbows with a satisfied grin.

Kal grinned back and wink as he stripped her and himself of their uniforms. He looked at her, taking in her gorgeous naked body.

"You are just too beautiful, Di."

"Thank you, Belov-" she gasped as he placed his mouth to her womanhood again, cleaning her up.

Diana laid back on her back as he softly continued to tongue-wash her sweetly and slowly.

"Kal..." her eyes rolled into the back of her head and she bit her lip. "You greedy...greedy man."

She arched her back still breathing a bit heavily and wondering what it was that came over him. Though, whatever it was, it was fantastic.

When he finally came up to kiss her, his face was drenched in her juices.

Kal wrapped his arms around Diana pulling her close and rolling over slightly for them to lay on their sides. He lifted her left leg and put his right leg between her legs, pressing his manhood gently against her center. Diana looked him straight in the eyes and they stayed that way for a few seconds. Diana let out a low gasp as he slowly pushed just barely inside of her.

They both moaned out feeling every inch of his hardness settling into her. Kal couldn't help but run his hands down her back all the way to her ass. He grabbed a handful and squeezed, pulling her tightly against his body as he was thrusting upward into her, keeping his slow steady rhythm.

"Oh, gods..."

"Diana."

She cupped his face and smiled before kissing him sweetly.

They held each other strongly and the moment was loaded with kisses and strokes.

Diana loved the feeling of Kal so close during their lovemaking, and him holding her, pressing her against him always gets her off.

They continued rocking steadily in sync devouring each other, lost in passionate kisses.

2 days later.... The Embassy

Diana happily hummed as she was walking to her office.

"Good Morning, Diana!" Councilwoman Phyllis Davenport greeted with a smile.

"Good Morning, Phyllis! How are you?"

"Oh, I'm fine. Another busy busy week but managing. And you? Seems you are glowing. It's a fair guess of that fine young man Clark Kent."

Diana smiled wider. "Yes. He is such a gentleman."

Phyllis smiled and nodded. "I know that smile and feel. I've had it for 30 years and counting. Good men are a rarity these days. We lucked out, girl."

Diana laughed softly.

"I'm sure he will be accompanying you at upcoming events."

"Yes, he will."

"Fabulous! Our men can get acquainted. I'm sure they'll be the best of buds!" Phyllis looked at her phone as it started buzzing. "Oh, I can't catch much of a break for more than 30 minutes. I must get going, Diana. Talk later!"

Diana nodded. "I understand. I have lots of papers on my desk to get to. Talk with you later, Phyllis."

As Diana walked into her office, her phone started to ring. She grinned answering.

"Hey, Love! I was just talking about you to Phyllis."

"Hey, Gorgeous. Phyllis? Uh... Davenport, right?"

"Yes, her. She said that I was glowing and already knew it was because of you."

"Ha! Wow! Have we made it that obvious already?"

"Yes, we have." Diana then placed her head on her head and let out a low groan.

"What's wrong?"

"I'm still feeling a bit lightheaded and nauseous."

"It's been a few days, Di. Was it because of using your power?"

"It comes and goes. No, It wasn't because of the use of my power. It was before that. It might have been the wine from back home. It is not the same as in man's world. It's much more potent. I hadn't had any in a while."

Dionysus had raised Pinot Noir and Chardonnay to a divine level. It was a special harvest straight from Dionysus' vineyards. Seedlings were given to the amazons as a gift and they made the wine in a special ritual, kneading the grapes naked, under the full moon, and singing to the god himself.

"Oh, yeah, your mother did mention how the first time you drank it, you were dancing and singing on top of the table and were challenging the amazons to fight."

Diana gasped then groaned embarrassed, putting her head on her desk. "My mother did not tell you that?!"

Kal laughed. "Yep. She sure did. That's payback for Ma showing you my baby pictures."

"But you were an adorable baby, Kal."

"Di..."

She laughed. "You were and you still are. I'll go to Hessia, Friday. I don't think there's anything major to worry about. I just won't drink as much next time."

"Alright, Di. I-"

"Hey, CK, is that Diana?" Jimmy asked. "Tell her I said hi. Let me talk to her."

"No, Jimmy she has to go."

Diana laughed. "Oh, Clark. Let me just say hi."

Clark sighed, giving Jimmy the phone.

"Hey, Diana! How are you?"

THE DARK SPELL

"Hello, James. I'm fine. And you?"

"Much better now hearing your beautiful voice. I see why CK is head over heels for you. You just don't know how much CK talks about you every 5 min-"

"Ok. We need to get back to work. Don't you have some pictures that need to be uploaded, Jim?"

"Yeah...yeah...anyway... bye, Diana!"

"Bye, James."

"He was seriously trying to flirt with you in front of me?!"

Diana laughed. "Oh, Clark, you two are so funny! And you talk about me every 5 minutes?"

"Well...I mean... yeah... I... Diana, every moment, I'm thinking about you."

"I'm thinking about you, too, Beloved."

"I love you, Diana."

"I love you, too, Kal."

"I'll see you at home. We'll cook dinner together."

"You mean making a mess with food all over us."

"The fun part is making a mess and the cleaning."

"Mmmhh...my sexy Kryptonian covered with cheese and pasta sauce. Dessert...Junior covered with whipped cream."

"Can't wait for my strawberries and peaches."

"Oooh...Gods, Kal. I can't wait."

"Me neither, Starshine. See you soon."

Hanging up, Diana squealed and leaned back in her chair.

No one could take this feeling of pure happiness away.

Two days later...Friday

Diana walked into Hessia's Dojo.

"Little Goddess!" Hessia said, embracing Diana.

"Hessia, I have so much to tell you!" Diana said, embracing her back.

"Just in time. I have about an hour and a half before my next class. Let's go to my office."

Diana sat down in the chair and sighed.

"So how are things?"

"Amazing! It's been such a whirlwind for Kal and me. Moving in together, staying the weekends in Smallville and Themyscira. All the time we spent together it's been incredible!"

"I can see it all over your face. You have such a bright glow, Little Goddess. You've always had it but this is a different kind. Being in love does that. The succubus has left you two alone I presume?"

"She did try to meddle when we were in Smallville and Themyscira but she hasn't since we've been back."

"Well, that's good. Did you talk about feeling lightheaded and nauseous on the phone? Did you feel any of that today?"

"Not really. I think it's our wine of ours. Mother told Kal about my first time drinking it."

"Oh, I remember that time. You tired yourself out so much you slept for nearly 2 days."

Diana laughed.

"Hold still for just a moment. Quick body scan," Hessia said using the purple ray.

"I believe that's what it is. I didn't start feeling this way until then."

"Hm...?"

"What is it?"

"Well, it's not the wine. Your body is going through hormonal changes being so active with Clark."

Diana frowned, confused, and tilted her head. "I don't understand."

"Your activity is healthy...very healthy. Though..."

"Though, what?"

"Quite fruitful..."

Diana pondered for a moment then gasped.

"Little goddess? Diana?"

"Am I...with child?! Hessia?!"

"Calm down... calm down.....no...well not yet. If you hadn't come here today and well...it is within the time."

"I do want a child with Kal and I know he wants a child too, but it's not the right time. We've been so caught up in...each other, we didn't think much of it."

THE DARK SPELL

"I understand, Diana. I have just the thing that will help but you have to follow the instructions. I will be right back."

Diana nodded.

When Hessia left out, Diana took a deep breath.

"A child? Our child."

It was true that they were so caught up with lovemaking, they didn't think beyond that a pregnancy could occur so soon.

She thought for a moment if it was to be, how would she have told Kal? There was no doubt how overjoyed he would be. Right now, though, was just not the time. But when it is their right time, she couldn't wait for that chapter of their journey together.

"Alright, Little Goddess, I have this for you." Hessia handed her a small bottle. "It's a mixture of herbs: hibiscus, ginger, wild carrot, lemon, and honey. Make a cup of tea and add a tablespoon of this every morning. Start fresh in the morning. Now the taste may be a little tart at first but just add sugar for a little sweetness and you'll get used to it. You must not forget because if you do miss just one day, 9 months from now there will be a new little goddess or god around here."

"Thank you, Hessia." Diana embraced her.

"Say hello to Clark for me."

"I will."

1 hour later...Metropolis, Clark and Diana's apartment

Diana walked into the smell of slow-roasted tomato, garlic, and prawn spaghetti.

"Oh, Goodness! It smells incredible!" Diana said walking into the kitchen.

She smirked seeing Kal shirtless and in jersey shorts.

"Di!" Kal wiped his hands on a towel then grabbed Diana pulling her into a passionate kiss.

Diana wrapped her arms around his neck and deepened the kiss, moaning into his mouth.

"Coming home to you as this feels like the first time every time. I love it."

"I love it, too and you," Kal grinned. "How was your day? Visit with Hessia?"

"She said to tell you hello and well... how about we discuss what she said after dinner?"

Kal then frowned immediately worried. "Di? You're okay, right?"

"Yes, Love. It's nothing to worry about, it's just something I do have to do going forward, however."

He quirked his brow. Diana smiled reassuringly and kissed him.

"Darling, just wait. It's nothing bad at all."

"Alright, Di."

"I'll be right back. Shower, put on something comfortable, then enjoy this delicious dinner prepared by my man." Diana kissed him again before walking away.

Kal slapped her ass making her squeal and looked back over her shoulder.

"Naughty, Mr. Kent."

"Can't resist my peach," he winked.

Diana laughed walking to their bedroom.

Kal couldn't stop smiling as he finished up cooking.

15 minutes afterward, he set the table and put the finishing touches on their plates.

"Kal?"

He looked up then did a double-take and his jaw dropped.

"Damn. You look...wow..."

Diana smiled and walked over slowly toward him seductively.

She was wearing a baby pink thigh-length lace trim double split satin nightdress.

Wrapping her arms around his neck, she kissed him deeply. Kal immediately responded, wrapping his arms around her. His hands trailed down, squeezing her ass.

"Mmhmm...I just want to be in your arms all night."

"Most definitely. But first, dinner is served."

Kal pulled out her chair for her.

"Thank you, Love."

While eating they talked about the rest of their day. Clark had finally finished his cultural write-up for part of his column and Diana, a guest speaker at an academy.

THE DARK SPELL

"The children were lovely, Kal. They love the League. We should get the others to one day, visit the schools."

"That's a great idea. Why not do that more often going to schools. That would be good for all of us."

"Especially Billy. Though we may need to coordinate with him being in school. As much as he wants to act like he isn't 14, he is still 14."

"Yeah. Downloading a video game to a high-tech database he wasn't supposed to be definitely what a 14-year-old would do."

Diana laughed.

After dinner, Kal cleared the table and placed their plates in the sink.

Diana wrapped her arms around him from behind.

"Darling, let that be for the morning."

Kal turned and kissed her forehead. He lifted her and Diana instinctively placed her legs around his waist as he walked into the living room over to the sofa. He sat down with Diana straddling him.

"Ok..so..what is it you wanted to wait after dinner to tell me?"

"Well, she did a full body scan with the purple ray. She said that nothing is wrong, I'm completely healthy. We are very healthy with our...activities." Diana rubbed her hands down his chest.

Kal smirked. "Oh?"

"However...we are so active, I probably would've been with child by now..."

He laughed then paused just staring at her for a moment realizing the seriousness of what she said. "Di...?" He started to question. "Wait?! Are you?"

Diana shook her head. "Not yet."

"So more practice for us then," he smiled, giving her a gentle peck.

"I knew that would be your reaction. But are you disappointed?"

"Huh? No. Why would I be? I mean we aren't ready just yet. We need to get ourselves a bit more established and balance civilian and heroic work but if we had a little surprise in the oven, we would adjust and I'd be shouting out to the world how happy I am! Diana, I love you. I want all of that with you but only if you want it when the time comes."

Diana beamed and cupped his face with both hands. By the Gods, she wanted to give him a child right then.

"I love you, too. When that time comes, we will take that step. Right now, I've been instructed to take herbal tea every morning and we can resume our activities as normal."

"We can handle that. Just let me know what else you need, Di. Whatever you want. I'm right here with you with any and everything."

"All I need and want I have right here. You holding me."

Kal smiled proudly. The rise and fall of Diana's chest filled his heart with adoration. He couldn't help but bring a hand up to rest on her cheek with all his attention focused on her lips and it wasn't long before he found himself leaning in towards her. With a slow sensual slide of her tongue across her lush, full lips, Diana watched his blue eyes darkened and before Diana knew it, he captured lips with his own so tenderly.

Diana trailed one of her fingers down Kal's jaw. Her other hand ran a hand down his chest and Kal opened his mouth, biting down lightly on Diana's lower lip. Diana gasped into his mouth, causing Kal to smile.

Suddenly, Diana deepened the kiss even further, pressing into Kal so they were chest-to-chest and poking her tongue into her lover's mouth. They were gasping for breath against each other, teeth and tongues clashing together. Kal ran his hands through Diana's long soft hair and Diana stroked her hands down Kal's massively strong arms.

Kal felt Diana continuing to run her hands over his body and he couldn't help but mumble her name quietly into the kiss. That was when Diana broke it and just stared into his eyes. She was breathing heavily and Kal felt each and every one of her breaths against his lips. Her closeness to him was driving him crazy with lust.

Diana ended up closing the gap between them and their lips crashed together again in a soul-shattering kiss.

After what felt like hours of kissing and roaming hands, they pulled away at the same time, gasping for breath. Kal trailed a hand down Diana's flushed face. Diana trailed her fingers down Kal's chest, smiling.

"I love you, Kal. You are such an amazing man and so good to me," she whispered softly cupping his face with both hands and kissing him all over his face.

THE DARK SPELL

"I'll do anything and everything for my gorgeous Starshine, my Moon," he whispered back. He pulled Diana's hand off his face and kissed her knuckles lightly. "It goes without saying that I love you too. Always."

A week had passed, Diana had gotten used to her morning routine to make her cup of tea, even Kal learned how to make it for her having it ready after her morning shower.

Diana sighed walking into the kitchen.

"Thank you, Love," she said picking up her mug taking a sip.

Kal smiled placing his arms around her from behind and kissed her neck. "Breakfast is almost ready."

"Hmm...you spoil me."

"Of course. It's my job." He kissed her neck again. "Are you okay with taking this?"

"The tea? Yes. I mean...I have to."

"You don't have to."

Diana put her mug down and turned in his arm giving him a confused, curious look.

"Kal, If I don't I'll-"

"I know, Di. But I just don't want you to be uncomfortable or feel like you have to do this because of me."

Diana laughed softly. "You know, making a baby does take two. This is for both of us, Kal. I'm taking what other women would take, but more herbal-based. This is our normal. Are you okay with it?"

"As long as you are. That's what matters to me." He cupped her cheek. "I guess I'm just worried or overthinking because I've never been in a serious relationship like this."

"I haven't either, Kal. But we are learning together. It's not easy. Not supposed to be. But we are going through this together."

"I love you, Diana. So much."

"I love you, too, Kal-El."

Diana kissed him softly. Kal immediately deepened the kiss lifting her.

"Hour and a half before heading out?"

"Mmhmm..."

2 hours later...WatchTower

The WatchTower was currently unoccupied.

BOOK BANK PUBLISHING

File downloading...
SECURITY DOWN
File download complete
File uploading...
AUTHORIZATION VOICE OVERRIDE
AUTHORIZATION CODE OVERRIDE
File upload complete.
SECURITY BACK ONLINE

Location: Daily Planet

Clark Kent walked back to his desk after he met with Perry.

"So what did Perry say?" Lois asked as she turned in Clark's chair.

"Lois? What are you doing at my desk?"

She shrugged. "I'm thinking maybe we could switch. This spot is better and a bit cozy."

"No. Unlike you or Cat, I like the little privacy I can get. It's enough having both of you and Jimmy hanging over me."

"What? Do you want alone time to have phone sex with your girlfriend now that you don't have to with your computer? I can't believe a big oaf loner like you have a girlfriend let alone she being Diana Prince."

"Lois, just because I don't go to happy hour or I don't tell every move I make doesn't mean I don't have a life outside this office. It's called a private life for a reason."

"I'm just saying Diana seems much more high class. She's a very sophisticated woman much like myself."

"She is sophisticated but she doesn't care for big luxuries and-" Clark paused and sighed. "Never mind. I don't have to explain anything to you or anyone, Lois. I thought that maybe you'd be happy for me to know I have someone since you seemed to care so much before."

Lois looked at him shocked. "Wow. Now that you have a girlfriend you got a backbone. Well, at least you have that going for you."

"Hey, guys! Hey!" Jimmy said. "Look at this!" Jimmy showed them his tablet.

"What the hell?! That should've been our story to break!"

Clark's heart dropped to his feet.

"I knew it! Superman and Wonder Woman getting it on!"

THE DARK SPELL

"Don't be immature, Olsen!" Lois said annoyed.

Jimmy snickered. "Sorry, Lois. I know you had a crush on, Supes."

"Wrong! Superman had a crush on me."

Clark's phone buzzed, Bruce, is calling.

"Yeah?"

"WatchTower. Now."

He hung up before Clark could say anything.

Clark quickly packed his laptop and gathered everything.

"Where are you going?" Lois asked.

"Follow up for a column," Clark answered walking to the elevator.

Lois frowned then shrugged. "He is one strange man."

Location: The Embassy

Diana's heart raced walking out of the Embassy. "By the Gods..."

"Diana!" Donna called running towards her. "Did you see the news?! That picture!"

Diana sighed. "I just saw it. Keep your voice down."

"How the hell was that picture even taken? And you too definitely were into it, though. Wow..."

"Please, don't say it, Donna."

"What? You and Clark getting frisky right outside the WatchTower?"

"I said don't. It's just a kiss."

"A very hot and heavy steamy kiss and him grabbing your ass like that. Yeah, I can see why he wants to-" Donna's eyes grew wide stopping herself.

"Wants to what?" Diana asked with a raised brow.

Donna laughed nervously. "Don't make that face, Diana. I was going to say he...he wants to be with you all the time."

Diana narrowed her eyes a bit still not believing her.

"What?"

"You've been acting strangely for the past 2 weeks."

"What? No...no..." Donna shook her head.

"Donna?"

"Diana."

"Fine. I'll just-" suddenly Diana's phone rang. She immediately answered. "Kal!"

Donna sighed relieved. "Nice save, Big Brother," she thought.

247

"I'm fine. I'm just shocked...okay...I'm on my way. Love you, too."

"Go! Go!" Donna said pushing Diana.

"We're not done."

"Diana, I told you. It's nothing. I'll talk with you later! Tell Clark I said hi!"

Diana huffed. "If you say so and I will. Bye, Donna." She flew off heading to the WatchTower.

Location: WatchTower

Welcome Wonder Woman

As Diana was walking to the hub she heard loud voices.

"How the hell could this happen, Bruce?! First some kind of shut down, breach, now this?"

"No one told you two to be right in front of the damn Tower camera!"

"It shouldn't matter. I told you to check the damn security. Do you think I wanted this to get out like this? Diana and I are already out publicly as civilians. It feels like even that should've been kept to ourselves. Now Superman and Wonder Woman will cause much more media frenzy. That's not what was supposed to happen."

"I warned you."

"You cared more about the League, not our privacy."

Diana's heart sank hearing how angry Kal was. She understood given their supposed private moment was now shared with the entire world but...it seemed there was something else. Was he now ashamed of their relationship? Was Superman and Wonder Woman together too taboo and to be kept secret but for how long?

She took a deep breath and walked in.

"Kal-El. Bruce. What happened?"

"Hey," Kal said and kissed her temple. "The attempted breach from a few days ago...whoever tried seemed to have been successful and leaked the photo," Kal explained.

"There's no lead to finding who did this," Bruce said.

"I see. Well, I believe Kal and I should address this before it gets even more out of hand."

"That's not a good idea."

"Why not, Bruce?"

THE DARK SPELL

"The photo came from here. You two speaking so soon would be like a publicity stunt."

"That's not how this is. It would be much better for Diana and I to at least let the public know the rest of the League isn't involved."

"Us not speaking will only fuel the gossip."

"No. You both know anything said will get misinterpreted."

Kal sighed. "We need to figure out what happened to the system."

"I've gone through everything. Cyborg did, too. It was no more than five minutes when this breach occurred. But no one was here. Even if it was some kind of invisible cloaking, it would've been detected."

"So you are saying someone did this remotely?" Diana asked. "It still doesn't make any sense because who could've known there was a photo? This was a premeditated plan."

"Let's...let's just go home. It's too much so fast right now. We'll think of what will be better to do next."

"Are you sure, Kal?"

"Yeah..."

Kal took Diana's hand. "If you get anything, Bruce. Just let us know."

"Seriously putting me in the middle of your relationship scandal?"

"Weren't you trying to put the entire League in the middle of it to guilt trip us for what was between just us in the first place?"

Bruce narrowed his eyes then turned to the computer. "Go."

Kal and Diana left out.

"Kal?"

"I don't know what's to gain with this. Worst, what if whoever did this has other confidential stuff."

"It seems like outing us being together was the main goal."

"That doesn't make sense, Di. I mean that's something you would expect to be news in a gossip column. Cat surely would love the story. This seems like some other kind of motive."

"Our relationship is the first target to a bigger attack on the League. It's a childish game."

"We'll figure it out before anything else gets out. We don't need any of that."

The rest of the flight home was quiet. Kal went to the kitchen to try to find something to cook for dinner.

Diana went to the bedroom to take a shower.

Kal sighed, closed the refrigerator, and walked into the bedroom. Walking in, Kal saw Diana was completely naked about to go into the bathroom.

"Hey..." Kal grabbed her by her waist from behind pulling her back. "You okay?"

"I should ask you that?"

"It's a surprise. I mean I didn't want our relationship coming out seeming like a publicity stunt or scandal."

"So you feel that going out together as even Clark Kent and Diana Prince is for publicity?"

"What? No. Why do you think that?"

"I overheard you and Bruce before I walked in. You said that even as Clark and Diana, our relationship should've been kept secret. Now with Superman and Wonder Woman public, it will only cause more media frenzy."

"Di..." he turned her around.

"Are you now ashamed of us?" she asked.

"What?! Di, no. No way in hell would I be ashamed of being with the most Gorgeous woman in the world....no universe! The woman that has been by my side through so much. My best friend, my Starshine, my Moon." Kal cupped her cheeks with both hands. "I'm so sorry for making you feel that way. I'm so, so sorry. It was such a shock seeing one of our private moments blasted like this. It was to be our choice. We are supposed to be in control and take our time. But before all this..."

"What? What happened?"

"Lois was talking about us. Well, I guess it was some kind of backhanded compliment of me having a girlfriend. But specifically you. She's surprised about us being together because she figured you wanted someone more of your league."

"What does that mean?"

"I'm not a businessman nor a politician. I'm just a reporter...a farm boy."

THE DARK SPELL

"I don't care for a business man or politician. Do you believe that's all you are?"

"No, but-"

"I fell in love with every part of what makes you the man you are. The farm boy, the reporter, the man from beyond the stars. You give me so much love and respect. How can I not love you?"

Kal sighed then smiled sympathetically. "I'm sorry, Diana." He kissed her all over her face then captured her lips softly. "It seems so much wants to come at us. I don't want the outside to try to taint what we have that's all I mean."

"That will never happen, Love."

"Clark Kent and Diana Prince. Superman and Wonder Woman. Together."

Diana smiled. "Will you join me in the shower?"

"Not even a question that needs to be asked."

Diana bit her lip seductively, took his hand, and pulled him into the bathroom.

The next day...

Superman and Wonder Woman flew off to the amusement park. One of the very popular rides had malfunctioned. Passengers were stuck upside down at the highest point.

"Diana, you get the passengers, I'll see what's wrong with the track."

She nodded and flew off ahead of him.

Superman then heard a creaking noise. A quick scan. The foundation was weakening and only a matter of time before it would collapse.

"Wonder Woman, the weight of the passengers is causing it to become even more unstable."

"Got it." Wonder Woman quickly flew to the passengers.

"Wonder Woman!"

"I'm going to get all of you out as quickly as possible."

Wonder Woman pulled the lap bar up and caught two passengers.

She flew down to the ground with them. Setting them down she smiled and nodded then flew back up.

"I'm Cat Grant from the Daily Planet. We're live at Metropolis Amusement Park where passengers are stuck upside on one of the park's most popular and oldest rides, the Turner Twister. Luckily, Superman and Wonder Woman are here."

Meanwhile, Superman was trying to figure out what happened.

"Hmm...?"

He touched a support pole and saw a scorch mark and light crack. There has been a storm a few days ago. It was possibly struck by lightning that caused the malfunction and the foundation damage. Using his heat vision, he sealed the crack however that still didn't seem like enough. The creaking noise was getting louder and the ride started to sway on its own.

"Wonder Woman?"

"5 more."

The roller coaster was starting to lean backward. The passengers screamed and started panicking to get out.

"Hold still, please. I have you. I promise."

Wonder Woman eased the lap bar. 3 passengers this time latched on to her.

"It's alright."

She flew down.

"Wonder Woman! My sons are still up there! Oh, I shouldn't have let them go!"

"I have them. What are their names?"

"Jeremiah is the oldest and Mason, the youngest."

Wonder Woman nodded and smiled reassuringly. "They will be safe with you momentarily."

Wonder Woman flew to Jeremiah and Mason.

"Hi, Jeremiah, Mason" Wonder Woman said.

"Wonder Woman...Wow!" Jeremiah blushed.

"You know our names?" Mason asked.

"You're Mother told me. She's waiting for you both."

The ride started creaking more and leaned back more. Jeremiah's lap bar unlocked and went up quickly. Wonder Woman quickly grabbed him. He looked up at her still with heart eyes and blushing.

The ride was still leaning back. Superman was trying to keep it held up and fix the supporting poles.

"You two hang on. We're going to help Superman."

THE DARK SPELL

"Cool!" Mason said

With Mason on her back with his arms around her neck and Jeremiah with his arms around her waist, she flew up using her lasso, hooking the railing and pulling it upright.

"Superman, hurry!"

He quickly flew around using his heat vision to seal the poles.

Superman flew up to Wonder Woman with a smile.

"Thanks for helping us out, Kiddos!"

"This is so much better than the ride!" Mason said happily.

"Wonder Woman's the greatest!" Jeremiah sighed with a smile hugging her waist tighter.

Superman quirked his brow then chuckled.

"Oh, sorry, Superman," Jeremiah said.

"It's alright, kid!" He laughed again.

Wonder Woman giggled. "Let's get you back to your mother, boys."

Superman and Wonder Woman flew down.

"Boys! Oh, I'm so glad you're okay!"

"Course, Mom!" They said in unison.

"Did you see, Mom?! We flew with Wonder Woman!" Mason said jumping up and down.

"Superman! Wonder Woman! You know me, Cat Grant."

"Hello, Ms. Grant," Superman said.

Cat instantly felt flustered. "Why Superman you can just stand there and still charm a girl. Now, we must know...is it true? Are you two an item? Was that photo real?!"

Superman and Wonder Woman glanced at each other.

"We-" Wonder Woman started.

"Are..." Superman finished with a proud smile.

Wonder Woman looked at him shocked. He winked and she couldn't help but smile back.

"Over the years, Superman and I have forged quite the partnership that has evolved."

"Oh my God!" Cat squealed. "Okay...okay..." Cat tried to keep her composure but she was so excited with this breaking news. "You heard it here first! Superman and Wonder Woman have confirmed the swirling years of rumors and speculation, this is the super romance of the ages!"

The crowd started to mumble and cheer.

"Kiss her, Superman!" Mason said.

"Yeah! Kiss her!" Jeremiah agreed. "Kiss her! Kiss her! Kiss her!" He started to chant.

"Kiss her! Kiss her! Kiss her!" The crowd started chanting and growing with more people.

Superman looked back at Wonder Woman. She smirked.

Superman wrapped his arms around her pulled her close capturing her lips in a searing passionate kiss.

The crowd roared with cheers.

"And there we have it! A super kiss to seal the deal!"

Location: At A.R.G.U.S

"Turn it off," Steve said lowly.

"What, Sir?"

"I said turn it off!" He yelled and stormed out of the room.

Location: WatchTower

"Wow...they really... am I seeing this right?" Green Lantern laughed surprised. "I mean good for them."

"Yeah, it's deserved."

"Now they don't have to be all sneaky flirty...wait?!" Shazam slouched in his chair. "Ugh! No! No! Now it's gonna get worse! They are going to be flirting more! I can't win with this! It's like parents getting all sappy weird!"

"What do you think, Bruce?" Flash asked.

Batman remained silent.

"Bruce?"

"They'll have to deal with the repercussions on their own with this broadcast."

Barry rolled his eyes. "We're already in the spotlight. Just let them be happy."

"Hm."

"I'm happy for them," Barry smiled looking up at the screen. "Always knew they'll be together. Won't be surprised if Big Blue pops the question."

Location: Valeria's Castle

THE DARK SPELL

"Oh...so the two have already adapted to the attention," Strife said.

"The mortals are doing what they do best. With every new little plaything they are happy for and praise but soon they will turn into the nasty creatures they are."

"A sprinkle of doubt goes a long way. The little civil war amongst them is quite entertaining. So shall we start the next phase?"

"Well, of course."

Later that night...Clark and Diana's apartment

Kal and Diana were in bed. After a long tiring day, Diana was fast asleep. Kal laid on his side with his head propped in one hand with his other hand running along slowly up and down Diana's side. He leaned over and kissed her lips softly.

He couldn't stop staring at her. She was so beautiful it was so surreal. He kissed her lips softly again.

Then he heard a soft melody as if something was ringing.

He eased out of bed and walked over to his laptop bag. He quickly went into the living room with it and took out the gemstone communicator given to him by Hippolyta.

A hologram of Hippolyta appeared.

"Hippolyta? Hi!"

"Kal-El."

"Um...one sec..." He flew into the room to put on a shirt then came back. "Sorry about that. Is there anything wrong?"

"You and my daughter have made the news."

Kal chuckled nervously. "How did you know so fast?"

"Fellow sisters are traveling, Dear. Word gets back rather quickly."

"Oh...ha! Well, that wasn't our doing. Someone got ahold of security footage from the Justice League Watchtower. We still don't know who."

"I'm sure you will find them. When you do, I would like a word with them as well."

"Don't worry, Hippolyta, I'll handle it. But then again, Diana will be sure whoever it was will have plenty of regrets, wishing they'd never even thought to do that."

"As she should."

"I know that part of Diana is happier now, though. Our relationship is completely public. Diana is all about living out the whole truth and that's what we are going to do."

"Have you decided on more plans for your proposal?"

"I would like for there to be four ceremonies. Clark and Diana, Superman and Wonder Woman, Kryptonian, and Amazonian culture ceremonies. I feel that's only right for us."

"Oh, that will be quite lovely!"

"Queen Hippolyta, your daughter deserves so much. She is so special not just to us but to the world. I want this to be unforgettable."

"It shall be, Kal-El."

Kal heard Diana moving in bed, waking up.

"Diana might be waking up. I should get back to her."

"Alright, we will speak again soon."

"Right, um...Queen Hippolyta?"

"Yes, Kal-El?"

"I know I keep saying it and I will continue to do so because I truly love Diana. Thank you for trusting me, for accepting me."

"Kal-El, you've shown you are worthy of my daughter's heart. A man of honor, loyalty, and respect. You've kept your word so far."

"And I will continue to do so, Queen Hippolyta."

She smiled with a slight nod. "Have a good night, Dear."

"Have a good day, Hippolyta."

Once Hippolyta's hologram disappeared, Kal placed the communicator back in his bag. He went back into the bedroom putting his bag back and took off his shirt, easing back in bed.

"Kal?" Diana mumbled. "Is everything alright? Who was that?"

"It was my laptop. Just checking up on something."

"Hmm...Darling, work can wait. Stay in bed."

Kal chuckled and kissed her cheek and lips.

"I'm not going anywhere, Di."

He wrapped his arms around her and pulled her to him. He adjusted himself rolling over on his back and pulled Diana to lay on top of him.

"I love you, Di."

THE DARK SPELL

He kissed the top of her head and held her tighter, listening to her heartbeat as she slept.

3 days had passed, Superman and Wonder Woman were still the talk of the world though Clark Kent and Diana Prince were going about their days as normal by their definition as they could be.

Friday evening: Clark and Diana's apartment

Diana was standing staring down at the 3 dresses she had laying on the bed.

"Hmm...?" She pondered. "Don't overthink. It's just a dinner, Diana. But with Kal's friends and colleagues," she said to herself. "I can't be too overly dressed."

Her cellphone started ringing. She smiled picking it up.

"Hi, Love."

"Hey, Beautiful."

"Are you on your way home?"

"Not quite yet. Heading to a warehouse in Ohio with Barry and Bruce. Got a lead on Penguin and Ignatius Ogilvy."

"Oh? Bruce is actually letting you and Barry help with this case?"

"Ha!" Yeah it's outside of Gotham so, it's okay for now for us to tag along."

"It's also for Bruce to apologize for his childish behavior without actually saying it. He wants to spend time with you because ultimately you are his brother."

"Yeah, you're right."

"So should I put my dresses up? We might miss the dinner."

"I was thinking that you could go ahead and get there and I'll meet you."

"Are you sure, Kal?"

"Yeah! I'm sure Jimmy would more than happy to keep you company until I get there. Take my badge and the invitation card. You are on the list with me and just let whoever asks know I'll be there. You won't be there alone for long."

"Alright...."

"Wear the one with the slit. Uh... it looks shimmery."

Diana smiled. "Mr. Kent, now how did you know I was trying to figure out which dress to wear?"

"You mentioned picking a few out the other night. I took a peek. Knew you would be sort of indecisive."

Diana scuffed then laughed. "You don't know me," she teased.

"Oh, yes I do. Every part."

"That's why I love you."

"I love you, too, Di. I'll see you at the dinner."

"See you then, Love." Diana sighed putting her phone down to pick up the dress Kal chose and couldn't stop smiling. "Perfect."

3 hours later...8:30 PM. Metropolis Plaza Hotel

Diana Prince walked into the Plaza. She looked around to the ballroom where the dinner was held.

When, she saw Daily Planet employees with their badges, she followed along with them.

"Good Evening, Ms. Prince! Will you be speaking tonight?!" A hotel attendant asked.

"Good Evening and no, I won't be speaking. I'm just a guest with Clark Kent." Diana showed his badge.

"Oh, and Mr. Kent is?"

"On his way," Diana smiled.

The attendant smiled back and nodded. "Mr. Kent is table four."

"Thank you."

As Diana was walking to the table, she discreetly took note of the stares. She was just about to pull out her own chair when someone grabbed her chair and pulled it out for her. She looked up with a smile but quickly dropped.

"Oh, hello," she said to the man. "Thank you."

"You're Welcome. You are stunning. Name's Lombard...Steve. Editor of Daily Planet sports column."

"Hello, Lombard Steve." Diana raised her brow a bit.

"Haha! I meant Steve Lombard. You have a sense of humor, too. I'm liking you more and more, Ms. Prince."

There was a momentary awkward silence.

"I'm sure Clarkie boy has mentioned me."

"I'm sorry but no, he hasn't."

THE DARK SPELL

Steve frowned a bit. "Oh...well this is the perfect time for us to get aquai-"

"Diana! Oh, you're here!"

Diana smiled. "Hi, Catherine!"

"Oh please, it's just Cat! Where is Clark?"

"Yeah, that's what I want to know," Lois said walking up to them.

"Wow...Diana, you are just so...wow." Jimmy's jaw dropped.

"Close your mouth, Olsen, before you start drooling all over the floor."

"Hello, Lois, James."

"This is your table, Diana?" Jimmy asked.

"Yes, it is."

"Sweet! We have the same table. I'm sure Clark wouldn't mind me sitting here," Jimmy said.

"So Diana, where is Clark?" Lois asked.

"He had a few last-minute errands."

"Hm. So you came all the way here from Boston or London? How's this long-distance relationship working?"

"Actually I live here in Metropolis now with Clark."

"Oh...really?"

"I do most of my work from home anyway. I can conduct meetings and such through the computer or calls. If I do have to travel, I've gotten quite used to flying."

"So you two are really serious?"

"Yes, we are," Diana frowned slightly confused.

"Oh, I'm so happy for Clark! He seemed to just spend his time with work," Cat said.

"No offense, Diana, but Clark just seems so...I mean he is a nice guy and all but I wouldn't take a woman like you of your stature would be interested," Lois said blunted.

"Lois!" Cat said.

"I see. Well, Lois, it is not my place exactly because I respect Clark's privacy. What he does in his spare time doesn't have to be broadcasted. He is a kind gentleman and we have a lot in common actually. He is quite an interesting man getting to really know him."

"Interesting? Are we talking about Clark Kent?" Lois asked with her nose high.

"Yes, Clark Kent. As I said, Clark doesn't broadcast what he does and he doesn't have to. What we do together goes along with that as well. As my mother says, the heart sees more than the eyes, it sees beyond critical vision, it sees who the person really is."

"Oh...spicy! You've met your match, Lane," Cat teased.

"Shut it, Grant."

"Listen Diana I-"

"Hey, guys!" Clark said walking up.

"Clarkie boy! We we just getting all acquainted with your lovely lady," Steve smiled and shook his hand.

Clark quirked his brow. "Uh-huh."

Clark smiled seeing Diana as she winked at him.

"Clark, I'm so glad you are finally here!" Cat said hugging him.

"Uh..thanks, Cat. Lois, Jimmy."

"Sup, CK!" Jimmy high-fived.

"Smallville," Lois said dryly.

"Excuse me, guys." He took Diana's hand as she stood up. "You're beautiful."

"Thank you. Although, you did help pick it out."

Clark kissed her softly and whispered in her ear, "I'm going to enjoy taking it off you."

Diana's eyes went wide and giggled. "Naughty man..." she whispered back.

Clark cleared his throat. "I would like a moment alone with Diana."

"Go ahead, you two love birds!" Cat said.

Still holding hands, they walked away out to the hall.

"They are cute!" Cat squealed.

"Cute. Sure."

"I'll say Kent is one lucky son of a gun. A guy like him gets a girl like that? No way."

"Oh come on, he totally took some pointers from me!" Jimmy joked.

THE DARK SPELL

Cat rolled her eyes. "Olsen, you can't even last a week with a girl. Lois, stop being so negative and Steve, please. You are nothing like Clark with your sleazy ways."

"Who do you think you are, Grant?" Lois frowned.

"I'm being a supportive friend to Clark."

Outside in the hall

Clark wrapped his arms around Diana's waist and Diana's wrapped her arms around his neck.

Diana smiled, "Hey, Beloved."

"I hope I wasn't too long for it to be too awkward or 21 questions."

"It was a little bit but I handled it."

"I knew it. What was said?"

"It doesn't matter right now, Love. We can talk about it later. You are here now so let's just enjoy the dinner."

"Okay...okay..." Clark kissed her softly. "But when I get you home..."

Diana giggled against his lips and cupped his face with both hands kissing him again deepening the kiss.

Jimmy, Lois, Cat, and Steve were peeking from the room entrance door.

"Wow...Clark getting that action?" Steve questioned. "Well alright!" He cheered.

Cat was in awe. "Clark seems to actually be a very...very good kisser."

"So that's how he got her," Jimmy said. "I need to write this down."

"Kent might actually have moves...but still lacking."

"Don't be a hater, Lane."

Clark and Diana pulled away slightly from their passionate kiss.

"Thank you for being here with me, Di."

"Darling, of course. I wouldn't want to be anywhere else. You always have my support and I will always be right by your side."

Clark smiled proudly kissing the tip of her nose.

"Ah, Kent!"

Clark looked over to see Perry and his wife.

"Mr. White, Mrs. White."

"Good to see you, son!"

"You too, Sir." Clark shook his hand.

"My wife, Meredith," Perry introduced.

"Hello! And you are Ambassador Diana Prince! You are such a lovely gracious young woman."

Diana beamed. "Thank you very much, Mrs. White."

"You are also the one that has Kent practically walking on air coming into the office."

Diana looked up at Clark still smiling. "Oh, really?"

"I see it in his work. Kent has always been one of my top reporters but in these recent months, there's been a big boost of the drive."

"Well, Mr. White, I am very proud of Clark. But I can't take that credit. Clark is an extraordinarily passionate writer all on his own. Once he is focused and especially with stories that should be taken note of by the public, he gives his all with everything."

"I like her, Kent! I really like her!"

Back with Cat, Jimmy, Lois, and Steve...

"I really like her..." Lois mocked. "Ms. Perfect has to have some flaws."

"Ha!" Cat laughed. "You are so jealous."

"No, I'm not!" Lois snapped. "What's there to be jealous of?"

"Diana has every man in here about to have their eyes pop out. Usually, with these functions, it's you or me. Clark isn't alone now to tease him and flaunt some kind of popularity dominance. You can't make him feel bad for not having a date now."

"So that's why he is probably paying her."

"Desperate delusion doesn't suit you, Lane. Just face the fact that Clarkie has grown up. He isn't the shy boy we thought he was. Obviously, there's something more to him than he let on. But with her...it's like he is a totally different person in a good way."

"Whatever you say, Grant. But I know there's something up."

After a couple of hours of chatting, eating, and listening to a few speakers either try to be inspirational or be standup comedians, the dinner party was winding down.

Throughout the whole time, Clark couldn't take his eyes off her nor stop smiling with the proudest grin. He placed his hand on her thigh, running his hand up slowly.

THE DARK SPELL

Diana looked at him blushing. "Clark..." she whispered so softly only he could hear.

His hand trailed higher up the slit of her dress and his fingertips glided over her inner thigh and up a little further brushing ever so softly over her center.

Diana immediately let out a low gasp and looked at him with surprise.

Clark leaned over and kissed her cheek. "I have to get you home. You ready?"

"Oh..." Diana blushed more. "Yes, Beloved."

Clark smirked and took her hand.

"You two are leaving?" Jimmy asked.

"Yeah, I-"

"Clark wants to make sure I get enough sleep for the morning. I have a few meeting calls," Diana said.

"Oh, it was nice talking with you, Diana!" Jimmy smiled.

"Thank you, James," Diana smiled.

"Gosh..." Jimmy gushed. "CK, you really lucked out."

Clark wrapped his arms around Diana's waist. "Thanks, Jimmy."

"You two are so adorable! Diana, I hope we can have more girl's chats! Clark won't mind, right?" Cat asked.

"Oh of course not!"

"Great! We will set up a lunch date soon! Lois will join, right?"

Awkward silence.

"Lane?" Cat nudged her.

"What?"

"Girls time with Diana."

Lois raised her brow. "You've got to be kidding me. I have-"

"Good! Diana, whenever you are free!"

"I will let you know, Cat. Good night, everyone."

"Good night!" Jimmy and Cat said in unison.

Clark and Diana started walking away.

"Oh, Clark, we didn't say goodbye to Mr. White and his wife?"

Clark looked over seeing Perry engrossed in a conversation with other colleagues and shook his head.

"I'll see him Monday. If we talk, we'll be head for another 2 hours."

Diana giggled. "Okay." She latched on to his arm as they were walking out the Plaza. "Could we take a walk before going home?"

"Yeah, of course."

It was a cool breezy night. Diana looked up at the full moon and smiled.

"This is nice. The dinner was lovely," said Diana.

"It was but you made the night. All eyes were on you."

Diana blushed and laughed softly. "Kal, I didn't expect that at all. I mean I was just a guest."

"Diana, you light up every room you walk into."

"Is that a good thing for us? For you? I know how you feel about your privacy."

"We still have privacy. I don't mind showing my gorgeous goddess off," he grinned. "And the fact that Superman and Wonder Woman are public now anyway, I don't see a difference besides the glasses and our names. It's still us. I had to realize that. I'm sorry it took me so long to."

"I understand now how much it means to have privacy and the secret identity."

"Yeah but Di, we still do. If you are worried about other photos, that won't happen. I'm sure of that."

"No, it's not that..."

"What is it?" Clark asked as he stopped walking and turned Diana to face wrapping his arms around her waist. "Di, tell me. What was said to you?"

"James and Cat are such a joy. Steve Lombard was trying to flirt-"

"Of course, he was." Kal rolled his eyes.

"Lois however. She questioned us...continuously. Made very snide remarks about us. You were right. She really doesn't believe I would want to be with someone like you."

Clark sighed. "She's saying that because I'm not falling at her feet. When I was an intern, I was excited and I was impressed by Lois, you know already being this star reporter. But getting to know her, working with everyone else, I started keeping to myself. Especially with Superman on the scene, too. I'm myself with you and the league. My parents and your family know me for who I truly am. That's what matters."

THE DARK SPELL

"I love you, Kal-El." She wrapped her arms around his neck and reached up to kiss him. "I love you, Clark Kent." She said against his lips before kissing him again. "I love you, Superman." Another kiss. "I love all of you." She kissed him deeply.

Clark responded immediately with his hands grabbing her ass bringing her impossibly closer. Diana giggled against his lips. She trailed one hand down his chest and further rubbed Junior through his jeans.

"I have to get you home, Di," he whispered huskily.

"Mmmh..." she moaned in his mouth. "Take me, Kal. Take me home now."

They started to levitate up. Then not a second longer, Kal and Diana flew up to the skies to their apartment.

Upon arriving, they went through the back stairway entrance.

Diana giggled as they were quickly going up the stairs. Kal placed his hands on her hips and pulled her to him kissing her neck. He then turned her around and pinned her on the wall.

"Clark..."

He smirked and kissed her.

"We are only a few steps away..."

"Few steps too many..." he whispered kissing her neck.

Diana moaned and closed her eyes as he sucked harder on her neck guaranteeing to leave marks.

Kal suddenly paused when he heard someone walking. He pulled Diana by her waist off the wall. Diana took his hand and they walked up quickly the rest of the stairs.

At the door, Diana turned and leaned against it. Kal wrapped one arm around her waist keeping her close. Diana cupped his face with both hands and her mouth is on him desperately. Kal unlocked the door and taking his key out, pushed it open. Diana walked backward inside never breaking their kiss.

Now inside, Kal kicked the door closed and reached back locking it. He threw his keys wherever they landed and wrapped his other arm around Diana's waist. Kal lifted her up and sat her on the entryway table. He kissed her neck and nibbled her ear making her squirm and press her body into his.

Sharp intakes of breath escaped from Diana's mouth. She could already feel herself getting wetter.

"Beloved?"

Kal glided his hands up her thighs raising her dress up. He ran his hand up farther the inside of her thigh to her center and pressed his palm against her, smiling as he felt her wetness.

He slid his finger deep into her, rubbing over her G-spot deliberately. Diana screamed and groped at his arm having a tight grip on his sleeve, her thighs closing around his hand and his lips attacking her slender neck.

Diana's breathing shifted as she approached her orgasm, and when Kal felt her inner muscles quivering around his finger, he stopped.

Kal pulled his hand away, set both hands on her hips, and pulled her to him, rocking against her in a slow rhythm, he bent down to kiss her, tongue brushing her lower lip.

"What's with you, tonight, Kal?" she asked him.

Kal kissed her again as an answer and slide both hands to her ass to lift her up. Diana tossed her arms around his neck and held on and Kal kissed her until she shuddered for breath, then lowered her to her feet.

"It's you and your dress," he said sucking at her throat, his tongue dragging across the sweep of her collarbone.

He dragged the thin straps of the dress down in the process of ravishing her neck and inching closer and closer to her chest.

Kal stopped his ministrations and gazed down from her face, dragging across her throat and the curve of her breasts peeking from her dress. He pressed his lips against the shell of her ear. "You look hot!" and slowly dragged the straps further letting her dress hanging from her hips, to reveal her bare skin.

Kal's eyes turned dark as the dress slipped over her taut nipples, revealing her naked upper body to him.

He lowered at his knees to directly stare at her naked chest until she felt so much heat building in her cheeks and his hands roaming in her neck, dropped down to brush her breasts in teasing sweeps.

His hands grab her hands and pin them down on either side of the wall.

"Perfect!" Kal moved forward and his tongue glides over the space between her breasts.

THE DARK SPELL

"Kal..." Diana moaned when she felt his teeth grazing her breast. She shuddered as she felt her nipples harden and heat pool in her lower abdomen.

He sucked her breast into her mouth as she gasped, rolling her nipple with the tip of his tongue. Diana swallowed hard when he slid across her nipples before gliding lightly around her areolas. She bucked against him and kneaded him to take more of her breast into his mouth.

Kal wrapped his burning mouth around her nipple which almost tipped Diana for sensation overload. She felt his tongue curling around her aching flesh, sliding around the circumference several times before finally caressing and rolling the tip between his lips.

He repeated it to the other side, wrap his burning mouth around her nipples and suck so hard.

Kal kept teasing her, he would suck on her nipples until they were red and swollen, once again, until Diana was nearly gasping as she struggled to hold still with him pinning her arms tight and he continued to kiss along the swell of her breasts.

When the twitching and shivers stopped, he will again close her nipple gently between his teeth, and brush his tongue against the throbbing tip.

Diana, screaming, palmed her fingers around his, as he continued to suckle on her nipple. Every touch of his tongue and every bit of heat from his mouth seemed to shoot straight down between her legs.

Ka drew his mouth away from her nipple and then leaned over to suck her other nipple into his mouth with Diana growing rigid as though she could come just with his mouth on her breasts.

Finally, Kal released her arms and continued to swirl his tongue against her sensitive flesh and one of his hands palmed her other breast, rolling and teasing the nipple beneath his fingers.

Lastly, he pulled away from her breasts and leaned forward to kiss her again.

He smirked and in a matter of seconds, to her surprise, Diana was completely naked with only her heels still on.

"Oh my..."

Kal stepped back to see her beautiful smile and her sparkling blue eyes. Curvaceous. Firm succulent double d's red and swollen from his action.

Long, sexy legs and thick thighs, glistening womanhood. Taking her in, Kal could feel Junior twitch and harden more.

"You want to break yet another table?"

"This one is a little bit more sturdier. But let's test it out."

Kal grabbed her and lifted her to sit back down on the table and pushed her legs wide, making sure she was comfortable, and brought her crotch to the edge of the table. He starts to make his way down her body. Kissing every inch and occasionally a playful nip with his teeth. He kneeled down before her placing her legs over his shoulders. He kissed her thighs and edged toward her glistening womanhood, driving her wild. He breathed in, smelling her aroma. Diana felt his hot breath on her clit keeping her in suspense for just a few seconds longer until she felt the very tip of his tongue flick over her clit and kiss her wet lower lips and at the same time reached up and stroked her sensitive hard nipples. Kal dipped his tongue into her and tasted her exotic nectar, feeling her wetness cling to his tongue and lips. Kal loved the way when he licked her his tongue became slick with her juices. Kal ran his tongue up to the pearl that is her clit and then back down to her perineum and back up again.

"Oh! Gods!"

Diana's head lulled back. She reached down gripping his hair.

Kal made his tongue as flat as possible so that he could cover as big an area as he could and taste as much of her. Diana flexed her hips to try and press her core against his lips.

Diana whispered and mumbled that what he was doing to her felt so lovely.

"Yes..."

His tongue moved quicker lapping at her and sucking in her juices. His hands were still stroking her hard sensitive nipples and his tongue was licking her hard. He then sucked on her clit and he heard her groan louder in pleasure.

Diana felt his lips starting to make their way back up her body retracing their earlier steps, then they were face to face once again. She bit her lip, glaring at him with lust-filled eyes.

Kal's chin glistened with her juices as she watched him, her chest rising and falling rapidly with her breathing. Kal leaned over and kissed her.

THE DARK SPELL

She let out a soft giggle before licking his lips and chin, tasting herself on him. Whilst doing that, Kal ran his index finger over her nether lips before slowly inserting it inside her warm tunnel. Bending his finger, he hooked it round to touch the area near her g spot, their kissing became more passionate.

Kal inserted a second finger and started moving them in and out of her. They were covered in her juices and slid effortlessly inside her. Diana bit his lips in between kisses. She put her arms around her and pulled him tight to her, digging her nails into his shoulders.

Kal broke their kiss and moved his mouth back down and start to lick her clit again hard and fast matching the speed of his fingers sawing in and out of her womanhood.

"Oh, Kal! Ah!"

Whispered words became his name over and over as she grabbed at his hair tighter, her hips moving involuntarily as her body began to peak. Whispers became cries as her climax overtook her, and Kal held on tight to her.

With her heels still on, her feet and toes stretched out, inner thighs twitch and she moaned deeply as an orgasm rolled through her and her juices flowed over Kal's fingers and mouth.

While Diana was enjoying her orgasm, Kal quickly undressed. His hard member bobbed up and grabbing his stiff rod, he rubbed it up and down her wet slit, making her squirm and moan. He lined up with her slicked center and thrust into her fast and deep, the height of the table was just right. Diana let out a loud gasp and wrapped her legs tighter around his lower back. Her heels dug into his buns of steel.

Kal held her tight against him, intentionally making his member throb inside her. He started to move, back out slowly, in fast and hard, moving the table with each thrust. Stroke after stroke, the sound of small grunts coming from between her lips each time he hit home.

He kissed her passionately, their tongues pushing against each other while their bodies seemed to melt together. With a couple of cycles of this pursuit, Kal's length was buried deeply in Diana's trembling body. Kal groaned and threw his head back. Diana had such a unique muscular control of her womanhood and he felt her taking hold of him within her magical walls and massaging the length of his shaft.

They got themselves moving in perfect rhythm as Kal pumped in and out of Diana's gripping pleasure womanhood; the warmth and wetness of her inner flesh created indescribable slick friction. A burning seemed to spread from their loins throughout their bodies, making them both flushed with heat and sweat. The pleasure seemed so intense that they wanted it to last forever, to be lost in this incredible everlasting pleasure. Kal's hands glided up to cup and play with her breasts, mauling them and squeezing them. He needed her, he wanted her.

Kal leaned forward and whispered in her ear giving her a running commentary of what he was doing to her. Diana was surprised yet loved it when he talked dirty to her, her nipples ached and her womanhood also ached as he thrust harder and harder in and out of her.

Diana reached up a hand to stroke his cheek tenderly and then a sultry voice said, "Gods, you are so good to me...OH GODS, YESSSSS!"

Lost in the throes of their lust, Diana threw her head back as she cried out her pleasure, her own voyage of delight enveloped her. Her thighs pressing more into him with her ankles crossed she pulled him down onto her while she pushed her core up to meet his thrust and bury him deeper inside her.

When Kal felt the orgasmic tension in her body build, he became more forceful with his thrusting, increasing until his body loudly slapped against her flesh and she writhed as her orgasm grew and then exploded.

"Yes...Yes...Oh GOD YEESSSSS!" echoed in the apartment as she thrashed about on the table.

Kal felt a reduction in friction as a flood of her hot juice surged from her core. He struggled to keep from releasing himself as he watched Diana's beautiful face contort in the ecstatic joy of her climax. He stopped moving, holding himself rigid as she trembled against him. When she finally recovered enough to open her eyes, she looked up at him with a smile.

"Wow!" she gasped. "Mr. Kent, you are such an incredible lover," She wiggled her hips and felt that he was still long and hard. "I can't help but be greedy."

THE DARK SPELL

"I'm here to serve," he smiled and lowered his head to her breasts to suck nibble of her hard nipples, which developed another shiver from her.

He started thrusting into her again, this time driving without the thought of holding back. He burned with the need to unload and he pounded it into Diana, all restraint released. She screamed out in both pleasure and pain as he ruthlessly filled her with his member. His groans and her yells became louder and more animalistic as they both approached a huge climax.

It felt like her womanhood turned into an electrically charged sheath made specifically for his sword. His manhood was being sucked into this warm vortex of energy that surged through his body until his complete awareness was focused on how he was absorbed into her. As he went deeper into her over and over, he was overwhelmed by the sensations pounding in his brain and realized he was fighting a losing battle to contain his release. He was on the verge of losing control and it was taking every last bit of willpower to keep holding back, hoping she would climax again soon.

Kal suddenly picked up Diana and slammed her against the wall. His hands squeezed her tight ass, cupping each perfect cheek. Diana's arms wrapped around the back of his neck and locked their lips together again.

Diana moaned and gasped into his mouth as he slid inside her, all the way, resting within her hot, dripping mound. Her ravenous womanhood clamped down on his length, squeezing and massaging. He gripped Diana by her hips, and drew back, until just the head of his length remained inside her, and then plunged back deep into her. He felt her whole body shudder against his own. Kal pulled back and plunged again, and again, the ferocity increasing with every single thrust.

Diana's moans grew louder and louder with each thrust, wrapped in waves of never-ending ecstasy, as his member teased her clit, before diving inside her walls to once again explore the warm depths of her sweet tenderness. Trapped between Kal's strong arms and toned torso, with her back pressed hard against the wall, Diana felt Kal penetrate her down to her innermost core.

He rammed into her and her gorgeous breasts danced with equal force bouncing up and down in time to every hard deep thrust, while her nails dug deep into the straining muscles on his back, letting him feel every bit of that sweet combination of pain and ecstasy he was making her feel down there. He pulled his mouth away from Diana's, slid down to her exposed, enticing neck, and bit down hard, sucking on the soft delicate skin.

They were now both close to coming. He could feel her tightening around his length, he could feel the weight of his balls as they filled to the brim. Kal and Diana both erupted at the same time, groaning ecstatically, jet after jet of hot essence shooting deep inside her, while her whole body shook against his own, convulsing uncontrollably. Diana let out one last wail and closed her eyes tight, rejoicing in the crashing waves of exquisite pleasure that overwhelmed her core, with Kal still holding her pressed against the wall.

A tiny droplet of a tear of joy escaped the corner of her left eye as she released her fingers from his back and spent a few seconds, enveloped in absolute bliss.

The room seemed incredibly quiet as they descended from that peak, the sound of their heavy breathing unnaturally loud. The aftershocks of their joined earthquake caused both of them to gasp and shiver, the movement of one of them triggering the same response from the other. They drew slightly apart, both with a satisfied smile playing on their lips.

Still holding Diana, Kal walked over to the sofa and sat down with Diana straddling him. Kal cupped her cheek and stared into her eyes.

"I love you, Diana. You are the most amazing, gorgeous woman in the universe. I'm grateful for you, Diana. I need you to always remember that. You've changed so much for me for the better."

"Kal..." Diana turned her head slightly to kiss his palm. "I am grateful for you, too. The gentleman you are, how godly handsome you are...I love you, too."

Kal leaned forward and captured her lips in a passionate kiss.

A few days later... WatchTower

Wonder Woman kissed Superman and embraced him.

"Hurry back home, Kal," she said.

"You know I will! It's a week trip, though. I'll make it up to you, I promise. Fortress." Kal wiggled his eyes and smirked.

Diana giggled. "I can't wait. I'll be counting down the days." She kissed him again. "I may have something for you when you get home."

THE DARK SPELL

Green lantern sighed. "Alright! Alright! Enough of all that! We got big intergalactic monster ass to kick!"

Kal rolled his eyes. "It's a peace treaty, Lantern. We're the witnesses and security is all."

"Yeah, but there's going to be a fight somewhere. Don't worry Diana, a space bar fight ain't nothing."

Diana frowned. "There will no fighting until absolutely necessary. If you try to get Kal into any of your childish games, Harold Jordan, you will have to answer to me."

"Wonds, I was just kidding. You are- wait a minute? Did you just call me Harold? Are you serious? No one calls me Harold but my own mom!"

"Well, I just did. It is your proper name after all and you know I'm serious," she glared.

"Way to kick me in my pride," he said sarcastically.

"Well, I mean it."

"Boy scout Romeo will be back in one piece and completely sober. The moment the treaty is signed and whatever else is secured, he'll be racing back."

"The only right thing you've said, Jordan." Kal kissed Diana's temple.

Diana reached cupping his cheek and kissed him passionately pouring all her love into the kiss.

The next night, Clark and Diana's Apartment

Diana lay in bed staring at the empty another side. She reached and glided her hands over the cold sheet. She missed her beloved's warmth so much.

She sighed hugging his pillow and inhaling his scent. She was unabashedly in love and this was no weakness. This was her happiness.

She thought back on the days of working, civilian or heroics, tirelessly and going home alone. Although, at first, especially during her first years of being in man's world and settling, she enjoyed that alone time. But finding herself becoming closer to Kal, the friendship they forged, her feelings evolved to wanting that companionship she saw on cheesy romance movies or civilian couples walking together hand in hand. She even admired Mera and Arthur's long-standing relationship.

To witness that kind of love was so beautiful yet so bittersweet because she thought she would never experience it.

Even by force of a succubus spell, having to confront their feelings was right. They wouldn't have done it on their own being convinced they couldn't be anything more than friends. It was too risky. But wasn't that what love was anyway. Taking risks but having faith to be guided in the right path? There's no selfishness in falling in love and being with that person. Why should it be any different with her and Kal-El?

"Oh...Kal..." She moaned suddenly rolling over on top of his pillow. She gasped. "Oh...no..."

She was feeling that burning sensation on the back of her neck again. The same as when Valeria cast the spell on her. She tightened her legs around the pillow, trying to hold it in. But this shouldn't happen. The spell had been lifted.

"Kal...she moaned out again closing her eyes. "Gods!"

She felt it in the pit of her stomach about to boil over. She rolled back over on her back and arched. Every moment they've made love, his touch, his kiss, his tongue, his hands were playing through her mind. It was like he was right there right now doing all those marvelously sexy things to her.

"Gods, Kal! Oh! Ah!"

She gripped the pillow and released it in an overflow.

She took a deep breath trying to calm herself. She kept her eyes closed only picturing him.

"Kal..." she whispered as she quickly drifted off to sleep

"Oh, you naughty little princess...That man truly has your heart and soul," Valaria said as she appeared over Diana. "It is not I anymore, it is only you and him. Such sickening purity. The passion has ignited such a fire that can not be tamed." Valeria sighed and lay next to Diana. "It was my fault for opening Pandora's box, but I just wanted to have a little fun." She trailed a finger gently over Diana's face. "The look of a satisfied woman." She smirked. "He truly is all over you, Princess." Her face dropped. "Though, I can not have Dionysus on me no longer. I need you and your lover, Diana. You and he will join me at a feast. You will pray to him and bring him out of his cowardly hiding. He will soon suffer the same as I all these centuries."

"You are becoming soft for them," Strife said annoyed appearing.

THE DARK SPELL

Valeria smirked and stood up. "Your plan of chaos is still in motion, Strife. Can't you feel the envy within the mortals? Their selfishness of trying to cast doubt in Diana and Kal-El's minds.

However, the bond between them is just too strong. Stronger than we realized. It will be very much used to my benefit. While you continue on with your mortal dealings."

They both disappeared.

2 days later...Afternoon: South Portland, Maine. The Maine Mall

Mera Curry dragged Diana into the Soma Lingerie store.

"Oh come on, Diana! You'll love it!"

"Mera...I don't think so. I mean anything I wear or don't, Kal doesn't mind."

"Diana, it's just having something a little sexy for the night or nights when he gets home."

"I have other means of-"

Mera raised her brow. "I knew you and Clark had a kinky side. Come on! Let's give it a go and be a bit spontaneous!"

Diana sighed. "Fine."

Mera laughed. "Yay! This is going to be so much fun!"

Diana scrolled through a rack. "Mera, I don't think I'll be able to wear any of this. It's so much smaller than usual."

"That's the point, Diana."

"So why don't I just not have anything at all? He has seen me plenty of times so it's no surprise."

"I don't know how to describe it. But men like the tease of the bodily reveal still."

"Well, yes that's true."

"So give him that." Mera took a teal bra set and held it up for Diana to see.

Diana tilted her head then shook her head no.

Mera shrugged and put the setback. "So, you know we haven't talked about the whole worldwide relationship reveal. I mean you keep deflecting the questions like bullets. Hasn't it quieted down now?"

"I'm not deflecting it's just...Kal loves his privacy. When we saw it, it was such a shock. I didn't know how Kal would react. It has quieted down a bit. However, our relationship is in the spotlight already as Ambassador and Reporter, Wonder Woman and Superman have been in tabloid gossip columns for years. With confirmation, it was a media frenzy we weren't prepared for."

"How does Clark feel about it all?"

"At first I thought that he was having regrets. I overheard him talking to Bruce, but didn't hear it all so I misinterpreted a few things. We talked at home and he explained everything and Mera..." Diana blushed and smiled. "The way that man expresses his love for me is so much of everything! I fall more and more in love with him every day."

"Aww! Diana, that's so sweet!" Mera picked out another set. A Jasmine plum babydoll set.

Diana smiled and tilted her head. "That's better."

"Finally," Mera teased. "If you don't be difficult, maybe we will be out of here in the next hour or two and get lunch. There's a fabulous restaurant called Gyro Express Mediterranean Cuisine."

"Oh, very nice!"

Diana walked over to another rack. She picked up a lavender sneak-a-peak lace bra set.

"Hmm...?"

"I was thinking something a little more sexy for a Goddess," someone said behind her.

Diana frowned and quickly turned. "Eros?!"

He smiled. "Apologies, Cousin."

"What are you doing here?"

"Trying to give some assistance."

"I don't need it. Especially with you meddling with Valeria. You've been hiding, haven't you? Ashamed?"

"No, no. Diana, I've been trying to protect you and your lover. However, now Strife has joined Valeria's game and-"

"Strife?" She gasped. "Wait...it was them. Wasn't it?! It was Valeria and Strife that sent out our picture?!"

Eros sighed.

"Eros, what are they trying to do?"

THE DARK SPELL

"All I know right now is Valeria wants to use you and Kal-El to draw out Dionysus from hiding."

"Dionysus? What does he have to do with anything?"

"He and Valeria were lovers centuries ago."

"Oh...Oh no! But why us?!"

"I don't know yet."

"And how does Strife factor? Nevermind. She doesn't. She just likes and has to be in the middle."

"Right."

"So what do I do to get out of this?"

"I'm not sure. Since Valeria's spell was casted and even when it was broken...there's still a connection. I've been watching you and Kal-El. Your love is an energy of some sort. A weapon."

"A weapon?" Diana frowned.

"For purification." Eros picked up a sexy bodystocking featuring sheer netted cups, a high scoop neckline with slashed trim, satin bow accents, halter ties, a sheer fishnet bodice with opaque center panel, slashed garter straps, an open crotch, and attached thigh high stockings with lace top detail. "This would catch the Kryptonian's eyes."

Diana raised her brow.

"As your friend said, be spontaneous. Also, I have a gift for you. Each clothing-"

"I hardly call this clothing, Eros."

"Whatever you want to call it, Diana, I will transfer it to a new special magic lasso. It is only to be used for these special occasions between you and Kal-El."

Diana gave him a questionable look.

Eros smirked. "You will thank me later."

"Diana? Who is this?" Mera asked walking up to them.

"A pleasure to meet you, Mera Curry. I am Eros, God of Love and Desire." He kissed her hand making her giggle.

"Oh?" Mera's eyes went wide surprised.

"I was just checking up on my favorite cousin as I would usually do. Would like to help her pick out a few things for her and Kal-El's enjoyment."

"I'm so glad you are here, Eros. Diana has no choice now."

Mera looked a Diana with a devious grin. Diana rolled her eyes.

A day later...Boston Embassy

Ambassador Diana Prince sighed, after a long day of meetings, calls, then rushing off to a few emergency alerts and right back to the embassy for more meetings and calls, she was ready to get home, take a hot shower and get in bed.

She picked up her bag and was just about to walk out of her office when her office phone rang.

She sighed and walked back to answer.

"Yes, Janine?"

"Madam Prince, there is a man here to see you for the last-minute meeting."

Diana frowned. "Um...who is he?"

"He prefers to see you first. Introduce himself to you."

"Oh... well I will be down momentarily."

"Ok, Madam Prince."

Diana frowned hearing Janine giggle. Of course, the guy must be a flirt.

Diana sighed and walked out of her office closing the door and locking it.

"Really hope this isn't long," she said walking into the elevator.

She leaned against the corner and took out her cellphone. She smiled looking at the screen of her and Kal. That handsome face with that charming smile of his and soulful eyes. She couldn't wait to see him. Only 1 or 2 more days.

Stepping out of the elevator she sighed and said a silent prayer to the Gods that whoever this was wouldn't take too much of her time.

When Diana walked to the lobby, she stopped abruptly and gasped.

"Ka-Clark?!"

"Hey, Diana," he smiled.

Diana rushed to him, jumping into his arms, wrapping her arms around his neck. Clark wrapped his arms around her waist.

Janine squealed. "Madam Prince, your...um... last meeting for the day." She couldn't stop giggling.

Diana smiled. "Thank you, Janine."

THE DARK SPELL

"Miss me?" Clark asked.

"More than you know!" Diana kissed him passionately.

Clark immediately responded deepening their kiss.

"Awww!" Janine gushed.

Other employees or visitors stopped and stared.

It was as if time stood still and everyone around them disappeared as they passionately made out.

Finally pulling back, Diana gasped. "You didn't go to the apartment first, did you?"

"No, I went to the... uh...The North place first. Why?"

"I have my own surprise for you. Didn't want you to see it yet." Diana embraced him. "I'm so glad you're home early."

"I am, too, Di. Wait... you have a surprise for me?"

Diana looked up at him with a seductive grin. "I do. As you promised, we will be at the North place so that's what I have prepared for."

Clark smirked and took Diana's hand.

"Thanks, Janine for helping me surprise, Madam Prince!"

"Oh, of course! Have a good evening!" she giggled again.

"Have a good evening, Janine," Diana said laughing softly.

Once outside, they walked down the steps and across the street to the park.

Standing near the park fountain, Clark wrapped his arms around her waist again, pulling her into another passionate kiss. Diana wrapped her arms around his neck and ran her fingers through his hair moaning in his mouth.

"Mmhmm...Darling, it's so good to be in your arms. I was so busy today I must have missed the alert you were back."

"No, I wanted to surprise you so I told the others not to say anything. It was even better with Hal getting drunk off his ass somewhere and girls keeping him occupied so I could leave alone."

"Oh?" Diana laughed. "He is celebrating the success of the treaty?"

"Yep! The leader wanted me to stay and celebrate too but I told him I had my own special celebration back home," he grinned.

Diana gave him a peck.

"So how about I get back to the Fortress, get dinner ready, while you get your surprise ready and everything at the apartment?"

"That's the plan, Love." Diana kissed him softly once more. "I'll see you in an hour."

30 minutes later...Fortress of Solitude

Kal through 5 frozen steaks into the air.

"Woof!"

Krypto, the Kryptonian direwolf hound used his heat vision to cook each steak and caught them all into his mouth.

"You're getting faster with all of that, Krypto. I hope you get full. Diana and I don't need any interruptions tonight or even all day tomorrow."

"Woof!"

"Yeah, I'll leave the steak chest unlocked. But don't go overboard!"

"Woof!"

Kal smiled. "Good boy."

Back in Metropolis, Clark and Diana's apartment

Diana hummed as she was packing with her tea for the morning, new special lasso, and a few extra civilian clothes she probably didn't need with the fact that she had plenty already at the fortress and she and Clark probably wouldn't even leave the Fortress let alone leave the bed.

Diana laughed softly at herself and blushed thinking about all the naughty things she and Kal will indulge in being at the Fortress. There were no limits to the unadulterated passion they were going to release.

Back at the Fortress

Kal finished setting the table and was just about to start making their plates when he heard Diana's heartbeat coming closer. He rushed to the front entrance of the Fortress to greet her.

His heart raced as the enormous doors opened and he saw his Gorgeous Goddess flying down to him. Catching her in his arms, he embraced her as tight as he could.

Diana smiled and sighed lovingly biting her face in his massively strong chest.

"I missed you so much, Starshine." Clark kissed the crown of her head.

"I missed you, too, Beloved."

THE DARK SPELL

"For dinner, I made Shrimp Puttanesca with asparagus and got a bottle of chocolate red blend red wine."

"Oh...delicious! And dessert?"

Diana looked up questionably when Kal didn't answer. He was grinning. Diana laughed.

"Well, Mr. Kent, I guess my surprise will be part of your dessert."

Kal licked his lips. "Can't wait." He kissed her softly. "Sweet sweet dessert."

"Let me go change into my robe and then we can eat."

"I'll go fix our plates."

Kal kissed her once more and as she walked away slapped her ass making her squeal.

Kal chuckled watching her. He loves this woman so much. Her laugh, her smile, the way she walks, the way she talks, the sparks in her eyes, long flowing raven hair, her gorgeous figure. Everything about her is perfect and he had every intention to show her that, worshipping every part of her.

10 minutes later...

Kal and Diana sat at the table enjoying their scrumptious dinner while Kal told Diana about his trip.

"Diana, the place was beautiful. It went better than expected. The people were a joy. I get the conflict of both sides was because of their separate beliefs but after the treaty was signed and celebrations started, they all ended up getting along great!"

"That's amazing, Love!"

"Hal was bored until he started drinking and dancing with about 15 women. There were no signs of alteration but I'm sure Hal would've started one."

Diana rolled her eyes and laughed.

"Di, I wish you were there with me. You would've really enjoyed it. Actually, when the King asked why wouldn't I stay, I told him about you. He invited us back anytime we want. It would be great for us, Di. A get-a-way to another planet entirely. Beautiful new scenery."

"I would love that."

"Seriously, Di, you are going to love it! Maybe holiday break we can go. Vacation for 2 weeks."

Diana stood up moving to Kal squeezing herself between him and the table sitting in his lap. Kal slid his chair out a little and wrapped one arm around her waist with his other hand on her though, mindlessly rubbing gently up and down.

"What's wrong? How was work and everything for you?"

"It was all fine. The usual really. Meetings, calls, training with Donna, a few emergencies...But the fun part was going shopping with Mera and Eros showed up."

"He did? Why?"

"He told me...well...he wanted me to know that he is on our side trying to protect us."

"From Valeria."

"And Strife."

"Strife?"

Diana sighed and looked down. Kal cupped her cheek.

"Di, what happened? What did they do?"

"Our picture. Strife and Valeria are the ones that had our picture sent out."

"What the hell?! Why?"

"Eros doesn't know the details and I believe him. What he did tell me is that Valeria wants us to help her with something. Something of her past with Dionysus."

"Trying to ruin our relationship, playing a game with our lives is not the way to get us to help her!"

Diana could sense his anger rising.

"I know. I don't know what all of this is. My family and their centuries of secrets, betrayals, conflicts. They all just don't care who is affected in the long run. I'm sorry, Kal."

He immediately calmed down hearing Diana unnecessarily apologize.

"Di, you have nothing to apologize for. Between reading my father's journals knowing the history of Krypton and Smallville, especially Smallville. It's a wonder how my parents were able to keep my secret." Kal gently brushed his thumb over her cheek. "It's with every family, Di. It's okay."

Diana gave him a sympathetic smile.

THE DARK SPELL

"What else happened?"

"2 nights ago, I was thinking of you...and it happened."

"What?"

"Valeria's... spell. I...thought that we had broken that."

"First, that's really sexy thinking about it. It's always been hot and sexy."

Diana sucked her teeth and playfully hit his shoulder. "Kal, I'm serious."

"I am, too," he laughed. "It wasn't her spell, Di. We aren't there any more of thinking our feelings were just some kind of infatuation being played on. What you and I feel is real. So that was real. That was us. That makes me proud as a man....as your man to give you that feeling. I love you, Di."

"That's all it should be. Us. I love you, too, Kal-El."

He pulled her into a passionate kiss. Diana kissed him back running her hand down his chest. She moaned in his mouth feeling Junior reacting underneath her thigh.

"Time for dessert, Beloved."

"Hell yeah!"

Kal quickly stood up with Diana in his arms carrying her bridal style. Diana giggled and cupped his cheek, kissing him as Kal floated to the Fortress bedroom.

In the bedroom, Kal set her down.

Diana smiled and took his hand walking over to the enormous bed.

"Sit down, Beloved."

Kal obeyed sitting on the edge.

Diana walked over to her bag and slowly unzipped it.

"I told you about Eros showing up at the store with me and Mera. But I didn't tell you what store it was."

Kal thought for a moment. "Oh no, you didn't."

She smiled. "It was a lingerie store. Mera's idea."

"Oh, Di, you know I-"

She nodded. "I told her that. But she had the idea that maybe you will enjoy a few sets. She said it's to be spontaneous."

Kal leaned forward even more curious.

Diana took a red lasso out of the bag and walked back over, standing in front of him. Kal sat back up again anticipating what she was about to do next.

"This is the gift from Eros. It is called the Lasso of Love, Passion, and Desire. It is for our pleasured use."

Kal smirked. "You mean you'll tie me up?"

"Oh, for sure...but be patient, Love. For now, I have a few outfits for you to see. Which would you like better for tonight. You know it's quite difficult getting in and out of those outfits. I know how impatient you are at times and may rip a few of them."

Kal quirked his brow them gave her a devious look.

"So the first, my Love..."

Diana twirled the lasso around herself and it started to glow. Her robe disappeared and her body glowed.

Kal's eyes went wide and his jaw dropped

The glow slowly faded, Diana's first outfit was revealed. A sexy chemise featuring sheer lace cups, a low scoop neckline with strappy detail, halter ties, a sheer lace underbust with a keyhole, and a fitted skirt.

Diana slowly turned around for him.

"Wow..."

"You like?" she smiled innocently.

"Yeah...yes...whew..."

Diana giggled.

"Ready for more?"

He was speechless mesmerized and only nodded.

The second was a sassy bra set that features all-over eyelash lace cups, a high keyhole neckline with halter straps, a hook back closure, and a matching lace g-string panty.

Kal felt Junior reacting, ready to be free of the confine of his jeans.

The third, a lingerie romper featuring a deep V-neckline with lace trim, gold hardware, adjustable spaghetti straps, a sheer mesh leopard print bodice, an elastic waistband, and a loose hem with side slits.

The fourth, a gorgeous red wine babydoll set features molded lace underwire cups with a criss-cross halter neckline, removable adjustable spaghetti straps, a sheer bodice with satin bow accents, hook and eye back closures, a flyaway open back, and a matching g-string panty.

Kal was salivating with each fit.

THE DARK SPELL

When Diana bent over in front of him, Kal reached out to grab her ass but then pulled his hand backbiting his fist.

A lace bra set featuring sheer cups, adjustable straps with a criss-cross back, a matching lace garter belt with adjustable garter straps, and a matching thong panty.

"So darling...which one would you like for tonight?" She asked teasingly changing into a seductive crotchless lace teddy featuring sheer cups, halter straps, a satin bow accent, a sheer mesh and lace bodice, an open back with a tie back closure, an open crotch, and a thong cut back.

"Every one of them..."

Diana giggled. "Darling, believe me...there are plenty more..."

The last for the night was a pleasing primrose teddy featuring sheer floral mesh cups with strappy bust detailing, a scalloped lace trim, satin bow accents, adjustable criss-cross spaghetti straps, a narrow bodice panel with fully open sides to let her lover's imagination soar, and a strappy, g-string cutback.

Kal reached for her grabbing her by her waist and pulling her to straddle him. Diana squealed as he squeezed her ass.

"No matter what you're wearing or not, Diana, you're so damn gorgeous."

"Thank you, Beloved," she blushed.

Kal turned them around sitting Diana on the bed as he stood up. He smirked as he took his own clothes off, giving her a little show.

Diana looked at Kal with her seductive cerulean eyes and pushed herself to the middle of the bed, sitting up on her elbows and spreading her legs wide. Her womanhood was glowing with anticipation, and she could feel the wetness sliding over her nether lips.

He took off his shirt tossing it to the floor. Then unbuttoned his jeans taking them off and kicking them to where his shirt was. He stood there proudly for a moment letting Diana take him in. A gifted godly man in his own right.

He was hers and she was his. Diana wanted nothing more than to feel him all over her. She wanted his lips on hers as their tongues did the dance of lovers.

Almost as soon as the thought crossed her mind, Kal crawled up the bed to her, on top of her, and stripped her of her teddy. He then wrapped a hand around her throat. His ocean blue eyes flared with wild passion, as he pressed his lips against hers for a feral kiss. As their lips broke away, Diana pulled her head forward, trying to prolong contact with his animal passion. When she did, his head whipped to the side as he violently dug his teeth into her shoulder. Diana gasped in surprised pleasure as his teeth clamped down.

His grip around her throat tightened as his mouth moved violently to her breasts. He kissed, licked, and sucked her breasts, her nipples. Diana writhed beneath him as he alternated between her two breasts. He was running on absolute passionate desire, when he began mauling her breasts to both their satisfaction, he ran kisses between her breasts and down her soft abdomen before he brought himself to his knees.

With his hair wildly disheveled and his eyes raging with hunger, his broad form became even more enticing making Diana's body immediately react.

Diana shuddered at his touch; her breath sucked in as he moved his hand from her neck down to her breasts. He caressed them for a moment, then his hand made its way further down her abdomen, tracing his trail of kisses.

He looked up at her and smiled then at the same time, he slid his hands between her thighs, spreading those lovely legs nice and wide and his Goddess responded by lifting them high above his head while keeping them spread wide.

His mouth hovers at her mound, kissing and caressing but never quite reaching any further. Diana felt herself getting wetter. She felt his hot breath against her clit. His sexy mouth was so close!

But he touched her wet, hard clit and began to massage it with his hand. Diana's eyes grew wide at the intrusion, then they closed again with the intensity of his touch. As he continued to massage her clit, stroking her faster, bringing her so close to the edge when suddenly, he pulled his hand away.

He put his fingers to his lips and said, "Damn, you just taste too good."

THE DARK SPELL

Diana suddenly felt his hot tongue begin sliding around her lips. All thoughts flowed out of her mind.

He kissed her thick lower lips in much the way he would kiss regular lips, complete with snaking his tongue out to lick off the tasty juices already there.

"Oh yes, that feels so good," she sighed, both hands clasping tightly onto the soft comforter.

Kal grunted something, his deep voice vibrating between her legs, but she couldn't make it out. Diana giggled to herself. It didn't matter, anyway. His tongue was still doing wonders, licking her from bottom to top, swirling around her lips, pushing in deep into her womanhood, then working its way up to her clit. Diana gasped as his tongue began gently circling the hypersensitive bump. Around in a circle, then licking up from inside her again and again and again.

She grabbed his hair in both hands, pushing his face into her center.

Pleasure rolled up her core in waves all the way up to her stomach. She could feel her legs starting to shake as Kal kept his tongue pushing in and out at just the right rhythm.

After a few minutes, Diana could feel that familiar pressure began to grow. She heard moaning, and not in a pretty way. Deep and guttural moans.

"Is that me?" She thought.

Though, she couldn't tell. Her mind was beginning to fog up. The pressure started to build more and more with each thrust of his tongue.

"Give me all your tongue. I want it deep in there."

Kal grunted something again, and then his tongue began to flick in and out, thrusting in deeper and deeper, curling up each time to brush the folds of her G-spot. There was almost too much sensation this time, too sensitive.

"That's so good, Love. That's it! Oh, that is definitely it."

He was going to give her much more.

He appreciated that giving his woman oral pleasure was an art form involving an arsenal of body parts, not just the tongue. For this particular excursion, he added multiple fingers, the palm of his hand, my lips, his nose, and even his teeth.

He licked up and used his nose to nuzzle the pad above her core while breathing deeply of her essence. His fingers pulled her lips apart and he rubbed them softly between the thumb and forefinger. She clutched his hair tighter. Her legs began trembling as they squeezed him to her tasty box. It was a little one. She groaned just a tad. Kal could taste her flavors becoming more savory after she came but he kept at it, adding the occasional side-licks at the marvelously tight, tiny porta just below her pie.

Holding onto both of Diana's thighs, he pressed his mouth against her core and licked her slit up and down before pushing his tongue back inside. As soon his tongue penetrated her again, Diana cried out.

He ran his tongue up and down her slit but don't touch her clit again, making her want to scream and grind her clit into his face. His tongue danced across her clit; it was heaven.

She gasped abruptly feeling his fingers inside her, two thrusting in her soaking wet womanhood and one in her tight little porta. They slide in and out together. Diana buckles her hips to meet his thrusts.

Diana held on to his head, with all four of her limbs fastened around it, made it impossible for him to break away... not that he wanted to. He continued to eat out his Goddess feverishly as the cage of her limbs grew tighter and tighter around him, her moans getting louder and louder. Soon he could feel her body tensing, an unmistakable sign of an impending orgasm. It encouraged him only to lick her as hard and fast as he could with the goal of making love come.

Diana tensed hard and cried out even harder as jolts of pleasure were now undoubtedly shooting through her sexy, delicious body. Kal continued undeterred to tonguing her, her body shuddering each time his tongue poked into her center. Diana held him in place for at least another minute before her orgasm subsided just enough for her to relax and release his head.

She sighed at the amazing sensation.

Kal delicately kissed his way back up her firm stomach, between her breasts again, and up to her neck. Diana may have had him weak in the knees, but the light brush of lips against her neck caused a similar, if not as intense, reaction in her. He looked up at her, momentarily staring into her beautiful eyes. Diana reached up caressing his cheek with a smile as their lips met in heated, passionate kisses.

Every time her hard nipples brushed the fine hairs of his chest she thought she was going to pass out. She pulled him closer guiding his manhood into her tunnel of love. Diana wrapped her legs around his waist and Kal's rigid member pulsing with unrestrained need before her aching womanhood. In the blink of an eye, he buried his length inside of her. A long moan escaped Diana's lips. He was such a well-endowed man, his desperate hunger never failed to shatter both their self-control. He slammed his throbbing rod all the way as much as he could filling her up, again and again, his gluttonous desire overwhelming his composed demeanor. With single-minded fury, he ravenously devoured her all too willing womanhood.

"Kal! Oooooh yes, just like that! Yes! Yes! Oh, Gods, yes!"

Kal felt drawn to Diana like a moth to a flame. God, all she had to do was look at him and he was under her control. He leaned into her body and kissed her deeply as he slid his member into paradise.

He slid up and down her hot center making sure he caressed her swelling clit. He listened to her moans and cries out for passion.

Diana took a deep breath and exclaimed, "Ooooh, Beloved! Oh, Gods!"

They moved in a rhythmic love-making motion as their passions mounted.

Diana's hips met his every thrust and then she pushed him over the edge and he began pounding into her deeper and harder. Kal plunged into her until it felt like he hit bottom. She was a tight fit even with him stretching her.

He could tell by her breathing she was close to an earth-shattering climax. He leaned down and bit her nipple and she trembled so hard, they were being lifted off the bed.

Diana milked his throbbing length as she ebbed the waves of climax.

She screamed, "Ooooooooooh, Love, keep going! Oh yes just like that...harder oooooooooh yesssssss arrrrghhhhhh!"

Every thrust of his member, he felt the surge of electricity go from the center of her womanhood to the center of his soul. He leaned back a bit withdrew his length almost all the way. He loved teasing her this way and could feel another orgasm building. He leaned over and sucked one of her nipples into his mouth and bit it while driving his member all the way inside her. He paused long enough to pull out again and then bit the other nipple as he drove it home repeatedly.

Kal was like a wild stallion. Diana was moving her head side to side, screaming and climaxing in a neverending wave overcoming her one right after the other.

"Ooooooooooh Yesssss!"

He let her catch her breath before turning her over on her hands and knees. Diana giggled wiggling her ass in the air. Kal smirked moving on top of her, moving her hair to the side, kissing down the back of her neck and all the way down her back.

He sat back and parted those beautiful butt cheeks. He experienced a feeling in her stomach of sweet anticipation. His heart was pounding. His naked Goddess before me, her beautiful ass glistening begging for him to enter.

Diana thrilled to his touch. The anticipation was driving her wild. Just the thought of his glorious manhood buried deep in her drove her crazy with desire.

His fingers gently brush backward and forward. He knew this had a powerful effect on her. Pleasure coursed through her and she whimpered and trembled.

He gave one firm cheek a slap because, honestly, how could he not spank her in that position?

Then he placed his hand on either side of her and spread her out again. Her womanhood was already glistening wet. Right above, her tight little porta stared back at him, waiting.

He pressed his lips to the grand curve of her right cheek. Her skin felt impossibly soft and warm to the touch, almost creamy smooth. He softly kissed and licked his way around her rear, and he loved it. It was the ass of his dreams, literally, and he was in heaven. He moved his mouth into that divine crevice between her ass.

He dragged his tongue through her crack and found the tight little rosebud of her rear opening. She took a sudden intake of breath as he

THE DARK SPELL

dragged his tongue across it. Diana pushed her ass out a little further, giving him easier access and unspoken permission.

Kal's manhood strained harder as he buried his face between her cheeks, licking her there in earnest. She moaned softly and let out a squeal of delight, as he worshiped her, and after only a few moments in that pose, he felt a spasm seizing his balls, grunting into her rear.

Long, slow licks, he worked his tongue all over her big, curvy ass. Kal felt her hand on the back of his head as he had so many other times before.

"Kal, the things you make me do," she said giggling and shoving his face deep into her ass.

He smirked. The feeling was mutual for him. His face was smashed up against her puckered hole. He stuck out his tongue and gave a tentative lick, enjoying the taste of her ass.

Diana removed her hand from the back of his head, gripping the sheet, but Kal kept his face buried in her backside. He was licking wantonly, really enjoying himself. Diana started to moan and encourage him on.

The way she was moaning was turning him on even more and he lapped at her vigorously. He couldn't get enough as he continued to worship her ass. He grabbed her round cheeks and squeezed, savoring the feeling as he worked that firm ass. From time to time, he would slip his tongue down to her womanhood to tease it a little.

Diana was really getting caught up in the pleasure which was completely surrounding her body.

With talented fingers, Kal entered her core while licking her ass, causing her to start making louder noises. Kal knew she would scream when she reached an orgasm and he wasn't going to stop until she got there.

With a harder push of his tongue, he entered, probing half an inch or so inside the warm, narrow crevice while his fingers probed deep into the cave next door.

Kal heard a loud "Oh by the gods" from his lover whose head was buried down on the pillow.

Using his fingers to rub her clit and penetrate her womanhood, he licked and sucked her ass furiously.

Short breaths and quick gasps of "Oh, oh, oh, yes, yes," told him that she was getting closer.

Diana was being driven wild with pleasure. "Yes, yes, oh yes!" she screamed loudly as her body went rigid with an orgasm.

When Kal moved back up her body, he kiss her asscheeks, her back all the way up her neck and her ear. Diana twisted her neck and captured his lips in a long kiss. She was very bold with her tongue, flirting with his, luring it into her mouth, and then sucking gently. She moaned tasting herself.

Diana felt the hot, hard head of length pressed against the entrance to her ass. The feel of him between her ass cheeks, brushing that hole that had never before been entered gave him the overwhelming desire to complete the deed, here and now.

It was here that their hearts began to pound from a mix of excitement and nerves of a new love-making experience.

Diana was very relaxed, which was good because Kal didn't want her to be tense for this next part.

"You ready?" He asked in a whisper

She nodded without a word, too calm to speak.

Kal leaned in, and slowly pushed the head in,

Both of them held their breaths. Kal paused to let her get used to the sensation of him and to calm his rapidly beating heart. Once he felt he was stable enough in there, Kal put both of his hands on his Goddess's hips, took a breath, and very, very slowly thrust forward.

Gently, he ran his teeth over her neck and shoulders. Diana immediately gripped the pillow her head was resting on and pursed her lips, making no sound, however. Silent as well, Kal slid one inch at a time into Diana's backdoor, entering as gently as he could.

Kal felt Diana thrust her head back and kiss his neck in that way she would when she let go of that inner passion.

With a gentle push from his hips and a raise of hers, Kal was careful not to push too hard, wanting Diana to enjoy this as much as he did, hopefully even more. He took his time and listened to her breaths and groans. Slowly length plunged a little deeper, and her ass gives way to receive him. Diana bucked her hips back to meet him.

Holding tightly to her hips, Kal began to slowly, so slowly, pull back and then thrust forward, just a little at a time and gradually working his way up to bigger strokes as he continued to observe Diana growing more and more comfortable with the intrusion.

Her tight anal walls closed in on his engorged manhood as he now steadily shoved it in and out of her. Before long he was picking up his pace hard enough to cause a steady smacking noise against her butt cheeks. The whole time, Diana kept her hands and head on the pillow, but each time he looked up at her face, she was smiling.

As he increased his pace, he reminded Diana to let him know if she needed him to slow down or stop. She assured him that she was enjoying it and sincerely wanted him to keep going, so he did. He chose not to go as fast as he could have since he knew Diana may have been just bearing it to not spoil the fun.

Besides, the rate he was going at was blissful enough anyway.

Kal felt Diana slowly start to rock her hips. The effect of him began to work its way in and out of her now stretched, but still an extremely tight ass. Her ass was so tight, it was squeezing him like nothing I've ever felt before.

For a few minutes he pretty much just held him in the same spot and let her work it into her, becoming more accustomed to this new sensation. They were getting a different feeling to vaginal sex. The narrower avenue down which Kal was heading gave him the sensation of being massaged firmly from every possible angle. He had about half of his length sliding in and out of her, the sensation was blowing his mind.

He got a little carried away. He pressed a little too deep and felt her flinch and pulled almost out, worried he may have hurt her and this special treat was over. But Diana pushed her ass back into his length and nodded.

"I'm okay...keep going."

That was exactly what he wanted to hear, and slid his member back into her accepting porta. He began again nice and slow, making sure not to go too deep. He probably had about 2/3 of his length inside of her, slowly pumping in and out.

Diana's ass raised more giving him permission to push a tiny amount further in. She was making deep, guttural moans as opposed to the high-pitched wails which he used to.

Diana laid flat on the bed with him still inside her ass. This was a better position for giving her the anal sex she deserved.

Diana thrust back against him, pleasure washing through her like the tide through the sand. He stop thrusting and just let it wash over her. That borderline between pleasure and pain was a massive turn-on for her. She clenched around him, staying in position for a few seconds. Diana gasped and turned her neck to look up at him with a dirty smile and a bite of her bottom lip. Kal knew that was his green light to really get this show moving faster

Deeper into the finest ass he'd ever seen, Diana's low-pitched moans turned to more familiar, higher-pitched wails as he quickened the rate at which I was thrust into. His hips met her ass cheeks with a loud slapping, amplified by their moist skin from the sweat.

Diana raised herself up onto her knees to give him even deeper penetration. She looked round to him with a look of sheer lust.

"Kal, take me harder," she commanded.

Upon his knees, with a strong grip of one hip, he gave a firm whack of his hand on her ass cheek, then pushed in as far as he could. Diana was bent forward on her knees and elbows. With the warmth of her back-channel enveloping member, he knew that it was going to absolutely explode when the time came.

As if reading his mind, she looked back once more. "Don't hold back," she said breathlessly.

Kal's eyes lit fiery red. Normal sex rules never applied to them.

With a grip of her hair, he pulled her body up to meet his as he pumped hard at her ass. He gave her several kisses on the neck and a caveman instinct hard bite on the shoulder. This sent her over the edge, he felt her body contort and her skin harden into goosebumps as she let out a loud, screaming orgasm. Instinct told him to move his head just as a potentially nose-breaking back-thrust of her head came past his ear. He wasn't going to slow down at this point and took a firm hold of her breasts as he was making love to her. Every once in a while, he just ran his hands lightly over her body like tickly little spiders crawling up and down.

THE DARK SPELL

He then trailed one hand down, working her outer lips and clit with his fingers. He slipped a finger inside her and she gasped. Diana felt herself licking her lips as she gazed up at the surprised but amused look in his eyes.

Diana's head was still thrown back over his shoulder in ecstasy as his manhood penetrated places deep inside which were never even thought to be explored. Her body was red with heat and sweat. The wild look of sheer lustful desire on her face was driving Kal crazy.

Diana planted a huge love-bite on the base of his neck, which was one sensation too far and he felt the tingle in his balls that meant he was going to blow. Every instinct inside him told him to pull out and shoot over her back, but he was under instruction to release inside her. He thrust into her ass harder and passed the point of no return.

As always, Diana sensed this and her screaming became high-pitched once again. She bent forward onto her elbows once again to get the best possible angle. Kal pushed inside her as far as he could, making the most of the last few seconds of this new-found route to ecstasy.

Diana slightly rocked her body back into his hard thrusts, making full sure that as much as possible of his shaft was getting sheathed in her ass. They continued pushing into each other for a couple of minutes before Kal reached his limit.

With a caveman-style roar, he shot the full contents of his essence deep inside her ass. Diana gave a loud shriek of delight and wiggled her ass as his love juice entered her back-channel.

Kal waited until every last drop was shot inside her backdoor, looking down watching his own manhood slide out, and watching his essence ooze from her down her asscheek. He was moaning pretty loudly too and needed to get a grip as he recovered. He was breathing heavily in an effort to compose himself.

Diana started giggling and then laughed joyfully, turning over as he exited her.

"That was so much fun...," she said breathlessly and hugged his neck pulling him to lay on top of her.

"You liked that? You okay?"

"I loved that! And I'm pleasantly exhausted," she teased.

Kal smiled cockily and gazed at her gorgeous, precious face.

"I love that I can experience things like that with you, Kal. The man that has my heart."

"It's my duty to spoil and worship my Queen. To give you an abundance of pleasure you deserve. I love you, Diana. I'm grateful to have these experiences with you, too."

He held her closer and captured her lips in a passionate kiss.

CHAPTER 9: LIKE HUSBAND AND WIFE

Fortress of Solitude: 9 AM

Diana woke up with a slight pleasurable ache between her legs and all the way up her ass. She looked around the room adjusting her sight to morning sunlight heaping through the Fortress ceiling. Although, they thoroughly cleansed themselves in the shower with Kal's new Kryptonian formula shower gel after their wicked last night session, her nostrils absorbed the sex still lingering in the air. The way he felt so warm and hard inside her...she giggled to herself slowly sitting up in bed, it certainly pained to sit flat on her ass now and she turned to look over to the handsome man still sleeping beside her. For him to still be asleep, she knew she wore him out just as much as he did her. She wondered what was his thoughts and how it must have felt for him having her that way.

Kal would wake up early every day whether as Clark Kent or Superman. He would spend an hour or two training and playing with Krypto. Post that, he would return to their apartment, take a shower and directly proceed to the Daily Planet. But after they moved together, he added to his routine to slide back into bed with Diana, with his hair wet tickling her stomach and would suck the nectar from her flower to a rhythmic tune.

Diana blushed and leaned over to kiss his cheek.

"I love you," she whispered.

His throat thundered a needy sigh into her hair covering his face and his lips found hers softly. "Love you, Di..." he mumbled in his sleep.

She grinned. Of course, he was still very much aware of everything.

Easing out of bed, she winced. She was sorer than she realized. She laughed softly to herself.

"Oh, Beloved, what have we done?"

Her thoughts drifted back on last night's moments of bliss and blushed. What a wonderful night. Diana fled into the bathroom and punched at the controls for the shower. She stood in it, hot water hitting on her shoulders, and she lubricated her hands with soap. Scrubbing her thighs, she hissed softly. It almost felt like she got a lethal blow from battle down there.

As water dripped down her skin, it started to feel sticky in her pelvis and rear area. Beneath it was reddened skin and light bruises. In the shower crystal wall reflection, she could see his fingerprints were still on her hips and the backs of her thighs and ass equally marked. She carefully avoided her clit which was overworked by Kal's hand and mouth and carefully rinsed her other parts washing his sex from her body.

After their shower last night, his tongue alone had given her 8 distinct orgasms over the course of the night and after that, they kissed for a long time before they drifted off to sleep in each other's arms.

Diana got out of the shower, put on her robe and floated over to her bag to get her tea. She didn't know what it was...maybe a side effect, but her sexual urges for Kal did seem to amplify even more now taking this tea. It makes even more sense as to why Hessia told Diana she must take it every day or the pregnancy was guaranteed.

She sighed thinking of when would be the day she wouldn't have to take this anymore. When will she and Kal plan for their family? Of course, right now, there was no rush but as a woman in love, she wanted nothing more than to have a family of her own without the dysfunction and drama. She wanted her peace and happiness. She knew with Kal, she would have that.

"Woof!"

Diana jumped slightly and turned.

"Good morning, Krypto!" Diana greeted patting his head.

"We have to be a little quiet while Kal is still asleep. Come on, help me make this tea. And well it seems like you've already helped yourself to your steak chest."

"Woof! Woof!" Krypto wagged his tail happily.

Diana laughed. "For such a big wolf, you act like such a tiny puppy!"

THE DARK SPELL

Krypto followed Diana to the Fortress kitchen area. Diana got a mug and a bottle of water.

"Heat this for me carefully please," she instructed Krypto.

"Woof!"

Using his heat vision, Krypto heated the water in the mug.

"Thank you very much. I won't say anything to Kal. You can have a few more steaks. I'll help get more later." She winked at the beast.

"Woof! Woof!" Krypto barked excitedly and flew off.

Diana took a sip of her tea. She developed a taste for it now. She flew casually to the Fortress lab. Kryptonian technology never ceased to amaze her. In the middle of it, the ship of the EL family was there. The one that brought him to her. The one that bridged two worlds.

She went to the trophy room with artifacts that not only Kal had collected but some of what his father collected from different planets across the galaxy. Then, Diana went to the planetarium where Kal kept otherworldly plants and animals he was guarding. On the left side of the stage, a suspended glass cage contained a wasp-like creature. It bounced off and come back to life sensing her presence. On the right side of the stage, a Sphere with a creature similar to Starro locked inside.

There was also a locked and secured portal way at the right corner of the stage to the phantom zone.

Diana went to the front foyer to the large statues of Kal's biological parents, Jor-El and Lara Lor-Van.

She noticed how obvious it was that Kal was their son. His facial and body structure from his father and eyes from his mother.

"I wish I could've met you both. I love your son. He is a very special man and he has done so many amazing things you'd be proud of. You are proud of him I know. Guiding him every day. You are always with him. Thank you, Jor-El, Lara Lor-Van."

As she strolled around the rest of the fortress, Diana finished her tea and went back to the bedroom.

She saw that Kal was now laying on his back, his face turned away from her and buried in the pillow, one arm above his head on the pillow and other extended towards the empty side of the bed, and the messy sheet dangling by his mid-thigh showed his long legs stretched and curled and her eyes narrowed on the Junior bulging from underneath the sheets.

Diana stood in the doorway and just stared. She smirked deviously and licked her lips. She floated over getting back into bed. She moved close to Kal, carefully not disturbing the mattress, and crawled, kneeling next to his hips. She saw her own love markings still on him and trailed her hand down his massive chest, tracing his abs.

It wasn't too much of a surprise by how much he trusts her by not even changing his breathing pattern when she shifted one leg to the other side of his hip.

Her kneading hands paused. "Kal, my Dear."

No reaction from him and Kal's face clearly showed him still asleep. For someone who is a light sleeper like him, he let her see his mouth open and lips smacking up against his drool while unconscious in sleep.

She laughed very softly and ran her fingers through his curls carefully without much disturbance and she leaned down, parting her lips and kissed his forehead.

She sensed his eye movement and carefully pulled back to not awake him.

Kal tilted his head in sleep and Diana caressed, kneaded, and rubbed his neck and shoulders softly. To her surprise, his ministrations helped. Gradually Kal allowed himself to drift deeper into the sleep with her touch. Diana could see slowly the tension began easing from him.

"Sleep, my Love," she whispered, running her warm, sure hands up slowly from the sides of his neck to stroke his clenched jaw.

Sliding her hands to caress his bare chest, she leaned down kissing his chest and her hand trailed down farther under the sheet until she felt his hard warm shaft and Kal moaned a little in his sleep as she gently took hold of him stroking slowly up and down.

Diana carefully studied his reaction to every little nuance of her touch as she caressed him and gently she pushed the sheet aside and pushed herself down until she was lying between his sprawled legs, one hand holding herself above him and the other endlessly stroking him.

A glance up at his face showed he is still breathing deep and evenly asleep with lips parted.

THE DARK SPELL

Her eyes drifted back to his manhood in front of her face. Her Junior. A good friend of hers. Thick and heavy and so beautiful in the palm, sticky from a few hours ago. She opened his foreskin and the head greeted her like a flower. She was looking at him too literally, the velvet crown, the veins, the testicles, the light curls of black hair sticking up in every direction.

She leaned down and breathed hot across the curls surrounding him. She lowered herself down on her forearm, sticking out her tongue to lick his hipbone just above his curls. She kissed him there again, lips parting and tongue tasting him, sucking at the skin. His member twitched next to her cheek.

With careful eyes on his face, she nibbed on his curls tasting herself on it and the skin beneath.

Diana can see his stomach spill on a breath and she licked a light, teasing circle around him then parted her moist lips and slowly licked the head. She inhaled the erotic scent of him and felt the heat radiate from his body.

Pulling her hair back, Diana teased the tip of his member with her tongue and closed her warm wet mouth around the head. Using all the gentleness she could muster, she slowly sucked his member into her mouth...just the first few inches. Holding it there, she enjoyed the feeling of the thick soft flesh filling her mouth. When she moved her tongue around the head, Kal moved a little more and moaned again.

Seeing the smile on his face, Diana wondered what he was dreaming about at the moment? But then again she had a good idea with his low mumbles that were of him saying her name a time or two.

Softly sucking, Diana soon felt Junior start to grow more, expanding in her mouth, getting thicker and longer. This slow, wet sucking and tonguing caused him to react just as she expected.

She pulled him out of her mouth with a pop, eyes the vein that runs under, and cocks her head, licking up from her thumb at his base to the very tip. Kal grunted when she reached the skin between the head and the shaft, so she licks it again.

Taking a breath, she pumped him with her hand and licked her lips. She watched his stomach muscles tighten and release, hearing tiny groans pouring from his lips into the pillow, then bent her head again, swirling her tongue around and around his ultra-sensitive tip.

She heard his soft moan of welcome under her ravishing kiss on the tip and Hera, she wanted him to feel good like this forever.

She looked at his testicles, cradling them in her palm, the skin tighter now than it had looked earlier and she angled her head to tug and lick his testicles. He flexed his hips and so she tugged and licked him again and again.

Diana leaned over to the inside of his thigh and nipped at his skin as he has done so many times to her, Diana released her hair, allowing it to flow across Kal's legs like raven tresses. She pulled back to look up at him, far harder in her hand than he had been, longer and the crown bigger.

Diana rose a little, placing her arms on each side of his body giving her better access to his engorged member. Diana pushed her head down, taking as much of him as possible, and then slid back to the head. His manhood was glistening, covered with warm wet saliva.

Diana began an easy slow rhythm of up and down. Each down thrust as far as her throat will allow, feeling his hardness hitting the back of her tongue and throat. It doesn't take long before Diana can taste pre-essence leaking from him. She sucked and swallowed and pressed her tongue up against him knowing he was getting close.

His hips jumped, pushing Junior deeper into her mouth.

"Sweatheart...Diana..." he groaned in a whisper.

Kal stretched up on his elbows, eyeing her with a passion in half eyelids. He lifted her hair, gathering it on top of her head until their eyes meet.

Diana pulled off of him, letting her hand slide along his slippery length, and she smirked and dipped her head back down resuming to slide her mouth up and down as much of his length as she can handle.

Kal's eyes darkened when he wholly noticed where the two of them are joined. There was a wicked gleam in her eye that told him she was reveling in his reaction. When she licked up the long vein with eyes on him, Kal dropped his head back to the pillow.

Diana went down on him again opening her sweet mouth wider, she took him into her throat, nearly gagging on the size of him, and she paused

THE DARK SPELL

there until he dropped his hand from her hair and clutched at the bedspread and chanted her name.

Diana could feel the pulsating beat of his heart deep inside her mouth as his manhood expanded even more. She closed her eyes, reveling in the scent of him in her deep throat, musky and sensual. His moans became louder, deeper, and longer as his swollen length moved even deeper, pulsating deep in her back throat.

Tears pricked her eyes and she gasped, letting him fall from her mouth but still holding him in her hands.

Kal lifted her hair again, Diana squeezed her hand on him in response, and when he made a little sound above her, she does it again.

She tugged with one hand, pumping with the other, and bobs her head, exploring the texture and ridges with her tongue. He moaned and flexed his hips, causing her to gag a little, and she sucked harder and moved faster.

Diana ignored her tired jaw and started humming, feeling his pulse against her tongue, his pre-essence flowed like a summer stream. Diana sucked him harder and harder, tonguing his slit, stroking it fiercely, and matching the jerking of her hand to the speed of her bobbing, feeling him shudder and throb from the onslaught.

The tears streamed down her cheeks again and she tasted them as she licked along his length. His breath coming fast, and he is virtually squirming on the bed. Diana knew he was about to release when he tightened his hold back to her hair and pushed his hips up more off the bed and held that position.

Diana moved her lips to the head of his member, lashing it with her warm tongue as she knew the load would fill her mouth.

"Aaarrrrrrggggg,...Ohhh Di...Diana! Shi-"

With that his member pulsated one last time as his steamy hot essence blasts from the small hole, hitting the back of her throat. Diana swallowed and gulped trying to accommodate his hot steamy essence. Each beat of his heart more squirting and gushing. Diana just kept swallowing blast after blast of him, moaning in satisfaction.

Kal stayed suspended while the pulsations and quivering continued. His body was hard as steel while his skin was covered with goosebumps. She continues to suck until his hips took in everything he was giving and soon he relaxed, lowering his body to the bed. His now empty member began wilting, the softening euphoric stutter of passion released.

Diana kept his length in her mouth, wanting to hold it as long as possible. She softly sucked and milked his member with her warmly, as his body relaxed.

Finally, she felt his heartbeat deep in his manhood return to normal, letting him drop from her mouth trying to prevent anything from falling out but drips some, catches some against her lips, swallowing the rest.

She licked her lips and her tongue flicked out to lick up drops of his essence on his navel.

Drained and sated, Kal looked down at her with half-lidded eyes and Diana looked up smiling.

"Good morning, Beloved." She licked her lips seductively.

"Morning, Gorgeous. Wow! What did I do to deserve to be woken up like that?"

Diana giggled and climbed up into his arms.

"Best 7 minutes of my life," He smiled at his beautiful Queen.

She stroked her jaw, "Seems like 5 minutes to me" she said mockingly.

Kal quirked his brow. "Come here." Kal pulled her up more, holding her tighter, and captured her lips, tasting the remaining flavor of himself in her mouth. "It was 7."

Diana looked at him with a raised brow. "No, 5."

"I can hold off much longer you know? But I can't resist you. But you, Ms. Prince. Just the slightest touch... you are undone in seconds. Having your time with Junior has you already turned on." He wiggled his eyebrows untying her robe to search for evidence.

Diana laughed softly. "Oh really? Is that a challenge, Mr. Kent?"

Kal smirked and quickly turned them over and grabbed Diana's wrists pinning her down on the bed.

"Challenge accepted."

"Kal, I took my shower already."

"Without me?! Well, that won't do." He buried his face into her neck, kissing, licking, and sucking. "I'll just have to get you dirty again."

"Kal!" she squealed and laughed. "I had to for some soothing from last night."

THE DARK SPELL

"What? What's wrong?!" He looked up at her concerned. "Are you hurt?"

"Darling, no. I mean it's just a little tender feeling. But I love it. To still feel my man's touch after hours of love-making and pleasurable experimenting." She smiled. "I know you will never intentionally hurt me. I trust you and you give me ultimate pleasure."

Kal smiled and placed gentle kisses all over her face. "That's all I want to hear, Di. Let me soothe you myself though, okay?"

Diana nodded.

"Be right back."

He rushed to the bathroom and back within 30 seconds.

Kal climbed back into bed, on top of Diana, and kissed her face again and again. Finally, he narrowed in on her lips and kissed her. He gently licked her top lip. A sensual tip of tongue teasing type lick and he licked and tickled across her bottom lip in just the same way.

As Diana opened her mouth to enjoy his kiss, he pulled his lips back. He darted his tongue forward and just touched his tongue to hers. Their tongues danced a sexy dance and Diana was in heaven.

Kal moved to her right and licked her neck. The tip of his tongue teasing the heck out of her. He nuzzled and licked her ear. All the while, slowly rubbing Junior against her already oversensitive center. Slowly he parted her robe and eager fingers found the evidence he was looking for. Diana was certainly dripping wet...no, flowing already and he knew it.

His hand brushed her bare core and Diana spread her thighs further as far as she could. Diana couldn't hold back the gasp when Kal parted her labia and slid his finger from her clit down to rest on her entrance.

He circled around the opening, then slid the tip of one finger inside her. Diana tried desperately to hook down on him and drive him, to hold him in place and pull him deeper, and to fill her with his fingers but he withdrew, his palm on her mound, holding her labia open with his finger resting against her clit.

"Told you. Under a minute..." he whispered smugly.

"Shut...up and-....AAH!" Diana gasped and then Kal pushed his finger into her.

Diana closed her legs around his hand writhing in pleasure but he drew out and returned with two-finger.

"Love you," he whispered into a kiss.

He quickened his thrusts, drove into her, and slid his thumb up to rub her clit and Diana arched her back being suddenly overcome by an orgasm.

"Less than a minute, Beautiful!" he said smugly and slid his finger into his mouth and closed his eyes to suck hard on his finger to lick her taste off his skin.

And after a few more luscious, sensual, and teasing licks with the tip of his tongue at her neck, and a few wonderful kisses, he drifted south. He kissed down her chest avoiding her breasts and slid to his left as he kissed her stomach.

When he ran his hands over her thighs, Diana parted them in invitation. He saw the now faint print of his hands and other marks still on her thighs. He kissed and licked her left thigh and then her right. He gently pressed a kiss to her slipped-open lips. Her juices string thickly to his lips. He licked her exquisite taste off them with his eyes closed. When Kal opened his eyes again, Diana was watching him, her cheeks blazing.

Kal kissed her slower and each kiss hitched her breath. He opened her inner lips, focusing on her clit, pressing his lips to it as lightly as he could. He kissed her clit a little firmer and nipped it between his lips causing Diana to tremor. Kal sucked her clit into his mouth and then kissed and licked down her left labia and up her right. Each time he used just the right amount of pressure, almost none, as only the very tip of his tongue caressed her labia.

Diana moaned loudly. She was slowly turning her head from side to side and was counting to five over and over. All of this was still those tantalizingly slow and delicate tongue teasing licks and Diana was on the verge of another orgasm, building like a wave forming in the ocean getting larger and larger as his tongue lashed on her beautiful jewels continued.

Nuzzling his nose against her clit, he pressed his tongue between her folds once more, he was rewarded with a loud, throaty moan. Tongue delved deep inside her as his hands held her hips down, keeping her pinned down as he tasted her.

THE DARK SPELL

Diana's juices covered Kal's face and She felt it is impossible to stop herself from climaxing as her thighs quivered. She came with a scream as she shook. Kal sits up looking quite pleased with himself. He wiped his mouth with the back of his hand.

With a smug look, he laid flat on the bed, and he pulled her legs wider and this time slammed his tongue up her again. Diana moaned loudly, loving this.

Her moans and cries became louder, and the rhythm increased until she locked his head between her thighs, as together they rode out her orgasm. Just like a wave breaking so did her orgasm crashing through her body causing her to shiver. She soaked his face as she took her pleasure, singing that beautiful hymn of female sexual energy.

Kal made his way up to the side of her, laying on his back as he let her, quietly, lie there while the ecstasy washed over her.

"That's 2 in under 5 minutes. You sure you want to do this challenge, Diana?" He chuckled.

She sat up with a glare and quickly moved over him, straddling his face. "Definitely," she answered.

Kal smirked as he held her thick ass. Kal ran his tongue along her slit, mapping every inch. Her moan was like music, starting low like a cat purring then building louder and louder as he plunged his tongue into her deeper and deeper. He licked upward toward her clit. Feeling her clit swell he put his lips around it and suck it gently. Diana began dripping onto his neck. She channeled her inner warrior to resist the temptation to climax. Her breath drew in sharply and she leaned forward a bit placing her hands on the wall as her body began to convulse with ripples of pleasure. Kal's tongue was everywhere and suddenly she felt him swirling his appendage like a tornado inside her. He firmly gripped her ass and started to move her on his tongue. When she is bouncing on his tongue, the foundation of her dam started to rattle. Her eyes went blind and she was still fighting to hold her breath to prevent an orgasm. Kal brought one finger in front to stroke her clit and the other kneads her curve as he tongued her. That sweet nectar she had been resisting to share was pouring out of her onto his face and chest.

"7 seconds." She heard him between her legs. His lips started to chew on her clit again. With a gentle bite on it, her legs gave up. Kal continued with a long lick and sucked it between his lips slowly relishing her taste.

"Not fair..." Diana turned and leaned over him, her breasts pressed on his abdomen.

Kal chuckled and slapped her ass. "Told you."

Diana took him in her hands again. He was already heavy and leaking. One hand dropped down to his balls. Rolling them in her hand and stroking him with others. She kissed the tip of his erection taking the head of him into her mouth a second time this morning.

Deep in her mouth, her tongue traced delicate patterns over him, making Kal shiver. He responded by licking her with greater intensity. He drove his own tongue deeper into her, swirling it to try and get all her honey.

The time stretched and both gave in to the taste of each other. They consumed like it was an addiction.

Kal began rubbing her soft ass cheeks, pulling her against his face with each rub. He took her moans as encouragement as his hand slid between her cheeks. The heat coming off her was intense, using one hand to pull her cheeks apart a little and slowly moving the other towards her tight little hole. He teased and rubbed closer and closer all while his tongue danced across her soaking wet womanhood.

It felt incredible as her body shuddered again. He pushed gently against her hole, just the tip of his finger going in. Diana snapped her head up and his length popped out of her mouth as she let out another guttural moan when he plunged his finger deeper into that hole. Kal began making circles inside her, small circles exploring her hole she moaned louder.

"Oooooh ... Love ... I ... I'm..."

Her body lost all control, where she clearly had a few smaller orgasms before they were nothing compared to this. Her legs clamped together. Her muscles convulsed as she shook. Kal's head was squeezed by her thighs up against her ass. He rode her orgasm out never letting his tongue slip out of her completely.

"Oh, Darling... that feels...so delightful!"

THE DARK SPELL

Her body convulsed again and another long low guttural moan escaped her lips.

Gently, Kal rubbed her clit with his tongue again as Diana slid his erection back in and out of her mouth. She needed to up her game. She sucked harder as it slid in and out and Kal sucked her clit harder.

Diana's voice was slightly muffled by his rod, but understandable. She slipped her mouth down as far as she could. Her tongue slithered up and down along his shaft, and he pulsed and throbbed.

Kal lifted his hips to penetrate deep in her throat as she licked and sucked on his manhood. His whole body started to lock up as he approached orgasm. He let out a muffled grunt to let her know. Diana locked her legs tightly around his head. Right as he began blasting his load into her mouth, she gushed all over his face. Kal gulped down as much of her nectar as he could. Diana sealed her lips around him and gulped down every drop of him.

Diana inhaled his length again, she moved a little lower and took his balls in her mouth. She tugged one in her mouth and washed him warmly with her tongue and then continued to the other.

She wanted him more and moved to his shaft once again. His taste was on her tongue and this time going all the way down as far as she could in one smooth move. As her mouth and throat swallowed him, her tongue was busy on his shaft, swirling all around and causing him exquisite pleasure.

Kal began to float upward and turned upright for Diana to be upside down. Diana crossed her legs around his neck. He groped two delightful handfuls of her ass as he furiously lapped at her core. Her legs started to tense.

Diana kept only the head in, sucking on it and licking underneath the crown. She was intent on what she was doing and it was driving Kal crazy. Kal was already feeling another orgasm starting deep in his balls.

Diana took him deep another two or three times and by that time he was ready to explode. She placed the head of him just inside her lips and put a lot of suction on the tip, and that was enough to make him let loose.

Pleasure flowed through Kal's body getting more and more intense as his body goes into spasm after spasm. He seemed to have no control over his body except his tongue, so he kept licking. He was rewarded with her orgasmic juices; pushed out by her own contractions. He licked deeper inside her, swirling his tongue in circles as she quivered. Her legs locked again in place. He kept his tongue moving, and she sped the action of her tongue up and down his shaft. Kal maneuvered a finger to her clit. When he very gently brushed it, he set Diana off again.

Diana place her hands on Kal's strong thighs, nails digging into his skin, as his hips started to thrust, pumping in and out; forcing her to open further, to take more and more of him. Her gush of nectar triggered him, and he sent jets into her eager mouth. He tried to drink as much of her love-juice down as he could. Diana sealed her lips around him and swallowed every drop of his.

Diana removed his length from her mouth and gave his tip a kiss. Kal licked her sweetness from her thighs and her slit.

After they both come down from orgasm, Kal found himself tingly all over and completely spent. Somehow he was still able to continue to lick her as he drifted back down to the bed laying on his back with Diana still on top of him. Diana slowly got up and flipped around so they were lying next to each other. She put one hand on Junior stroking him slowly and laid her head on Kal's shoulder saying, "That was wonderful."

"You certainly are," Kal grinned. "I think we should let this round be a tie."

"Hmm...I can agree with that...for now." Diana laughed teasingly.

They leaned in capturing each other's lips in a passionate kiss. Both moshing in pleasure tasting the now mixed flavors of themselves.

Pulling away from their kiss, Diana sat up with a devious smile, "Race you to the shower," and flew off quickly

"Hey, Diana! You didn't say when!"

Kal was out of bed and right behind her in seconds. Diana gasped and squealed as he swooped her up in his arms.

Going into the bathroom, Kal turned on the shower, adjusted the temperature, and stepped in under the steaming hot water with Diana. They both smiled and came together for a deep kiss, their tongues and lips melding under the heat of the water. They hungrily made out with water

THE DARK SPELL

flowed down over their necks and down their chests as their hands over each other's backs.

Diana admired the curve of his back and with a smirk, she acted on the impulse and raked her nails across its contours, creating angry red lines in his skin. There was a lift to the corner of his mouth, a sensuous curve, which constituted as a smile.

Kal advanced on her, gripping her waist to pull her body impossibly tighter against his own and then he bent to trace her skin with his lips. Teeth dug into her neck and she moaned, quietly, at the sensation of it. Diana's hands scrambled for skin, settling with his shoulder blades as her head tilted to accommodate his lips. They covered a broader surface, nibbling along the way.

A shuddered breath flew from her lips at such touches and she could not help but return the favor. Accordingly, her nails pierced his skin like talons and held tightly to it. In response his arms tightened at her waist, kneading her flesh as his hands inched toward her thighs. The skin was smooth beneath his touch. His fingertips danced along the skin until they reached her inner thighs and here he parted them, idly tracing her most sensitive of flesh with a soft, masculine chuckle.

Diana's knees buckled and she grasped him all the tighter, lust engulfing their bodies and spreading like a flame.

Kal reached for the bottle of body wash. They each poured the soup into their hands, lathering up and rubbing against each other. Diana spent a fair amount of attention with Junior in her hands as Kal spent an equal amount of attention on her breasts.

Kal laughed and turned her around, facing away from him and at the wall of water jets that were shooting out to rinse off her front and, as the changing colors of lights cast by the fixtures cast their ethereal glow in the steamy shower, he began massaging her shoulders.

"Mmmm, this is nice," she moaned.

Kal took his time, working his thumbs into her muscles, moving from her shoulders to her neck, up the back of her head, running his hands through her scalp and massaging it, then working back down to her shoulders and continuing down her back. He worked his way down to her lower back, then knelt behind her, kneading the area above her ass with his thumbs, working them into the dimples in the skin there and around them, then lowering to her ass, working to release any pent-up tension in her muscles and, of course, spreading her cheeks from time to time for a view. Then he carried on to her legs, working away at her hamstrings and her calves, gripping her and loosening her muscles, feeling the tension release as she gave the occasional moan of relaxation.

"Turn around," he commanded, and she quickly obliged, and he continued to work on her legs, starting around her ankles and studiously keeping his head angled down, denying himself the view of her womanhood for a moment.

Sliding his hands higher up her calves and then to her quads, he took more time than he probably needed, wanting to draw out the experience for her.

And then his hands were higher, his thumbs brushing just under her center.

Finally, slowly, he ran his thumbs along the fleshy part between her quads and her core, brushing at her labia as he continued to massage her, but much more gently now. He stood up and took the showerhead from its latch on the wall. He sat down on the shower bench and pulled Diana down with him to sit on his lap. She said nothing but gave him a curious look.

His hand twisted the grey circle around the head with all the icons of the different styles of spray until he picked one he liked. Holding out his arm he let the water spray him as he adjusted the temperature.

"Perfect, you ready?" he asked.

"Ready for what? You going to wash my hair for me?"

A mischievous grin crossed his face. "Oh, no. You'll see. Just hold on to me and lean back against the wall."

Diana gave him a wary look but did as he said. She put her arm around his neck and leaned against the back corner of the wall.

"Like this?"

Kal nodded his head, "Perfect. Now just relax."

Taking the shower head in his left hand he used his right hand to push her legs open. The spray of water hit her womanhood without warning, sending a rush of ecstasy throughout her body. Her breath caught in her throat, the impact of the water stream had surprised her in its intensity. The shock quickly turned to immense pleasure as he moved the stream up and down her slit. A million tiny fingers are what she imagined, all with one purpose in mind, to make her climax.

His right hand left her leg, she no longer needed the encouragement to keep her legs wide. They had a mind of their own and opened even wider. she closed her eyes and she moaned loudly.

Kal watched the pleasure as it spread out across her face. Her moans came faster and deeper as he moved the shower head up and down, allowing the stream to cover her entire womanhood. Slowly he moved his right hand to the showerhead, hoping she hadn't noticed. With a twist, he moved the ring over one slot to power spray. All the exterior holes closed and redirected the water to the middle nozzle in one full hard spray.

Diana's body jerked involuntarily.

"Kal! OH, GODS!"

The force of the water took her by complete surprise. Her core was already super sensitive from everything he had already done and the water just sent her over the edge. Her hips bucked hard into the air and she arched her back. She felt the hard spray of water following her every motion.

Kal had grabbed her right leg as soon as her first spasm erupted to help hold her in place. With his left hand, he held the shower head as close to her as he could to keep up the constant stream of water into her swollen center.

"Oh Gods!" she screamed.

Diana tightened her grip around his neck as she arched her back one last time. Her orgasm ripped from her body in one last convulsive shutter before she relaxed. She shifted curling against Kal. Her breasts heaved up and down tantalizingly with each deep breath she took. Her nipples were hard erect points that stood a full inch from her body.

"Wow. That was... That was amazing," she finally managed to get out between deep breaths.

Kal rubbed his right hand over her. Slowly, he slid two fingers inside her. Caressing her, working his first two fingers around inside her, he felt her grasping him as he maneuvered around, teasing at her g-spot.

"Oh, I...I...love...this..." she moaned, running her fingers through his hair and scratching at his shoulders.

As Kal continued to thrust his fingers into her as Diana occasionally flexed her muscles and spasmed with jolts of pleasure.

Diana gave a quick intake of breath, but she didn't stop him, continuing to tug at his hair and squeeze his shoulder as he entered her deeper with his fingers and he sped up his thrusting. Her hips thrust harder and harder, and then she let out a long, loud moan and he felt her spasming, losing all control as she rocked against him while he continued to toy with her g-spot and her clit. Diana sat back more against the wall, her chest heaving, and her face totally slack in full relaxed pleasure.

Kal leaned over to kiss her forehead gently, before finding her lips and giving her a peck, just brushing his against hers.

"I want to stay like this forever," she moaned, throwing her arm around his neck and pulling her torso toward him until he was supporting most of her upper body as she buried her face in his neck. He stroked her back and kissed the top of her head.

"Me too," he said.

It was several long minutes before he slowly released her and eased up for them to stand. He placed the showerhead back then turned Diana to face toward the shower wall and slid his member into her. With her hands pressed on the shower wall and his hands on her hips, he drove into her hard and fast.

"Oh gods," she repeatedly cried in pleasure.

She turned her head to look behind her and they shared a look of fiery lust. After a few more moments like this, he pulled out and spun her back around. Their lips met again, full of heat and passion. Kal then picked up Diana and pressed her up against the wall. She spread her legs, resting a foot on the bench. This provided Kal with the perfect position. With a forceful thrust, he plunged his hardness back into her. Diana wrapped her arms around his neck and shoulders, pulling him closer in with every push, and clamped her muscles on him with each thrust. Heated breaths and moans flowed over her lips as she was overcome with his lustful takeover.

"Kal! So...so good! Yes!" she screamed as her back was pressed into the wall and the water continued flowing over their passion.

THE DARK SPELL

"I love you, Di," he breathed in return with a sultry smile.

"I...love you...too," she moaned and hungrily returned her lips to his.

They continued their hot, wet, passionate love making in the shower for a while...until suddenly the water finally went ice cold.

When Kal and Diana emerged from the bathroom in luscious soft white towels, Kal swooped Diana back into his arms.

"Breakfast?"

"Yes, please!"

Kal set her down for them to get dressed. Well half-dressed. He slipped on his boxer briefs and Diana slipped on her thigh-length sheer see-through robe.

The fortress kitchen was just as an ordinary kitchen would be with crystallized walls and much more technical with its appliances.

Diana leaned over the counter watching Kal make his way through chopping vegetables, mixing eggs, flipping the pan. She smiled and walked over to him wrapping her arms around him from behind.

"It's so sexy of you showing off your cooking skills, Chef Kent."

Kal chuckled. "I should show off more often."

"Oh, you do. Especially in the bedroom...or wherever we are for the moment making love." Diana laughed and kissed between his shoulders blades. "Darling, the fortress is just so fascinating. The planetarium, the trophy room, your lab. My sexy scientist. I can't wait to see what your working on."

Kal paused with widen eyes. "You went into the lab?"

"Yes. Was I not supposed to?"

Kal quickly turned around to face her with a nervous yet reassuring smile.

"Oh, yeah, yeah, of course, Di. I just want you to be careful. There are just a lot of things in there that are dangerous. I wouldn't know what to do if something ever happened to you because of that."

Diana smiled and kissed him softly. "You are so protective."

Kal embraced her and kissed the top of her head. He sighed in relief.

Yes, it was very dangerous things in his lab but there was also something very special he was working on. Something Diana couldn't know about until the time was right.

Location: Valeria's Castle

"I love to hate them but hate to love them." Valeria scoffed watching Kal and Diana. "Love? What is Love? A succubus destains the thought. Yet I...relish in their purity. Why?"

Flashback:

From the 16th century to the 18th, Covent Garden, and in particular, Drury Lane, was London's prime location for the sex trade. Sir John Fielding, the magistrate of the Bow Street Police Court, called it "the great square of Venus," and it certainly lived up to the name. The market may have raged in the daytime, but at night men flocked to the square not for perishable goods, but for two things: theatre and sex.

"And you are?"

"Valeria. Valeria Messalina."

"Valeria? What a gorgeous name."

Valeria smiled seductively. "And you are?"

"Dionysus."

"Like the God?"

"I am the God."

"Oh?" *She laughed.* "Well as head Mistress of this fine establishment. It would be an honor to pleasure a God."

Valeria took his hand guiding him to a private room. Once inside, she closed and locked the door with a devious smile.

"So Dionysus I-"

She gasped as she was immediately pinned against the door.

Dionysus smirked and inhaled. "The scent of wickedness. A beautiful demon. A beautiful...poisonous flower. My Aconitum."

Valeria's eyes are glazed. "Unhand me now," *she warned.*

"And what will you do...Succubus?"

Valeria was shocked. Dionysus smirked again and threw her to the bed.

"You may have made fools of the likes of Hercules and your beloved Emperor Husband, but me, Succubus, I can take the poison. Show me your true form, my Aconitum."

Flashback End

THE DARK SPELL

Valeria looked into her mirror to see Kal and Diana feeding each other breakfast, kissing, and embracing.

She scoffed. But felt a tremble run through her body and she could only think of...

"Dionysus..." she moaned. But suddenly, "No!" She snapped into a rage. "He shall pay!"

2 hours later: Pennsylvania - King of Prussia Mall

King of Prussia Mall is the largest retail space in the U.S. and the largest shopping mall on the East Coast with seven major department stores and more than 450 stores, boutiques and restaurants.

With Kal holding their bags, he and Diana strolled looking to see which store they would be interested in going into next.

"This is amazing, Love! I don't think we can get to all the stores in one day!" Diana said as she latched tighter onto Kal's arm.

"Ha! You know we can just fly back anytime. Busy work schedules be damn. Making time like this with you is priority."

"Darling, we have time. You know I know our work comes first. It's sexy when you work, it makes the end reward even more satisfying."

Kal moved behind Diana and wrapped his arms around her waist from behind as they kept walking. He kissed the side of her neck.

"Ah, so putting in work for the wonder? I can handle that."

"Well if you want that to be another one of our sexy challenges?"

"Challenge accepted. Putting in work is what I do best."

"Hmm..in more ways than one."

"Yeah...full body work." Kal kissed the side of her neck again.

"Oh, Kal, you are such a naughty man!"

"You just don't know what I'm thinking right now but once we ge-"

Kal stopped walking abruptly.

"Kal?"

"Mom! I can't find my mom!" he heard.

"Trouble. A kid's lost. No one is even trying to help."

"Oh, no! Let's hurry!"

Kal took Diana's hand as they started running toward the direction Kal heard the child crying.

The little boy fell to the floor kicking and screaming. Other costumers passed by completely ignoring or mumbling amongst themselves believing he was just a child throwing a tantrum.

Kal handed Diana their bags and ran over to the child.

"Hey, hey, sport...come on. Calm down. It's alright."

Diana smiled watching as Kal picked him up, embracing him, trying to sooth him. Kal was always great with kids. She remember fondly the times the Justice League would visit children hospitals or orphanages, be part of festivals and parades. The children loved having Superman take them on a flight or to hang and swing on his massive arms and even read to them, reenact a battle in the most comedic way or have a puppet show. During Christmas time, Kal would dress up as Santa with bags full of toys. He would also use his laser eye to craft small wooden sculptures. Super Santa, they would call him.

Diana couldn't help but think that one day, yes, it was very possible for them to have their own children and deep down that is what she truly desired. A family with her best friend and the love of her life.

"I can't find my mom!" The boy still cried.

"Promise we will find her."

The boy sniffed and looked at Kal then looked down.

"You're very tall, Mister."

Kal chuckled and set him down.

The boy then noticed Diana.

"You're very pretty!"

"Why thank you," Diana smiled.

"What's your name, little guy?" Kal asked.

"Benji."

"I'm Clark and she's Diana."

"How old are you, Benji?" Diana asked.

"7." Benji looked at them both. "Are you married?"

Their hearts dropped and they glanced at each other.

"Yeah, we are!" Kal said without any hesitation and smiled making Diana's heart drop even further and butterflies in her stomach.

Diana placed her hand on Kal's shoulder.

"Where did you last see your mother?"

THE DARK SPELL

"I don't remember. I saw toys and went there. I didn't like them. I went back to where she was but she was gone."

Kal nodded. "Hmm..." he listened through the crowd.

"Have you seen this little boy?! Excuse me! Please! Can you help me! My little boy is missing. Please can anyone help me!"

"Ma'am, calm down," a security officer said.

"How can I calm down when my son is missing?! Benji! Benjamin!"

"Is your mom wearing a sweater with a drawing printed on it?"

Benji gasped. "Yes! That's my drawing!"

Kal smiled. "Alright, little buddy. Let's get you back to your mom!" Kal kneeled down. "Hop up!"

Benji climbed up Kal's shoulders. He gasped and laughed as Kal stood up.

"I'm tall!"

"Heh. Sure are kid! I'm sure you can spot your mom now."

Diana couldn't stop smiling as she latched onto Kal's arm again. He looked down at her with a proud smile and winked.

They went down the escalators heading to the large fountain.

"Benji!" They heard yelling.

"MOM!"

The woman quickly turned and smiled with tears running down her face uncontrollably. "Benjamin! Oh goodness!"

As she ran towards them, Kal set Benji down for him to run to his mother.

"Oh, Benji!" She embraced her son, crying harder. "I'm so glad you're safe!"

"I'm sorry, mom. I just wanted to get a toy."

"I know. I'm sorry, too just being all over the place."

"Mom! Clark and Diana helped me find you! Clark is really tall and Diana is really pretty!"

The woman looked up and gasped. "Oh... Mr. and Mrs...?"

"Kent," Kal said with a proud smile.

"Mr. and Mrs. Kent. Thank you so much for finding my son and bringing him back to me." She shook Kal's hand. "Oh..." she smiled staring at Kal's godly handsome face.

Diana looked off trying to hold back her giggle.

"Mrs. Kent?"

The woman was also taken aback by Diana's divine beauty.

Diana looked at the woman and smiled, nodding slightly. "Benji is such a very sweet boy."

Kal kneeled to Benji. "Okay, kiddo. Be sure not to walk away from your mom again. Just have patience and you'll find the right toy."

Benji nodded. "Okay. Yes, sir."

Kal held up his fist. Benji laughed and fist bumped Kal.

Diana bent down and cupped his cheek. "Be good, young man."

"Yes ma'am," Benji grinned bashfully.

"Thank you so much again."

"No problem at all."

"Mom! Can we get ice cream?!"

"We sure can. We just won't tell your dad."

"Yes!" Benji cheered.

She glanced at Kal then looked at Diana. "You have a good one there."

Diana smiled proudly. "Thank you. I know."

Kal and Diana watched as Benji and his mom walked away. Benji looked back and waved.

Kal and Diana waved back.

Once they weren't in sight blending with the rest of the busy crowd, Kal placed his arm around Diana's shoulders and kissed her temple.

"In or out of the suit, you will always save the day."

"You too, you know. A woman of wonder that has me tied in her lasso."

Diana giggled. "Is that a hint of what you want me to do to you when we get home?"

Kal wiggled his eyes brows and grinned as he took their bags from her. "Let's go home, Love."

"Want to pick up some dinner on the way?"

"Much much later. I'm still stuffed from breakfast," she smirked.

"Ah, then I'll stuff you again some other way," he winked.

Diana giggled.

2 hours later: Clark and Diana's apartment

Diana sat down on the couch with Kal and sighed.

THE DARK SPELL

Kal wrapped his arm around her pulling her closer and kissed her forehead as she curled more against him.

"What's on your mind, Di?"

"I just can't stop thinking about how you had Benji smiling and laughing. He had such a cute little laugh."

"I can't believe no one tried to help him."

"I think that someone would have."

"After how long though? It's like sometimes the world feels like it's going backwards."

"It does but, Darling, that's why we are here. We are here to help move forward. We know some of the most amazing good hearted people and we meet others almost every day around the world. It takes time is all. I believe the term is stubborn in their ways?"

"Ha! It's stuck in their ways. Yeah, yeah...I know, Di."

"Benji's mother was certainly eyeing you," she teased.

"What?! No way!"

Diana laughed and nodded. "This very charming, sexy, strong man brought her son back to her. You are always so great with kids. She even told me I have a good one." Diana caressed his cheek. "I told her I know."

Kal smiled back. "I'm all yours, Di."

Diana paused for a moment then looked up at him with a serious expression.

"May I ask you something, Kal?"

"Of course, Starshine!"

"When Benji asked were we married...you said yes?"

"Oh... Uh..." Kal cleared his throat. "I'm sorry, Diana. It was in the moment of trying to cheer up the kid. Make light of the moment a bit. I was surprised he asked really. I mean...I wouldn't have expected a kid his age to ask that? But then again, kids his age does say and do things unexpected. I don't want you to feel rushed or pressured. If I made you feel that way, I'm sorry. I've told you, I'm grateful for just being with you like this. I know that things have been happening so fast with us. I just...I shouldn't have said that I..." Kal kept stumbling on his words.

Diana shook her head and smiled.

"Oh, Kal...Beloved...Weeks ago we were on the verge of conceiving our first child. That moment of possibility brought me such joy. Seeing you with Benji or any other child, I've imagined our own. From what I know, we've done things a husband and wife would. We are spiritually bound together, Kal. This path we are on together, I wouldn't have it anything other way."

Diana moved to straddle him and placed her hands on his chest. She loved when he was shirtless and only in drawstring pants or his boxers for easy access to her pleasure. Kal just as much, loved Diana wearing a tank top or one of his shirts and thong. He moved his hand down, slowly started to knead her asscheeks.

"Hmm...Madame Ambassador Diana Prince-Kent? Diana Kent. Diana Prince Kent -El. Prince -El Kent....Or should it be Clark Prince?" she laughed. "So many combinations!"

Kal's grinned "Whatever you want, Di. Sexy either way."

Diana smiled and leaned in capturing his lips softly.

"Darling, we spent a few years denying what we deeply felt for each other but our relationship has been a thrill with all we've been through together. It doesn't matter how it happened, all that matters is that we are together now. Completely open and honest about it. No one else can make me feel what I feel. I can't get enough of us making love. The way you hold me in your arms. The way you protect me. I want..." Diana paused, cupping his face with both hands and looked deeply into his eyes. "I want it all with you, Kal-El. To say "I do" and to have our own little ones. It may take more time but we will get there."

"Diana, to hear you say that..." he paused and reached up cupping her cheek. "I love you, Diana." He placed kisses all over her face. "I love you so much. My incredibly gorgeous Starshine. My Goddess. My Queen. My peace. Through all the battles, missions, hours at the Planet trying to meet deadlines, I'm the luckiest man in the universe to come home to you."

"I love you too, Kal-El. So...so...much. You incredibly sexy man. My man."

Kal smirked and placed his arms back around her waist and slid down to her ass again. Diana ran her hands over his warm chest again as he pulled her closer to kiss her neck, lightly sucking and nibbling. Kal was pulling

THE DARK SPELL

off her top and she barely remembered to lift her arms up, listening to his appreciative groan as he caressed her double D breasts, making her so wet. He licked and teased her hard nipples through the lace, switching sides as he went. Always licking, biting, and pinching. Her thong was getting soaked through. Diana untied his pants. Kal stood up, changing places with Diana on the sofa.

Diana grinned and opened her legs for him, snuggling into the cushions. Kal kneeled between them, pulling her closer and ran his hands up to her waist. Her thong with a see through, patterned front, was such a tease to him. Her womanhood was drawing his attention like a magnet. He kissed up the inside of her left thigh as Diana closed her eyes and moaned in anticipation, then up the right thigh as he hooked both sides of her thong and maneuvered it under her and down her thighs, putting it aside after she freed her ankles from it and spread her legs again, revealing a glistening, moist center, ready to be eaten.

Without hesitation, Kal kissed Diana's engorged clit, clearly visible between her nether lips in her arousal and Kal buried his talented lips in her core. His tongue found the right spot immediately and he himself sighed deeply. It was all too easy to lose oneself. A small gasp followed by an encouraging moan greeted him as he kissed again, then extended his tongue to slide the whole of it over her clit, tasting her beautiful womanhood as he did. He focused his effort solely on her clit to start. He flicked, rubbed and circled the little button with his tongue, his hands holding her thighs in place as she bucked her hips in pleasure, meeting his tongue work with moans and gasps. It only took a couple of minutes for his efforts to be rewarded with a long, loud moan as Diana's body stiffened and her back arched into the sofa as she came, orgasmic juices flowing from her core.

Diana grabbed the back of his head as Kal was lapping her core with his tongue, savouring the taste of her juices. He then slowly rubbed her clit with his thumb, bringing shivers of pleasure from Diana as he drew the orgasm out for a little longer, allowing her body to finally relax before returning his tongue to her clit. As he continued to manipulate her, he brought his right hand round from her thigh and slid first, one finger, then a second into her soaked center. Diana moaned as his fingers easily slid into her well lubricated hole. Kal slowly moved them in and out, pleasuring her with his fingers before he began to speed up.

Diana was gasping, "Oh God," repeatedly, as his fingers thrust into her faster and harder, his tongue still flickering over her clit. Her gasps and moans became louder and faster as he worked her hard with his hand, and she came again with a squeal shortly after, her walls contracting hard around his fingers as another flood of orgasmic juices washed over his hand.

Diana's body came to relax after a second intense orgasm, her eyes closed and her mouth open in an O. Taking a chance as Kal knelt up slightly, away from her soaked center, he reached up and placed his two fingers into her mouth. Diana's eyes opened in surprise as she tasted her own juices. Recovering quickly, she gave him a sultry look and sucked his fingers clean, licking around his fingers to ensure she got every drop.

Her urge to kiss him clearly became too strong as she dragged him up to her. Kal offered his lips willingly. Diana just wanted his tongue in her mouth and to put hers in his.

Diana turned their bodies, breaking their kiss, and pushed Kal down to sit on the sofa. She slowly dropped to her knees to remove his pants. She smiled as his thick 9.5 inches sprang up in front of her. It was time to do her own teasing.

After throwing his pants to the side, she leaned up for a brief kiss. Diana ran her hands down his chest and well-formed abs. Her hands went around his shaft and she stroked him. He sucked in a breath and as she stroked the length of him, she couldn't help biting her lips.

He was so hard and his excitement was glistening on the head of his manhood. Diana loved the sight of him...so long and hard...and she couldn't wait any longer to get a taste of him. Diana opened her palm to lick up the length of his shaft, savoring every inch of him, and once she reached his head, she licked him clean with a swirling motion. Diana flicked her tongue and smiled devilishly as she heard him moan with pleasure. She swirled her tongue now all around his tip and she felt his muscles tighten quickly in response.

Diana then parted her lips and Kal felt a sudden rush of sensation as she took him into her mouth, as deep as she could. She squeezed his thighs with her hands as she continued to move up and down taking him in again and again. His breath came in moans and gasps as he tried to stay quiet. She could see his hands bunched up in the pillows on each side of him.

Continuing to take him into her mouth, Diana felt him tense further as she sucked and flexed her tongue. She worked her way up and down as far as she could take him into her mouth, getting into a steady rhythm now with her hands.

"Damn, Di," he moaned, helpless to do otherwise, "shi-."

Kal's hands came to get tangled in her hair and cradle her head. Diana moved her right hand to caress his balls, gently pulling and stroking.

"Di," he gasped and stopped her after a bit when the pleasure became almost too much.

Diana looked up at him and he looked at her, sitting between his legs with his manhood in her hand. She could see the desire in his eyes. He groaned as he gently pulled her up to stand in front of him.

Diana straddled him again. As they embraced, Diana couldn't help but to sigh feeling his hot, smooth skin pressed against hers and the strength of his embrace with his arms around her and holding her so tight. Diana leaned back a bit as Kal lifted his hands to her breasts, cupping them in his palms. Kal begin to caress the sensitive skin and lowered his mouth to one breast and teased her nipple with his tongue again. Diana tilted her head back and moan softly as she grasped his shoulders and just enjoyed this moment of pleasure.

After a few moments of teasing her this way, Kal pulled her body back to his. Kal took a moment to just stare into her eyes, the piercing cerulean blue, deep and intense with growing passion. Kal held her face in his hands and kissed her gently on the forehead, Then he begin to trail kisses all over her face...her eyes...her nose...her cheeks...and finally her lips, kissing her deeply, enjoying the taste of him and her on each other's lips. Diana wrapped her arms around his strong shoulders as they kissed more fervently now...their tongues teasing and flicking against each other.

Diana rubbed herself against him. One of Kal's hands went down Diana's stomach, the side of her thigh and then inwards. Kal cupped her mound, groaning low in his throat and Diana gasped against his mouth as he slid two fingers between her nether lips and found her swollen clit. He rubbed her clit in circles and Diana lost control, whimpering against his demanding mouth and his strong hand.

"Kal," she was already climaxing, "Oh Gods!"

He captured her lips again and his kiss got fiercer. He crushed her to him with his free hand. His fingers left her clit for a moment, to let her feel his member against her core.

Diana rose a bit positioning herself above him, reaching down to hold him in place. She lowered herself and slid down his length slowly, inch by inch. They both moaned as he filled her. Kal loved the warmth and wetness of her tightness encasing him, every millimetre of a sensation as the slick walls pressed against him. Diana sat there for a moment with him fully embedded inside her, her soft thighs and calves pressed against his thighs and her erect nipples brushing against his chest. Then, she started to slowly move up and down and got a steady rhythm going, she brought her lips to his and slipped her tongue into his mouth.

Kal's fingers returned to her clit and started to rub. Diana rode him slowly, his fingers bringing her to the brink of sanity.

"Oh, Gods..." Diana breathed against his lips.

Diana felt her climax start and she knew she didn't have long to go. She thrust down on him harder and he responded, bucking upwards to meet her, his fingers firmer and faster. Diana clutched his shoulder and the sofa back as she frantically held on to anything she could get her hands on. Her breath was mere gasps and she whimpered again. She caught his eyes and he was staring right back at her.

Kal brought his hands up to her breasts, fondling them, caressing the soft, smooth flesh while running his palms gently over her hard nipples as he savored the feeling of her hot, wet womanhood sliding up and down his manhood. He then leaned forward to take her nipple into his mouth as she rode him, feeling like silky heaven. His tongue and lips alternated on her nipples.

"Oh by Gods, Kal! My Love!" she screamed.

She began picking up her pace and riding him harder and faster. Kal released her breasts at this point and leaned back so he could watch them bouncing enticingly. Diana straightened up on his lap and threw her head back.

THE DARK SPELL

Kal ran his hands along her waist and reached around for her full, round ass, squeezing and caressing it, as it bounced up and down on his lap.

Diana's eyes were closed but her expression was blissful, which was definitely nice to see and made Kal smile. Kal pushed up into her to make sure she was getting all she could of his manhood as she was getting closer and closer to climaxing.

Diana moaned loudly and nearly continuously as she approached another orgasm. It felt as though her core was becoming even hotter and more slippery, though Kal wouldn't have even thought that possible when he'd first slipped into her.

Kal's gaze was still on her bouncing breasts but his focus was on making her climax again and she was nearly there. Diana dropped down hard on his lap and just remained there as her orgasm coursed through her, causing her entire body to tremble. She still rocked her hips subtly so that she could feel him moving inside her but mostly she just sat there moaning and shaking. When she finally went still, she let out a long sigh and continued sitting there with her eyes closed.

Kal was feeling the stirrings of his own orgasm and could feel the gooseflesh under his hands as they continued to caress Diana's bare skin. The look on Diana's face went from concentration to ecstasy then a big smile took over. When she finally opened her big, beautiful eyes again, she was still smiling and she looked at him before kissing him passionately.

He groaned and Diana felt his smile against her lips.

She broke apart, becoming everything and nothing for a moment before returning to her senses. Kal leaned them over sideways into the sofa. He had her underneath him, still inside of her, still hard and so ready for release. Becoming hungry again, Diana lifted her ass a bit to take him in deeper and Kal gasped with a smile.

"You," he moaned, "You're wild."

Diana smirked raised her head up to claim his lips.

"An Amazon can't be tamed, Mr. Kent. But try it if you dare," she whispered to him seductively.

"Heh," he grinned slyly as he pinned her down on the sofa.

Kal thrust in and out of her at a hard yet slow pace. Diana licked and bit his neck as Kal plowed her into oblivion.

The smack of flesh on flesh filled the living room. He groaned roughly and held on to her ass as his powerful thrust became even more deliciously intense and Diana climaxed around him. Diana trailed her nails down his back and finally rest on his ass, squeezing firmly as he was thrusting into her again and again. Diana wrapped her legs around his waist and thrust up toward him taking all she could of him in. She moved her hips in a seductive circle and she could feel him stroking every inch of her inside. Diana moaned out his name breathlessly...drawing out every syllable.

Diana felt Kal's body tense and his breathing becoming ragged. She could tell that he was getting close. Kal began to say her name over and over and Diana swore that there was no sexier sound on this planet or any other. Within half a dozen hard thrusts, she felt the inevitable warmth building within her again, then slowly focusing until a wave of pleasure washed through her. She shook violently as a strong orgasm flowed through, then she felt a super hot warmth filling her womanhood.

She nodded and whispered, "yes..." in his ear. She wanted ever last drop of him.

Kal rose up off her.

"Kal," she groaned and whined as he slowly slid out of her.

She watched Kal's face and as soon as she felt the cool air of the room against her burning flesh she knew he was staring at her most intimate region. The vision of this gorgeous man kneeling in front of her giving her such rich pleasure simply drove her more and more wild.

His long thick member flopped on her stomach making her gasp and giggle.

Diana looked down and reached with the fingertips of one hand and stroked the silky skin of his head, gathering a clear drop of essence on one finger, putting it to the very tip of her tongue, delicately tasting it. She took that finger into her mouth, closed her eyes and savored it. She reached again and took another drop, licking it, rubbing it along her lips. Kal watched her in awe.

"My, my...Darling, please...more..."

Kal lifted her legs high into the air, and yanked her closer placing her legs against his chest. He look down between her legs at his own member. He squeezed her legs together and pulled back then pushed forward,

THE DARK SPELL

teasing between her nether lips gently. He pulled out from between her thighs. Once again rubbing against her slit; feeling her puffy outer lips, wet, soaked with his abs her juices, coating him. Kal pressed forward half an inch, her outer lips part, rubbing against her soft wet flesh, then, another half inch.

Diana whined. "Kal-El...now..."

He smirked. "Patience..."

She whined, groaned then gasped in surprise as Kal sunk into her. Her eyes snap open, a hiss of breath taken through her teeth. She arched her back, her head presses into the sofa, both hands gripping the cushions.

Kal pushed forward, Diana's thighs began to tremble, her mouth opened, another gasp of breath.

Kal pulled back and, just as he was about to slip out, he pushed back in, a little further this time. Pull back, push forward; this time he didn't stop, a long slide all the way in, his hips pressed up against her buttocks, squeezed up against her, pushing in as far as he could go. Her back relaxed, she sunk back into the sofa.

"Oh! Ahh!"

Grinding up against her ass, short tight thrusts, Kal shifted the angle inside the swollen walls of her womanhood, rubbing against her sensitive spots. Her thighs trembled again, back arching again, pulling the cushions. Long deep thrusts with a little grind each time his hips pressed against her.

Diana's head was pressed back more and she was panting through her open mouth, her body shivering each time Kal thrust into her. The exquisite feel of her womanhood around his flesh; all the sensations to tip him over the edge, to tempt him into pounding into her and, to take his pleasure and pump his load into her again.

But not yet.

Not until he'd savoured every minute of pleasuring this woman nice and slow. He looked down at his manhood burying in her body and he groaned out loud as once again the sensations threaten to overwhelm him. Kal closed his eyes and tried to concentrate on not releasing but this only seemed to increase the awareness of his senses; her perfume and hot sex, the sound of his length sliding in and out of her wet core, the feel of her ankles against the sides of his face the feeling of her ass against his balls, her juices soaking his balls and upper thighs, the hot liquid grip around him and the extremely sensitive skin of his glans as it rubs against the walls of her womanhood.

God damn this was just too good.

Diana's panting breath was changing, becoming imperceptible moans and cries, barely above a whisper but the more Kal plunged into her the louder they got. Her hands reached out and trailed down his abs to his hips, urging him on, the telltale tingling starts to build even more inside him

Responding to the overpowering sensations and her urging, his pace increased; hips slapping against her ass, length pounding into her.

Kal gritted his teeth as he held off for a few more seconds.

Diana started to gasp, her eyes squeeze tight shut, arms flung out to the side fingers splayed wide, Kal can feel her insides clench:

"Ohyesohyesohyes! YES!"

With one more pounding thrust the tingling exploded; with his balls crushed against her ass, Kal felt long jets of essence pulse again and again, he pulled back and smacked into her, another pulse, giving her everything he could, but pretty quickly, as his orgasm rippled through his body, his hard, pounding thrusts deteriorate into short slow unsteady movements until he stopped and pressed up hard against her; rasping breath, head down, eyes tight closed as he savored what had just happened.

Then, Diana's body began to relax, her face too, a long sigh from her as Kal's own orgasm also diminishes with a shiver. He released his grip on her legs, ease them down off his shoulders, back around his waist. Kal slumped back and his member slipped from her.

A few moments on his knees, still breathing hard, he stared at his Goddess. He waited for her to catch her breath completely. When she did, Diana pushed herself up on her elbows. She looked to see Kal smirked.

"What is it?"

"Your beautiful and I can't get enough of you."

Diana raised her brow and looked down to see Junior still at attention.

She smirked. "Such a man of resilience and you are taking this stuffing literally."

Kal smiled boyishly. "Turn around for me." He directed his eyes to the back of the sofa.

THE DARK SPELL

Diana smiled, sitting up on her knees and adjusted herself to lean against the back of the sofa, her hand already gripping the back edge and her her legs spread for him. Kal took the time to admire her ass once again, running his hands over it, kissing it and tonguing her. After pleasuring her smooth cheeks, Kal positioned himself, kneeling behind her. He took his swollen manhood in his hand and teased her center and clit with it...just slowly sliding it back and forth.

He guided his manhood back into her hot, dripping womanhood, once again mixing their juices. They both moaned as he slowly slid all the way into her and his hips touched her ass. Kal took her by the hips and started off slowly but, as Diana started pushing back against him, clearly still very worked up from her recent orgasm, he picked up the pace. Diana reached back running her fingers through his hair then gripped and pushed his head forward to hers and their lips mashed together in a brief kiss.

Diana continued pushing back against Kal's incoming thrusts, so anxious to have him fully embedded in her as he was.

Breaking their kiss, Diana pressed her face against the seat of the couch and she reached down between her legs to stroke her clit as Kal thrusted into her. Her womanhood was still so nicely snug but also incredibly slippery, making for a very pleasant friction on his throbbing member.

As Kal slipped his hands up to fondle her breasts, Diana moaned louder, quickly approaching another orgasm, right on the heels of another. God, how her womanhood felt heavenly sliding up and down his member just as her breast did in his hands, and Diana was enjoying herself just as he was.

Kal moved his hands back down to her hips, giving her deeper penetration with long, full strokes and after a few full thrusts deep, he felt her body tremble as she came once again. Kal let everything lose, pounding into her, feeling her pulse around him, holding on every minute and then every second he could...until finally with a huge breath, he exploded into her releasing everything and allowing the sensation to wash over then both.

"Oh my Gods!"

"Di..." he kissed the side of her neck and trailed her shoulder before slowly pulling out.

He laid back on the arm of the sofa and Diana adjusted herself to lay on top of him with Kal immediately wrapping his arms around her.

After a few minutes lying in a breathless pile, they shared a sweet kiss.

"I'm surprise we didn't break the sofa," Diana teased.

"Ha! It's sturdy enough to put you in all sorts of positions. But I can definitely put in even more work to see just how it really holds up."

Diana laughed. "That's a very good excuse just to say you want more of me."

"No excuse needed. I would shout that out to the world."

"I think we were already loud enough for the neighbors to hear."

Kal chuckled. "Yeah, you were extra loud."

Diana playfully bit his neck.

Kal squeezed her ass. "You know I'm telling the truth."

"But who's fault is it, hmm?"

"I most definitely take full responsibility."

Diana smiled and kissed where she bit him on his neck.

They laid their for a moment in silent bliss. Kal ran his fingers through Diana's hair as Diana was drawing hearts and their initials on his chest with her finger.

"It feels like we're already are married."

"Yes, it does. That's what makes this all the more special."

"Diana?"

"Yes, Darling?"

She looked up at him and their eyes locked.

"I love you."

"I love you, too."

Kal caressed her cheek and pulled her up closer to capture her lips in a soft kiss.

Location: Valeria's Castle

Valeria, Eros and Strife watched them from Valeria's mirror.

"Well...quite a show that was," Strife said sarcastically taking a sip of wine.

Eros smirked. "Jealousy is becoming of you more and more."

"Jealously?! Why would I be jealous of low rank gods?!"

THE DARK SPELL

"You know there's nothing low rank about Diana and Kal-El. They have the power to level us all. Kal-El can rival your father."

"Watch your tongue, Eros. You wouldn't say that in the presence of Father."

"I wouldn't have to anyway. He knows as well."

"Enough, you two with your childish bickering! Have either of you found the serpent?"

"No." Eros answered sternly. "I've said before, Dionysus does not want to be found."

"He is a coward! But he will face what he's done to me."

"Valeria, I warned you not to get them involved."

Strife scoffed. "Don't worry, Eros. Diana can handle herself or is she too much of a spoiled princess that can't be touched?"

"What are you after, Strife?"

"You dare go against your Queen?" Strife questioned back.

"It's sibling rivalry, Eros," Valeria teased.

"Strife, this is not the time. Diana is not at fault for your father's misdeeds."

"She exists. She's nothing more than a slut for that second rate Sun God like her mother was for Father!"

"What's between Diana and Kal-El, even you know is not something that should be compared with Zeus and his conquests. His passion for the Amazon Queen couldn't be denied. Zeus seduced Hippolyta just as he's done times before with others."

Strife glared. "The others are just as worthless."

"I said that's enough! Diana and Kal-El will help me. They are the only ones who can anyway. You know that, Eros....and besides... they are protected being their own guards of one another. Kal-El is the epitome of male specimen. He is neither a god nor a mortal yet he represents both. One after another of pleasurable tidal waves. I know I counted more than 15 of Diana's awakenings we just witnessed. A godly lover. If it wasn't for that special herbal concoction, there would be dozens of half-breeds infiltrating Olympus. Kal-El has the ability to populate a new world. His love for Diana is boundless. All the more reason to counter the impudence of Dionysus."

"Once we find Dionysus, I will have a word with him myself. Then you shall do as you please," Eros glared.

Valeria smiled. "You'll love the gathering I have planned. You say Dionysus doesn't want to be found, Eros? This is only a game to him. He will make his presence known soon enough for the mortals' festivities."

A week later: Clark and Diana's apartment

While Diana was on the shower, Clark was on the phone with Martha. "Yeah Ma, everything is fine."

"Well seeing you two on TV fighting like that always worries me."

They came back from a briefing at the WatchTower after a long grueling battle against Titano, the Super-Ape and Karaqan.

"I know. But we don't want you to worry, especially Diana. She would assure you of her battle training and would say making a sacrifice is an honor for the greater good and protecting the innocent."

"She's such a sweet strong young woman. So when will you..." Martha paused. "Where is Diana? I'm not on speaker, right?"

Clark smiled. "No speaker, Ma. She's in the shower and to answer your question...it'll be soon. We still have a lot to take care of first though. And I'm still getting it all planned out. Her mom and sisters, all our friends are getting prepared too. I have to put a few more touches on the...gift. It has to be perfect, Ma. Diana deserves it."

"My boy. Now a grown man making such an important decision. I'm so proud of you!"

Clark could hear Martha starting to cry.

"Thanks Ma. But it's all because of you and Pa. You both showed me what it meant to being in love. You know how it was for me growing up. I had Lana and Pete and a few other friends but I just couldn't truly be myself around them. Lying to them everyday. Lana found out by accident and I was happy for at least her to finally knowing. But with Diana, there's no hiding anything. No secrets. Honest from the start. Ma, the day I met Diana, I knew she was the one."

"I remember the first time you brought her here. You couldn't take your eyes off her, not even for a second. I hadn't seen such a smile you had that day since you were a child at Christmas. I knew she was special to you then."

THE DARK SPELL

"She has me smiling like that everyday," he admitted. He heard the shower turning off. "She's getting out now."

"Oh! Well let me get off the phone before I run off at the mouth being so excited. Let her know a little later I checked up on you two. I love you both and so proud!"

"Will do, Ma and love you, too. Tell Pa to be careful on the tractor."

"Ha! You sure do know your stubborn father. Let me go out and see what he's up to now. Bye, Son. Talk again soon!"

"Okay! Bye, Ma."

Clark hung up the phone and set it down on the counter. He quickly went to their bedroom bathroom. As Diana was wrapped the towel around her body, he swooped her up.

She gasped then laughed. "Oh, Kal! What are you doing?!"

He smiled and kissed her softly.

"No clothes for the rest of the evening, Di."

"Hmm...I'm loving where this is going."

"Dinner and a movie marathon...but naked. And it's guaranteed we won't make it past the first 5 minutes of the first movie," he smirked and kissed her again.

Another week passed: The Embassy

Clark Kent walked in with a devilish smirk but then walking up to Janine, he flashed his charming smile.

"Hi, Mr. Kent! How are you today?" Janine asked.

"Just fine and you?"

"Fairly well. Madam Prince will be with you momentarily. She's in another meeting. Please have a seat."

Clark nodded slightly and smiled. "Ok. Thank you."

Clark sat down looking at his notepad.

"Of course, Ms. Romay, my sister, Donna, will be in touch to make arrangements for the photography."

"Thank you so much, Diana! I'm so excited about the festival and banquet. All the talented little girls and boys performing will be lovely."

"Yes," Diana smiled.

"I will see you soon, Diana! Enjoy the rest of your day!"

BOOK BANK PUBLISHING

They walked to the lobby. Diana smirked seeing Clark sitting in the waiting area.

"Oh I plan to," she said under her breath. "Enjoy the rest of your day as well, Ms. Romay!"

Clark looked up and his jaw immediately dropped seeing Diana wearing a vintage deep v neck double split backless halter Grecian dress.

"Good afternoon, Mr. Kent."

He quickly stood up. "Afternoon, Madame Prince."

Diana bit her lip glancing down to see his quite obvious erection he wasn't even trying to hide. She turned and started walking away.

With a sly grin, Clark kept his eyes on her as he followed her. He couldn't take his eyes off her. The way her hips swayed and those beautiful cakes he loved so much with a jiggle. Clark couldn't help thinking how it would be to place his palm against one of those cheeks and just squeeze, definitely bend her over.

They walked into the elevator however they were not alone with 5 other people. Two other men couldn't help but sneak a glance at her. Another woman in the elevator rolled her eyes. Clark was amused with the different reactions Diana would always get from people. While he stood closely behind her, Diana couldn't help herself to teasingly push back against him.

She looked back at him and winked. Clark cleared his throat trying to maintain discreetness.

The elevators opened on the second floor.

"Excuse me..." Diana said as she walked out.

Clark watched her for a second with a smirk then walked out as well.

Once in her office, Diana closed and locked it.

"Please, Mr. Kent, have a seat."

Clark sat down in a chair while Diana sat on the lounge sofa seductively crossing her legs. Clark was given a full view of those long glorious smooth sexy legs. The splits of her dress opened to show off her thick thighs and his trousers started to get tighter and tighter. He wants so bad to be in between those legs right now.

"Madam Prince, I wasn't aware of that dress?" He quirked his brow.

"Will this be on the record, Mr. Kent?"

"Just between you and me. Our private record."

Diana bit her lip. She had him right where she wanted him. Easy win for this round of their sexy little game.

"Oh, this was just one of the few things I've had. Hand sewed by my Amazon sister, Maizie. She would design and with the help of others sow incredibly beautiful dresses, skirts, tunics, even jewelry. She told me that some of these certain designs are meant for special occasions."

"This is one of those special occasions?"

"Very much so."

Diana uncrossed her legs and stood up walking over to him.

"Let's see how much self-control you have," she said in a teasing voice.

Clark smirked when she leaned over, unbuckling his belt and unzipping his pants. Diana slowly got onto his lap and Clark knew exactly what she was going to do. He watched her as she began to rock back and forth. He dragged his eyes down her body taking all of her in. He felt the fabric of his boxers getting damp from the wetness of her.

His hands wrap around her waist, holding her still and their eyes boring into each other's as their lips become ever closer with each passing second. Both wanted to so badly kiss in the moment but he evaded her by crashing his forehead into her shoulder with a groan and his hands softly running up and down her bare thighs, slow and teasing.

"Come on, Kal. Give up!"

Her breath hitched, her hands gripping his shoulders as she continued to grind herself against him, feeling his hard muscle tense and flex underneath her.

"What are you trying to do to me, Diana?" His lips teased along her jaw, grinning when she moved her head to the side to give him better access. "I know the spots, Diana. The ones that will make you scream.."

She gasped when he slapped hard on her ass and gave it a wild squeeze.

Knowing she was losing the game she started, Diana raised from him and pulled down his boxers, his manhood immediately sprang out of its confinement. Clark shuddered, feeling her fingers wrap around his length, making it throb lustfully.

Diana moaned seeing him already leaking. She gazed up into his eyes and licked her lips erotically.

"Give in now, Kal."

"Diana..." he growled.

She let him go. "I will wi-"

To her surprise, Clark grabbed her by her hips turning her around. He lifted her dress up and slid her thong down her legs to her ankle. He then pulled her down to sit on his lap, her back against his chest.

"What was that?" he questioned. "You'll win this round? Sure about that?"

Diana giggled and leaned back fully into him, kissing him on the lips.

"This surely wasn't what you left home in," he whispered in her ear. "We wouldn't have gone anywhere."

"It was a surprise to get this exact reaction." She moved against him.

Clark smirked as his hands did the one thing they wanted to do, running them up and down her thighs. The skin was like velvet silk, smooth and taut. After he got his fill, he ran them right up her side to cup and squeeze her breasts. The feeling of his hands squeezing her breasts made Diana's cerulean eyes widen, gasping and moaning.

The intensity of Clark's erect manhood throbbed throughout his body. Every little movement and sound just increased their desire.

"You know you can't be too loud, Diana," Clark whispered in her ear.

Diana bit her lip. "We should soundproof my office then."

"I'll get right on that."

After a moment of pause and heavy breathing, they threw themselves at each other and frantically kissed in a sexual frenzy. Diana kissed hard with her lips that were soft and warm.

Diana began moving her hips back and forth slowly, causing his length to slide against her nether lips and between her thighs. Diana leaned further into him, angling her body so her clit would maintain pressure against his rod.

Seeing where this was going, Clark quickly stood them up, moving forward, turning Diana, lifting her off her feet, and set her on the desk.

He looked at her, his gaze was dark and wild and something else that sent a shot of pleasure straight through Diana's body. Never once did he break that contact and his hands slid back down her body, grazing her

THE DARK SPELL

nipples until she shivered and traveled down until he reached her slit on her thighs.

He dipped beneath her and she felt him kissing up her thighs. She let out a small sigh as his lips latched onto her skin, nipping and sucking in a way she knew there would be a trail of marks all along her inner thighs.

Diana trapped her lip between her teeth, "You're such a tease, Kal"

Kal pointed to her dress and asked her back, "Who is the tease here, Sweetheart?" and pecked a few soft kisses along her thighs, a small whimper escaped her lips at how sensitive she was when she felt him softly bite down on her skin before soothing the spot with his tongue.

Biting her thighs on last time, he stood back up and shifted her, bending her over the desk.

"Our meeting will run through lunch," he growled in her ear. "I'm pretty hungry, actually."

"Oh? For what?" She asked him as she felt her dress lifted from her back and the cold air caressing her ass.

Being blind to his actions, Diana felt his warm breath passing down her back and over her ass as he kneeled down. Clark groped her ass, filling his hands with her cheeks, spreading her ass a bit, and nipped a kiss to the round curve of her cheek.

He teased his nose and tongue along the curve of her ass and slowly his tongue approached and licked down her crack. She gasped and moaned, wiggling toward him. His tongue circled, causing her to moan again though a little louder.

"Yeeesss! Gods!"

Clark was pleased, and pressed his tongue against the sensitive hole, pushing in, while his fingers pulled it open more from the sides. His tongue tickled her sphincter as she made soft sounds of pleasure and satisfaction. He did his best with a firm tongue, in and out, back and forth, up and down, teasing her. He then made sure to give her womanhood attention, moving one hand to her front, his thumb stuffed between her lips and pressing into her clit. He was ramping her orgasm up quickly. Her body was quivering.

After several delicious licks, Clark kissed the insides of her ass cheeks and blew cool air up and down her crack. He looked down to see her womanhood glistening from this new excitement. Diana was gyrating her hips ever so slightly. Clark plunged back into her ass, now with more intensity. He flicked his tongue quickly against her hole, then gave short, firm licks directly and circled around her rim.

"Oh Gods, this is good!" she breathed out.

"You are so sexy..." was all Clark could get out before returning to her ass.

Diana looked back at him. Clark felt her hand glide to the back of his head, gently grabbing a fistful of his hair, and pushed his face more into her ass. Not that he needed the encouragement, he could do this all day.

Doing this made him feel a little out of his mind. He couldn't believe this beautiful woman was letting him pleasure her like this, and he was determined to satisfy her. The only thing that was even more gratifying than the feeling of her pinching around his tongue was the sound of her simple moan of pleasure.

"Ohhhhhhhhhh, ahhh!" Diana stammered, leaning more against the desk.

Clark's thumb continued to stroke quick circles around her clit and then after swirling her wetness around her core, he thrust two fingers deep inside. At the same time, continuing to thrust his tongue into her ass. Diana was quickly approaching orgasm, not able to keep herself from grinding down on his fingers. She gave a tiny squeal as she clenched down on his fingers, gushing across his hand. She panted heavily through her orgasm, her stomach muscles shivering and her womanhood refusing to let go of his fingers. Clark was bathing her ass in saliva, stroking his fingers in and out slowly as she came down from yet another one of the best orgasms she'd ever had because of her man.

Clark stood up and Diana tilted her head back, eyes hungry with anticipation, intending to give him a kiss.

Clark grinned as their lips touched. Diana moaned softly and her hand still on the back of her head, stroked down his neck. Kissing gently, tentative tongues reached out, yet slowly building to intensity.

Clark hovered just a few inches from her tight, slippery thigh gap. He realized how easy it would be to slip into a different area entirely, but quickly waved the thought away. Not just yet, as much as he wanted to. In

THE DARK SPELL

the meantime, he fully planned on enjoying the next ride he was about to give her.

Despite her eagerness, Diana was still pleasantly surprised by the sudden contact, gasping in delight as the tip of his manhood slid gently between her thighs. Clark gradually filled that small triangle with throbbing flesh, groaning with every inch. He reminded himself, however, to push slower. He applied just a slight amount of pressure against her labia as he slid forward, teasing her with his erection. The veins in his manhood were bulging along its length, adding a bit of texture as he pressed against her labia and clit.

Diana shut her eyes and moaned louder, not daring to catch her breath until his hips were firmly seated against her ass. The sensation of being between her legs alone was more than he'd bargained for. The warmth of her body gave way to cooler air, the head of his manhood now within her sight on the other side.

"How does that feel?" Clark asked, already knowing the answer.

She turned her head slightly back to him, biting her lip. "Wonderful, Beloved. I thought I had you but...it seems I've surrendered."

"We'll count this as another tie is all. It's always a win/win anyway."

Clark pulled himself backward, the head of his manhood disappearing again into her gap and rubbing against her lips. Diana moaned and Clark looked down at the sight of her arousal covering him. There was no way he was going to let it go to waste, and he quickly pushed back into her, filling that triangular void as if it were the tight little hole just above.

Clark thrust faster and harder as her little gasps of pleasure filled the room.

"Oh Gods!" she gasped between thrusts. "Please, don't stop!"

"Not until I feel you flowing down your legs," he answered, glad to find that both of them were enjoying themselves.

Clark remained firm against her womanhood.

The tingle returned to the tip of his manhood, reminding him that Diana's little tease had brought him closer to orgasm than he would have preferred. Clark closed his eyes as he envisioned the mess he would leave between her thighs and on her backside, that would soon transpire.

It was in this moment, lost in his own thoughts, that a slip occurred. Clark pulled back just as Diana's arms began to go weak with ecstasy. She tried to compensate, pushing herself higher and straightening her arms. Her body angled once more, just as Clark thrust forward. Rather than the squeeze of her thighs, he felt the tip of his length begin to penetrate her. Clark froze, immediately aware of the mistake they'd made.

Diana gasped in what he could only assume was a mixture of surprise and pleasure. At the same time, Diana made no movement away from him. And so Clark stood there, head and crown still sheathed in her slippery warmth.

"You couldn't resist anyway, Mr. Kent," she teased.

"Junior couldn't."

Diana giggled and pulled his face closer for a long, passionate kiss.

Clark pushed forward, slipping deeper inside her. Diana's muscles gripped him and then Clark started to move his hips, slowly at first, so Diana could just enjoy the feel of him inside her. And she most definitely enjoyed it. Clark knew that.

Diana cried out, pushing her ass back against his pelvis to take more of his hard member into her tight, slick heat.

Clark placed his hand over her mouth and Diana placed her hand over his to muffle her scream of ecstasy as Clark pumped his immense shaft in and out of her. As her wetness increased, he thrust even faster. The sound of their breathing and him slapping against her is the only sound in the room.

Diana closed her eyes, hunched over her desk as the intense pounding continued.

The heat inside Diana increased until, when she thought she would not be able to bear it any longer, it suddenly exploded and as the intensity of her orgasm pulsed around him, Clark thrusts become quick and deep and suddenly he tensed, groaned, and came inside her wet depths. Diana moaned feeling the warmth of him spilling into her and it was wonderful.

"Diana..." he groaned out, shooting himself into her receptive body. He leaned over and kissed her neck and as he slowly withdrew, brushing his tip against her lovely ass. He smeared it with his essence.

THE DARK SPELL

After a second of catching her breath, Diana turned, looking at her handsome lover. Her fingers came up to his cheek, gently caressing his skin. She kissed him sweetly.

From her lips, Clark moved his mouth down to her chin and along her neck and collarbone.

"Darling, you need to get back to work."

"I'll get there..." he whispered against her neck. "Unless...you want me to go."

"Having my way, I would've already had you tied up and doing whatever I wanted to you. You wouldn't be going anywhere."

Clark immediately felt a stir below. He smirked and smacked her ass making her squeal.

"You've got your lecture with Julia for your night class. You just don't know how sexy you are with that."

Diana laughed softly. "Giving a lecture is sexy?"

"Diana, everything you do is sexy."

"You are making this so difficult. I want you to take me again."

"I'll wait until we get home. Take my time." He kissed her neck. "Nice and slow." He kissed and sucked harder on her neck determined to leave a mark before having to leave.

Then suddenly, Clark's cellphone rung. He paused and sighed.

"Darling, answer. It's probably work."

Clark sighed and answered. "Yeah, Jim?"

"Clark, where are you? Lois is having a fit because of the story you sent in Perry for the front page."

"I'm having Diana for lunch."

Diana's eyes went wide, gasping and slapped him on his shoulder.

"I mean... I'm having lunch with Diana."

"Oh! Sorry! Tell her I said hi!"

Diana giggled. "Hello, James."

"Man, she has the voice of an angel!"

"Yes, she does."

Diana leaned over kissing Clark's neck.

Clark held down a groan. "Well alright, Jimmy. I'll be on my way."

"See ya, man!"

Clark quickly hung up and set his phone on Diana's desk.

Diana was smiling as she was buckling up his pants.

"I really can't believe you said that."

"Jimmy didn't know the difference. But I mean I was just being honest."

Diana laughed. "Naughty man."

Clark smirked and kissed her softly. Diana moaned in his mouth wrapping her arms around his neck, deepening the kiss.

Clark then broke their kiss with a dramatic sigh and groaned.

"What is it?"

"An alert."

"Oh, duty calls. We shou-"

"Nope." Clark kissed her again. "I'll go. It's on my way back to Metropolis. I don't know how long this will be with whatever is happening at the office and hopefully nothing else comes up but I'll be right on time for your lecture tonight, too."

"Darling, you don't have to."

"I wouldn't miss my sexy Goddess speaking about ancient Greek history."

Diana blushed. "I love you."

"I love you too, Di." He kissed her once more. "See you in a few hours."

Clark quickly fixed his clothes and picked up his phone and laptop bag. He kissed her for a final time.

"I couldn't help it."

"I know," Diana winked.

Clark left out of her office. As the door closed, Diana walked over to sit on the sofa.

"Goodness that man." She couldn't stop smiling and bit her lip.

KNOCK KNOCK

Diana stood up making sure her dress was fixed and quickly went to her desk to straighten her papers.

"Come in!"

"Madam Prince, Mayor Corbett is waiting on line 3."

Diana looked at her phone to see it was off the hook. "Oh...Thank you, Janine." Diana picked up the phone. "Hello? Hi, Mr. Corbett...."

THE DARK SPELL

Janine nodded trying not to laugh as she closed the door. She didn't know exactly what had occurred but she could imagine.

30 minutes later...Metropolis: Daily Planet

Clark took a deep breath as he knocked on Perry's office door.

"Come in, Kent."

Clark opened the door to see Lois frowning with her arms folded and Jimmy looking for a an entertaining show.

"Perry?"

"Have a seat, Kent."

Clark slightly nodded and sat down.

"So now we can hash this out like adults."

"Perry, before anything else, I want to say to go ahead and give Lois the headliner front page."

"You sure?"

"My story will still be on the first page just not the headliner. It'll be online and aren't we trying to get as much traffic on our site and personal profiles? My focus is on that."

"CK's right," Jimmy co-signed. "The traffic on the site has been skyrocketing. Especially after Superman and Wonder Woman's big kiss and relationship reveal."

"As long as the stories get out, that's all that matters," Clark said.

"Anything you want to say, Lois?" Perry asked.

"This shouldn't be a discussion in the first place."

Lois stood up and left out of Perry's office slamming the door.

Perry raised his brow. "This seems much more personal?"

"She's just jealous of Superman and Wonder Woman. Also, Clark having a girlfriend means she can't use that anymore as a joke Clark doesn't have a girlfriend."

Perry paused for a moment and sighed. "I don't have time for this playground nonsense. We have news to report. Get to work and squash whatever this is outside this building!"

"Yes, Sir," Clark and Jimmy said.

Clark and Jimmy left out of Perry's office.

"Why did that just feel like leaving the principal's office?" Jimmy questioned.

"Because that's exactly what it seemed like." Clark frowned and walked over to Lois' desk. "So could you tell me what the issue is?"

Lois ignored him.

"Lois?"

"I'm working."

"You're not typing anything and that's a shopping site."

Lois slammed her laptop closed and turned around in her chair.

"Ever since you've started dating Ms. Perfect, you've been talking a lot of shit and smelling yourself. Get this through your think skull now, you miraculously found a backbone, but you are still low on the totem pole for getting anyone else's attention. Ms. Perfect sees an opportunity. You are more than willing to write up anything she says to get in her panties."

"Really Lois? You're still on that? What makes it so hard to believe that I'm with Diana? Are you that mad at your own self because you were wrong about me? You thought you had me figured out? Well I'm sorry that I ruined your streak of thinking you are always right. You can talk about me all day long but I will not let you talk about Diana."

"Wow, Smallville. That's the most emotion you've ever displayed. You're completely whipped. If this is the way to show your being a man more power to you. It would be actually impressive seeing you defend Diana against another man instead of whining to me."

"I'm the one whining? Lois, you are acting unreasonable with this stuck up attitude more than usual. But fine, whatever. When you find someone you care about, you'll understand how it feels when someone questions you and your relationship. But I sincerely hope that you don't have to because you won't know how to maturely handle it. I wish you the best Lois and congrats on top front page headline as you wanted."

Clark walked away going back to the break room leaving Lois stunned.

Going into the break room, Clark sighed. He reached into his pocket to get his phone but then he felt a very thin piece of silk like material. He smirked and carefully took his phone out to keep the material in his pocket.

I got a gift :)

Took you long enough to find it ;)

I'll tell you what happened later but finding this made things much better

THE DARK SPELL

Whatever it is, Love, you should already know it's all okay
With you, I know it is. I love you, Di
I love you too, Clark

Clark smiled proudly looking at his screen saver photo of Diana.

"Hey, CK! Need your help with picking out some photos."

"Alright, Jimmy."

3 hours later, Back at the Embassy...

Diana was walking out talking with Hessia on the phone.

"Yes, Hessia, everything is just fine! There's no effect with the tea besides Kal and I being even more active...?"

"Oh? Haha! That's very much expected. But it's also more to the fact that you two are young and in love."

Diana couldn't stop smiling. "Hessia, he truly is so much of everything. We talked about marriage and children a few days ago. He wants that with me just as much as I want it with him."

"Well I believe I'm ready to be an Aunt again."

"Thank you, Hessia. Really."

"Of course, Little Goddess. I just want you to be happy."

"I am...very much so."

"Tell Clark I said hello. I'll check back with you within the next two week or if you need anything be sure to call me."

"I will, Hessia. Thank you again and I'll talk to you again soon."

"Bye, Little Goddess."

As Diana hung up and was just about to take off, she heard her name called.

"Diana?"

She turned surprised. "Steve? Why are you here? "

"I needed to talk to you without the red cape around."

Diana sighed. "I can't believe you came all the way here. I don't have time. I need to get to the university."

"I can take you. We can talk on the way."

"What is it you need to talk about?"

Steve moved closer. "Diana..." he shook his head and sighed. "I'm sorry. You know I would never try to hurt you. This is just frustrating. It's ridiculous. I can see something special with us. Everyone can see it but you. You're trying so hard not to."

"Who is everyone?"

"My crew. My friends..."

"I see..."

"Diana, come on, don't make this hard."

"I'm not making anything hard. I've made things very clear of my feelings."

"You and I both know that with me, the Justice League image stays in check. I am the one that can make the others tolerable. We can be in the ranks together. Maybe one day you can be my First Lady...."

Diana raised her eyebrow.

Steve paused and looked down realizing Diana had the lasso touching his hand. He pulled away quickly.

"Stop. You don't need that with me. Diana, I love you. You know that's the truth."

"You don't love me like you think you do. You love an idea. A fantasy of me being on your arm to be paraded around in front of your friends and ranks. You want me as a showcase."

"A showcase? You were the one with your tongue down another guy's throat on national television!"

"Oh, now I understand. Kal isn't just a guy. He is the man I am in a relationship with. I told you, Steve, I'm not that naive girl anymore. It's been almost 10 years since I first came to man's world. I've learned so much on my own. I am happy with what I've accomplished and established. I will not apologize for not putting my happiness to the side for someone else. I will not apologize for not allowing someone to take advantage of me or try to guilt trip me into something that is not true. I will not change who I am for anyone else's comfort."

Steve frowned a bit noticing a faint mark on her neck.

"You changed for Superman."

"No. I am who I am and he sees that. He loves and respects me for me. He puts how I feel first."

"What did he do? How did he get to you so easily?"

THE DARK SPELL

"You don't know what Kal and I have been through together. When I opened my heart to him, it wasn't easy. I don't have to explain anything further."

"Are you serious?!"

"Yes, I am. Just as Kal and I are very serious."

"You owe me a reason why."

"Excuse me? I don't owe you a damn thing! You don't own me, Steve. Don't you ever think you can even try to threaten me and insult my relationship with Kal. What's between you and I has been strictly professional and nothing more will ever be. You and Etta was my first friends of man's world. I will always cherish that. But this, with you, I will not tolerate. Now you can go back to your base, Colonel. I have somewhere I need to be."

"Don't walk away from me, Diana."

"I'm not walking. I'm flying."

Diana made sure no one could see her flew off.

Steve watched her enraged. No matter how hard he didn't want to believe but it was true. Diana wasn't the innocent, sweet girl that rescued him from the plane crash. The girl that was amazed with first arriving to man's world and he knew he was going to be the one to show her everything. To teach her. But somehow she slipped away. She was warped by the Justice League, especially Superman.

Though she will see one day. It's only a matter of time.

"I'll be waiting..."

Valeria smirked looking down the scyring pool.

"Poor poor mortal...you are not the one the Amazonian Goddess is bound to. The mortal mind is fascinating. The mortal emotions are even more so fascinating. When the mind and emotions are confused, it's pandemonium. Infatuation and lust veiled as love will only cause more heartbreak and even tragedy."

"You're learning, Valeria," Eros said.

"Learning?" she questioned. "Eros, I am Queen for a reason."

"I know. Before Dionysus further corruption, you were the chosen succubus. The one that balanced the scale of love and lust. The one that was somehow pure."

"I want what was taken from me, Eros. I want to be free of what has tarnished me. I was imprisoned for thousands of years. It was my doing to choose Dionysus over my husband but I was bound to him or so I thought."

"Dionysus is a God of charm. Just as any other God. Taking pleasure in selfish deeds."

"I will take pleasure in seeing him suffer for all he has done."

4 hour later... Boston University

"Demeter is the goddess of the harvest and presides over grains and the fertility of the earth. Although she was most often referred to as the goddess of the harvest, she was also goddess of sacred law and the cycle of life and death," Diana stated.

"So do we like pray to these Gods or make a sacrifice and poof! Dreams and wishes come true?" A student asked.

"No, they are not genies or fairies. Though, if you believe in the Gods, they will guide you."

"Do you believe, Professor Prince? You are of Grecian decent."

"Yes, I do. It is part of my culture and ancestry. I know you all have a fascination with the Justice League. Wonder Woman is a Demi-Goddess and she is Grecian as well."

"A very HOT Demi-Goddess!"

The students laughed.

"Her dad is said to be Zeus, bro. The freaking KING of the Gods!"

"Professor Prince? Will we have a discussion about the League in comparison to the Gods?"

"Hmm...I've thought about that but didn't know if any of you were interested."

"Yeah we are!"

"Yeah!"

"That would be so cool!"

"Alright. Alright. In time. Now back to this lesson. Demeter being the Goddess of earth as producing fruit, and consequently of agriculture, whence human food or bread is called the gift of Demeter." Diana looked up to see Clark sitting in the last back row. "My Love's parents are farmers and I am from a tropical island. Everything was fresh and homemade."

"Wait what? She's married?" Clark heard a student whisper to another.

"Seems so. Reporter dude with glasses over there."

"Seriously? Damn. Lucky as hell."

Clark smiled to himself. Yeah, he was damn lucky.

"So like fishing? Making your own bread?"

Diana nodded. "Yes. On the farm, there are vast beautiful cornfields and both of our home lands have other vegetables naturally grown, we've picked berries, there are apple trees. Younger, I watched the creation of natural medicines, even wines."

"So do you prefer that over instantly going to the store for processed items?"

"Well because of growing up that way, I enjoy it. Though, going shopping in stores is quite an adventure at times especially during those times with sales or holidays!"

The class laughed.

"It's also mentioned that Demeter is the Goddess of marriage?"

Diana smiled. "Yes. She was worshipped especially by women. Her priestess also initiated young married people into the duties of their new situation."

"Wow! Having a Goddess initiate weddings would be so cool and romantic!"

"It sounds like a bunch of fairytales, really."

"You can believe in all we have talked about today or not. It's up to you. But just know that the bases of life is spiritual connections and having faith in whatever you believe in. There's bonds forged within us all with everyone we know and on different levels." Diana glanced at the clock. "Okay, that's it for today. What a lovely discussion and I'm very proud of all of you for participation. Be sure to read the next two chapters and your essays will be due next Thursday for Professor Kapatelis."

As the students walked out of the classroom, they all said bye to Diana and couldn't wait for her next class.

Diana smiled proudly hearing them still talking about the presentation.

As she was gathering her papers and shutting down her presentation, Clark walked up to the desk.

"That was great, Di!"

"Thank you, Love."

Clark quirked his brow and went around the desk.

"Hey? What's wrong?"

Diana took a breath and turned to him.

"Diana?"

She gave him a quick peck then wrapped her arms around his neck embracing him.

Clark still a bit confused wrapped his arms around her waist holding her tight.

"What happened?"

Diana pulled back slightly.

"Steve came by the Embassy when I was leaving."

"What? Why?!"

"He wanted to talk to me without you being around. He is convinced you've done something to me and holding me against my will to have fallen in love with you. He threatened the League and me saying we all need him to be tolerable. He also wants me to be his First Lady and dependent solely on him."

"I see. Well first, yeah, I might have done something to you which is just treating you like the Queen you are. If that's bad then I'll be bad then. He doesn't know and doesn't have any right to know what happened with Valeria but we've moved passed that and it's us together as it should be. He talks about the League being superior when he and his military buddies act like they are the superior ones. They want to control us. We've given them no reason to be against us except for not bowing down to their whims. That won't and never will happen." Clark cupped her face with both hands. "It seems that a few want to be against us and that's okay because they don't matter. What matters is us. Our happiness. Diana, I am grateful for being with you but if you are ever unhappy, I-"

Diana shook her head. "No, Kal. I will never be unhappy with you. Just the thought of you makes my heart soar and my whole body burns for you. Your touch, your voice...I can't get enough." Diana ran her hands slowly up and down his chest then back around his neck. "I gave my heart to you because you have shown me so many times how much of an amazing, honest, hardworking, respectful, trusting man you are. You're right. No one has to know what we've been through. All they need to know and understand is that you are my Love."

"Damn right!" Clark captured her lips in a soft kiss. "You know I didn't take Steve as a politician. I think he has been hanging around Sam Lane too much."

Diana laughed.

"Enough of that. Tell me what happened with Perry."

"My article will still be on the first page but second story at the bottom." Diana frowned. "That's not fair, Kal!"

He smiled and kissed her nose. "You're so cute when you get angry. But no need. I let Lois have it. I'm tired of this competition thing. People are going to read my articles on the daily planet site. My profile gets a lot of traction already. It's fine. Even if I didnt have as many readers and only had 1, at least someone's reading."

"Darling, you know I'll be that one but the way you articulate your words and the important subjects you bring to light. That's why I love you."

"I love you too, Di." Clark kissed her softly. "Really really sexy watching you teach, Madame Professor Prince."

"Really? Well...I can teach you a few things, Mr. Kent. Private lessons."

"I was thinking I could give you some lessons to in the Kryptonian style Kamasutra," he smirked.

Diana gasped. "There is?!"

"Ha! No. But that doesn't mean we can't create it ourselves."

"Oh, you naughty, naughty man."

Clark wiggled his eye brows and grinned devilishly pulling her into a passionate kiss. Diana smiled against his lips and moaned in his mouth.

Clark groped her ass.

"Let's go grab a bite to eat then we can go work on our lessons."

"Ooh, lovely!"

After Diana locked up everything, Clark and Diana left the university heading to Ma Maison.

Ma Maison remains faithful to the classics of French cuisine reserving the right to surprise and tease the palate with unexpected interpretations of favorite recipes. A boutique wine list and an exciting cocktail menu compliment the elegant ambiance. Warm wood accents, leather banquet and silver trays on the walls invite diners to feel as a private guest at the house of the owners.

45 minutes later...

The food was simply fantastic, cooked to perfection. With each bite Diana took, it left her desperate for more. With every morsel inserted into her mouth; a literal orgasm occurred among her tastebuds. She just couldn't get enough.

However, the orgasm inducing entrée, was nothing compared to what was on the menu for dessert.

As she stared across the table at her broad shouldered, thick armed, handsome partner, she bit her lower lip. Looking at him scantly across the table, she straightened out her leg and stroked her foot up his inner thigh, beginning at his knee, she applied the right amount of pressure to get his attention and moved it up towards his groin.

The motion caused him to look up from his meal and meet her sparkling cerulean eyes. His face matched hers with a look saying he knew exactly what she wanted, and he was going to satisfy her every need.

Clark smirked. "Dessert to go?"

Diana smiled and nodded.

After paying for their meal, they left the restaurant, walking along the street, arm in arm.

"You know, I was thinking about when you called me your Love in front of the class."

"Well you are," Diana smiled. "Most of them know who you are already."

"I overheard two believing we are officially married."

"Oh, really?"

"Said I was lucky as hell. He was right. I am damn lucky to have you, Diana"

"Well next class I will refer to you as my husband," she smiled.

Clark smiled back and in one swift movement he pulled her closer, smothering her mouth with his. Diana clung to him as the kiss deepened and became more passionate, Clark's fingers tangling in her long raven hair as their bodies entwined.

"Oh right on time for us all to join in..."

THE DARK SPELL

Clark and Diana quickly pulled apart surprised.

"What the hell?!"

"Valeria?!"

They looked around to see they had been transported into her castle. They were surrounded by succubi and incubi touching themselves and one another.

"What do you want?!" Kal asked angrily.

"Calm down, Kryptonian."

"Eros?! Why are you here?" Diana asked.

"Oh, Diana...you reek of this being."

"Strife?!"

"Diana, apologies but there was no choice," Eros said.

"There's always a choice!"

"Now, now...no need to bicker over me. All I want is simple. You two find Dionysus and bring him to me."

"We are not going on a wild goose chase for someone we don't know!"

"You will know, Diana. I'm asking nicely."

"No. We will not partake in this foolishness! We are go-" Diana abruptly stopped talking.

"Diana?" Kal could hear her heart rate picking up.

Valeria smirked.

"What are you doing to her?!"

"Disobedience never goes unpunished."

Diana couldn't move though she felt that familiar feeling on the back of her neck that sent a chill down her spine and rocked her to her core.

"You said this was no more!"

"Yes, well...I changed my mind. Though, it can be over once and for all if you help me find that serpent."

"No, dammit! Stop what you are doing to Diana and let us go home!"

"You know once this spell has been casted, only you can break it."

An incubus and succubus flew over to Diana.

"Don't you dare touch her!"

"Kal-El, don't you want Diana to have even more pleasure?"

Valeria went behind Kal. He felt paralyzed.

"Let us go."

"You see, Kal-El, Dionysus enjoyed watching someone else pleasure me, though I so desperately wanted him. Will you enjoy watching Diana?"

"Let her go!"

"Oh? No?"

The incubus ripped Diana's blouse open.

Clark's eyes immediately went ablaze.

"Valeria, this is too far!" Eros yelled.

"Relax, Dear Cousin, enjoy the show," Strife said.

Eros glared.

"Dionysus loved watching...until he didn't. Instead, he wanted me to watch him be pleasured by others until one day he didn't want me to watch at all. He didn't want me at all anymore. He tricked me...betrayed me...used me. Afterwards, because of his misdeeds, I was imprisoned! I was once a beloved Empress. Regardless of my Worshipped by all. That was taken from me. I can not get that back but I will have immense pleasure with his slow tortuous demise."

"Let us go, Valeria!"

"Is it a deal, Kal-El?"

Diana dropped to her knees as her body started to glow, her breathing was heavier.

"Ka-Kal..." Diana whispered.

"I said let her go, DAMMIT!"

Valeria gasped feeling Kal's rage. To her surprise, he broke her paralyzation spell and quickly dashed toward the incubus, grabbing him by his neck and slung him across the room. He narrowed his eyes at the succubus who flew off to help the incubus.

"Oh my..." Strife gasped.

"His passion for her is remarkable. I warned you two not to go too far."

Clark slowly picked Diana up. Her body was trembling uncontrollably.

"You pull some kind of stunt like this again, there's no telling what I will do!"

Valeria smirked. "I love a challenge, Kal-El. Continue on..."

"This is not a game! I'm tired of your twisted shit! Diana and I just want our peace but every god damn turn there's something trying to disrupt us! I'm not having that anymore!"

THE DARK SPELL

Clark looked down at Diana. Her eyes were such tight and she was gripping his shirt. She was trying to hold off her orgasm.

"Make this one last deal with me, Kal-El. You will not have any regrets only rewards. That is a promise I shall keep."

"Kal..."

He looked down at Diana again. She nodded.

"She'll keep her word...if she doesn't...I'll behead her myself."

"Ooh...no need, Diana. The only violence needed is against Dionysus. Between all of us is passionate love. Just give me this one last thing."

"Kal..." Diana nodded.

Clark sighed. "We'll find him. But if you try anything else!"

Valeria smirked. "Juri, take Kal-El to the room. He and Diana need...time."

"Yes, Empress."

Clark was a bit hesitant.

"Go on, Kal-El."

He glanced at Eros and Strife then followed Juri.

Eros sighed. "I will gladly join them in your beheading, Valeria. I'll have a golden bullet with your name as well."

"Eros, don't be so vicious. It will all go accordingly. As I said, Kal-El and Diana will be rewarded."

In a room within the castle...

Clark walked in and looked around.

"This is the room we woke up in the first time we were here."

"Yes, Kal-El. I will leave you to your duty."

Clark quirked his brow.

"Ah!" Diana's body convulsed. "Oh, Kal..." she groaned.

Clark nodded and quickly went to the large bed and laid her down. He stripped her of her and himself of their clothing. Diana felt him climb on top of her and he pressed his now fully uncovered flesh into hers. He took her into his arms. She gasped when she felt his hard member head rub at the edge of her dripping center, desperate for him to fill her. Her body was extremely hypersensitive to his touch.

He crashed his mouth into hers and kissed her with such passion and force, it took her breath away. His mouth was rough on hers, his soft lips and tongue dominating her, melting her into a puddle of pure lust. Diana let her hands run over his chest and back, her fingertips greedily exploring the terrain of his body

He broke off his kiss and said, "I got you, Di."

If there were any solid bones left in her body, they melted with those words.

The entire time he was talking, his hands had slowly moved their way up to her face. His thumb was slowly caressing her cheek as he spoke. She could feel the roughness of his hands on her skin and her body was on fire. His voice was like a sultry melody that was talking directly to her body. When his thumb touched her bottom lip it was too much and Diana moaned with desire.

Kal slipped his thumb just barely inside her mouth, grazing her tongue. His hand instinctively came up to grab his arm. She wanted him inside her any way she could so she pushed his thumb inside her mouth deeper. She ran her tongue slowly around his thumb almost keeping the same swirl pattern as his fingerprint. His eyes lit up red like they were on fire. He removed his thumb from her mouth, running through her hair, slowly tracing down her neck, and stopping at the top of her breasts. Diana was struggling to keep eye contact with him. Each touch was like an explosion being set off inside not only her body, but her mind as well. As far as she was concerned they were on a cloud high up in the sky and everything else was gone.

His hands were seemingly all over her body at once. Clark pinned her arms over her head, worshiping her breasts with his lips. Gentle bites, kisses, and his tongue ever so gently running across her skin.

"Kal...Oh Gods!"

Diana felt the waves of heat and ecstasy his hands were lavishing on her body. The need for release was so intense.

With that, his hands went still. His eyes locked with hers.

"With me...please..." It was barely above a whisper, but his eyes told her he heard every word clearly.

Her womanhood was quivering with need and something had to be done immediately to fix it. She opened her legs to him and wrapped them around his hips. Squeezing her thighs together and pulling him into her.

THE DARK SPELL

Clark grunted as he eased into her. He let out a groan and Diana's back arched, pushing him deeper inside of her. Diana's body buzzed in pure delight, and tingling sensations traveled down her legs. Every nerve in her body was in overdrive and each agonizing inch he gave her only served to fan the already inferno level fire within her. Diana started to rock her hips forward to force him further within her. She wanted to feel him all the way inside, completely full of his hard throbbing member.

Each time she pushed against him, he would pull farther back only to fan the flames even higher. His teasing her was driving her mad. He knew it would only take a few strokes before all hell broke loose and she would climax. Her dripping center was involuntarily quivering against his member, pulling him in further; Diana was no longer in control. All Diana wanted was the release she knew he could give her.

Their bodies were one.

A united being of pure passion.

Their eyes...their whole bodies began to glow. His of red and hers of blue.

She began to moan uncontrollably, and he let out grunts in pleasure. Clark was pushing into her with such strength and passion. Diana's body started shaking, building and then she bursted into a climax.

"Oh, Gods, Kal!"

He growled from somewhere very deep. He spared her no gentle accommodation as he slammed into her thrusting through her orgasm.

"Ah! Gods!" She screamed.

Clark slid one hand down to her core and quickly found what he was looking for...her sensitive clit.

His desirous stare filling her entire view. With her body pressed into the bed, he began to rub it, harder than he normally would but it was such a turn on for both of them with the rough touch feeling absolutely incredible. Her body was just a puddle of nothing, melting into the bed; yet it was humming.

He continued the assault on her womanhood and her mind as he growled sweet nothings in her ear, knowing exactly what she needed to hear to get there again.

After a few moments he took his hand back and Diana whimpered at the loss. Though, he grabbed her wrists and pinned them above her head, looking her dead in the eye. He began to thrust harder, sawing his manhood in and out of her soaked slit and hitting every sensitive spot inside her.

Clark's hunger, need, and benevolent intent of complete and total claim of her body rested on the surface of his face. He didn't hide that he knew she's his and he is hers as he watched her cycle through her pleasure of their impossible connection. They both know that part of why they belonged as one was due to the ability to do this to each other...to know each other, and see each other, and the loop of both of them getting exactly what they needed was the rarest form of pure decadence.

He had already over taken the spell. He brought her to several crashing orgasms, all the while his incessant, pounding, perfect rhythm continued on as he was working towards his own need to release.

Diana screamed. Loud, long, and so high-pitched that it made the hairs on the back of Clark's neck stand up. And she kept screaming. The sound whistled in time with him driving her into the mattress. It only stopped for a moment when her eyes went wide, she sucked in a frantic, noisy gasp of air, and exploded into orgasm.

She convulsed beneath him, her range of movement limited by his weight pressing down on her bent legs. Screeches and squeals emerged from her wide-open mouth, and she constricted around him.

Clark was still thrusting mercilessly as she came.

Her screams turned to squeaks and choked yelps. Her face contorted into a mask of beautiful agony. Her back arched high above the mattress. Her mouth was agin open in a silent scream, and she was trembling as though there was an earthquake inside her.

He leaned down low as his breathing grows erratic and shallow. He looked directly into her eyes again, gazes locked and foreheads pressed together tightly. Diana doesn't look away. She doesn't even blink.

The increase in speed the echo in the room of their panting and the bodies hitting increased. Diana pushed her head back in the pillow with her mouth wide open and eyes rolled back. Her hands stretched out to wrap around his neck. She pulled him close till his face was buried in her neck. He kept on moving back and forth to make her cry in the pleasure.

THE DARK SPELL

Clark moved his hands underneath her back and penetrated with all the love he had. Diana's lower body raised slightly off the mattress made him hit a spot which made her throw her hands on bed as she pushed her lower body up pushing it on him shouting his name at the top of her voice.

The entire castle was now shaking.

Clark continued at the same pace which was fast enough to keep her shivering as she kept on shouting her vocal cords out with her hands gripping the sheets and her body raised on his pushing so heavily that her breasts kept on dancing.

The pace was picked up even more without them even realizing it and while he kept his eyes locked with Diana's, they were only half open and glazed over; in that happy place only go to being well on the way to an orgasm.

Pounding into her with pure abandonment, he held nothing back. Harder and harder. Filling her to the limit with each thrust. She could feel her juices gushing around him inside her. Diana was overwhelmed; riding out yet another all encompassing orgasm. Stars and clouds; they were all there and it was like getting thrown in a pool of pure ecstasy. Her legs were shaking. Clark leaned down and kissed her hard, his tongue probing her mouth. His lips then traveled down her neck and chest.

Clark raised up pulling Diana with him. As Diana straddled him, he grabbed her thighs, sliding his hands around her ass, grabbing and squeezing. Holding her close to him.

Their mouths come together in a clash. Hot and heavy they battle with their tongues. Clark bounced Diana up and down on him. The feeling was so exhilarating. Something came over her and she placed her hands on his broad shoulders and helped him. Every time she came down he slammed up against her. Soon Diana was all but thrashing against him as another orgasm rocked her entire soul.

Diana cupped his face and kissed him. It started off tender, but quickly turned savage.

"Oh, Kal! Yes!"

Her mind was completely gone. She was lost somewhere in sensation.

"Di!" He responded, "Aurgh!"

The headboard was thumping, the bed was creaking.

Diana was alternating between incoherent words and moans.

This was an absolute plowing, Clark was going as hard, as deep, as fast as he could. He was getting close to climaxing when out of nowhere they heard a loud, "Kkrr-SNAP!"

"KKkrr-SNAP!" They heard a second time.

The bed had totally gave way but neither faltered or took pause. Diana started to grind on him unleashing a wave of moans. Groaning and breathing heavily, the movement of her hips meeting his thrusts. Her excited screams and her orgasm causing her to clench around him pushed him to climax.

As Clark let out huge load, Diana gasped, her mouth wide open in silent pleasurable agony as he twitchingly fills her, while he hissed through gritted teeth continuing to thrust into her through his own orgasm.

Diana bucked her hips, desperate to feel him bottom out inside her, and was rewarded with a hot splash of his essence coating the inside of her womanhood. He moaned with her as he emptied his balls into her with powerful final thrusts, Diana's body still shuddering around him with the intensity of her own pleasure.

Diana screamed out in pure erotic euphoria, letting the sound muffle as she bit into his shoulder and her nails dug into his back. Her body continued to pulse around him, and he just held her there, nestling his head in her breasts.

They were shaking and moaning, in their own little orgasm world.

As Diana came back down, she could feel one of Clark's arms around her while the other was stroking her hair. She took a deep inhale and let her body melt into his as she released the air back into the room. Clark kissed her forehead and the only response that Diana's exhausted, quivering body could produce was an unintelligible murmur. She could feel him grin and he whispered, "That's it, Starshine. I told you, I got you."

They both caught their breath. Their bodies slowly coming back to normal no longer glowing. They remained locked together, a lewd tableau of two bodies connected at a fulcrum point of twitching, throbbing slippery heat.

Diana looked up at his face, seeing a look of adoration and compassion. Clark captured her lips in a passionate. Their kiss lingered for several

THE DARK SPELL

delicious moments and Diana settled more into him so that he could rock their bodies gently. He was still inside her, not actually moving, but Diana could feel his pulse inside of her. His body, then her body, then his again would shudder.

Clark then caressed her cheek. Diana opened her mouth slightly, nipping at his finger as it moved into her mouth.

"Hmm." He smiled amusedly then replaced his finger with his lips and tongue again.

Diana moaned in his mouth feeling Clark hold her to him tighter; arms wrapped protectively not possessively around her.

"Are you... Are you okay?" he asked between pants and kisses.

Her hair was tousled, but beautifully so. Her eyes are tired, but brimming with excitement. Her smile has some pain in it, but also resilience.

She nodded. "Yes. We broke the bed."

Clark shrugged. "Not paying for it," he joked.

"Kal, we have to find Dionysus."

"I know. As much as I don't want us to be part of whatever the hell this is, we have to, to keep Valeria away for good."

"I'm sorry," Diana said looking down.

Clark frowned and raised her chin back up. "For what?"

"She's part of my world with Dionysus being technically my brother."

Clark chuckled. "You know dysfunctional family drama comes with the territory of the whole in-law thing. I'm up for any and every thing with you. We got this together."

Diana reached up twirling his S-curl then caressed his cheek.

"I love you."

"I love you, too, Di."

He captured her lips once more in a searing kiss, holding each other in total erotic bliss.

Location: Valeria's throne room...

"He truly does cherish her. His kisses, touches still very much visible all over her body."

"Your pets are...?" Strife questioned looking around to see the succubi and incubi laying all over each other exhausted.

Valeria smirked. "Kal-El and Diana's energy had over taken them. Never had they felt such immense purity of pleasure. Kal-El and Diana have also purified the entirety of this castle."

"Only for you to taint it again," Eros scuffed.

"Now, now, Eros. It's about balance. This occurrence was just that. They can have every room to themselves to break every bed. I don't mind."

"When Dionysus and you reunite, this inevitable clash is only between you two. Either you kill each other or fornicate. I don't give a damn. But Diana and her beloved will no longer be involved. Is that understood?"

"Well that is the plan, Eros. Diana and Kal-El have a connection and future I can not...will not tarnish. The power in which they hold together is quite pleasing. All I want now is Dionysus."

Prague, Czechia: K5 Relax Adult entertainment club

Take parts of the strip club experience, parts of the brothel experience, and parts of the escort service experience and combine them to make a single establishment, K5 Relax would be the result.

"After all this time, Valeria. I admire your persistence," Dionysus chuckled taking a sip of his wine. He leaned his back against the bar counter. "Father chose wisely. Impregnated the Amazon Queen. Powerful earth daughter chooses an equally powerful mate that has Apollo burning with resentment. Heh...interesting. I shall soon introduce myself."

"Are you just going to stand and stare tonight?"

Dionysus looked to see a curvaceous woman smiling seductively with her hands on her hips. Sandy red shoulder length curls, green eyes. She was wearing a and a flirty, curve-hugging mini sheer tube chemise fit featuring an all over rhinestone shimmer, a strapless neckline, and sheer mesh cups.

"And you are, lovely lady?"

"Imani."

"Well, Imani..." he grinned. "It's a night for celebration. Let's have a few rounds."

CHAPTER 10: TO BE LOVED

Location: Valéria's Castle

Diana sighed as she was about to put back on her blouse but the front was too torn to close.

Kal sat on the edge of the broken bed with her handing his T-shirt to her.

Diana puts on his t-shirt, "I can't believe we are here. I expect Strife to have it out for me given she resents my mother but I'm disappointed with Eros. He has the power to stop this nonsense, yet didn't say much of anything and continued to let it be."

She leaned on him, resting her face on the side of his broad shoulder.

"Because it was not his place to stop, Di. I understand it now. The spell. Valeria was able to catch us off guard because for so long we were holding back our feelings. We still have a lot more making up to do for the years that I should've been honest with my feelings for you. How deep they truly are." Kal held her hands within his and gave a little peck at her fingers which are poking out from his grip.

"But Kal, neither of us wanted to risk losing our friendship if we weren't truly ready to go farther. It was unspoken but we knew there was more between us even if we didn't act upon it yet. Nights alone, I longed for you in ways I surprised myself for having the thought of." Diana would have never told these words louder even to his ears but the dimly lit bedroom of wicked Valeria's castle had brought the amour out of her.

"Now you have me. All of me. I'm yours, Diana. And you can have me, however, whenever you want. Dionysus is just part of getting rid of Valéria for good. There's something else that has to be done and I'm the only one that can," he assured her.

"What are you going to do?"

Kal smiled and leaned over to kiss her forehead.

"It's nothing like what you think it might be, Di. Far from it. Don't worry."

"Gods, I love you!"

Diana immediately straddled him pushing him down on the bed.

"We're going to end up going through the floor if we start again," Kal joked.

Diana giggled and bit her lip. "Mmmh...Darling, what a tempting idea. Though...I'd rather we be in our own apartment."

"So what are we going to tell the landlord?"

"Weak flooring? Though my very sexy handyman can fix it right on up before anyone notices the extent of the damage. Gladly the apartment below us is vacant."

"Yeah...but we still have the neighbors on our floor knocking on our door."

"Oh, Gods!" Diana buried her face in his shoulder laughing. "Mrs. McCowen certainly gives me a look every time I see her."

"She's mean to everyone no matter what. I talk to Mr. McCowen from time to time. He just ignores it."

"Is that how we will be older?"

"You mean in about 100 or more years? We will be exploring more dimensions. Our kids will be on their own. We'll probably fuss a bit because you know that Amazon stubbornness..."

"Hey!" Diana scuffed playfully hitting his arm making him laugh.

"We will make up afterwards."

Diana smiled and kissed him softly.

The door opened.

"Oh..." Juri bowed. "You're already ready."

"Hell yeah, we are," Clark stated. "Time for us to go home!"

"Very well... Mistress will meet with you first."

Location: Valéria's Throne Room

Valéria smirked taking a sip of wine.

"Mistress, Kal-El and Diana are ready to depart back to the human realm."

"Was last night pleasing, Diana?" Valéria asked.

THE DARK SPELL

Diana glared at her. "I am in no mood for your antics. Besides, you already know the answer to that."

Valéria licked her lips. "You're angry with me. I know. But as I said, you will have a very satisfying reward."

"Uphold your deal, Valéria, or I will keep my word with my blade," Diana warned.

"Mmmh...how I envy that flame of yours." Waving her hand, she opened a portal. "Goodbye, Lovers. We will meet again once you've found the serpent."

"We are not your lovers!" Kal and Diana said in unison taking each other's hand and walking through the portal.

Valéria laughed. "Oh, they are so amusing. Dionysus, you don't know what you are in for with those two."

Location: Metropolis: Clark and Diana's Apartment

The portal opened in the middle of their bedroom.

"To be home!" Diana said happily as they stepped out of the portal.

"Yeah, this is so much better. Come here." Kal pulled her into a passionate kiss.

He then placed gentle kisses all over her face.

"Shower?" she asked rubbing his naked chest.

"Oh, yeah!"

Pulling Diana into the bathroom, Kal turned on the steaming hot water, stripped her and himself clothing, and stepped in under the steaming flow.

Tightly embracing, the shower warmth was comforting and Diana's skin was soft and tender. Their lips mashed together. Then Kal cupped one of her breasts and massaged the aureole. Still kissing each other, tongues in cue, and both his hands now roaming her breasts, Diana let out a slow moan in his mouth.

Touching each other this way was just so hot. Feeling their bodies and hearing their breathing over the roar of the shower.

Kal broke his kiss on her lips and traced her neck with his tongue. Then traveling his tongue to her ear, and sucking her earlobe. Diana again gave out another slow moan. Kal took his kisses to the hollow between her collar bone and laved there. Then taking his kisses further down he caught her right nipple between his lips. His tongue underneath and his mouth clamped over the top, and he began to suckle. Diana placed her hands atop Kal's head, pushing him closer to her breast. Kal suckled a little harder, before switching breasts. After a few minutes of suckling, he came up and laid a kiss on her so deep, that Diana felt it all the way to her toes.

Kal took a washcloth off the rack and handed her one. They begin soaping up each other's bodies. Kal paid particular attention to her breasts, her neck, and down her legs while being sure to tread her womanhood lightly for now. Once Diana started washing Junior, she was immediately transfixed by it and soon she was stroking him with both hands. Kal responded groping her ass.

Diana giggled and looked up at him with fire in her eyes. They breathed into each other's mouths.

"I like touching you," she murmured against his mouth. "I like that you're showing me how much you like it, too."

Diana could feel Kal quiver and smile at her touch. Her hand stroked up and down his length faster now as she felt it throbbing in her hand. Kal broke their kiss and sucked air in through his teeth, barely restraining his overwhelming desire for her.

"Diana...Ah! Shi-!" he whispered.

They both looked down to watch as she jerked his manhood, squeezing at the base and pulling up the length. Kal leaned forward to kiss and bite her neck and he moaned as Diana slid her thumb over the tip, coming away slick with pre-essence. Diana felt his moan originate deep within him and resonate through to her throat where his lips were.

The smell and taste of her smooth, firm skin, her sounds of pleasure simply from touching him. Kal pressed one hand to her hip as the other cupped the back of her head, his fingers wound into her wet hair. Kal smirked and walked her back into the cascade for them to rinse off.

Diana let him go and turned around his arms. She rested her head back on his shoulder, just feeling his touch on every inch of her torso. She pressed herself into his chiseled body, feeling his swollen length against her ass. Diana moved her hands behind her and took him in her hands, massaging him between her fingers little by little. Kal moaned in satisfaction. He ran his tongue sensually along the side of her neck, making Diana's knees buckle.

Diana bit her lip as the fingertip from Kal's middle finger traced a line straight down her stomach and to her womanhood. Kal press a finger between her nether lips and drag slowly vertically, it slid easily due to her excitement and Diana shuddered as he grazed the nub of her clit.

Diana moaned tilted to head to press her soft lips to his and their tongues swirled together. As he entered her with two fingers, Diana pushed back against him, grinding her ass against his length. Kal curved his fingers round to rub against the sensitive g-spot.

"Yes..." whispered Diana.

Kal nipped her earlobe lightly causing Diana to groan again.

He moved his fingers faster, using his thumb to roughly play with her clit.

"Darling, beloved, your hands...such a...gift..." she murmured again.

Diana squeezed her eyes shut and was overwhelmed with all of these sensations all so fast. She was breathlessly overtaken by crashing waves as her body opened itself to Kal's hand. Her orgasm shattered her and Diana uttered the coup-de-grace to this temptatious game and let out an unstifled moan as she started to come. Feeling her tense up around his fingers, Kal kissed her neck, slowing the pace of his fingers until he was sliding them in and out slowly.

"Gods, you are so good to me." She said

As Kal withdrew his fingers, Diana turned to face him again. Kal wrapped his arms around her tightly and kissed her fiercely, Diana letting him suckle her tongue again. They were so consumed with their combined passion for each other. Kal felt her moan and collapse into him, holding him around the waist. Her shoulders quivered against his chest, but her legs weren't shaking as much, and she put effort into the kiss.

Kal reached to turn off the water. He grabbed the towels for them to dry off as they stepped out of the shower and began to dry Diana's body.

"It's only fair for me to dry you off," Diana smirked starting to do so.

With both of them reasonably dry, Diana put on one of Kal's shirts and Kal put on his boxers. Kal swooped her up and walked over to the bed laying her down. While Kal was starting to kiss her, with his mouth working on her lips, then her ear lobes, then her neck, Diana wrapped her arms and legs around him, rolling them over for her to be on top.

She sat up with a smile and trailed her hands down his massive chest and abs. Kal reached under the shirt massaging her ass.

"Now, this is all I want to do. In our own bed with my man."

"We can break our own bed, too," Kal smirked.

Diana laughed softly and took his face in her hands.

"The bed, the couch, the kitchen counter, bathroom counter... and everywhere in between."

Diana kissed him, deeply, her tongue making more exploratory movements into his mouth, Kal respond in kind with hers, breathing as one.

"No chasing a God because his succubus ex wants revenge. Sounds like a soap opera. We don't even know where to begin to look."

Diana laughed. "I don't want to worry too much about that right now."

"Excuse me, Cousin, Kal-El. I can help with that."

Diana gasped quickly turning her head and Kal sat up.

"EROS!?" They yelled angrily in unison.

"Calm down, Cousin, please."

"Oh, no! You!" Diana jumped off the bed and grabbed her sword pointing it at his throat.

"Di, no!" Kal jumped from the bed and grabbed her by her waist and arm. He tried to lower her arm but she wasn't budging.

"Di..."

"Listen to your lover, Diana."

"Eros, I thought you were the one I could somewhat trust but you are just like the rest of them! I expected it from Strife but not you!"

"My deepest apologies, Diana. You know that I am one that is on your side."

"How did you get wrapped into Valéria's scheme?"

"I was already cleaning up one of Apollo's messes. She casted her spell and it was too late. I couldn't break nor reverse it."

"Why are you here?" Diana's asked irritated.

"I know where Dionysus is."

"What?! Why didn't you tell Valéria instead of us involved?!"

THE DARK SPELL

"Diana, this battle is no ordinary battle. Only you and Kal-El can mediate this. Valéria is not the succubus you believe her to be. She was once respected by all. The chosen sort of speak that balances the scales of lust and love. In order to understand love, you must understand lust and vice versa. She relishes in both the tainted and the pure. Though, because of your powerful union, her...tastes have drastically changed. However, she is slowly consumed by her own rage and resentment. Diana, Kal-El, what's at stake is the mortal world being entirely transformed into her playground. Mortals consumed by other succubi and incubi only knowing of lust and deceit."

Diana sighed. "Eros..."

"Diana, I plead to you."

"There is no need for pleading. It is our duty to protect this world."

"We meet in Olympus in an hour."

Eros disappeared.

Diana dropped her sword and turned to Kal embracing him.

"Hey! Woah Woah?!"

"I despise getting caught in the middle of their childish games!"

Kal kissed the top of her head embracing her tighter.

"Diana, look at me."

She looked up with a pouty expression making Kal chuckle. He kissed the tip of her nose.

"Don't worry about it. I told you earlier, that's how family is. A little crazy and dysfunctional. It's just the crazy and dysfunction has been upped a bit given they are Gods. I'm with you through and through."

"This is why I love you so much!"

"You're stuck with me, Starshine!" He kissed her softly. "Let's get going."

Location: Mount Olympus

Diana and Kal-El arrived, met promptly by Eros and Hermes.

"Cousin," they greeted in unison.

"Kryptonian, we have not been formally aquatinted," Hermes said shaking his hand.

"Right...well no time like the present. But would've preferred different circumstances."

"No worries, Chap!" Eros assured. "We will have plenty of time for family familiarity."

"Eros, where is Dionysus?" Diana asked.

"He was last in Prague. He enjoys being amongst crowds. That is why Valéria and Strife should not know his whereabouts."

"And where is he now?"

"He is moving fast. A sort of cat and mouse game it seems. He knows of you two. Wants you to find him."

"We don't have time for games!" Diana said angrily.

"Relax, Cousin. It's an easy task. I assure you. One that you and Kal-El will enjoy taking advantage of."

"What do you mean?"

"Enjoy yourselves on this trip. Your flight awaits."

"Wait a minute? What? To where?"

"Barcelona, Spain. Everything has been handled for you."

"Eros, this isn't the ideal vacation for us."

"It is, Cousin. Enjoy."

"Ero-"

Hermes snapped his fingers. Diana and Kal were transported to boarding the plane.

"Oh! I can't believe them!" Diana sighed as they sat down in their seats.

Kal chuckled and took her hand. He raised the back of it to his lips placing a gentle kiss.

"Relax, Di. We are going to get this over with but Eros made a good point. Vacationing in Barcelona is very good for us."

Diana smiled and leaned over kissing his cheek. "I still wish it was of our own planning."

"Yeah, but we will make the best of it."

Diana nodded. "Okay, Love."

Diana held his hand and laid her head on his shoulder.

3 Hours later, El Prat de Llobregat Aeropuerto

"We're here!" Kal announced.

"That didn't take long at all."

"Let's go find our luggage and see which hotel we should check into."

Suddenly, someone cleared his thought, "Clark Kent? Diana Prince?"

THE DARK SPELL

Kal turned to see a short middle-aged man wearing a tuxedo with their luggage.

"I am Hughes McPherson. I was hired by Mr. Roma as your guide," he said shaking Kal's hand.

"Mr. Roma? Huh?" Diana raised her brow and smiled. "It's a pleasure meeting you, Mr. McPherson."

"I'm sure you two are ready to get to your hotel so we should get on our way."

Kal and Diana walked hand in hand following Hughes to the car.

Kal opened the door for Diana while Hughes placed their luggage in the trunk.

"I understand this is your first vacation together?"

"Sort of, yeah, but we don't really count this too much with...work that needs to be done," Kal said.

"Yes, I understand. It is a bit tricky with having such a beautiful woman at your side."

"Diana and I are a team, no doubt. Definitely going to make this trip worth it regardless."

Hughes smiled and nodded.

Location: The Pulitzer Hotel

"Well, this is all very lovely!" Diana complimented looking around the room.

"Mr. Roma made sure that everything would be to your liking," Hughes bowed. "I shall go now until my services are needed."

"Thank you, Hughes." Kal shook his hand. When Hughes left out, Kal grabbed Diana lifting her in his arms. "So, Mr. Roma kept his word."

"Eros Roma better had."

"Impressive last name. Took me a minute to get it."

"Roma, amor backward..."

"This is the least he could do for us being in the middle of this demon god battle of the exes. But we are definitely going to have fun with all these rose petals." Kal wiggled his brows.

Diana laughed.

Kal smiled. "There it is! I needed to hear that beautiful infectious laugh."

Diana blushed.

"How about we go out for a bit? It's still early."

"I would love to!"

After a quick shower and changing clothes, Diana wearing a sleeveless top and ruched midi skirt and Kal wearing a casual zipper polo shirt and shorts tracksuit set, they left their hotel walking down the sidewalk already in awe of the atmosphere and scenery.

"Regardless of why we are actually here, the fact that we are together here makes it so much better."

"Come here."

Kal felt the need to kiss her. Diana kept smiling at him as he brought his lips to hers. Her lips were soft and warm, just as they always were. And it sent chills and shivers up and down Kal's spine whenever he kissed those lips.

They didn't pay attention to any of the locals and tourists that were watching them.

Diana's lips parted for him almost instantly, and Kal let his tongue wander. She had such a heavenly taste and scent that always made his head spin. Kal ran his tongue all around the inside of her mouth, earning a few rewarding moans from her. Their tongues battled each other and she repeated everything his tongue did to her mouth.

Kal let his hands wander up along her waist and into her hair. She did the same to him. He could still hear everything that was going on around him, but he simply didn't care and choose not to pay attention. Suddenly, while he was sucking on Diana's tongue, she began to laugh.

"What's funny?" He asked pulling away slightly.

"You are getting even bolder with the PDA."

Diana kept laughing lightly. Kal couldn't help but smile too.

"Can't help it. I'm in love with the most gorgeous woman in the galaxy. I have to show you off every chance I get."

Diana took his hand and started dragging him away from where they were standing.

There were couples all over the boardwalk. Then Diana stopped and so did Kal. She let go of his hand and turned around to face him. She was

THE DARK SPELL

giving him her sultry smile. The smile that only he got to see and he smiled back at her.

"I'm following your lead, Di," Kal said.

Diana and Kal wandered through the streets of Barcelona. They took as many pictures as they could everywhere they went. They couldn't wait to get to major sights including the Capella de Santa Àgata, Barri Gòtic, and the Torre de Collserola.

The Barcelona Cathedral towered above the heads of the many tourists littering Pla de la Seu, also snapping pictures or staring at the building in awe.

"Oh, this is glorious!" Diana grinned.

"It is!"

Kal wrapped his arms around Diana, holding her in place while Diana let her arms wrap around Kal's neck. Closing the space between them, their lips met in a soft kiss.

When the two parted, Diana was blushing furiously.

Kal kissed her forehead and intertwined their fingers, continuing on with their walk.

Parc Guell, one of the many Gaudi sights, had a great view over the city. This was so perfect. Breezy afternoon and the park was relatively empty, a weekday in late summer, with few tourists milling about. The mosaics and sculptures are interesting.

"The detail in these sculptures, the mosaics, all these intricate tiles. They really are beautiful, especially the way the light hits them."

"Yeah, it's a very interesting designed park with a lot of character."

"When we get home, I would like to do more research on every sight we're going to. I want to document everything wherever we go!"

"Course, Di!"

There was a little trolley around the corner that sold ice cream.

"Oh, Kal, please? It won't spoil my appetite for dinner."

Kal chuckled and kissed the tip of her nose.

"I got you, Starshine."

They took their ice cream to the plateau overlooking the city, Kal leaned back against the parapet looking back at Diana. His tall, massive, muscular frame folded over the edge looking out across the city, down to the sea, the light sparkling, bobbing in the slate water. The sun was peaking in and out of the clouds, a beam every now and then backlighting the raven hair goddess, casting her silhouette in gilded light. Kal's stomach flipped, and he grew quiet, contemplative, trying to get a grip on his emotions. At that very moment, he wanted to propose.

"Where should we head next?"

Diana's tongue traced the length of the neapolitan ice cream piled high in her cone, Kal's eyes were drawn to her lips, gaze lingering, momentarily forgetting himself. Kal didn't answer just kept staring at her. Diana quirked an eyebrow, a look crossing her features, too quick to catch.

"Kal?"

"Huh, what?"

Diana frowned slightly. "What's wrong?"

"Oh, nothing! Nothing at all!" He smiled reassuringly. "I was just taken aback by how beautiful you are." He stood up. "Hold on."

With his phone, he snapped her picture.

"Damn that's beautiful. I had to get this moment. Every moment after."

"You are the sweetest," Diana kissed his cheek. But then she realized she put ice cream on his cheek and licked it off slowly sending chills down Kal's spine. "I love that combination of my man and ice cream."

They gazed at each other for a long moment, Diana pulling her bottom lip between her teeth. Kal slowly reached up, fingers barely brushing Diana's cheek, thumb lightly touching her chin. Holding her gaze, his fingers stilled slightly, he slowed as if making a decision, then he lifted his thumb to trace Diana's lips. Diana's tongue darted out lightly to lick the tip of his finger. Kal let out a low groan, closing his eyes.

A couple of children, trying to race and outpace the other, bumped into Kal and Diana, giggling as they did.

The moment between them was lost, but Kal would remember it, tuck it away so he could recall the look on Diana's face as he traced her lips. A small seed of hope was blossoming by the moment.

"Let's go to the next spot."

After finishing their ice cream, they took a 30-minute walk to La Sagrada Familia.

THE DARK SPELL

They walked in companionable silence down the wide avenue, the spires of La Sagrada Familia just barely visible. Diana couldn't contain her excitement, making Kal laugh.

"Kal, this is so wonderful!" she said simply, smiling at him.

As they neared the entrance, they noted the rather dramatic crowd of tourists all around. They walked around, taking in the odd curve of the buttresses, the traditional archways.

"It's so different when such things are mentioned and you can imagine it a bit. Pictures don't always do justice to being right here. Seeing all of this makes our jobs even more important. Protecting the people and preserving every piece of art and history."

Kal stared into Diana's eyes.

"That spark in your eyes. Listening to you talk...your enthusiasm for everything in the world."

Kal moved forward, closing the space between them.

Diana blushed. "Kal..."

"I can't help but fall more and more in love with you, Diana."

She grinned. "Your sweet talk, the way you look at me and hold me make me fall more and more in love with you."

"Di...I..." Ka looked around and smiled. "This might not be the right moment to have this talk. Let's go look at some more sights. Grab a bite to eat, then there's an outdoor theater I want to take you to on the beach."

Diana kissed him sweetly. "Okay, Love."

They walked into the stone structure, which was lit up with the most extraordinary rainbow of colors, yellows, oranges streaming in from the west façade, a smattering of blues, greens, soft white speckling the marble floor, the stone archways, and buttresses coming in from all other angles.

Diana let out a loud gasp, slowly spinning around, and looking up. When she came to a stop, her head was still tilted back, looking at the ceiling, eyes darting this way and that.

Kal didn't look about the cavernous room, he was instead focused intently on Diana, her whole body lit by a rainbow of color and the features of her face alight with joy.

Diana dropped her head, now looking about the space, the intricate pillars all radiating out from the center of the room in slight variations of size and color of pale marble. She was mumbling, almost whispering to herself. She walked a little away from Kal, lost in her exploration. She ran her hand up and down a column, noting its changing form.

"Oh, Goodness! This is so beautiful!"

Diana ran her finger down the center, leaning down, bringing her eyes closed.

She sighed, then turned in a slow full circle, looking for her beloved, wondering if she'd been talking to herself. She saw Kal then, walking toward her with a soft smile on his handsome face, lit orange as if by a sunset.

Diana grinned back. "You're glowing Kal-El. A Sun God in your own right."

"You're glowing too, my Moon and Earth Goddess."

"It's like we're lost in a magical stone forest, look..." She pointed up to the canopy.

Diana looked back at him who had become quiet, seeing an expression she couldn't place. Kal looked distracted, his mind somewhere else. Diana looped her arm through his.

"Hey," tilting her head to the side, "where'd you go? Everything okay?"

"Everything is just perfect, Di," he assured and kissed her temple. "Seeing you happy, spinning around in this room, the light dancing around you," he closed her eyes, exhaled, "it's all perfect."

Diana placed the flat of her palm on his neck and Kal leaned into her instinctively. Diana pulled him down for a light kiss, all soft lips, not tentative, but not pressing.

She pulled away, Kal's handsome ocean eyes looking at her.

Diana's whole body thrummed. Kal took her hand and intertwined their fingers.

They walked out to the courtyard on the other side of the basilica. Looking back to take in the façade, Diana was the first to speak.

"I'm still just so in awe!"

Kal smiled at her thinking of how grateful he was for this time to really give more to the ever-growing connection between them.

"Let's go somewhere for dinner."

THE DARK SPELL

Diana squeezed Kal's hand, their fingers entwined as they walked through the city.

As they walked leisurely through the streets, Diana noticed the small avenues and shops give way to centuries-old stone, water-stained and dark, passages narrowing, a closed-in, damp feel even in the heat of the afternoon.

They passed boutiques and food stalls, bakeries, and full shops, all nestled in plazas and squares.

Kal was surprised when Diana drew quickly to a stop, a smile on her face as she breathed in deeply.

"What? I miss something?" Kal mused, looking around.

"No, Love," she said as she lightly shook her head. "I'm just taking all this in."

She grinned and pulled him to a pastry shop, Dolceria De La Colmena.

They walked into the cloying smell of chocolate and brown sugar, overwhelming them in the small space.

"No spoiling your appetite for dinner, huh?" Kal teased.

Diana giggled and looked at him innocently. "I can't resist sweets like I can't resist my man."

Kal shook his head and smiled. "What would you like?"

"An assortment of all of them if possible."

He nodded and ordered for her.

"Thank you, Love," Diana kissed his cheek.

They left the shop with a large box of truffles and found a nice spot to sit to try them. They sat talking, people watching, Kal couldn't help but notice Diana's easy laugh, her warmth, leaning against him every now and then when she made some cheeky remark about eating the different flavored truffles.

Diana pointed out a few of her favorite truffles, Kal tried them in turn, savoring them. Somewhere during this truffle tasting, Kal's free hand drifted between them to Diana's, fingertips tracing an open palm, and lightly entwining their fingers.

They were having one of the most carefree days in memory.

"This is beyond anything I imagined with us."

"Hmm...what do you mean?"

"The actual experiences we've had over the past few months. It's been a whirlwind but these calm moments bring it all together."

"Oh...yeah," he nodded, "yeah, you're right."

"I love you, Kal," Diana said softly, almost a whisper, squeezing his fingers between hers.

"I love you, too, Diana."

Diana's eyes drifted to Kal's lips, biting hard at her own.

Kal leaned in, pulling her hand away from Diana's, and bringing both hands to her hips, squeezing lightly, pulling their bodies into closer contact, fingers threading against her lower back, tongue tracing Diana's lips for entrance. Diana's hands slowly moved up Kal's strong arms, until she reached his shoulders, looping her hands behind his neck and pulling Kal closer to her.

After a long moment, Kal pulled back.

"Mmhh...the taste of Kryptonian flavored truffles...I like that very much."

"Heh...I've got plenty for you," Kal smirked.

"Oh, I know..." Diana blushed.

"It's almost close to the time we need to get get to our last spot before it gets crowded."

"I'm so excited for this theater at the beach!"

Kal smiled. "You'll love it."

"How do you know where to go already?" Diana asked arching her eyebrow curious.

"I went on and took a peek at an itinerary and overheard a few other tourists," he winked.

Diana laughed. "The perks of super sight and hearing."

"Yep! Now we need to get something more solid than ice cream and truffles. Not sure how long we will be at the beach."

"Are you asking me to dinner, Kal?" Her tone was playful, as per usual.

"I'd rather have you for dinner but, would you like to go to dinner with me?" He was equally as playful.

"Mmmm, once we go back to our hotel you can have as much of me as you want. We have a rose petal-covered bed to test. Though, for now, yes, my Love, I would love to go to dinner with you."

THE DARK SPELL

Next to one of the main arteries of Barcelona, the Via Laietana, and a few steps from the central market of Santa Caterina, is the Arcano restaurant. Located in an old stable from the 17th century, with a beautiful Romanesque stamp, arched shapes, and stone walls that crown a large part of its spaces.

Entering the restaurant, romantic interior, warmly lit, Diana was already in awe yet again. It was cozy, but with a sort of elegant presence.

As they sat down, Kal ordered cocktails.

"Oh, Goodness, I'm not sure what to order!" Diana giggled and drew her lip between her teeth.

"We'll just ask for specials and what they would recommend since it's our first time here."

"Lovely!" Diana grinned.

As plate after plate was brought out, the waiter explained the inspiration for the dishes, very briefly. Kal and Diana enjoyed every dish. The conversations between them didn't let up as they ate and sipped their cocktails.

Nearly an hour and a half passed afterward, Kal reached for Diana's hand and met her eyes. Diana's lit face with a question.

"Darling?"

He leaned in, kissed her cheek, and lightly traced his thumb over her knuckles just once, then intertwined their fingers.

"Let's head down to the beach."

Diana smiled slightly squeezing his hand in hers.

"Okay."

They walked out into the night in comfortable silence. Diana sighed happily as they swung their entwined hands slightly.

Kal smirked, catching Diana by surprise, and pulled her to him, crashing his lips on hers. He tentatively ran his tongue over Diana's bottom lip, and she opened eagerly. Their tongues moved slowly, twisting their heads and letting out soft small sighs of pleasure.

"I love you," Kal whispered breathlessly as they pulled away, their foreheads resting together.

"I love you too," Diana smiled.

They walked aimlessly, fingers still intertwined and as they neared the beach, Diana leaned down, slipping off her sandals.

The crash and whoosh of the waves were a backdrop to what they were feeling. They were happy, carefree, breathing in the scent of the sea. Lights from the city and the harbor danced on the water, smears of green and red and blue twinkling in the distance. The moon was just starting its assent, quarter full, the sliver still casting the beach and waves in a soft white-blue glow. There weren't many people on the beach, but a hundred yards beyond, there were some people still around the beach bars.

"I forgot the real reason why we are here," Diana said nudging his shoulder.

Kal kissed her temple. "We should just keep forgetting for a little while longer." He quirked his brow. "As a matter of fact, hold on a minute."

"Where are you go-...?"

Kal rushed off but within less than a minute, he was back with 2 blankets.

"Wha-?"

"Ready for a movie on the beach?"

"Yes, I am!"

"There are some other spots but this one, we get a little more space and not many people at all it seems."

They walked along the beach for ways, hand in hand, stopping now and then to lean into each other and look out at the waves. Then they came upon a secluded bit of beach, still able to see the movie screen.

Kal pulled his hand from Diana's, it felt empty and cold at the loss of her. He laid out the blanket, and slowly sank down, the cool, fine sand leaching heat through the blanket, pulling Diana down to sit next to him.

Kal's fingers brushed Diana's cheek, looking deeply, seriously into her eyes. As he leaned in, their noses just brushing, Diana met his eyes directly. They kissed, slow, tender, at first. But as Diana slipped her arms around his neck, cradling the back of his head, pulling him closer, gaining leverage, the kiss deepened. They pulled into each other, tongues sliding in and out, hot and needy. Kal lightly sucked Diana's tongue into his mouth, a moan escaping from Diana's lips.

THE DARK SPELL

Diana broke away, breathing deeply the scent of Kal: sandalwood, vanilla, musk, mingled with the salty air, the breeze fluttering around them.

"My Beloved Kal..."

She nuzzled into him, placing hot, open-mouthed kisses along his jaw and neck. Then she stopped, still pressing into him, burying her face in the crook of his neck.

When the movie started, Diana felt rumbling from Kal's chest.

"Hm? What is it, Love?"

"1953 classic, Roman Holiday."

"Oh? What's it about?"

"A bittersweet love story about a Princess and a Reporter."

Diana looked up at him with a smile. "Quite a coincidence. Though our love story continues on..."

Halfway into the movie, Diana's roaming fingers managed to glide up and down Kal's chiseled abs.

Batting away the skilled fingers, Kal was tempted to watch the movie in peace. His girlfriend, however, had other ideas. Deftly sliding her hand under the waistband of his shorts and boxers, Diana brushed her fingers against the tip of his manhood.

He let out a low groan. "Di..."

She let out a quiet giggle. "Just a little play, Love."

She smiled innocently as she began to slowly stroke him causing him to moan and his hips began to move in rhythm with her hand motions. All the while, Kal does his best to conceal what she was doing with the blanket. Kal moved closer, cupping Diana's chin until their eyes met. His other hand looped around her waist.

Diana's hand was setting him on fire. It wouldn't take much before he was on the verge of exploding. She knew this too, so she slowed down and circles his member with her hand, teasing the head with her fingers. Kal let out some hard, sudden breaths. Diana continued stroking again in a slow, full-length manner.

"You are something else, Ms. Prince."

He pulled their bodies even closer together as he captured her lips in a soft kiss. His tongue pressed against her lips and slipped into her mouth. He felt her tiny moan reverberate through his own mouth.

Diana jerked him as his hand slid down her thigh and then up under her skirt and underwear. He effortlessly moved his fingers against her swollen clit. He dipped his middle finger in and hooked her G-Spot immediately. Kal stifled his own groan of pleasure as he saw Diana's eyes roll back, her mouth slightly open. Diana jerked her head as she gasped. Her body stiffened before relaxing. He fingered her slowly as her body started to rock in rhythm with his hand movement. Diana matched Kal's rhythm with her hand on Junior. He started stroking her with tiny little movements and finally inserted one finger, then two, inside her. Diana couldn't help it, she moaned; almost exploding right then and there. Kal moved his fingers in and out; both feeling and hearing the suction pulling his fingers deeper inside. He managed to keep doing it and use his thumb to rub her clit at the same time. The combination of the physical intensity, and the public location, set Diana off and she moaned again, louder than before.

Diana laughed delightfully and moved her head into his chest, before suddenly remembering where they were and checking to see that no one was looking.

Kal pressed her clit hard and move further on the downstroke, heading down to her opening. Changing the angle of his hand, he slid his fingers into her. She jolted again as he pushed his fingers as far as they would go into her soft, wet womanhood and then bring it up and over her clit again. He continued fingering her like this, gradually speeding up the tempo. His own breathing is quite heavy, and his erection was hot and throbbing. Diana's eyes squeezed closed, the expression on her face is one of sheer ecstasy.

He kissed her cheek and neck. His lips trailed up to her lips and kissed her again but only briefly as the pleasure they gave each other with their hands caused their breathing to increase. Kal's fingers slipped faster up and down, in and out, occasionally flicking across her clit, extracting soft moans every time.

Kal kissed her neck and cheek again, and licked and bit her ear, which tipped the scale for Diana. Her back arched, her eyes closed, and she bit her lip, trying to stifle her pleasure moans as the waves of pleasure rippled through her body.

THE DARK SPELL

The whole time, they made hardly any noise, or at least nothing that can be heard over the movie. Kal's hand was now moving as fast as it could under the blanket. He wanted to take her over the edge. He wanted to finish her. He brought his focus to her clit, rubbing two fingers over it side-to-side as hard and fast as he could. Diana's mouth dropped open into voiceless moans, her head tilted back. Her hips buck violently, her legs occasionally hitting against his.

In a single moment of release, her body tensed up and jerked back. He felt a squirt of liquid on his fingertips. She had climaxed. He was amazed she managed to do so without screaming as loud as he knew she could, let alone without her voice making even a sound.

Diana opened her eyes, panting, looking completely spent. She looked into his eyes and bit her lip in a mischievous smile. Kal move her panties back in place and brought his fingers up to his face. Diana watched blushing as he licked his fingers tasting her sweet juices.

"So, so good..."

Diana smiled and sped up her stroking. It was bliss. Kal closed his eyes and tilted his head back. The bit of slippery liquid that had collected at the tip was perfect. There was just the right amount of friction as she moved her hand up and down his shaft. Kal continued thrusting with his hips and Diana heard the mix of gasps and moans that meant he was getting close. Diana kept up the steady rhythm; she rubbed the head of his manhood with her fingers to spread around more of the fluid that was oozing out.

Kal felt the tension in his balls as his whole lower body started to tingle and throb. He opened his eyes and looked at Diana. They both know he was arriving. She's a clever woman, slowing down her strokes to prolong the moment.

Kal's eyes widen and he panted heavier. A couple of more significant, stronger thrusts, a louder moan, Kal couldn't hold his own climax any longer, shooting stream after stream of hot, sticky essence oozing all over Diana's hand and into his boxers. It just kept on coming. He shuddered a few last times and was still. As Kal caught his breath, Diana's hand was still on his throbbing erection.

Diana brought her hand up from under the blanket. Kal's essence was all over and a thread of it hung down from her thumb. In the most beautiful moment of all, she discreetly and causally sucks it from her hand, being sure to get every drop, eating it as she goes. She only made a sound as she sucked the last drop of it. A cute sucking noise and a satisfied moan.

No one noticed anything and the movie was near its end. Kal chuckled as he fixed his shorts.

He looked at Diana and they smiled at each other again with unspoken connectedness. There's a little spot on the corner of her cute mouth. Kal watched her lick her lips and the corner of her mouth.

"You don't know how sexy you are and how much I love you," he said.

"Hmm...well I have some kind of idea but how about we take to the skies and you can show me when we get back to our hotel?" she asked softly.

Kal smirked. "Let's go."

They got up, Diana's carrying their blankets and they walked a short way not to be seen before flying up.

Location: The Pulitzer Hotel: Kal and Diana's Suite

Closing and locking their room door behind him, Kal immediately started undressing along with Diana. He wrapped his arms around her now naked body pulling her against him. Their noses barely touching before Kal leaves a sweet chaste kiss on her lips.

Diana loved how the sweetest of kisses makes her weak in the knees. She placed her hands on his arms, feeling his biceps contract beneath her.

"Shower," she whispered.

Kal nodded and smiled against her lips as he kissed her again, deeper this time. Diana's arms wrap around him, body melding with his. She moaned into his mouth, feeling his tongue parting her lips to meet hers in a familiar dance.

Kal lifted her up and Diana wrapped her legs around his waist as Kal floated into the bathroom. Diana reached to turn on the water while kissing Kal deeply, her legs still wrapped around his waist.

With her back against the white tiled wall of the shower, Diana's skin erupted in goosebumps as she felt the cold meet her, a salacious juxtaposition to Kal's hard and heated body melding with her front.

Taking his right hand from where it rested right on her lower back, Kal trailed it slowly up her body, blindly finding her breast, gently massaging it before using his thumb to tease her nipple.

THE DARK SPELL

Diana groaned into his mouth, feeling her skin burning with a fire he set in motion.

Kal parted from her lips then with a loud smack, not wasting any time to trail his mouth down to her neck, hearing her short breaths in his ear. His lips trail further down still until they meet her chest, drinking in the droplets of water between her breasts. He savors her skin slowly, without hurry, knowing it'll only drive her crazy. He covered her breast with his mouth, teeth and tongue taking turns to nibble and suck, his other hand playing homage to her other one, tugging her nipple to attention.

"Clark..." she called out to him and she tugged his head up, claiming his lips with her own as soon as he reached her. Her teeth nip at his bottom lip, using her tongue to soothe the spot over and over.

His hands trace invisible patterns on her stomach, feeling her muscles contract as he reached lower. Upon reaching the apex of her thighs, his hand stills.

Diana groaned against his mouth, a frustrated noise that lets him know he better get to it, or else. She doesn't wait for him though, taking one manicured hand, she rakes her nails down his arm, scratching his skin as she goes before reaching his hand, guiding him to her. He smiled against her lips and gave her what she wanted, dragging one thick finger against her. He growled as he felt her wet and ready for him already, a feat he will never get over.

Suddenly, his lips left her own, but before she could protest, he was staring into her eyes, their ragged breathing the only thing she can hear. She placed her hand on his chest, right above his heart.

"Kal-El..." she whispered, the ache between her legs almost paling in comparison to the way her chest swells at the intensity of his gaze.

"I love you," he told her, simply, honestly, and it takes everything in her at that very moment to not let her tears fall.

Diana gave him a watery smile, grabbing the back of his head to guide him into a kiss, whispering against his mouth, "I love you, too."

Holding her body even closer to his, making sure he had her secured and wrapped up in his arms, Kal made sure to tease her clit for a mere second, hearing her gasp into his mouth at the touch, before he finally sunk into her.

Their lips continue to glide against each other, breathing becoming a challenge as their movements grow uneven and rapid, each too wound up to take things slow.

When he felt her muscles contracting around him, Kal sped up the process, lips parting from hers as they claim her neck, kissing and suckling her skin there.

Holding onto him, Diana began to feel the familiar tightening in her lower abdomen, closing her eyes as the sensations from every inch of him bring her closer and closer....

"Diana..."

Diana feels more than heard his words against her, and she tightened her hold on him, muscles gripping harder around him still.

Kal watched as her eyes remain closed, mouth slightly open as a quiet moan escapes her. He pulled out of her just long enough to hear her whine of protest before he rammed inside her.

"OH GODS!" She groaned, lip trapped between her teeth as her head collapsed on his shoulder.

Kal felts her nails gripping his biceps harder, leaving angry marks as he drove into her, just the way he knew was an inevitable pathway to drive her over the edge. Her teeth were suddenly on him, biting his shoulder, stirring more fire within him and he made his movements more rapid, matching the rhythm of her grinding against him.

"That's it," Kal told her, voice low against her ear, kissing her temple in encouragement.

It's his words that do it for her, a soundless cry escaping her lips as she quaked in his arms, letting him hold her steady as she slowly came down from her high.

When her breathing has returned to normal, she lifted her head to look at him, expecting to see a smug smile on his face, but instead sees his eyes glassed over with arousal. She took one last steady breath before she speaks again, voice dripping desire.

"Fill me..."

Kal pulled himself almost entirely out of her then thrust back into her.

"Oh Gods!" she gasped.

"I want to hear you sing, Diana. Sing like you always do."

THE DARK SPELL

Diana met him at every thrust, then their pace became a crescendo as they rocked towards the peak of their love making. Diana buried her face in his neck as he entered her and began bucking her hips against him, a twinge of pleasure racked her body as she clung to him, her legs coiled tightly around his middle, almost as if she was trying to trap him even more deeply inside her.

The moment Diana looked up at him, Kal crashed his lips against hers. Sucking at one another's mouths, their tongues tangled as they swirled within each other's mouths. With each stroke of Kal's length gliding in, Diana's moans became more drawn out and louder. Both their tongues became more entangled as well.

As he continued to pound into her, each thrust stretching her around him as he thrust harder and faster. Deeper and deeper. Diana felt like she might split in two, but the friction of his hard member sliding in and out of her made her entire body quiver with unadulterated pleasure.

"Don't stop," she begged. "Oh Gods...don't stop!"

Diana's moans grew increasingly louder as Kal's thrusts grew more intense- with every passing minute Kal's breathing grew laboured as his member got harder and thicker as he continued pumping into her relentlessly until she was moaning and gasping with pleasure.

"Di..."

"By the Gods!" she pleaded. "I want all of you. Yes! Yes!"

Diana threw her head back against the wall, moaning louder as Kal's mouth trailed down her neck, licking and sucking. She felt herself tightening around him as her orgasm built up inside her.

"Gods! Kal, I....! " she gasped out incoherently through the haze of pleasure.

He nodded, thrusting faster into her. Diana screamed as her orgasm overtook her, holding on to him as tight as she could to pull him deeper into her as she came. Diana felt Kal swelling up inside her. The increased tightness was too much for Kal. He let out a deep guttural groan and began to pump even harder, pumping his essence into her. Diana climaxed again with increasing volume as Kal came in a hot, sticky explosion filling her completely. They came together, each other's names a soft mantra on their lips, mutual groans accompanying them, swallowing the sound of the running water in their small enclosure. Their bodies momentarily shuddered as they held each other.

Their lips met softly, gently, tenderly, but still deeply and powerfully. When they broke apart after what felt like an eternity, they were both smiling.

Kal tentatively ran his tongue over Diana's bottom lip, and Diana opened eagerly. Their tongues moved slowly, twisting their heads and filling the atmosphere with small sighs of pleasure.

"I love you," Kal whispered breathlessly as they pulled away, their foreheads resting together.

Diana kissed him again, passionately.

"I love you, too," Diana sighed lovingly.

Slowly, Kal let her legs untangle around him, a satisfied sigh escaping his lips.

As Diana stood, Kal gently pulled her to him and moving her under the water.

Kal got a bottle of body wash and squeezed out a generous amount of it on his hands and started to lather it on Diana, having his hands on her made her melt. The way he did it was so slow and sensual, massaging his hands over her delicate body and Diana looked up into his eyes lovingly. He started on her arms, then her neck, then her torso, his eyes of complete concentration darted to her own and a smirk played on his lips as he lathered her torso but never touching her already taut breasts. He gently moved down to her legs, not once touching her center, and he could see her struggling wordlessly because he was saving the best for last.

He poured more of the soap to his hands and started to lather her back, slowly inching lower and lower until he cupped her ass making her bite her lip. He started to knead her cheeks as he lowered his own lips to her, not letting his tongue dart out but simply nibbling Diana's swollen lips.

Having satisfied himself, he gave Diana a lustful look and started to lather her voluptuous breasts. Kissing her more deeply, he kneaded her breasts rhythmically, the soap causing almost no friction, making Diana almost squirm underneath him, then he caught her taut nipples between his fingers and started to pinch them, making Diana gasp into their kiss, granting a satisfied smile from him.

THE DARK SPELL

"Are you being a naughty man, Kal-El?" Diana asked, moaning softly.

"Maybe." Kal grinned as he continued to play with Diana breasts for a bit.

His fingers closed in on her nipples, flicking them with his fingertips, pinching the tips gently just to drive his Goddess wild. Kal stopped playing with Diana's breasts and moved his hands further down her body, until Diana swatted his hands away.

"It's my turn to wash you," Diana said.

Kal looked at Diana as she poured body wash and lathered it up in her hands. She began to wash his chest, then up to his shoulders and up to his neck, repeating the process on him. The sweet and innocent Goddess continued on, soaping up his stomach and his pelvis before she poured more of the soap in her hands and moved down to Junior. When she wrapped her fingers around his rod of pleasure, moving her hand up and down on it nice and slow, he almost buckled.

"And you said that I was being the naughty one," Kal chuckled.

Diana smirked and giggled. With her hand still on her boyfriend's manhood, she wrapped her other arm around his neck and kissed him tenderly as their wet, naked bodies were pressed together. Kal wrapped his arms around Diana's waist, holding her tightly while she kept stroking him. He kissed her back making the kiss more passionate as their arousal for each other kept growing. Kal ran his hands up and down Diana's back, making her shudder from his touch. His hands moved down to her lovely ass again to squeeze it for a bit and giving it a hard smack, making Diana yelp into the kiss.

When all the soap was rinsed off their bodies, Kal turned the water off. Diana was just about to get a towel to dry off when Kal picked her up, hoisting her over his shoulder.

"Kal? What in the Gods names are you doing?"

Kal smacked her ass again carrying her to the bedroom where he playfully threw her onto the bed.

Diana sat up on her elbows looking at him. Both still dripping wet.

Kal stared down at her with the most unadulterated lust filled look Diana had ever seen him have.

"You never cease to amaze me, Diana. Surrounded by those rose petals right now and having them all over you like that."

Diana blushed realizing the petals on the bed were sticking to her wet body.

"Come here, Love."

Kal crawled up the bed to her. He took her into her arms and no other thought than him came into her mind, not even concerned that their bed was completely soaked. Although a soaked bed, they are used to it with their sexual endeavors anyway.

He placed his lips to hers, his tongue explored her mouth.

Kal smiled pulling away from their kiss and sat up flipping Diana over, surprising her. He moved her hair to one side, laying a kiss on the back of her neck.

Diana laughed. "What are you doing?"

"Dessert."

He trailed his way down with kisses to the small of her back.

"Oh..." She gasped and squealed as he squeezed her ass then bit her left cheek. "Kal!"

She loved how sensual he was being, lightly massaging her gorgeous ass. And she had one fine ass. A world class ass. A full, round, woman's ass. It was an ass built for comfort, for love, for adoration. An ass that a man could get happily and comfortably lost in.

"I can't help myself. The only kind of cake I want at any hour of the day."

He kissed her ass giving each and every inch its due time. Then he stuck his tongue out and place the tip of it at the top of her crack.

"Oh, you naughty man!"

Diana can't help but moan; she tried to turn over but Kal held her down; she quickly gave up and laid there.

Kal gently caressed the smooth flawless sun kissed skin of her ass. Every part of him wanted to love and adore her ass until he dropped. He was one hungry man and her ass looked like the best feast he had ever seen. Pure nourishment.

Diana looked back at him. The hunger and fire in his eyes stirred her in all the right places. The scene in front of her blew her away. Here was her best friend, the love of her life, the sweetest, humbled, respectful man in the

THE DARK SPELL

world, on his knees before her ass. She and all her assets was the object of his love and adoration...love and adoration that she knew she wanted more than anything else, and from no one else.

"Mmmmm... you don't know what you are doing to me, just staring the way you are," she said softly.

Kal smirked and gently placed a warm kiss on the full part of her right ass cheek.

"Mmmmm..." she purred.

His lips would brush gently across her skin. Her ass pushed out, reaching for his affection. He breathed deeply the beautifully intoxicating mixture of her aromas and the rose petals still on her. Her scent swirled in his brain. It was a unique scent he never grew tired of and only became more addicted to. He kept asking himself how he ever got so damn lucky, blessed even.

"Beautiful... perfect... absolutely gorgeous..."

Diana's eyes widened at his words. She blushed. She laughed a deep, full laugh.

Kal loved the playful look on her face. He wasted no time burying his face in the soft, warmth of her anal valley. He flick his tongue causing her ass to loosen up while he massaged her ass cheeks apart. He slowly inserted his tongue and Diana couldn't believe how deep it went as he spread her with his hands. Kal continued to shove his tongue in and out while also taking a break to kiss and nibble on her ass cheeks.

"I love you," he mumbled as his lips kissed her. "Damn, how I love you," he said as his lips and tongue began a long anal adoration session of her delicious rosebud.

Diana responded eagerly to his affections, twitching, tingling and pushing out at him.

Diana almost levitated off the bed. She tingled from head to toe. That feeling that she was truly being made love to, his touch had affected her so strongly. The heat and passion and hunger she felt pouring from him into her bottom. Her hand reached back. caressing his head and pushed his face in farther.

Her passion fueled his. Kal tried to fill her ass with his tongue. For the next while the only thing that existed for either of them was the connection between his face and her ass, totally abandoning himself to his passion.

Diana found herself blown away by the amount of tenderness, affection, and passion he showered her ass with. Things stirred deep inside her. Diana felt an orgasm building just as Kal placed his ring finger above her clit. Diana cried out and tore the sheets off the bed as Kal simultaneously rubbed her clit ever so lightly and shove his tongue into her ass. Both move at the same time increasing the sensation ten fold. Diana's orgasm racked her body and she shook all over him.

Kal lifted her ass up higher, kissing her thighs. While Diana continued to moan from her previous orgasm, Kal moved toward her womanhood. He started to lick up her soaking juice. Diana tensed up as his tongue separated her lips. Flicking her with his tongue so quickly causing waves of pleasure to flow through her body. His hands move up under her, cupping her breasts, rolling her erect nipples between his finger as he ate her out from behind.

Kal then quickly adjusted their position. His tongue only momentarily losing contact with her clit, he turned to lay under Diana and pulled her to sit on his head. Diana could now look down into his eyes as he ate out her womanhood. His tongue worked expertly bringing her to another orgasm. Diana threw her head back and smothered him as she came and filled his mouth with her juice.

Diana slowly turned herself around so she could give attention to Junior as Kal continued to give attention to her womanhood and ass.

Kal placed a chaste kiss, only a press of the lips, against the petals of flesh. Diana's heart swelled at his tenderness. Diana got lost with him in her throat.

She moaned around the flesh as Kal's tongue slipped between her lips one long stroke at a time. His tongue roots deeper, as his hips thrust up his manhood in a slow steady rhythm.

Kal savored each muffled gasp and whimper that comes from her lips, listening for the different sounds each movement creates and losing himself in the sensations of the moment. The whorls and dips of his tongue, the thrusting savageness followed by tender caresses, every motion calculated to bring Diana closer and yet keep the end just out of reach.

Abandoning her swollen clit just before she could give in completely to the feelings tightening her body, he chuckled at the sounds of her desperation.

The animal sound that swelled in Kal's throat, escaped in a heated moaning howl to undulate along the quivering walls where his mouth was buried, pulling at the chords tightening inside Diana, demanding an answer. Diana's responding purr shimmered down the length of his shaft, choking off her air for just a moment as he pressed deeper.

As soon as Kal felt the slight pressure of Diana's hands pushing at his thighs, he pulled completely out of her mouth to let her catch her breath.

Taking him back into her mouth, it was as if he grew even harder and larger, stretching her throat each time his velvety head passes over her tongue. His shaft began pulsing in her mouth.

Diana relaxed her jaw and let his hips do the work of thrusting into her mouth. There was no hope of her keeping suction while he was pounding her with such zeal so she gave him free rein with her throat.

The sensations coming from her core have more of her juices flowing freely onto his questing tongue. Her hips grind upwards seeking that final incredible release that she knew was so near. Kal's fingertips dip into her and Diana's throat opened deeper for him as his passionately pumping manhood strangled the first cries of her orgasm. The throbbing of his shaft shoots the first long string of seed against the back of her throat and she instinctively swallowed.

Kal's fingers thrusting into her, his tongue pressing against her clit, his manhood filling her with heavy bursts of essence, everything combined to send Diana hurtling over the edge into an orgasm that ripped through her entire body.

Diana tried to keep up with the ropes of essence flowing from each pulse of him but she could feel it dribbling out the sides of her mouth and down her neck. She gulped what seemed like gallons before Kal rolled them over to their sides.

Diana took a breath as he pulled out of her mouth.

They lay there breathing heavily, recovering from the emotional upheaval as their bodies soften and return to their natural state.

Kal rose to his elbow, slowly and gently rubbed the inside of Diana's thigh, up the curve of her hip, and cheeks with a chuckle before he said, "I won't ever apologize for being greedy when it comes to you."

Diana laughed. "Don't you ever dare," she said softly as she turned around and moved up to him, gently kissing his lips.

The taste of them combined sent more shivers through them. She kissed him again, slowly.

Kal gently slapped her ass. Diana's eyes widened with surprise and pulled away from their kiss. She loved the playful twinkle in his eyes.

"I love you," he said.

"I love you, too."

Their lips met again.

The Next Morning...

The sun was rising slowly, rays of sunshine gradually hitting his face. With his hands under his head, Kal was looking up at the ceiling listening to Diana's soft breathing as she slept. He looked over to her and smiled. The covers were only covering up to her waist, giving him a full view of her beautiful back. He smiled, admiring her figure. Those voluptuous curves, and he was the lucky one that could admire them as much as he liked. He picked up a single rose petal and ran it slowly over the side of her body, the gentle touch lingering on her waistline. Kal saw her move faintly under his touch, but kept on caressing her back with the petal slowly.

"Mmh...I felt you staring," she mumbled lowly giggling.

Kal reached over to brush a strand of hair from her face. He then leaned in kissing her cheek.

"I can't help it. Waking up to this gorgeous Goddess still feels so surreal."

"It does feel like a dream."

Diana's eyes fluttered open and turned to face him.

Kal wrapped an arm around her pulling her closer to him into an embrace, letting no space between their naked bodies. Their skin was being caressed by the light covers and each other's body. They remained still and

THE DARK SPELL

silent for a long time. How long, they had no idea. They just enjoyed each other's warmth, smiling faintly and caressing each other's skin gently.

Kal let his arm rest on her waist while Diana reached hers to his head, running her fingers through his hair. He moaned slightly because of the pleasure her touch gave him. Diana would often do this, play gently through his hair, while he closed his eyes and tickled her side. When she stopped and removed her hand, he opened his eyes again and looked at her lovingly, still saying nothing.

Then, slowly, he buried his head in the crook of her neck, not forgetting to put a small kiss on it, thus sending shivers down her spine. With Diana still in his arms, Kal turned on his back so she would be positioned over him. She laughed softly and rested her arms on his chest and her chin on her arms. That way, she could look at him while being so comfortable.

"Slept well?" he inquired.

Diana placed a small peck on his lips.

"Mmm...very well," she answered with a smile, before putting another, longer kiss on her lover's lips.

While Kal was running his fingers up and down her back, Diana was kissing him all along his jaw and down his neck. Kal caressed her lower, over her perfectly rounded ass and her soft thighs. Diana went back up to kiss him fully on the lips, not like the previous innocent kisses, but a deep and passionate one. Kal grabbed her by the hips and sat up in the bed, his lips never leaving hers. His hands left her waist to go up on her stomach all the way to her breasts. He massaged them gently, running his thumbs over her hardened buds. Diana moaned slightly and arched her back in appreciation of Kal's broad and slightly calloused hands on her body.

"I...haven't...my...tea..." Diana muttered in between kisses.

Kal nodded, knowing what Diana was trying to say.

"I'll go get you some," he stated breaking their kiss.

"Thank you, Love."

Kal caressed her cheek and kissed the tip of her nose.

She moved off of him for him to get up to quickly get dressed.

After getting dressed, Kal walked over and sat on the edge of the bed.

"Are you okay?"

"Of course, Love. Why wouldn't I be?"

"I mean with having to do this everyday?"

Diana smiled. "One day I won't have to but as for now, in order for us not to have a little league of our own too soon, I don't mind it."

Kal nodded. "I just want to be sure."

"Yes. Very sure. Now hurry so afterwards you can put me in that position you like so much."

"Which one?" He smirked. "I like every position I put you in."

Diana giggled. "That's what I meant, Love."

He chuckled and kissed her softly. "Be right back, my gorgeous rose."

Diana laid back smiling thinking of the possibility of children. "Yes, one day, my Love. One day."

Hours later...Museu Nacional d'Art de Catalunya

"Pose for me, Di," Kal said grinning.

"Okay!" She said with a light chuckle.

She placed one foot in front of the other and her hand on her hip. She was wear a sexy tie dye two piece set: One shoulder crop pop and ruched midi skirt.

"Perfect!"

"We have to get pictures together, Love."

Kal switched the camera on his phone for them to take a selfie. Diana kissed his cheek, letting her lips linger.

After taking that picture, Kal turned his head to capture Diana's lips. Diana smiled into the kiss as he took that picture.

"Be careful showing off our pictures, Kal. Superman and Wonder Woman's photo was just from the WatchTower security camera. Wouldn't want Clark Kent and Diana Prince's intimate photos especially the lingerie ones getting out."

"Oh, of course not! Those pictures are for my eyes only. But..." he grinned and pulled her closer. "I'll say, every picture of you is damn gorgeous though, having you in my arms is even better."

Diana smiled. "I'm all yours, Beloved."

As they were about to kiss, the ground started to shake.

"What?!" Diana questioned.

"An earthquake?"

THE DARK SPELL

"No...I can sense...magic." Diana looked around. "There's something else going on."

Kal looked around as well, scanning the city.

"It's something happening near La Rambla."

Kal and Diana quickly flew off changing. Kal's supersuit generating and Diana twirled her lasso around her body.

While flying, they saw tourists and locals running away from something.

"Maaaa!"

"What the hell?" Kal couldn't believe what he was looking at. "Is that a giant goat?!"

"Dionysus is near. This is his doing. He's hiding like a coward somewhere."

"We'll find him."

Diana nodded.

"How do we deal with him though?" Kal asked.

"I'll talk to him. You go get as much hay, fruits and vegetables available."

"He will actually eat what a normal goat eats?"

"Yes. We just need a lot of it."

Kal nodded. "On it then."

While Kal flew off, Diana turned her attention to the giant goat. It looked harmless. Though, confused and scared.

"Now, now... Superman is going to get you food. I need you to remain calm for me so you nor anyone else will get hurt. I'm sorry you are used for my half brother's scheme."

"Maaa!" The goat stepped back a bit from Diana.

"Be calm."

She flew closer to the goat and reach out slowly to touch its forehead.

"Monstre! Fuig! Fuig!"

Diana gasped and turned quickly to see a group of local men.

"No! Surt ara a la seguretat!"

One threw a bucket though Diana blocked it.

"Atureu-ho ara!"

"MAAA!"

Diana felt the aura of the goat becoming angry.

"Marxa ara!" Diana demanded.

As the goat was just about to charge at them, Diana flew up lassoing one of its horns to pull it back.

"No!"

Suddenly, Superman flew down with a truck bed full of food for the goat. He turned his attention to the group, frowning.

"Has sentit a la senyora. Ella va dir moure's."

The men tried to stand their ground although trembling.

"Marxar..." he said sternly.

The men were still a bit hesitant but ran off.

"They're gone, buddy. Calm down," Kal said flying up with the hay. "Here. Hungry?"

The goat sniffed then opened its mouth for Kal to dump the hay into its mouth.

"There you go, bud."

Diana flew next to Kal as they watched the giant goat eat all that Kal brought.

"What should we do now?"

"I'll have to see if Hermes can take him somewhere safe or...?"

With a gust of wind, there was a faint whistling sound.

"Maaa!"

The goat turned and started walking away.

"Where is he going?"

The goat was slowly disappearing.

"As I knew. It was a grand message from Dionysus telling us he is around."

"What do we do now?"

"Go back to our hotel for a moment. Maybe he'll send another message? I just fear what that would be."

Kal and Diana walked into their hotel room.

Diana sighed and walked to the balcony.

Kal was just about to take off his shirt when he noticed a bottle of wine.

"Di? Did you order this?"

"Order what, Love?"

Kal held up the bottle.

THE DARK SPELL

Diana frowned confused. "No, Love." She took the bottle. "There's a note. Χάιντ."

"Hyde?"

"It's a night club. We meet him at 11."

"Alright. This all ends tonight."

Hours later...

"Damn..." Kal said wide eyed as Diana walked out of the bathroom wearing a sexy silver cross wrap cutout backless glitter halter bodycon dress.

Diana blushed. "I'm glad you like it." She trailed her hand down his chest. "My handsome Spaceman."

Kal wore a plan black under shirt with a quilted lined full zip river plaid jacket and dark denim jeans.

Diana trailed farther down caressing his manhood and giggled. "Seems Junior likes my dress too."

Kal grinned and kissed her. Diana moaned in his mouth feeling his hands travel down to grip her ass.

"We have to go..."

Kal sighed. "The faster we get this over, I can have my cake again."

Diana took his hand dragging him to the door. "Come on."

Location: Hyde Club Barcelona

Walking in, Diana immediately caught the attention of some of the men at the club. Kal chuckled and caressed Diana's hip.

"So much for being discreet..." he joked.

"I should've worn a different dress."

"No matter what you wear, Starshine, your gorgeousness can't be hidden."

Diana smiled and kissed his cheek.

"Do you know what he looks like? I mean, even if in disguise?"

"I will know. For now however, let us enjoy a dance."

Kal grinned and placed his hand around Diana at the small of her back and leaned closer. His hands caress her hour-glass body up and down as she swayed her hips. Diana loved the feel of his shoulders, the smell of his cologne, and the feel his warm breath on her ear. Kal leaned in and kissed her neck and she eased her head back.

Kal's hand then made contact with her leg. Tingles start to ride up Diana's spine. She continued swaying her hips. His fingers stroke her thigh, gentle strokes, gliding smoothly. He kisses across her jaw line to her lips. They lock together, swaying, fingers stroking under Diana's hemline. Warm tongue probes into her mouth, deepening their kiss. She felt a twinge of excitement between her legs. No one else seemed to notice or care.

After what seemed like eternity, they broke apart. Diana glanced over to the VIP lounge area.

She saw a man chug down a whole bottle of wine with women surrounding him.

"He's there."

Kal turned his head. "You sure that's him."

"His ring. The goat."

Kal nodded. "Well let's go."

Hand in hand, Kal and Diana walked to the VIP area.

Dionysus spotted them and smiled brightly.

"Well, well, well! My young sister and her companion! Come! Have a drink with me!"

"Dionysus, we are not here for a drink. We are here for you to come with us and face Valéria."

Dionysus stared at them for a moment then bursted out laughing. "Valéria...Ah...she just can't let go of the past. We are in the now!"

"She was falsely imprisoned because of you. She has disrupted our lives because of you."

"Disrupted? Looks more to me as she has actually done a good deed with you two finally giving into your temptations and truthful to the love you share."

"We didn't need anyone's interference," Kal said sternly.

"I'm honestly surprised. Diana, you are our father's daughter and an Amazon. To commit yourself to this being?"

Diana glared. "What does that suppose to mean?"

"You have the right to enjoy yourself such as I and others do. But yet you choose to enjoy just one?"

"I don't expect you to know what true love is. Once you have true love, all you ever want and need is just that one."

THE DARK SPELL

Dionysus laughed. "Can never escape Aphrodite and Eros influences. You should know love isn't necessary to breed. Father can attest to that. Isn't your species extinct, Kryptonian? Tell me, what is your intentions with dear Diana, the beloved Princess of the Amazons and Father's favorite offspring. Are you hoping to revive what was lost to you?"

"What?!" Kal's eyes start to turn red.

"Kal, no. He isn't worth it."

"Diana, I'm not about this drunken idiot disrespect us, especially not you." He clenched his jaw and fists.

Dionysus took another drink from a wine bottle and stood up.

"Yes, Kryptonian, show your strength! Show me why the daughter of the King of the Gods would waste opportunities and carnal knowledge on the likes of you, a false God and last of his kind!"

Kal angrily lunged at Dionysus, punching him in the face. Dionysus fell backwards on the sofa. The women that were surrounding him screamed.

"Ha! The strength is there but you are no match for a true God!"

"I've faught Gods before. You are nothing!"

It was Dionysus turn to lunge at Kal. Kal dodged quickly and his fist connected with Dionysus's face again. There was blood this time.

Dionysus wipes the corner of his mouths "There won't be a third."

"Want to bet?"

Dionysus frowned. He was becoming serious now. The building started to shake.

"Diana get everyone out of here now!"

"Kal, you are not fighting him!"

"He's not coming with us if I don't. Don't worry. I won't hurt him too much," he winked and smirked. "Now go."

"Be careful, Love."

"I was trained by the best."

That sexy confidence of his. Diana kissed his cheek and flew off to the crowd.

"Alright, Dionysus. It's you and me."

Dionysus cracked his knuckles. "You will learn never to challenge a true God again."

Kal and Dionysus uneasily danced around each other, each trying to anticipate the other's next move. Dionysus came at Kal and the battle was on. They both moved swiftly, though Dionysus was stumbling.

"This is insane!" Kal thought to himself. "Fighting a God drunk off his ass. But gladly Diana got everyone out of the way."

"Pay attention to me, Kryptonian!"

With Kal only seconds of being lost in his thoughts, Dionysus was able to finally land a blow on Kal's cheek and sent him sprawling backwards crashing into chairs and tables.

Kal rubbed his face and leered. "Lucky shot but that won't happen again."

He lunged again. Dionysus dodged him, colliding with a wall in the process.

"I can see it in your eyes. Feel it with every strike. You are motivated by her but why? You are with power yet you do not pursue the luxury of more. There are plenty more."

"Diana is already everything and more. I'll do any and everything in my power to protect and love her. She is my best friend and I don't expect you or anyone else to understand. It's not meant for anyone else to but me and Diana."

Dionysus smirked and moved swiftly. Kal kept his eyes moving on him as he jumped up but then he disappeared and before Kal's could react to dodge, Dionysus slapped him down hitting the bar counter. Kal quickly recovered and uppercuts Dionysus. Before Dionysus could recover, Kal punched him again, crashing through the front window to the street and now in front of the the crowd.

Diana gasped. "Oh, no...."

Kal flew out, his fists clenched. Dionysus stumbled trying to get up. Kal grabbed him up by his shirt.

"I'm done with this! Either you come with us or I'll keep kicking your ass all the way there!"

Dionysus looked at Kal puzzled and laughed.

"Good show! Good show! That was the most fun I've had in centuries!"

THE DARK SPELL

Dionysus waved his hand fixing everything within the club and the window. The crowd of people only remember seeing him and Kal brawl in the street as if it it was a normal brawl between drunk idiots.

"You can let me go now, Kryptonian."

Kal let his shirt go. Diana rushed over to him.

"Kal?" She wiped the blood off corner of his mouth.

"I can now see why you've chosen this one...only one. The strength of Father though much less pompous. Father will surely like a word."

"This is none of his concern."

Dionysus shrugged. "Once Father is done with his current...conquest. He will want to properly meet the one who has his daughter."

"You make it sound as if I'm a prisoner."

"You are. A prisoner of love."

Diana rolled her eyes. "Watch your tongue, Dionysus. You think Kal-El was a challenge, you don't want to test me."

Dionysus laughed. "I like you two more and more. Let's not have Valéria waiting any longer. Eros and Strife will be accompanying us, too? Quite a family reunion. I should bring more drinks!"

"No! No!" Kal and Diana said in unison.

"You've had plenty enough," Diana said.

Suddenly, a portal opened.

Dionysus sighed. "Until next century or maybe sooner, Mortals!"

Diana sighed and rolled her eyes again pushing Dionysus in. "Don't be so dramatic."

Location: Valéria's Castle: Throne Room

"Honey, I'm home!" Dionysus joked with a loud laugher stepping out of the portal.

Though, he was met with chains being wrapped around him and a hiss in his ear.

"Oh, Valéria, don't be like that. I expected a much better welcoming from you."

Valéria appeared in front of him. Rage in her eyes.

"Playing a petty game of cat and mouse was in poor taste for you, Dionysus," Eros said.

"You sound more bitter than Valéria," Strife teased Eros.

"Strife! You..."

Kal grabbed Diana by her arm and shook his head.

"Strife isn't who we need to watch out for right now."

"What do you mean?"

"Dionysus is still playing a game. Valéria isn't having it."

"You will pay for all you have done!" Valéria yelled.

Dionysus smirked. "My...my...my...you haven't changed...haven't learned. The succubus I met long ago didn't know her place and you still don't!" Dionysus broke out the chains and grabbed Valéria. "You are still weak."

Dionysus slapped her.

Valeria held her cheek glaring. "You coward!"

She attacked him, though, Dionysus is much more powerful than she, regardless of her rage fueling her own power. She clawed his face.

Diana and Kal watched in shock and horror as the battle between the God and demon ex lovers went on. The entire castle shook violently.

"You made your choices on your own accord!"

Tears fell uncontrollably from Valéria's eyes.

"I chose to love you because you promised me that the lives of the succubi will change!"

Dionysus laughed. "You are blessed and cursed. Blessed with such power to have any and every one fall ate your feet. Yet cursed because your heart and mind is of a mortal. Weak and gullible." He back handed her. "You were chosen to understand and balance the nature of pure love, lust, seduction. You lost control. I thought you could be by my side, but you failed."

As Dionysus was about to strike her again, his hand was being pulled back. He looked to see the golden lasso around his wrist.

"Diana...you dare?"

"I sure as hell do! Lay a hand on her again and I promise I will cut off both your damn hands!"

Dionysus laughed. "Is that a challenge, little sister? I accept."

Dionysus gripped the lasso and yanked Diana forward.

"Diana!"

THE DARK SPELL

Kal reached for her but she had already caught herself and kicked Dionysus in the face. He was sent flying across the throne room.

"You defended me?" Valéria asked shocked.

"It's what we do, no matter who it is," Diana smiled reassuringly.

Strife rolled her eyes. "And here we go with Ms. Goody-Goody."

"Jealous, Strife?" Eros taunted.

She glared. "Never!"

"Sibling rivalry, Diana?" Dionysus questioned. "You dare take the side of a succubus? One that has tormented you and your lover for months?"

"While Valéria has been pestering, she did help Kal and I realize the love, the desire, and the passion we share could no longer be suppressed. She never failed. Regardless of anything she has done, you took advantage of her and I will not stand for that!"

Diana lasso'd Dionysus again and flew up with him, swinging him over and slammed him to the ground. Diana then flew down slamming down on his back.

"It is your turn to now be imprisoned!"

Chains appeared cuffing his wrists, ankles and neck. Though, this time he could not break them.

He frowned then smirked. "This won't hold me for long."

"Dionysus?!" Eros called.

He scoffed. "You're going to shoot me with pheromone bullets? What a pleasure."

"You mock me?" Eros shot him right in the middle of his chest. "I should put a bullet through that big hallow skull of yours! Though, I believe Diana and Kal-El has done most of the work bringing you down. Because of you, my work was disrupted. This cat and mouse game is over! Valéria has plans for you. You may enjoy them...you may not. Either way, get used to the chains. You will be in them for a very long time."

"Eros, you can't do this to me!"

"Yes, I can. So as I said, get used to it."

"Juri, have him taken to the dungeon," Valéria ordered.

"Valéria!"

She flew to him with a wicked smile. She caressed his cheek then slapped him as hard as she could clawing his face again.

"I've been waiting so long to have you as I please. The pain I felt, you will now feel too."

Dionysus yanked the chains but still could not break them.

"Strife! Don't you just stand there snickering! Get me out!"

"Oh no...this is so much fun! Such chaos and drama! You know how much I love this! Let go, Brother. I want to watch this preparation of torment Valéria has in store for you."

"Strife! Eros! Diana! I swear, you all will be dealt with! Father will make his presence known and when he does, be prepared. Especially you, Kryptonian!"

Dionysus was dragged away with Strife following along amused.

"What was that suppose to mean?" Kal asked.

"No need to worry, Kal-El," Eros assured. "Dionysus is only acting as a child. Know that he is paying for all the chaos he has caused over centuries without punishment."

Diana latched onto Kal's arm.

"As much as I want to go back to Barcelona, I'd like to go to our home instead."

Kal nodded and kissed her temple.

"But our belongings are still in the hotel and we didn't check out."

Eros smiled. "Not to worry, Cousin. Taken care of."

"Diana, Kal-El?"

They turned to Valéria.

"Thank you both. I cannot get my past back but I can start over. Diana, will you wrap your lariat around me."

Diana raised her brow questionable making Valéria laugh.

"No, no, as much as I would love and it's so so tempting, I can not partake in that endeavor."

Diana wrapped her lasso around Valéria.

"Kal-El, you take it as well."

He too was hesitant, but took hold of the lasso with Diana. The lasso began to glow as bright as it ever has.

"This is my truth. I, Valéria Messalina, Queen of the Succubi, along with Eros, the God of Love, are the gaurdians of your love and devotion.

THE DARK SPELL

You will go on to achieve what you deeply desire together. However, it will not be an undemanding journey."

Eros stood beside Valéria and took hold of the lasso.

"You are both ready."

"We are," Kal and Diana said in unison.

Valéria and Eros glanced at each other with smiles.

Being released from Diana's lasso, Valéria opened a portal.

Kal intertwined his fingers with Diana's as they were stepping into the portal.

"Our next encounter will be a bit more delightful," Valéria smiled.

"We congratulate you both."

Kal looked back at Eros and Valéria. They both winked. He smiled to himself and gave them a slight nod.

Valéria sighed as the portal closed. "Oh, how I still wish I could've had some fun with them. Breaking a few more beds would've been quite the thrill."

"Your thrill awaits you with Dionysus but knowing you, you'll be watching them."

Valéria laughed. "Yes, I will. They gave me back something I truly missed. I may have dabbled in a little disruption for power but it feels divine and even more power is emanating from them."

Location: Clark and Diana's Apartment

Diana took off her shoes and jumped on their bed.

Clark smirked and jumped on the bed on top of her making her laugh. He kissed her cheek then Diana turned her head and captured his lips.

"What do you think Eros and Valéria meant with congratulating us?"

"Oh...hm...?" Clark knew exactly why but of course couldn't say."Diana, we've been through a lot and for us to get passed it all and be where we are now deserves celebration."

Diana smiled. "I agree with that. Our love should always be celebrated!"

"Yep, and I'm thinking of some many ways we can do that."

Diana giggled. "It all involves us completely unclothed and staying in bed for hours, doesn't it?"

"Well...I mean it depends on how you want it and where we are."

Diana gasped. "Oh!" She laughed. "How risqué!"

"I love you, Di. I love everything that's you, everything we do together, everything we are together."

Diana turned to lay of her back to completely face him. She reached up and caressed his cheek.

"I love you, too, Kal. You are such an amazing man. I never thought I'd be at this point in my life of having such a love. I put that aside because I didn't think it was for me. But with you, any and every thing of this life is possible. I never want this feeling to go away. I never want to lose you and what we have."

"Di, you will never lose me. I will never lose you." He took her hand placing it over his heart. "It's true that it's a long, tough journey. But we are a team, partners through and through. No matter what happens and come our way, we can handle it."

Diana nodded and reached up kissing him softly.

Hours later...

Diana was happily humming as she finished cutting up avocados and placing them in the side salad to go with her Moussaka dish.

She washed and dried her hands then leaned over the counter flipping the pages of one Clark's cook books.

Clark walked in with a smirk. He shook his head chuckling to himself and licked his lips eyeing her ass. She was wearing one of his oversized t-shirts and a thong.

He walked over to her wrapping his arms around her waist, bent over her and kissed her cheek.

"Smells really good," he said huskily in her ear.

Diana smiled. "I'm surprised I was able to follow everything with such ease."

"Di, you have to stop doubting yourself with cooking. You've been doing amazing. I just don't want you to do this, thinking you have to or obligation."

"What do you mean?"

"Like what your mom and sisters think."

"Oh, Darling, no!" She turned in his arms and wrapped her arms around his neck. Her eyes twinkled as she kissed him softly on his lips. "I love doing this! I don't think of it that way at all! It's so sexy seeing you cook and I'm comfortable being just like this. We take turns."

Clark grinned. "It's sexy seeing you being this comfortable. You're a vision, Di."

He captured her lips in another soft kiss but then the oven timer went off.

"Hold that while I check dinner."

Diana went over to open the oven then closed it adjusting the temperature.

"Seems another 10 or 15 minutes and- ah!"

Clark was behind her, chest to her back, his erection pressed against her ass.

"Kal...dinner is almost ready."

"You said 10-15 minutes. What about an appetizer, Diana?"

Diana smirked and playfully bit her lip. "I made us a side salad. You can go set the table."

She went over to the refrigerator and opening it, she purposely bent over farther than needed knowing he was watching her.

She placed the salad bowl on the counter. Clark took the bowl and walked over to the table setting it down along with their individual plates and utensils. Coming back to Diana, she was standing at the sink washing dishes. Clark stepped behind her again. Though, Diana bent back bumping him with her ass.

"No," she said seemingly sternly.

Clark quirked his brow when he heard her very low giggle. He watched her as she dried her hands and went over to the oven to take out the Moussaka.

Once she set it down, Clark came up behind her again, though, this time was quicker to wrap his arms around her and pull her tight against him.

She bursted out laughing. "You're relentless!"

"I'm a very hungry man, Di."

"Well dinner is ready," she teased.

"That's not the kind of hungry I'm talking about."

Diana moaned moving her ass against him.

"Tell me then, how do you want me?"

"I can show you better than I can tell you."

Clark moved her over to the other side of the counter and bent her over. He got on his knees, running his hands down her amazing body as he went. Diana pulled the t-shirt up, fully expose her ass and Clark ran his hands over the soft, smooth flesh. He gave her ass a squeeze before he slid her thong down her legs and she stepped out of it.

Clark kissed her cheeks all over. Then spreading her cheeks as he worked his way down, he planted his upturned face firmly between her beautiful cheeks. He heard her gasp when his tongue found her sweet spot.

Diana thanked the gods everything was done because his relentless affections causes her to lose focus on anything else.

As his tongue found its way deeper inside her, he lost himself in the ecstacy of being on his knees behind her, desperate to please her. Clark had this need to lick every spot between her legs royally. The taste between her legs was absolutely exquisite. A taste that he absolutely cannot be without. Warm, majestic, feminine tasting. It has flooded the inside of his mouth numerous times and smeared all over from his forehead to his chin often, leaving his face, the bed and sometimes the floor a wet sticky mess.

His hands ran up between her legs up to her dripping wet womanhood. He slid his fingers inside, quickly finding her spot, and slowly begin fingering her.

"Oh, Gods..." Diana moaned.

It drove him crazy, his desire to please her, his need to make her climax, his longing to feel her body tense and hear her screaming. He was determined to bring her to orgasm. To finger her to completion while making love to her backside with his mouth. He let out a growling moan into her body, hungry for more, hungry to please, hungry for her to climax.

He turned his hand around and begin rubbing her clit with two fingers and his thumb slid inside putting pressure on her g-spot. His other hand was squeezing her ass, spreading her cheeks open so he could bury his face further in her.

Diana gasped loudly and her eyes rolled back. She spread her legs more, giving him even more access. He fingered her faster as he hungrily ate her out. She began grinding her perfect ass into his face, moaning

THE DARK SPELL

louder, throwing her head back. She reached back and grabbed the back of his head, digging her nails into his scalp, scratching behind his ear. Clark groaned as she pushed his face more between her cheeks, urging him to lick deeper. He happily obliged.

His fingers picked up speed on her clit and his thumb on her g-spot. She grabbed the counter with both hands and her body tensed, pushing into him before she exploded into a powerful screaming orgasm. Her whole body shaking above him, her ass grinding violently on his face. She collapsed onto the counter as her knees started to buckle. Clark held her steady, softly licking and kissing her perfect ass as she came down from her orgasm.

Diana gave a small shudder and a quiet moan every time his tongue found her sweet spot. She slowly danced on his tongue, her approval of a job damn well done. Clark smiled, proud of giving this to her. He leaned forward, gently making out with the world's most beautiful wondrous ass. Diana ground back onto him, softly moaning, smiling to herself as she danced. Clark stood back up behind her, lightly massaging her back as he went, admiring her incredible body.

Diana leaned back up, struggling to catch her breath. She turned to look at him. She was even more beautiful in her post orgasm glow. She grabbed his neck and pulled him into a deep passionate kiss, moaning as she was tasting herself on his tongue.

She bit his lip as they pull apart.

"Mmmm...are you satisfied with your appetizer, Mr. Kent?" she whispered through her smile.

"I am and now it's dinner time. So let's get this..."

He got the tray of Moussaka setting it down by Diana and got a fork for them to share.

Diana took the fork from him as he lifted her up sitting her on the counter.

As Clark dropped his pants, Diana took a forkful for him to taste.

Diana moaned at the sight of Clark taking the fork into his mouth and then he slid his erection into her tight heat slowly.

"Damn good."

"The food or me?" She asked teasingly.

"Both. But the way my Goddess tastes and feels, nothing can ever compare."

Clark thrust up pushing farther into her slick channel. Diana groaned and gasped softly, biting at her lip.

"I love us having such a creative way to have dinner."

"Yeah, no better way than this."

"I love you, Kal."

"I love you, too, Di."

His thrusts remain slow and steady and Diana wrapped her legs tighter around his waist as they continued to feed each other Clark leaned in and kissed her. A slow, sweet lingering kiss. The kiss that led to another kiss, the passion growing with each touch of lips against lips.

No more than 5 more minutes within taking a few more forkfuls of the Moussaka, the tray was pushed aside. Clark's thrusting picked up pace and Diana leaned back more on the counter screaming, "Yes, My Love! Yes! Yes! YES!"

CHAPTER 11: CHERISHED, AND WORSHIPPED

2 months later.... Smallville, Kansas

Clark and Diana arrived at the Smallville town fair, finding a parking spot in the large field.

The main street was blocked off for the vendors and rides to be set up. Saturday afternoon they stop all the traffic on that block for an hour long parade.

"We're right on time to see the parade."

"Oh, this is so exciting! I can't wait to see your parents faces when they see us!"

"Yeah!" Clark smiled and leaned over to kiss her cheek.

"I'm glad you're happy to be here, Di."

"Of course, Kal! Smallville is such a wonderful joyous place. We need to be here."

"Simple, quiet vacation."

"Exactly, my Love," Diana agreed and kissed him softly.

Clark got out of the truck and quickly went over to the passenger side to open the door for Diana.

"Thank you, Love."

He took her hand helping her out and shut the door for her. They wandered hand in hand to the ticket booth to get their wrist bands.

"I can't wait to eat everything and watch the fireworks! Nothing's going to stop us from having a good time," she insisted, finishing her statement with a kiss to the corner of his mouth.

"The league is taking care of things for us if need be. No meetings, conferences or deadlines, no chasing demons or Gods. Just you, me-"

"Your parents and the farm!"

Clark smiled proudly and kissed her temple.

"Oh wow! It's quite a crowd!"

"Yeah, Smallville is quiet any other time, but guarantee lots of people from neighboring towns join in with this!"

"Do you see your parents?"

"Yep! Right in front as always!"

"I really hope Clark and Diana gets here. I wouldn't want them to miss any moment."

"They'll be here, Martha. Don't worry."

"I'm so so proud of our son!" Martha beamed. "I was worried when Clark left. He just seemed to want to be alone. So reserved as he always been. Never once did he seemed to want to settle down. But now he has really opened up more and just seeing him so happy with Diana. She is just such a nice, sweet girl. She's the one."

"Hey, Ma, Pa!"

They both turned happily surprised.

"Clark! Diana! We are so glad you made it!"

Martha hugged them both.

"Course, Ma. Wouldn't miss it. Especially with this being Diana's first parade, too."

"My boy!" Jonathan shook Clark's hand then hugged him.

"Diana, you look beautiful as always!"

"Thank you, Jonathan!" Diana smiled at Martha. "And thank you as well, Martha," she winked.

Martha hugged her again.

The parade started.

Martha took note of Diana's excitement. How her eyes sparkled watching the different bands and dance teams. She really lit up seeing the children.

"Oh, they are so adorable!"

"Clark was in the parade a few times for school," Martha told her.

"Oh really, Clark? I know you were just as adorable," she smiled.

Clark averted his eyes making Diana giggle.

"Still shy as always," Martha teased.

"He is the same when we have press conferences or events for the League. Though, it's a joy when he does the addresses and seeing him with the children," Diana kissed his cheek.

THE DARK SPELL

After the parade, while the Kents went to set up the food eating contests, Clark and Diana went to play a few games.

Oh! This is so much fun!" Diana took hold of Clark's hand as she pulled him towards the games while giggling.

Clark then looked around hearing a group of men, one sounding all too familiar. He glared at them eyeing as they were eyeing Diana.

"Beloved, do you know them?"

"Back in high school..."

"Oh, I see." Diana smirked. "Well then..." She reached up and kissed him passionately.

Clark smirked back into the kiss wrapping his arms around her waist. Diana moaned in his mouth as Clark held her tighter, moving his hand to her ass and deepened the kiss.

Diana pulled away slightly and glanced over at them who looked in disbelief.

"I think that gives them an answer."

Clark grinned. "You are-"

"Yours. I'm all yours, Clark."

Clark kissed her softly once more before they headed off for the games.

Clark won a few and got all the prizes for Diana. But there was one game he knew Diana would be interested in to play herself.

"Let's try that one." He grabbed her hand and gently pulled her to follow him towards the game stand.

"Welcome! Come on and try out our dart game!" A man announced.

"Hi, Mr. and Mrs. Braga. How have you been?" Clark asked.

Mr. and Mrs. Braga were long time neighbors to the Kents.

"Oh! Well, well! Kent boy! Haven't seen you in quite a while!"

Clark shook his hand. "Yeah, busy with a lot of work. I came back a few months ago but couldn't stay too long."

"Clark! You've gotten so much...taller, bulked up quite a bit! Always been so handsome!"

"Thank you, Mrs. Braga."

"And who is this young lady with you?"

"Hello, I'm Diana Prince, Clark's girlfriend," she stated proudly.

"Oh, you aren't from around here for sure! Lovely accent. You look quite familiar. You've been on television before?"

"I'm from an island in the Mediterranean. Moved to Boston upon first arriving to the states. I travel a lot for work as an UN Ambassador and University professor."

"Yes, I knew it! Oh my! You are even more gorgeous in person!"

Diana smiled "Thank you!"

"So will you two test your luck with a game of darts?"

"Yes, she will."

"Alright, young lady! Here you go!"

Mr. Braga handed her her the darts.

Diana concentrated for a moment then threw one right after another. All three flew at the board so fast that anyone who blinked, missed them. All of them had hit every balloon and landed in the bulls-eye. She looked back at her boyfriend, grinning proudly at herself. Clark winked at her.

"How...What?" Mr. Braga was both amazed.

"Archery as a child," Diana smiled.

"Well, congratulations! We have a winner!"

Diana picked out her praise, which was a stuffed teddy bear with a sun on its shirt.

"Thank you!"

"Later, Mr. and Mrs. Braga."

Clark took Diana's hand as they walked away.

"I think I'll name him, Kal. He has a sun on his shirt and very cute. Reminds me of someone in particular."

"Haha! Cute, Di?"

"Uh huh!"

Clark chuckled and shook his head slightly. "Come here." He grabbed her by her waist and pulled into a kiss then kissed her nose. "You're cute."

Diana blushed and smiled giving him a soft peck.

Later, after playing more games and eating all the fried foods, pies, and other desserts they could, it was time for the fireworks show.

Clark and Diana met back up with the Kents as everyone went to their cars and trucks for the view other the lake. Many couples and family sat on top of their trucks or laid the the truck beds.

THE DARK SPELL

Martha looked over with a smile seeing Clark and Diana cuddled together.

"Would you look at that, Jonathan. How adorable they are."

"Heh. Yeah. Young love. Reminds me a lot of us back in the day."

Above them all, sparks of wonderful color and design danced with the stars, and the many Ooh's and Ahh's were almost audible from the huge audience.

Clark has his arm wrapped around Diana. A few gasps of amazement slid past her lips as Diana witnessed the beauty of the fireworks, but her attention was drawn away from the display when Clark tightened his grip around her waist and looked at her. He stared at her for a short bit, before she finally grew curious.

"What is it?" she asked, cocking an eyebrow.

He smiled dreamily, and his melting blue eyes caught her in their trance.

"I just wanted you to know that today was amazing. Everyday with you is amazing," he stated.

Diana's face reddened.

"The feeling is mutual, Love," she replied, "So much fun! I want us to take time for more things like this, Clark. Just as going home to Themyscira, we will come here to Smallville."

Clark nodded in agreement and before either of them knew it, their lips were inseparable. Clark raised his hand to Diana's cheek, stroking a finger down her jaw line and coming to a stop under her chin. Diana smiled through the kiss, and she moved even closer to him so their bodies were practically pressed together.

Diana took a deep breath, and then parted her lips. She had sent the invitation, and Clark accepted. He slid his tongue in swiftly, caressing her mouth in ways she had never imagined. She replied with equal terms, and her hand slithered up behind his head.

A soft laugh escaped her, lost into the wind and noise of the night, only to be heard by the one she truly loved.

"I love you, Diana," he whispered against his lips.

"I love you too, Clark," she whispered back.

They sealed their love with another passionate kiss as the last firework flew up in the sky.

Kent Farm, The Next Morning...

Diana quietly closed Clark's door as he was still asleep and went downstairs to the kitchen to make her morning tea.

She tried remain as quiet as possible not to wake the Kents.

"Oh, it would be much quieter with the use of heat vision."

She placed the mug of water in the microwave, wincing at the beeping sound. She leaned against the counter and closed her eyes for a moment.

"Good morning, Diana!" Martha greeted.

Diana gasped opening her eyes. "Oh, Good morning, Martha. I'm sorry. I didn't mean to wake you."

"No, you didn't at all. I'm usually up even earlier than this!"

"Oh..." Diana sighed relieved taking the mug out the microwave and stirring it slowly with a tea spoon.

"I didn't expect you to be up this early?"

"Well..." Diana took a sip. "...it's just a routine of mine. I have somewhat of a certain time to have my tea."

"It's mandatory that you have it? Is everything alright?"

"Yes! Yes, it is! It's just...um..."

Martha could sense Diana getting nervous and smiled at her.

"Diana, you can talk to me," she assured.

"I know I can," she smiled back. "A couple of months ago, I went to my friend who's also a fellow Amazon and doctor. I wasn't quite feeling well after coming back from Themyscira. I thought it was too much of the wine but..."

"But what?"

"She explained a bit to me about Clark and I..."

Martha gasped. "Oh my! Are you pregnant?!"

Diana shook her head. "No. But it was a high possibility. Especially with us..." Diana paused and blushed.

Martha nodded understanding. "You are young and in love. That's the only thought for the moment."

Diana sighed. "We both want children...one day. It's not time right now. We have responsibilities and obligations that takes so much time. We

THE DARK SPELL

want our children to have a stable home. On the surface, knowing that your parents are superheroes especially Superman and Wonder Woman may seem exciting but Clark and I know all too well of the burdens of feeling alone. We can't have that for our children."

"Diana, your children will be surrounded by so much love. Never to have the feeling of loneliness. I understand both of you have taken on such a responsibility bigger than anything imaginable but...you do have your own lives to live and enjoy. You will know when the time is right. There's no rush right now, however, don't wait too long. Jonathan and I aren't getting any younger," she joked.

Diana laughed softly. "Thank you, Martha. And I understand. Clark and I want our children to spend a lot of time with their grandparents."

Martha smiled proudly. "Oh! I just can't wait to be called grandma! Haha!"

"Thank you, Martha, for welcoming me."

"Well of course! You are part of the family!" She hugged Diana.

Close to an hour later, Clark and Jonathan were walking down stairs to the smell of breakfast.

"Mmhmm...nothing like the good ol' smell of fresh hot pancakes and buttery biscuits!" Jonathan laughed. "Mornin' Martha! Diana!"

"Morning, Hon!"

"Good Morning, Jonathan!" Diana smiled.

"Morning Ma!" Clark hugged Martha.

"Morning, Son!"

Clark turned his attention over to Diana, who was finishing cooking the eggs, looking her up and down licking his lips. She was wearing a sleeveless v-neck Henley tank top and dark denim high rise shorts. He wrapped his arms around her waist and kissed her cheek.

"Morning, Diana!"

"Good morning, Love!"

"Yep, it's a very good morning....and..." His voice lowered to a deep husky whisper only she could hear. "Pa was right...Nothing like good cakes. Especially these." He grabbed her ass cheeks giving a squeeze.

Diana jumped slightly and let out a low gasp. "Behave yourself!" she whispered back.

"No promises..."

Diana turned her head and glared while Clark had a cheeky grin.

"Sit down, right now, Mister!"

Clark chuckled and kissed her cheek again before walking over to the table to sit down.

Through out breakfast, while Martha and Johnathan were occupied on conversation Clark and Diana stole glances at each other. Clark couldn't help but keep eyeing her cleavage.

Diana got up to warm up the rest of her tea and Clark got up with her.

"I'll say! These eggs are perfect!"

"Diana did a fantastic job!"

"Thank you both! But Martha gave a lot of guidance as I'm still learning."

"And you are a fast learner, Dear!"

"Absolutely perfect." Clark brushed up against Diana. "Delicious..." he whispered.

Diana glared at him. "Not in front of your parents!" she mouthed.

Clark gave her a wicked grin.

As Diana was putting more sugar in her tea, Clark stood behind her.

"Stop it," she whispered.

"Can't help myself. I have a craving for some melon."

Diana gasped lowly and quickly covered her mouth as he cupped her breasts.

Diana was so glad Martha and Jonathan had their backs turnt.

Clark kissed the side of her neck.

"I love you," he whispered huskily.

"I love you, too. Now go sit back down and finish breakfast."

Another 20 minutes, and they were all done.

"Come on, Son. Got work to do now!"

"Course Pa!"

"Well that leaves me and Diana going through more photo album you didn't get to from last time."

"Oh, no, Ma! No!"

Diana giggled. "I would absolutely love seeing more pictures of Clark as a child!"

THE DARK SPELL

"Di...no."

She reach up and kissed his cheek. "You're adorable!"

Clark sighed. "There's no way of stopping you two anyway."

Diana and Martha laughed.

30 minutes passed.

"We'll be back in about 2 - 3 hours max," Jonathan said as he kissed Martha's forehead.

Clark embraced Diana and kissed her passionately.

"Hey, Romeo, I said 3 hours, not 3 weeks," Jonathan teased.

Martha laughed nudging Jonathan.

Clark and Diana pulled apart smiling.

"Be back, Di."

"Okay, Beloved."

Martha and Diana watched as their men got into the truck a drove off, continuing to wave until the truck was distance away.

"The hours will go by fast," Martha stated. "They'll be back in no time. So let's hurry and let me show you as many more pictures of Clark as I can then we can start preparing lunch."

Diana laughed softly and nodded.

With Jonathan and Clark

Jonathan glanced over at Clark and laughed.

"I'm the same with your Ma even after all these years. Can't be away from her long. Hearts racing, blood boiling..."

Clark smiled. "I'm going to propose to her soon, Pa."

Jonathan grinned widely and reached over ruffling Clark's hair.

"That'a boy! Ma and I had a feeling you would eventually. When you first brought Diana to meet us, we thought that's what you were going to say. When you told us she was just a friend, we knew otherwise."

"It's been complicated for us. It took us...fighting against a demon to protect our feelings for each other."

"Wait a minute? You're talking about a real demon, aren't ya?"

"Yeah...it was unbelievable. But none of that matters now. Diana and I are moving forword. I have everything all planned out. I just need you and Ma to be there."

"Of course, Son! Proud of you! Watching you grow into being your own man, there's no other greater accomplishment to a father."

"Thanks, Pa!"

"I assume grandkids eventually?"

"Would've already been a few months ago actually."

"What?! Son, I'm sorry."

"Oh, no, Pa. That's not what I meant. With us being...uh...we didn't think to..." Clark was stumbling on his words a bit.

Jonathan pondered for a bit deciphering what Clark was trying to say then laughed.

"Ha! My boy! I get it. I get it."

"Diana went to her doctor and she gave her an herbal mixture for tea she has to take in the mornings. I don't necessarily like it because it feels like she is obligated to just because of me."

"Son, when Martha and I were trying to have a child of our own, I felt the same way. She was the one who had to go through a lot more and stayed strong through it all. There's nothing like a woman's strength, Son. She's going to be stubborn sometimes but you just have to support her no matter what because she's going to do what she wants. Just be sure to protect her."

Clark smiled. "Yeah...Diana is quite stubborn and of course I'm going to do everything I can to always protect her. We've been through a lot already and from what we've been through, we can make it through anything else."

An hour later, back at the Kent Farm

Diana was sitting at the table helping sort peas when she heard a gasp and slight scream behind her.

She quickly jumped up.

"Martha?!"

She was met with cake mix flying all over the place and on her face. The cake mixer was going out of control.

"Oh Gods!"

"I can't get the darn thing unplugged trying to hold it."

With more mixing flying all over her, Diana quickly unplugged it for her.

Martha gasped then laughed. "I'm so sorry, Deary!"

THE DARK SPELL

"Oh, it wasn't your fault at all," Diana laughed along with her.

"Jonathan told me to get an another mixer but I didn't listen. It's just much easier using this thing to prevent hand cramping."

"Should I call Clark so they can stop by a store to pick up a new one?"

"No, I'll do it later myself. I don't want to hear Jonathan's "I told you so's" just yet. And this has to be cleaned up before they get back."

"Do you have more mix? I can help you with anything you need, Martha. Have this all clean and another cake made in no time."

"You're a dear-heart, Diana. Thank you!"

Another two hours had passed. Clark and Jonathan finally made it back home.

"Ma? Diana? We're back!"

"Told ya wouldn't be two long. 3 hours max like I said. And it's not even close to noon yet."

Diana came to the foyer to greet them.

"Martha is in the kitchen waiting Jonathan."

He nodded. "Right, right!"

"Clark..." she kissed his cheek.

"You changed?" He asked.

She was wearing a floral print off-shoulder crop top and mini skirt.

"Your mother and I had a mishap earlier with the cake mixture and cake mix went everywhere."

"Oh, dammit! I missed helping get you all cleaned up?" He pouted wrapping his arms around her waist pulling her closer. "I have to have my cake," he kissed her neck.

Diana giggled and moaned.

"You know...after your stunt from earlier, you shouldn't get anything for at least a week."

"What?! Oh no, Di. No. Don't do that to me, Starshine."

Diana smirked and leaned over to whisper in his ear. "I want you to beg..."

Clark felt a jolt below.

Diana licked her lips slowly and pushed him slightly away. Clark watched as Diana walked away back to the kitchen.

He smirked, quickly catching up with her and gave her ass a squeeze before they walked into the kitchen.

Diana looked back with a raised brow.

"Diana, you are of many talents! Beautifully designed cake!"

"Thank you, Jonathan!"

Clark again took full advantage of Martha and Jonathan turning their attention on preparing for the outside picnic lunch.

"Beautiful cake..." Clark whispered in her ear.

Diana waved her hand slightly for him to stop. Clark just chuckled amused.

1:15 pm

Clark carried the large picnic table setting it in the open area of the yard. Diana placed the table cloth on top and Martha set the first dish, potato salad down.

"I got everything else, Ma!"

Clark had the rest of the food set up on the table in seconds.

Jonathan came with the pitches of iced sweet tea, lemonade and water.

"Lovely!" Martha beamed. "We hadn't had times like this in so long! To sit out here and Clark couldn't sit still for not even 5 minutes. He just had to run around the field going back and forth eating. Especially with learning his powers."

"I remember when Clark landed face first in the pie because he was floating upside down above the table and lost concentration."

"That's not funny, Pa."

Jonathan shrugged. "Lesson learned, right?"

"Right..."

Diana giggled and leaned over to kiss Clark's cheek.

For the next hour, the Kents were telling Diana more stories of Clark younger.

As embarrassed as some of it was, Clark loved to hear Diana's beautiful laugh.

She looked at him with an all too innocent smile. She leaned over and kissed his cheek again. As Clark was about to return the kiss, he jumped slightly feeling a squeeze on his thigh. He glanced down to see Diana's hand trailing farther up and started rubbing Junior through his jeans.

THE DARK SPELL

He looked up at Diana and she smirked then licked her lips slowly. Clark gulped and shook his head slightly.

Diana raised a brow and gripped him a little harder making him jolt again.

"Are you okay, Clark?" Martha asked.

"Yep! Just fine!"

He looked over to Diana with a slightly glare and all she could do was still smile ever so innocently. She noticed some salad dressing on the corner of his mouth. She took the opportunity while Martha and Jonathan were looking down at their own food to lean in and lick the corner of Clark's mouth.

She went up to his ear and whispered, "There's nothing like Kryptonian farmboy flavor."

"Di..."

"What was that, Clark?"

"Oh... I was just telling Diana thanks for getting a napkin for me."

"Still making messes?" Martha raised her brow. "Mind your manners."

"It was an accident, Ma."

"Don't worry, Martha. Clark keeps thoroughly clean. You should see the apartment. Always spotless."

"Well that's good to know!" she smiled.

Diana leaned over again to Clark and whispered. "It's Junior that likes to get very messy. I'm more than happy to help clean up."

With another jolt, Clark stood up.

"Uh...I hear the phone ringing. I'll be right back."

He quickly raced to the house.

"Ah, probably, Reilly. Told him to call when the new pick up is ready."

"You're taking full advantage with Clark here."

Jonathan chuckled. "No, but he's a big help and doesn't at all mind."

"Jonathan, he is suppose to be taking it easy from work with Diana."

"Oh no, Martha. Jonathan is right. Clark is just fine. Believe me, this is him taking it easy. He loves helping around the farm! He loves working," Diana assured.

Another 20 minutes passed.

"He must be still on the phone. Reilly can talk anyone's ear off."

"Oh, I'll go check then," Diana said.

While Martha and Jonathan continued their own conversation, Diana went to the house to see what was taking Clark so long. She couldn't help but smile to herself having an idea.

"Beloved?" Diana called walking in.

It was silent.

"Oh, Clark, my love?"

Still not a sound.

She went upstairs to his room.

"Clark?" She called opening the door and giggled seeing him laying on the edge of the bed, on his back, with his arms across his eyes. "Beloved, what's wrong?"

"What do you think?"

She giggled again seeing the obvious straining tent of his pants.

"Oh, Junior's not behaving?" she asked teasingly leaning on the side of the door.

"Can't think of anything else but you."

Diana smiled wickedly. "That's what you get for your earlier stunts in front of your parents."

"Diana..."

"Well..." she walked into the room and closed the door locking it. "How about I help relieve you?"

Clark uncrossed his arms and looked at her as she was walking over to him.

"Dammit, Diana..." His pants was getting tighter.

"Relax, my Love, and let me."

Clark sat up delightfully surprised when Diana fell to her knees in front of him, her slender fingers, loosening his belt, unbuttoning and lowering the zipper.

"Di...?"

"Let me..."

"Do we have time?"

"Yes. Now let me take care of this for you."

Clark raised his hips for her to pull his jeans and boxers down. His entire rock-hard length and the smooth flesh of his scrotum were now

THE DARK SPELL

exposed. Diana paused as it twitched. She smiled loving that. She gently grasped him in her left hand and stroked it while admiring the just over 9 inches and thick gift of his. Her hand moved to cradle his solid balls as she leaned down, and through pursed lips blew hot breath at them. Diana felt the wetness of his pre-essence on her hand and heard him sigh in relief as she gave his shaft a nice hard squeeze in her fist, and giggled in delight as she was rewarded by another bead of pre-essence that oozed out to run down his shaft and onto her hand.

Smiling up at him, Diana raised her hand to her lips, licking the salty fluid off. She made a show of savouring his flavour, closing her eyes and moaning with pleasure. She felt his hands begin to caress her hair unconsciously. Clark struggled to keep himself from going wild. Diana knew he was desperate to feel her mouth on him and was ready to put him out of his misery.

Clark softly moaned. Looking down at this gorgeous woman kneeling in front of him, with those enormous eyes and beautiful mouth, he wouldn't have been able to deny her even if he wanted to. And he damn sure didn't want to.

He gathered her hair in a tight hold at the crown of her head. His eyes were now fixed on hers and widened some when Diana extended her tongue and dragged the tip from his frenulum down along the bulging urethra until it sank beneath the flesh at the base.

She softly sucked one of his balls and rolled it around over her moist tongue. He moaned again a little harsher than before.

After giving that one a juicy tongue bath, she let it slip from her lips with a resounding popping sound. Its mate entered her warm wet mouth and received the same sensual treatment.

Letting it slip from her mouth, she reversed her trek up his shaft, teasing the urethra with her tongue.

Diana wrapped one hand around his member just above the base drawing the head toward her open lips.

She knew that this precise moment was the one Clark dreamed about, the millisecond just before her sexy mouth engulfed his length. Clark's eyes widened again as she touched the head to her soft smooth lips.

He groaned as her moist lips closed around him just below the head.

"Shi-," he said as the head slipped along her wet tongue.

An elated groan escaped Clark's lips when she grabbed at his balls. She just takes inch after inch of his length into her mouth until he was pushing into her throat. His member was so incredibly hard, throbbing intensely as little by little more of his shaft slid between her lips, wedging against the back of her mouth, but didn't let it slip through to the even softer flesh of her throat yet.

Diana slowly lifted until the head slipped out of her mouth, several strands of salvia stretched from her lips to the head of his member. Clark threw his head back in contentment, and pulled hers closer as his hips begin to thrust forward involuntarily, needing more. Her warm fingers continue to massage his balls and rubbed against his thigh. Diana swallowed around him, moaning deep in her throat, which nearly brought him to climaxing. Clark growled and dug his fingers into her scalp.

Diana grunted around his girth, and Clark hissed out a breath. By now, he was panting, his groans long and deep in his throat.

Feeling his grip tighten on her hair, she fully expected Clark would drive his rock-hard length through her mouth and impale her throat, but instead he slowly pulled her mouth down. His delicate movement caused Diana to softly moan. He enjoyed the sensation of her moist tongue and slippery flesh provided. His hands moved her mouth up and down slowly and each time he drew her down, his head got closer and closer to the entrance of her throat. As the tip of his head pressed, Diana inhaled deeply, filling her lungs with air, knowing that in a moment his throbbing member would block her airways.

Clark's grip tightened on her scalp and he thrust off the bed burying his pulsing member in her throat.

"Diana!" He exclaimed as he surged in her throat.

Clark's hips settled back to the bed, his hands released her hair a bit, and Diana slowly lifted her throat off him. It slipped from between her lips and she slurped the excess salvia that clung to the head back inside her wet mouth.

"It feels so god damn good when you do that," he remarked.

Diana smiled at him then said, "I know...That's why I'm going to do it again."

THE DARK SPELL

Diana lowered her mouth to his scrotum and teased his balls with the tip of her tongue circling each solid testicle several times. Clark sinfully moaned and kept his eyes fixed on Diana's face. Once she coated his sack with even more moisture, she started a sensual slide up along his bulging urethra. That sensitive tube that carried his essence from his balls pressed against her tongue as she orally climbed his pulsing member.

"So good," he remarked, as she neared the top.

She leaned back just a little and extended her tongue more and licked at his frenulum which caused Clark to twitch.

"God damn!" he exclaimed confirming this was one very sensitive spot.

Diana's tongue continued caressing him there, and he rewarded her with a drop of pre-essence which ran down from his length head onto her tongue.

"Hmmm, you taste so good," she said after his essence coated her taste buds.

Diana's wet mouth surrounded his head again and closed her lips.

"Yes," he softly whispered, as the warmth and moisture of her mouth engulfed him again.

Diana bobbed up and down repeatedly caressing him with her smooth lips, but she wanted to feel his member in her throat again.

Very slowly her lips slipped further down his shaft. Little by little, his throbbing erection approached the opening of her throat. As her mouth and throat swallowed him, her tongue was busy on his shaft, swirling all around and causing him exquisite pleasure.

Diana took a deep breath and then slowly and steadily swallowed his member and much as she could. And then she started bobbing her head up and down in Clark's lap and at an increasingly faster pace. That, alone, was quite a show.

Clark couldn't believe how far Diana went down each time and returned all the way back up to the head and how incredibly hard she was sucking. It was like her lips were constantly squeezing him as she moved up and down.

He was practically out of his mind with pleasure. What she was doing was something on an entirely different level. Diana settled into a rhythmic pace of throating his beautiful manhood only lifting when she needed to breathe.

She came back up and kept only the head in, sucking on it and licking underneath the crown. She was intent on what she was doing and it was driving him crazier by the second. He was in ecstasy and urged her on. The tip wedged into the back of her mouth and Diana felt Clark's hips lift some as she took him inside. His member felt so good entering her throat, and Diana softly moaned as she swallowed him.

Diana held him deep until she needed to breathe and then lifted enough to recharge her lungs before engulfing his throbbing length again. She took him deep another two or three times and by that time he was ready to explode. Clark's breathing became ragged, and his stomach began to convulse.

And then he exploded into orgasm, one mind-bender that caused him to yell out in ecstasy. Diana eagerly moaned as she felt his member expand to an impossible size deep in her mouth before bursting with flavorful essence. He erupted down her throat with a string of curses, Spurt after spurt of pent-up essence spilling into her ravenous mouth. Diana swallowed everything he gave her without wasting a single drop.

"Mmmmmm hmmmm..." Diana moaned.

As the flow of fluid coming from his member began to slow, he thrust his softening member into her mouth hard. With each heave, pulling her face hard into him with his hands. He gasped for air as he gyrated his hips into her oral cavity, unleashing the last few drops and spurts of essence into her.

When Clark's breathing, and hers, returned to close to normal, Diana slowly removed his member from her mouth and gave it a kiss. She licked her fingers clean, swiped her tongue around her lips and sat up.

"Feeling better, my Love?" Diana asked with a smile.

"Hell yeah..." Clark said, with a satisfied sigh.

He stared down at her for a moment.

"I really enjoy pleasing you," she added, lifting up on her knees, her hands clutching at his thighs. "We should now get back to your parents before they do try come up here."

"Yeah...right right..." he smiled, nodding, and stood up.

THE DARK SPELL

Clark and Diana went into the bathroom to clean themselves up.

Emerging from the bathroom, Clark grabbed Diana and held her face in his hands, looking into her eyes. He placed his lips on hers and she immediately responded. They kissed for long moments, tongues tangling together, lips locked in heated passion.

"Goodness..." she panted as they finally came up for air.

"I love you, Diana."

"I love you, too, Clark."

She gave him a soft peck.

Walking downstairs, Clark had finally keened in on another voice outside.

They went back outside smiling hand in hand.

"Oh, it's Lana!" Diana waved. "Hi Lana!"

"Diana! Hi! Woah..." Lana paused looking at them both. "You guys look like models!" she laughed and rushed to them hugged them both. "It's good to see you guys."

"Likewise!"

"Good to see you too, Red!" Clark smiled. "Sorry, Ma, Pa. Diana and I had to take care of something important after Reilly called. Ready to go, Pa?"

Jonathan nodded. "We won't be long, hopefully."

"Yeah, not too long." Clark gave Diana a gentle peck.

"Me and Diana can have girls' talk," Lana smirked.

Clark looked at her with disbelief. "Please, no. Ma and Pa embarrassed me enough."

Diana giggled. "Oh, Clark. I'd love to hear even more stories from Lana."

"No, you don't."

"Yes, I do. Now go with your father."

"Diana."

"Go," she said raising her brow.

"Fine...fine..." he gave her another peck.

Diana and Lana smiled and waved as Clark was walking to the truck with Jonathan.

"Clark might be taller and muscular than he was in high school, but he's still the hopeless adorakable romantic."

Diana smiled. "He is for sure!"

"I'll let you girls have your time to talk while I go out this up in the fridge."

Diana and Lana sat down.

"How have you been, Lana?"

"Oh, fine! Working. But I'm sure not as hard as you and Clark with the superhero stuff, Clark reporting and you working with the United Nations as well being a Professor at one of if not the top universities in the country!"

"Lana, I-"

Lana grabbed Diana's hand and smiled. "I'm so proud of Clark. When we were in school, Clark had always thought of everyone else. He stood up for any and everybody. When I accidentally found out about his powers when he saved me for the first time, as a kid, of course it just seemed like fun. But as we got older, I started to understand why Clark felt to keep it a secret. It was so dangerous. He was so reserved, careful and still a bit distant. Now that I see him with you, he has changed so much and for the better."

"Clark is still very much reserved, in a very calming sense and that's what I love about him. He isn't like any of the men my mother and sisters have told me about or that I've witnessed on my own."

"With being here in little ol' Smallville...isn't it a drastic difference from where you are from? The luxuries and all...don't you miss that?"

"It may seem luxurious but to me, I see Smallville with some similarities as Themyscira. I used to run and train in the fields and forest. Exploring the beauty of nature. It's so quiet and relaxing yet full of liveliness and joy when coming together for things such as family gatherings or the town fair. The time Clark and I spend here together is wonderful! I don't care for luxuries in that way. If I did, I would've stayed on my home island. This is luxury to me."

"Diana, I'm going to be honest."

"Yes?"

"I wanted to be very protective of Clark when I first met you because I love him. I mean...when Clark was talking about you even before then...I

THE DARK SPELL

pictured you much differently. Seeing this woman who looks like a Goddess is actually a Goddess?!"

Diana laughed. "Yes, I know. You two shared a lot as children and grew up together. That is something very sacred."

"But that's the hard part of it all actually. Clark was my childhood best friend and in high school, I fell in love with him. He and I did share a lot and had our firsts...we thought that we would have a life together. But senior year...I don't know...I just...I knew we were heading toward different paths...especially with his powers."

"Do you have regrets? Are you still in love with him?"

"No, I don't. I believe that the right decisions were made. We've both moved on to where we are suppose to be. I'm still just a small town country girl. The everyday city life like that isn't for me. Part of me will always be in love with him and to know that he has someone that will never break his heart, someone that can love him and be with him as Smallville adorkable Clark having powers and all that comes with that, makes me very happy."

"He makes me very happy. Clark and I have been through so much together. I never thought that I would fall in love or even have time to find love given I was so focus on work. But I was drawn to Clark from the moment we met."

May I ask something, Diana? I mean I don't mean to get too personal."

"No, it's alright. You can ask me anything!"

"When he is with you...intimately, he isn't nervous or anything like that, right?"

"Nervous? Oh, no. I mean...he makes sure that I'm comfortable. But..." Diana blushed. "He is an incredible lover."

Lana laughed. "I know we were inexperienced teens at that time but I don't know, it just all comes down to how careful he is because of his powers."

"I understand. Clark is a gentleman so like I said, he wants to make sure I'm comfortable. We are both careful but not exactly with each other more...of our surroundings."

"Huh? Oh wait...?" Lana's eyes widen. "Seriously, Diana?!"

Diana laughed. "Yes!"

"Oh my God! Haha! Clark has really really changed! Didn't know he had a wild side! I love that for him!" Lana laughed then reached over and hugged Diana taking her by surprise. "Thank you, Diana. Thank you for taking care of Clark and loving him."

Diana hugged her back and nodded.

2 hours later...

Jonathan came into the house to hear Martha, Diana and Lana laughing.

"Well looks like you ladies had a nice time."

"We certainly have!" Martha said.

"Clark is going to get an earful, huh?"

"Oh, yes, Mr. Kent! I told Diana enough that she will be teasing Clark about for weeks on end!"

"Where is he anyway?"

"Out unloading the truck."

"Oh, well I need to get going. Catch him outside." Lana smiled. "It's always nice to come visit ya'll, Mr and Mrs. Kent!"

"Always glad to have you, Lana!"

Lana then hugged Diana.

"I'm glad we were able to really talk and get to know each other a bit more!"

"I am, too, Lana! I hope that we can have more times likes this?"

"Of course, Diana! Next time actually, we can go somewhere around town for girls' time!"

"I would love that!"

"Great! Remember to call me anytime!"

"You do the same!"

Lana hugged her again before leaving out.

Martha gushed. "That's really nice. You two becoming friends so fast!"

"Lana and I have quite a lot in common," Diana smiled.

Outside, Lana saw Clark standing at the truck. She knew he could hear her foot steps no matter how quiet she was trying to be. But still, she tip toed a few more steps before jumping on his back.

"Clark!" She laughed.

"Woah! Lana, what's up?"

"Diana and I had a great time talking and no, nothing too embarrassing."

"Thanks for that."

Lana jumped off his back and leaned on the truck.

"Remember what I told you when you were leaving for college?"

"Uh? That day you said a lot. Especially with us going our own way and all."

"Well reminder... I told you that one day you would meet someone you will be able to share that super powered life with. It's not a life I'm set up for. But Diana? She's amazing, Clark."

"I know she is, Lana," he chuckled.

"Clark, I'm serious right now."

"Yeah, I get it. I'm serious too."

"She really loves you. The way she talks about you, how she lights up even brighter than she already is to your name. She thought that everything I told her about you was so cute and adorable. Don't screw this up!"

"I'm not!"

"Clark Joseph Kent!"

"I'm not! I'm not! I love her, Lana." Clark sighed. "Diana and I have been through hell and back. I would kick my own ass if I ever screwed this up with her. But I know for damn sure I'm not. We want a life together. We've talked about it and I'm... I'm going to propose soon."

"You what?! Oh my God! Really?!" Lana gasped and smiled jumping to embrace him. "Yes! I'm so proud of you! So happy!"

"Lana, she hasn't said yes yet."

"She will!"

Clark smiled. "Thanks for your support. I have everything all planned out. I want to make it as special as possible for of course both of us but her especially."

"Clark, I will always support you!" Lana embraced him again. "I have to go but I'll catch up with you later. I can't wait for the wedding invitation!"

Clark nodded. "Of course! Bye, Lana."

"Bye, Clark!" She happily waved.

Clark watched as she got into her car and drove off.

He smiled to himself thinking back on how far things have come along and changed.

20 minutes later...

Diana was walking outside with a glass of freshly made lemonade. She smiled seeing her man shirtless and hard at work.

"Hi, Darling!"

"Hey, Di!" He smiled closing the truck tailgate.

Diana pecked his lips, handing him the lemonade.

"Made this with Martha. I think I'm doing alot better in the kitchen already in this short amount of time. Your mother is a fabulous teacher!"

Clark smiled and kissed her again. "I'm glad you are enjoying yourself. You and Lana had a good time embarrassing me." He quirked his brow.

Diana giggled. "It wasn't at all embarrassing. We had a lovely conversation and she even wants us to have some girls' time."

"Yeah, Lana told me she didn't say anything too embarrassing but girls' time, huh?"

"She's very fun to be around and funny!"

Clark couldn't help but smile. He took a gulp of the lemonade but then couldn't stop until he drunk it all.

"Wow! That was great! I can tell you made it."

"Oh? How?"

"Ma puts just the right amount of sugar in it. But you put about two extra spoon fulls in."

"You noticed that?"

"Di, I notice every little thing you do even when I'm not around."

She grinned and blushed. "That's why I love you so much!"

"I love you, too, Di...I love you more than I can say."

"Mmmhmm... but you can show me, later."

"How about right now? I need more to drink," he smirked.

"Your parents are wide awake we can't just go upstairs, no matter how quiet we will try to be."

"I didn't mean in my room, Di. I meant the barn."

"Oh? Oh..." She bit her lip. "Very tempting but would we be too wide op-"

Clark silenced her with a passionate kiss.

THE DARK SPELL

"Clark, you-"

He pulled her back into an even deeper kiss with his hands traveling down to give her ass a squeeze.

Diana giggled against his lips.

"You are so tempting..."

"There's blankets already in there."

"You planned this didn't you?"

"Uh... well not really but I was prepared just in case."

Diana laughed and then whispered in his ear. "Take me, Kal-El."

"Don't have to tell me twice!"

Clark took her hand as they ran across the field and driveway to the barn.

Diana laughed as she was running with him the time.

"Clark!"

He looked back at her with a devious grin pulling her into the barn. He then quickly closed the large door and locked it.

"It's locked. So in a way it's saying do not disturb."

"But your parents? They'll still come looking for us."

"No, not at all." Clark placed his hands on her hips and moved her back up against the wall. "Now relax and let me have some more to drink."

Diana smiled and wrapped her arms around his neck. She yanked him closer and kissed him. Her tongue darted over his lips as they shared a deep all consuming kiss.

Clark pressed himself closer. He lifted her a bit, and crushing her to him. Diana moaned and Clark felt blood rushing to his crotch. Diana was so soft and yielding. The smell of her was intoxicating and above all, she felt so good against him. With one hand, her fingers ran through Clark's hair, lingering at his nape. She knew he liked that best. The other felt the skin of his chest underneath her palm. It felt like he was burning up and she imagined him stretched over her, both of them moving in rhythm.

Clark pulled away from the kiss momentarily. He stared the longest at her lips, crushed from the kiss. Finally, he looked her in the eyes.

"Kal-El..."

Her voice was deep and heavy with lust, the same lust that coursed through Clark's veins, lust that throbbed in his pants.

"Cla..." she said again, but before his name was fully out of her lips, he crushed them to his.

Without breaking the kiss, he pressed his crotch into her. He had to make her feel how hard she made him. He had to make her feel how he felt. Once she started to grind against him, he moved one hand over to her breast. He squeezed it hard through her blouse. His other hand searched for one of hers and pinned it above her. Diana laced her fingers through it. Her other hand was on his nape again. It sent electric shocks through his body to his crotch.

Clark broke the kiss and nibbled on her ear. Diana moaned, arching towards him, almost setting them off balance. Clark tightened his grip on her hips as his lips trailed along the side of her neck. Then he reached under her skirt to stroke across her panty-covered mound.

"Oh Gods," she whispered when he slipped his hand under the waistband of her panties to tease her further.

"I've been wanting to do this all day," he whispered back as his fingertips slid over the fleshy expanse of her outer lips.

"Mmmmmmm," she nodded.

He slid lower then, finding the dampness at her entrance and easing just the tip of his finger inside of her.

Diana strained her hips forward into his touch, seeking more. He pushed further, sliding his finger all the way in and allowing Diana to grind against the palm of his hand for a few seconds before pulling it back out. Now dampened by her juices, it slid easily back upward to find her clit, still buried beneath its protective hood.

The lazy circles of his fingertip against her button and quiet whisper of teases brought forth another moan and emphatic nod, as Diana continued to strain forward into his touch.

"Diana, I need to taste you..."

"Yes! Please!" She groaned against his cheek. She turned her face back into his kisses. "Darling, have me," she sighed into his mouth between kisses.

Clark kneeled down on his knees, lifting her left leg and put her thigh on his shoulder. The look in his bright blue eyes was unmistakably devilish

THE DARK SPELL

when he turned back to capture her gaze. Diana sighed with heady anticipation of what was to be next.

Diana found herself achingly aware of her already labored breathing then, watching him, lift up her skirt more. His right hand sliding up, skimming lightly over the sensitive skin of her inner thigh, until his fingertips made contact with the moistened fabric of her underwear.

Diana's heart pounded furiously beneath her breasts as he snagged the edge of the material and pushed it to the side, teasing across her warm, wet flesh until he exposed his prize. Diana felt herself blushing under the scrutiny of his gaze, not able to hide the extent of his effect on her. Clark dipped his finger down until he found the moisture collecting around her opening and slowly drew it back up the length of her slit until he reached her clit again, now beginning to swell and peeking free from her hiding place, begging for his attention. Diana felt her eyelids flutter, but forced them to stay open and continue to watch as his fingertips brushed delicately over her most sensitive areas. Finally, just as she almost couldn't withstand the suspense anymore, he leaned in closer.

Diana sigh softly as she watched him descend, almost in relief that he would soon put an end to the tortuous knot already forming deep within her. Diana came to the quick realization that her feelings of relief were premature when he stopped just short of contact, preferring instead to allow only the warmth of his breath to join in with the play of his fingertips along her exposed mound. Her breath caught in her throat at this madness. She felt herself screaming inside, begging for the release she knew he would provide, as her hips strained, seeking contact.

Finally, he saw fit to end her torture and moved his face even closer. All the air escaped Diana's lungs at the first touch of his tongue on her heated flesh. His tongue was warm, firm, as he drug it along the fleshy expanse of her outer labia, still teasing. Warmer still when he slipped it between to find the more sensitive skin of her inner lips. Even hotter when he made love to her with his tongue, pushing his tongue deep inside to collect the juices spilling from her opening. Diana gripped the back of his head and began to move her hips to meet the thrusts of his tongue.

Diana was trying so hard to hold off, to match the slow teasing pace of his seduction, but the knot of her orgasm had been building for far too long. She reached up and bit down on the side of her fingers to quiet the screams bubbling from the pit of her stomach. The slight rasp of his tongue when he withdrew and found her clit sent her over the edge in a single stroke. Each flick of his tongue brought forth another spasm, and another, and another as he lapped at her, merciless to the cries she muffled into her hand. Finally, the thrash of her hips bucked her away from him, and the spell was broken, leaving her spent, gasping for air.

Within seconds, he raised back up, finding her mouth again with his own. Diana tasted herself in his kiss and clung to him. She made quick to unbutton his pants. Diana slid her hand inside to stroke him through his boxers, reveling in the feel of him stiffening beneath the smooth skin on the palm of her hand. Their kisses continued as Diana tightened her grip on his shaft and stroke him through his boxers.

"These need to be off, Kal," she whispered placing a kiss on his neck.

Diana stepped forward, making Clark start to walk backwards until the back of his knees hit the large stack on hay. Diana broke their kiss, removed her hand from his pants and pushed him down to sit on the blanket covered loft of hay.

"It's really cute how you made this look like a bed. Very creativity," Diana stated as she leaned down and kissed him.

Then, kneeling down on her knees, this time, she pulled his pants down and off tossing them where they landed.

Her fingers came into contact with the heated flesh of his thigh, and she stroked him there for a few moments, feeling the way that the muscles there rippled, watching, enraptured, as his head tilted backwards. Curiously, she continued to stroke him there gently, feeling the hardness beneath her palm. Clark's ragged breath was the only sound that could be heard in the barn, his hands clutching at the blanket.

Currents of pleasure ran through Clark's body, making him shiver. He bit his lip hard as he felt himself twitch in his Goddess's grasp. He was quickly beginning to realise that he was coming in at a disadvantage because Diana had him undressed, and she herself was still fully clothed. And, with her hand stroking him in such a way, he was fast losing his ability to do anything about it. The way that her fingers were flexing against

THE DARK SPELL

him was sending streams of gratification jolting through his body, and his throat worked desperately to stop himself from groaning aloud.

"Why are you doing that?" Diana breathed when she saw the expression on his face. "You said we couldn't be heard."

Her words and the lusty quality of her voice had him stifling a grunt. It was true but it was also easier said than done for both of them knowing how loud they could get. They were here in this barn with no one else for miles around, no one else to know or care about what they were doing. The Kents were occupied with their own thing, yards away, in the house. And it was so very difficult to keep silent when Diana's hand was doing the things that it was doing...

Diana bit back a triumphant smirk when her beloved submitted and let out a groan of appreciation. His head fell forward to rest against her shoulder, and she couldn't resist nudging his face so that he turned to look at her dazedly, and she let her lips travel teasingly over his face, touching her tongue to the raindrops that had collected there as he'd done to her earlier. When her mouth finally relented and found his, he kissed her eagerly, his breath hitching and his throat vibrating with the sound of smothered noises. Diana knew exactly what to do to bring her lover pleasure and she let her fingernails graze him gently as she let them travel back up his length.

Heat seared from his loins, and she wrapped her hand fully around his length, gently pulling him forward and then pushing back, mimicking the action of their lovemaking with her hand. She breathed heavily in his ear as she worked, feeling his every tremble and twitch as she worked, feeling her own body beginning to respond more eagerly to his, anxious to answer the primitive call. Her spare hand, previously resting on his thigh and kneading the skin there, began to travel up his back, feeling the ripple of his muscles, the flex of his shoulder blades, up his neck to the nape, the heat of his face, gently twining her fingers through his hair and using it as leverage to pull him gently away from her shoulder.

"Clark," she said softly.

His answer was a guttural moan as she squeezed him lightly. It was no longer enough to touch. She needed to feel her beloved's hands on her too.

"Clark, I love how I get to have this with you. How Junior response to me with such excitement."

She lower her mouth to Junior and slowly licked from the base to the head, swirling her tongue around the tip. She teases him licking up and down for several moments before she swallows him. He let out a low moan causing her eyes to flicker up.

Gods, he was so sexy and it was even sexier having him under her control.

Clark locked eyes with her as she started to shove more and more of his length down her throat. He was a goddamn lucky man to be orally pleasured twice in one day just between a few hours.

Diana managed to get half of it down her throat and used her hands to stroke the rest over and over, matching her sucking movements. She was intentionally driving him wild, as her did to her.

Clark threw his head back again. Mouth was open, silent, but telling Diana all she needed to know. Deep inhales and exhales from his chest. Shuddering with arousal. The quiet sound of Diana's controlled gagging became audible gulping around him in her mouth.

Clark looked down again. Eyes meeting hers as she look up at him, half of his massive, throbbing hard on buried deep inside her mouth. He could see her throat begin to convulse, and feel it tighten around him as more barely audible gags emit from deep within her.

Clark felt a boiling in his balls now as he approached the point of no return. Clark tangled his hand into her hair and thrusts forward. He felt his member hitting the back of her throat before pushing it further down.

He held her there for a few seconds before releasing her completely.

With a final massive convulsion, Diana pulled her mouth back, releasing a thick, soupy downpour of saliva from her lips as she gasp for air, hovering over his member and continuing to stroke it. Clark groaned as he felt her well lubricated hand sliding up and down his length, and soon feel her lips join that stroking appendage as she bobbed up and down on him, for one more deep throat, moaning with undisguised lust.

Before completely releasing him, she licked and kissed the tip.

Clark growled as he threaded his long muscular fingers into Diana' hair again and pulled her lips up to his. They're flavors mixing in a very intimate way as their tongues met at the edge of her lips.

THE DARK SPELL

"We taste so good together," Diana hummed across his lips, drawing the bottom one into her mouth and rolling it between her own before she released it slowly, trailing her tongue over it, savouring the very last ounce of flavour that she drew from his mouth.

She then stood up with a seductive smile. She unzipped her skirt letting it fall to her feet. She took off her blouse, letting it fall where he skirt was, then slowly slid her underwear down her long sexy legs. She stepped over her clothes and stood there in all her gorgeous naked glory.

Clark's mouth watered and Junior twitched with anticipation as she turned slowly for him to get a full view of her body.

"Damn..."

Diana blushed.

"C'mere, Di."

Diana walked back to him and once in reach, Clark wrapped his arms around her waist. Diana placed her hands on his shoulders as she straddled him.

"Oh, Gods..." Diana groaned descending onto Clark's member.

When he was sheathed inside her, she sat still for a moment. Clark moved his hands to her ass and held her to him, pushing her breasts firmly against his chest. He was totally captivated by her body hugging him so tight. He squeezed both her ass cheeks, that felt so good in his hands, so soft and luscious. He gazed at her sultry lips and beautiful face.

Diana started to move up and down, grinding at a slow pace, both of them moaning softly.

They both instinctively came together for a kiss. It was a soft and closed mouth kiss at first. Clark sucked the edge of her bottom lip in between his lips and gently nibbled on it. Diana's arms wrapped around his neck as he kissed her full on the lips. Clark moved his tongue over her lips, and she let it slip inside her mouth, swirling around it with her own. Their lips parted and he let his tongue drag down over her chin.

"Yes...yes..." she whispered and continued slowly grinding a little harder against him while Clark's hands held her ass.

Clark kissed her face, from the corner of her mouth, along her cheek to the little spot behind her ear, along her neck, down over her collarbone, and then back to her mouth again. Their kisses were becoming more passionate and suddenly, their mouths opened and mixed saliva as their tongues were dancing with each other. Time seemed to standstill as they enjoyed each other's taste.

Clark slowly let his hands move up and down her sides, massaging, then moving up her her back to her shoulders.

He then leaned back momentarily and gazed at her. Diana's mouth was slightly open with a seductive smile and her eyes were somewhat glazed over. He could see the fire, the same fire in him, smoldering in her, as he gently started to rub her stomach. Then they were at it again, kissing each other's lips and cheeks.

Eventually, Clark slid his lips down under her chin and started kissing her there. Diana's breathing became more ragged and her chest rose and swelled. Clark continued kissing down her neck and brought his hand up along her ribcage until he was rubbing that area just below her breasts. Clark kissed his way down her neck to her chest, then nibbled and sucked his way into that heavenly valley between her breasts. Then he kissed and nibbled the inner sides of her breasts.

Diana's breathing was heavy and she started to moan and as she did, Clark kissed his way back up her chest and neck to her lips. They were in a passionate lip-lock. Clark moved his hand up and palmed her breast. Diana groaned and pushed her chest out into his hand. They were kissing each other like crazy again, all over each other's face.

Then Clark leaned back and gazed again into her eyes.

She was magnificent. Her beautiful breasts bouncing. He couldn't wait to go to work on them. He cupped her breasts in his hands, leaning forward, and bending his head down to began the oral assault of her breasts with his mouth and tongue. He didn't waste any time when his mouth connected with the taunt peak.

Clark lightly kissed her left nipple and Diana moaned her approval. He took her breast into his mouth, as much of it as he could, and gently sucked and slurped on the taut nipple. When his mouth was on one side, his hand was on the other. Diana arches her back and grinds her hips on him. She was looking toward the ceiling of the barn with her eyes closed, and that pushed her chest out even more.

THE DARK SPELL

For the next fifteen minutes he gave his full, undivided attention to her breasts.

"Mmmmmm..." she shuddered a little and said, "Oh, gods... So good... So...so...good..."

Diana's beautiful moans fill the barn. It was like a lullaby to Clark, along with her heady scent intoxicating his mixture signaled him to bite, nipping at the skin as he sucked.

Diana blathered almost incoherently and her mouth turned dirty. She kept this up while Clark battered one breast, then the other, switched again.

"Oh, god! Yes! Yes!" she cried. "Oh!"

She bit her lip when he bites down at the sensitive area, pulling her nipple.

"You don't know how that... There! Right there! Gods, yes!" she hollered as he moved his hand from one nipple to another, pinching and pulling.

The pleasure heightened to a new level and forced a choked moan from Diana's throat. Both her hands were pulling his head hard into her chest and she was moaning and groaning while saying, "Oh, gods! Oh, yes! Yes!" over and over.

Clark continued this oral attack for a few more minutes and then, with final hard bites of each nipple, he released her breasts. He smiled at the markings he made on her skin. They were red from his onslaught and her nipples were distended, hard, and wet.

"You talented man! You are so good to me," she said softly, smiling.

Her gorgeous smile was the most beautiful expression of desire he had ever seen.

"I'll do any and everything for my Goddess. Sweet, delectable...so god damn sexy. I can't get enough."

Clark pulled her into a new kiss, now somewhat more demanding, to which she was willingly succumbing. Her moist lips velvety in touch; making him desire more. His tongue darted into her mouth instinctively, on its own. Diana gasped and trembled under the touch of his tongue on hers. The fiery kisses were raising the temperature rapidly, soon becoming a furnace. Their lips seemed to have amalgamated into one while tongues battled for domination.

Back at the Kent Main House

"Clark and Diana have been out for a long while. Hope they are okay?"

"Heh..."

"What's funny?"

Jonathan kissed Martha's cheek. "They're just fine. I saw them heading to the barn earlier," he informed nonchalantly.

"The barn? Oh! Oh my...well...I guess we will have dinner night with just the two of us."

"Yep! They'll join us for breakfast in the morning...or lunch. Maybe we should just have brunch."

Martha couldn't help but laugh.

Back in the barn...

Diana suddenly came down hard on Clark causing her to scream.

"BY GODS!" she yelled as he filled her even more.

This angle heightened her pleasure, so she moved faster. She lifted herself up and came down harder as if she were galloping on a wild horse, her hair flailing.

Her moans became louder, and Clark took pleasure in watching her express herself from their coupling.

"My Love!"

Clark's hands on her hips. He claws at her skin, helping her move more on him. Diana grinds on him, causing Clark to close his eyes, moaning and growling.

"Diana!"

He began the float up and leaned back slightly again and Diana also leaned back slightly, moving up and down the length of him as they're grinding growing more intense. They looked into each other's eyes, both of them moaning. Clark had this hot sensual woman in his grasp. Diana was breathing heavily as they humped harder and harder against each other.

She loved the control in this one. Shutting her eyes in obvious blissful delight as she she was drilling herself more onto him. She looked simply spectacular, arousal on her moaning face, hair lashing her shoulders, breasts bouncing and his straining member vanishing at her slit.

THE DARK SPELL

She leaned towards him again, lifting and lowering her hips to take however much of him she wanted inside her, the action easily visible for Clark.

He wrapped his hands at the back of her neck, looking hard into her eyes, his hard as steel manhood went unbelievably deep inside her, with his balls slapping loudly against her skin. Her eyes were quite simply inflamed and crazed. They were both moaning, grunting or groaning. He was able to stay still and let her be in control for some time, but such passion fest was stirring the beast in him fast and there was only so much time he could keep it from being unleashed. No idea how long that took, but eventually, he pressed his hand on her back pushing her down. Diana held on tight to him. Her face right next to his; her body shaking and trembling. He simply could not prevent his beast from rising anymore: with his manhood throbbing, her womanhood pulsating against him like mad and balls tingling, his desires had priority. Her ass lifted up slightly now gave him sufficient space. He placed both of his palms on her ass cheeks; a powerful, secure grab.

He started moving, fast from the get-go. Her ass was pushed down onto him adding to the stabbing action.

"Oh my...! OH BY THE GODS!"

She screamed against his arm, gripping it tightly herself. She was in his power. He was filling her completely and more; it was demanding and insistent.

He only needed to push her ass down onto it a few times before Diana knew what was expected of her; although he kept his hands on her ass, nonetheless, she dropped it down soon onto his length in union with his thrusts, adding to its force as it tore through her. Forceful and harsh, this was a position of dreamlike friction. She shouted into his arm, bit into it, and kept landing her ass against his member the whole time.

Her supple graceful body kept delivering as his member ripped through her. In his debauched state, with the beast released and in control, he slapped her add several times and a bizarre combination of words was there, completely lost on him at the time.

He kept his hands on her ass, a clear indication of being in control, which she loved, that much was obvious, as much as having been in control before; but he now let her lift herself up again wanting to see her as he kept thrusting into her. Her expression was gorgeously strained, almost pained, tensed up by the intense never-ceasing waves of pleasure. She kissed him, passionately, panting into his mouth, whimpering and grunting.

Clark feel that familiar tightening around him and Diana screamed again louder than she had and quivered with ecstasy.

Though, they still weren't done and Clark was determined to give Diana everything she wanted and needed until they were. Clark was not so much moving in and out of her as he was moving within her, her pubic bone and clit pushing against his body.

Clark gave her ass another squeeze and helped her rock back and forth. He had a new wind, and he was moving her slowly.

They fall into rhythm again and hold each other, looking into each other's eyes, kiss, and finally Clark felt one last incredible squeeze from Diana as he sucked on her tongue. Her whole body shook against him as the orgasm traveled through, moving involuntarily, and she whimpered out the moans as a few tears well up in your eyes at the indescribable pleasure ripping her from reality and taking over her mind.

She then put both hands on her round breasts and started rubbing them. Arching her back, she quickly moved one of her hands to her clit, rubbing as he filled her with his essence. He loved watching his length going in and out of her dripping womanhood as she played with her clit. He could not imagine a hotter sight as they made love to each other with such abandon.

Clark slowly drifted back down to lay on the loft of hay. He reached for another blanket he had near and covered them both. They both just laid there for a moment, enjoying the afterglow. His lips met hers again, but this time they were gentle and tender instead of filled with lust and need.

"This is such an amazing experience," Diana smiled.

"You think so? I mean it's still nothing lavish. It's simple...in a good way but-"

"Kal, I love being here with you. Why would you think otherwise?"

"I don't know. I guess..." he sighed running his fingers through his hair and placed his hand behind his head. "I just want to give you everything you deserve. Seeing that gorgeous smile everyday and being part of the reason for it, I take pride in that. You were so in awe when we were in Barcelona. I want to take you to places like that all over this world and even other worlds. I want you to-"

Diana silenced him with a kiss.

"Places like that are beautiful and I can't wait for us to take trips more often to go sightseeing but, Darling, my heart is so full when I'm here with you and your parents. It reminds me of home."

"Diana, this is your home, too." Clark placed her hand over his chest and kept his on top of hers. "Always remember that."

"And...This will be the home for our children as well."

He grinned. "I've thought about that. Little rascals flying around in the field...Or thinking the tractor is a gigantic toy to be lifting like I did when I was a kid."

Diana laughed. "Taking them to the town fair, teaching them how to fish...Oh, it's so much I can't wait for!"

Clark cupped her cheek.

"I had a conversation with Martha earlier this morning about us having children. I had to tell her about the tea. She understood, though, she really does want grandchildren."

"Kinda had the same conversation with Pa, too. He noticed the tea. I told about how I feel with you taking it. The obligation."

"Darling, you know I would never do something I didn't want to. I don't see it as an obligation in a negative way. I see it as being responsible because if I don't, we will have little ones around sooner than expected. What we just did, we couldn't do if we didn't take the precautionary measures."

"I just want to make sure, Di. We are a team and I want to make sure I'm doing my part."

Diana smirked. "Oh, Beloved, you are doing your part and so much more." She sat up. "We should get back to practicing in the meantime."

"Ah..." Clark grinned and sat up with her.

They leaned towards each other, face-to-face, capturing each others lips, kissing sensually yet sweetly, lovingly, blissfully. They're soft lips, moist, feeling the warmth of each others' faces, cheeks, and feeling the energy of each others presence and affection.

"Remember that activity we did when we were having our oil massage?" She asked blushing cupping her breasts in her hands.

Clark pondered for a moment then eyed her breasts and smirked.

"Oh! You mean when Junior got comfortably acquainted in between those glorious soft personal pillows."

Diana giggled, biting her lip and nodded.

"I want to do it again," she told him motioning him to bring Junior up a bit.

His erect shaft, completely upright, stood in the cool barn air.

Slowly, she enveloped his length with her breasts, first softly and presently with a bit more pressure. The underside of his shaft was held in place against her warm, sensuous mounds, while he could enjoy the sight of her bared, stiff nipples and areoles.

Her breasts were so supple, so soft, so warm, and feeling them in a lockhold around his length was marvelous.

Diana gently began to massage him with her breasts, gently sliding them up and down, very slowly.

Clark watched while the crown tip of his length appeared then disappeared into her cleavage. He shut his eyes for a moment, simply enjoying the sensation of being stroked this way.

He lay there while she continued to work Junior rather masterfully, squeezing her breasts around him more firmly.

Clark opened his eyes again, and watched her choking his manhood with the firmness of her breasts, with the slightest, self-assured trace of a smile on her lips. What he saw was equal parts playfulness, equal parts lechery, and the rhythm of her rubbing him was gradually speeding up.

He felt himself approaching climax, the essence rising from his balls into his shaft, trying to hold it back a little bit so he wouldn't come too fast. And yet, the sublime sight of his manhood being massaged by these two lovely orbs with their nipples showing was incredible.

He was starting to moan more loudly now, as the sensation was becoming warmer, firmer, more climactic. The muscles of his manhood were feeling more sensitive, the head swelling with blood, essence, and energy. He fixed a trance-like stare at her as she continued to milk him with her breasts, almost as if she was on a mission, a mission to make him come,

THE DARK SPELL

to make him come as hard as he possibly could. It all mixed together, her breasts, her nipples, her areoles, her lovely face, and the forceful motion of her trying to get his manhood to surrender, over, and over, and over, and over...

He felt his muscles give way. He couldn't hold it in anymore. Her breasts were too beautiful. She was too beautiful, her lovely face, her long raven hair, and the loving way she spoke to him. He'd seen and loved every part of her but right now, the focus was all about her nipples, and her deep, cavernous cleavage.

On one downstroke of her breasts, a blast of essence shot out, up into the air, hitting her on her lower chin. On another, several streams began to pool in her cleavage but she held his manhood tight within. He watched while more streams shot across her breasts, reaching her shoulder, even going over her right shoulder at one point.

Still, she kept insistently squeezing his member, over and over, another thick, stream hitting her hair.

Clark moaned audibly, unable to contain his excitement.

Another six or seven strokes, and she rested, still cradling Junior in her breasts' cleavage, a puddle of essence sitting on the crown of his manhood.

After he came, she continued to cradle him in her breasts very softly murmuring, "I love you. I love you so much." And Clark still felt like wanting to come some more. He felt his glands working feverishly at producing essence way down there, even though he'd just shot off. And it felt so good.

He was done for. They were both breathing heavily at this point. Out of breath, trembling with energy still, they reached for each other and held each other in a long, close hug that lasted minutes. Clark kissed her lips, and as he drew back, marveled at her being covered with him.

The wind outside was still quietly humming in the background. Their breaths supplemented the sound. Clark reached for her, and gathered her fully into his arms and spooned her, holding her from behind. She rested her head on him, and he rested his on the back of her shoulder.

Clark broke the silence after a few moments.

"That was..."

"Mmmmm," Diana quietly cooed. "It was very satisfying."

"Experiencing things like this with you, Diana...I never thought I could...or would but with you..." he kissed her shoulder. "...with you any and everything is possible."

"Yes, my Love. Any and everything is possible with you and I together," she said, pulling his body around hers.

There was just something about the sensation of their love making experience overall. Being so unadulterated, so soft and gentle, affectionate, emotional and loving.

Clark hugged her more closely.

There was certainly the thing of carnal, the erotic beauty of it all. The warmth, the support, the emotion...they felt all of it through each other.

They lay there silently, Clark's arms wrapped around this amazing Goddess, quietly marveling at the experience they shared.

"Could we go to the lake tomorrow? I'd like to go fishing and swimming...unclothed..." she quietly ventured.

"Absolutely," Clark replied kissing her shoulder again.

"I love you, Kal-El."

"I love you too, Diana."

And then they drifted off into the most blissful sleep.

The Next Day: Afternoon

Clark and Diana were standing at the edge of the dock of the lake.

"This feels incredible! So refreshing!" Diana smiled gleefully as she looked around the lake.

"Yeah! Hours fishing and swimming!"

Diana looked at him deviously. "How about we take that swim now?"

"Oh, yeah, want to get to swimming naked before fi-" Clark paused mid sentence as he was pushed.

He quickly turned to see Diana giggling then smirked and grabbed her hand pulling her with him.

She gasped. "Kal!"

They both fell in with a big loud splash. Resurfacing, they were both laughing.

"Di, we were suppose to be naked," he smirked pulling her against him.

"I know but I couldn't resist. We can still have a delightful swim unclothed and it's hot enough for our clothes to dry."

THE DARK SPELL

Clark wrapped his arms a little more tightly around Diana. He leaned down and kissed her.

Diana closed her eyes and wrapped her arms around his neck, deepening the kiss.

After a few moments, Diana leaned back slightly, breaking it gently.

"Kal-El," Diana sighed.

"What's wrong?" He looked worried as Diana ran her fingers through his hair.

"Nothing is wrong, Love. Everything is perfect!" she smiled sweetly. "I love you."

Clark kissed her nose and grinned. "I love you, too, Di. I love you, too."

2 weeks later: Metropolis - Clark and Diana's Apartment -11:30 pm

"Yeah, it's finally done, Bruce. It's perfect for her," Clark said over the phone as he stood at the front door of the apartment.

"Does she suspect anything yet?"

"Course she does but I'm not making it any better almost slipping with what I say. To say that she can't go with me to the Fortress has been difficult."

"Since it's done, take her there. You have it somewhere she can't find, right?"

"Course. Locked and secured away until time."

"Then there you go."

Clark sighed. "I'm not rushing the days but I am...I'm ready for this. I just hope that Diana's won't be too mad at me afterwards."

"Dammit, Clark! Stop worrying. I know you aren't getting cold feet and trying to make excuses?!"

"What?! I just said I was ready! I'm not making excuses and I sure as hell don't have cold feet. I just..." He sighed again. "It's a big step for us, Bruce. I want it to be perfect. I want to give Diana what she deserves."

"Come on, Clark. Everything you do is perfect to her! Don't overthink."

"Ha! I'm getting advice not to overthink from the main guy who does that and is paranoid all the time."

"It's called being aware. Anyway, I have to go."

"Have fun with chasing Selina from roof to roof."

"Funny." Bruce hung up.

Clark chuckled unlocking and opening the door. He quietly went in shutting and locking the door.

Normally, Diana would be awake but this past week of long hours at the Embassy, lectures at the university and heroics, exhausted her.

He quickly made a b-line to his laptop bad taking out the communicator Hippolyta gave him.

"Hippolyta!" He whispered happily seeing her hologram.

"Hello, Kal-El! Is everything alright?!"

"Taking the opportunity while Diana is asleep. I wanted to call and tell you that it's done."

She gasped. "Oh, joy! I can't wait to see it!"

"I'm proud of it. Thank you for helping with the rest of the band and the last jewel piece."

"It was a pleasure, Kal-El. It has been an honor being part of this grand surprise and celebration for my daughter. I mean I do understand this is for you both."

"Hippolyta, you're right. This is for Diana. Celebrating her, the love I have for her, the bond we've built, shared and strengthened throughout all these years. I can't say it enough how grateful and thankful I am that you have given me your blessing."

"I trust that you will keep your word, Kal-El. You have proven so."

"And I will continue to do so. Have a good day, Hippolyta."

"Good night, Kal-El."

Clark placed the communicator back in his bag. Going to their bedroom, he saw his sleeping naked Goddess sprawled out on her stomach on the bed.

He took off all his clothes and having been drawn to her slender legs on display, before he could stop himself, Clark was lightly brushing his fingers along Diana's calf. He couldn't help it that Junior responded at the same time. He loved the feel of her smooth skin under his hands.

Diana moved in her sleep but she didn't wake. Though her movements had made the duvet rise more than it already was exposing the backs of her upper thighs.

THE DARK SPELL

Clark resumed his exploring, slowly moving his hands towards Diana's thighs. He started massaging her thighs with more pressure, running his hands up and down, slowly trailing up the outside of her thighs, then back down towards her inner thighs.

His hands rubbed up and down the backs of Diana's thighs for several minutes, knowing that as he did so, he was slowly inching his body closer to hers.

Clark couldn't help himself any longer, so he leaned over and traced his lips along her leg that was closest to him, trailing small, soft kisses all the way up to the backs of her thighs.

He climbed onto the bed, straddling her thighs.

Unbeknownst to him or maybe he was aware, Diana was slightly awake and she was quite enjoying his slow exploration. She felt a fluttery feeling, low in her stomach and instinctively pulled her legs together, but that only caused her to become aware of the dampness that was already collecting between her thighs. Diana felt her breasts pressing more into the bed underneath her, and she felt her nipples had begun to harden in response to the attention of her lover's hands.

Since he was now straddling Diana's thighs, Clark moved to trail his fingers lightly up and down Diana's back. His hardness pushing against her ass.

He slowly eased back from her thighs to perch himself further down her legs.

Clark felt Diana squirm slightly under him. She soon settled again and let out a soft sigh. She felt him continue to rub her back, down lower and then to the top of her ass cheeks.

She smiled a little in her sleep and whispered, "keep doing what you're doing".

Clark smirked. "So you were awake."

"A tiny bit."

Clark allowed his hands to wander further down onto Diana's ass, slowly caressing the curvy globes. Diana felt Junior harden even more and detected a bit of pre-essence leaking. Clark began to massage her ass more firmly. Diana let out a soft moan as he was grasping her cheeks and moving them up and down and side to side.

Before he could stop himself, Clark was massaging Diana's ass cheeks underneath the edge of the duvet. Her skin was soft and silky smooth, and Clark found himself roaming his hands around on her ass and towards her hips, then back again. He massaged the supple skin, watching how it stretched under his fingertips.

"You miss me?"

"Of course, Beloved."

"I missed you, too."

His big strong hands were really moving around now, from her ass cheeks, across to her hips, down her side slightly to the back of her thighs, and then back up to her ass. Each time he was moving his hands up her thighs, Clark slowly allowed his thumbs to dip between her legs just a little. He didn't linger in one area, though he was allowing his thumbs to really manoeuvre between her legs with each new journey around her ass. Clark could even feel the heat emanating from between Diana's legs.

"Did you finish your tasks at the Fortress?"

"I did and now we can go anytime you want."

"Will you show me what you were working on?"

"Yes, eventually...but not just yet."

"Clark..."

"Shhh...let me work my magic, Starshine."

"Why can't you?"

"Why can't I what?"

"Show me. Why wait?"

"Because it's not time."

Diana raised her hips a little towards him making him groan.

"When will the time be?"

"Soon, Starshine...soon."

She sucked her teeth. "How soon is soon?"

Clark laughed. "Diana, relax. Don't worry about it."

He was entranced with what he was doing, and slowly leaned forward to nuzzle into Diana's ass. He used his thumbs to gently ease her cheeks apart a little, and he kissed her softly where he had exposed more skin. Clark's tongue snaked out of his mouth to lightly lick at Diana's inner ass

THE DARK SPELL

cheeks. He licked further towards her puckered entrance with each new swipe of his tongue.

Diana moaned and pushed her hips back a little, as she could feel Clark was really getting into her ass now.

Clark's hands slowly grasped at her hips, using his thumbs to pull her ass cheeks apart, allowing his tongue easier access. Diana couldn't help but moan louder and push her ass back to encourage him to continue.

"Oh Gods..."

She felt each swipe of his tongue along her entrance. He was slowly drawing his tongue further down each time, and Diana could feel it brush at her nether lips.

However, Clark eased away all of a sudden, and Diana groaned in disappointment. He was soon assisting her to turn over on her back, so he could access her from the front.

Diana opened her beautifully piercing cerulean eyes to him. She was clearly a little overheated.

As Clark gazed down at Diana on the bed, he noticed her face and decolletage was slightly flushed and her breathing seemed to be a little bit faster. Since Diana had been moved, the duvet had worked its way up over her hips, and Clark now had a clear view of her delectable womanhood before him. His mouth salivated seeing a shiny slick wetness on her lips.

"Kal..." she blushed. "The way you stare at me."

"You're breathtaking, Di. I can't help myself."

Clark eased towards the juncture in Diana's thighs, settling himself between her legs. He was looking at her gorgeous womanhood and inhaled her arousal, when he glanced up to see her blushing profusely. Her breathing was still a little faster.

He reached out with one hand and gently stroked Diana's inner thigh, enjoying the smooth skin under his fingertips. His hand continued its journey, his fingertips moving towards Diana smooth nether lips. With a fingertip on each, Clark traced down her lips and then slowly brought his fingers back to the top of her mons. He did that several times, each time moving slightly closer to be parting her lips with his fingers.

"Oh, Clark..." she moaned and wriggled a little, unconsciously pushing her womanhood towards Clark's touch.

Clark used his thumb and forefingers and gently eased Diana's puffy lips apart. Finally, he could properly see her inner lips, slick with her nectar. With his fingers holding her lips apart, Clark edged his mouth towards her, eager to taste her. his tongue to swipe from the bottom of her pussy all the way up to her clit. She involuntarily pushed her hips towards his mouth, welcoming the intrusion. Diana glanced down to see this amazing man's head between her legs, unable to see his face while he was busy lapping at her womanhood. His tongue was teasing her, slowly taking long swipes up, reaching her clit and then starting all over again. She felt him nuzzle in a little more and then he was licking and kissing all around the top of her womanhood but not directly on her clit.

He just needed to get onto her clit, and Diana was frustrated with trying to push her hips to guide him.

"Stop teas- AH!"

He latched onto her clit and sucked, causing Diana's hips to undulate, her back arch and her eyes flutter close. She enjoyed the pleasure he was giving her. He was swapping between the flicking with his tongue and sucking, with the occasional long swipe up of her core.

Diana moaned a little louder, and Clark momentarily stopped his ministrations to glance up at Diana's face. His tongue involuntarily ventured out of his mouth to lick up some of Diana's delicious nectar that had smeared around his mouth. Diana laughed seeing his chin smeared with her nectar. Clark smirked and directed his gaze back to the task at hand.

While his tongue had moved away from her, Clark had kept a few fingers in its place instead. His index finger and ring finger were on either side of her womanhood, while his middle finger was directly stimulating her clit.

As he moved his mouth back towards his tasty night snack, Clark eased his middle finger down her slit to slowly tease at her entrance. His tongue edged out of his mouth and began to lap at Diana's clit again.

Diana's hips were moving slowly up and down, as if trying to direct him where to stimulate next. He just followed wherever she went and continued his delicate assault on her most private sensitive part. The finger that he had started to tease at her entrance was now moving slowly up and

THE DARK SPELL

down the slick folds, dipping into her every now and then to capture some more nectar to spread around.

Diana's hips continued to move up and down, but slightly faster than before and more centred on one place, her clit. Clark was sure that along with the juices that were flowing from her and the way her movements had changed that she was very close to an orgasm.

Diana felt that amazing orgasm building deep inside her, and she was determined to get there just as much as Clark wanted to get her there. She started to move her hips up and down a little slower, to make sure he focused his tongue on just the right spot. She could feel his finger dipping into her womanhood further and further each time, gradually getting to the limit of how long his finger was. At the next movement out of his finger, she felt him plunge back in again, only this time there was more than one finger.

At the same time as the added fingers were plunging in and out of her center, Clark's tongue seemed to kick into overdrive and flicker even faster over Diana's clit. She was right on the precipice and just needed a little bit more to get over the edge.

Without even thinking about it, Diana sat up a little and reached down with both hands to grab a hold of his head, partially bunching her fingers in his hair. The movement made his mouth come even closer towards Diana, and he sped up the movement of his fingers moving in and out.

Diana's orgasm crashed over her like a massive wave at the beach, exploding from within her. She could feel it spread out all over her body and she gripped the Clark's head a little more desperately, letting out a small triumphant cry of joy and pleasure at the same time. His tongue continued to lap at her clit, while his fingers continued to move in and out of her core, helping to prolong the orgasm.

Clark loved the taste of Diana's orgasmic release of nectar, simultaneously continuing to lap at her clit and take long swipes at her center with his tongue. His fingers continued to pump in and out of her, but he was slowing them down as he could tell Diana's orgasm was fading.

Diana's fingers started to relax from the grip on his head, alerting Clark again to the receding orgasm. She had stopped moving her hips up and down as well, and so Clark slowly eased off with his ministrations, taking shorter swipes of his tongue and slowly withdrawing his fingers from inside of her.

Clark gradually worked himself away from between her legs. As he slowly reversed backwards from her, Clark glanced up licking his lips.

His gaze was met by a bleary-eyed Diana, with a pleasured look on her face. She was still feeling the aftereffects of her orgasm.

Clark moved to the right side of her adjusting the pillows to lean against the headboard. Diana slowly sat up. Clark wrapped his arms around her, bringing her in for a bear hug and Diana immediately melted into his embrace.

Clark smiled and leaned in for a kiss. His lips gently locked into hers. Warm pecks on her lips, jaw, and neck. By the noises coming from her throat, she was loving this. Their hearts were thundering. Clark cupped her soft cheek in his palm, and kissed her slow again.

"I love you, Di."

"I love you, too, Kal."

He kissed her eyebrows, and booped her nose with his own. She giggled, and butted her head up into his neck. Her eyes were half shut, Clark cradling her.

"Will you hold me like this for the rest of the night?"

He smiled and held her tighter. "Of course."

Diana brushed her lips against his neck then reached up and kissed him deeply.

A few weeks later: WatchTower

"Are you sure we won't get attacked?" Hak asked with a quirked brow. "I mean I don't want to spear getting stuck up my ass."

"Nevermind him, Big Blue. Is there anything else we need to do?"

"No, everything is set, Barry."

"So like I can go too right? I'm tired of being left behind." Billy asked.

"Of course, Billy. But please, don't be embarrassing."

"What?! Me?! No way! Who's embarrassing is Jordan talking about spears and wanting to flirt with the Ama-"

Flash nudged him to shut up quickly as Diana, Mari, and Dinah walked into the conference room.

Diana immediately noticed the awkward silence.

THE DARK SPELL

"Hello, gentlemen. What have you all gotten yourselves into now?" she questioned.

"Oh nothing, Wondy! Nothing at all! Big Blue was just telling me about your-"

Flash hit him in the back of the head.

"Ow!"

"Telling what, William?"

"Billy was complaining about not going to the adult meetings and Big Blue was saying that if he goes he can't be an embarrassment. Or else you will deal with him."

"But it's Jordan that's the embarrassment!" he whined.

"William, given that you are still a child, I still expect you to act as your age of 17. Harold, we've had this conversation before."

Dinah, Mari, Barry and Billy snickered. "Harold..." they teased.

Kal smirked and walked over to Diana placing a soft kiss on her cheek.

"Aaaww! How sweet!" Dinah gushed.

"If all of you are done with your antics, we have a briefing to get through," Batman said sternly.

"Way to ruin atmosphere, Bruce," Dinah scoffed.

"The faster we get through this, the faster I can get back to Gotham where I'm needed and you can get back to rehearsals."

"Didn't know you actually cared."

"What were you all really talking about?" Diana asked Kal in a whisper.

"Nothing to worry about."

Diana raised her brow.

Kal kissed her cheek again. "Don't worry. Fortress after the briefing okay?"

Diana rolled her eyes and sighed. "Okay."

2 hours later... Fortress of Solitude

"You sure you aren't hungry, Di?" Kal asked as they were floating to the bedroom.

"I'm sure."

Kal quirked his brow noticing her answers were short and she was barely saying anything else otherwise.

"Hey..."

He grabbed her hand and pulled her to him. He cupped her chin, raising her lips to his though as he was trying to kiss her, Diana turned her head slightly. Kal looked at her surprised.

"What's wrong?"

"That's what I should be asking you." She frowned and pushed away from him. "I'm going to bed early."

"Diana?"

She rolled her eyes. "You are such a terrible liar."

"What are you talking about? I'm not lying about anything and you know I would never ever lie to you!"

"So why do you keep trying to change the subject or say don't worry about whatever this is?!"

"Because there isn't anything to worry about, Di." He tried to grab her hands but she yanked away. "Diana, trust me."

"That's all I've done!" she yelled in frustration. "But right now, I don't know! Tell...no...show me what you are hiding from me! Why have you been coming here alone?! Why has the League even been so secretive?! I'm trying to give you a chance to be honest and not use the lasso."

"Diana, come on. Right now, no, I can't. But I will in time. When it's the right time!"

"And when is that suppose to be?"

"Soon. I promise."

Diana rolled her eyes. "Soon? The last time you said soon was 3 weeks ago!"

"Diana...Starshine...please..."

Staring into her eyes, his heart broke. He couldn't tell her the truth. Months of planning, he couldn't ruin this for them.

Diana glared at him. "Ugh!"

She turned away from him, about to walk off.

"No, don't! Diana, I'm not letting you walk away from me!"

He grabbed her arm and yanked her back to him. Diana gasped and yelped when she felt a stinging slap on her ass and Kal groping her.

"Wha-?!"

He grabbed her by her chin and kissed her deeply.

THE DARK SPELL

"Don't you ever doubt my trust and honesty. Don't ever doubt my love for you," he said sternly staring deeply into her eyes.

Diana's heart skipped a beat, surprised by his actions.

"I love you so damn much, Diana. Trust me, Starshine. Trust me."

Before she could speak...or even blink, he had her stripped of her attire and thrown on the bed.

"Clark?!" She gasped seeing his eyes ablaze, his suit degenerating and her lasso in his hands.

"I would never hurt you, Di. Never lie. But what this is, it's very important. I can't tell nor show you right now. I won't. But eventually you will see. Be patient. I promise."

Diana nodded slowly just staring at him, anticipating his next move. She didn't even want to protest whatever he had in mind, curiosity getting the best of her. His demeanor as well, so assertive, sent a shockwave straight to her core.

His grip on the lasso tightened.

"That stubbornness of yours is sexy as hell but I can't have my Moon doubting me."

"Kal...I just didn't understand why-"

He shook his head. "Di, you doubted me." He gave her a sad puppy dog look.

Diana tried not to laugh and maintained her seriousness. "That look won't work on me."

"Diana, I know how much you like a challenge. I wasn't expecting it to be that easy."

"What are you...?"

Diana gasped as suddenly, she was flipped over. Kal quickly wrapped the lasso around her wrists, tying her up with her ass up in the air.

He spoke into her ear, "Never doubt me, Di. Never doubt us."

"I don't..."

"I love you," his voice, raw with emotion. "You are my Moon, my Starshine."

Diana whimpered, "Kal-El, what has gotten into you?"

"You think I would ever lie to you or hurt you?"

A sharp sting of his hand came across her supple ass.

"Kal!" She cried out and visibly shivered.

His hand came down on her ass again, followed by a series of smacks.

Diana heard him drag in a ragged breath as he skimmed his large hand across her ass.

"I'd never take for granted this luxury..." she heard him whisper, then...

SMACK!

Kal landed a punishing blow on her ass that caught her by surprise and she cried out "AHH!" gripping the lasso.

SMACK!

"CLARK!"

Diana looked back at him over her shoulder. His eyes were fiery red of lust and passion. He rubbed his hands up over the backs of her thighs, over her ass, her back and shoulders. His hands were rough, gripping, and tight on her body.

Kal leaned in and kissed her neck and a moan escaped her lips as she lost her breath. He slowly worked his way around to her front kissing along her neck, up to her ears, and across her eyes, nose, lips, chin and back to her other ear and back to her neck. Then he nuzzled into her hair. He could feel her tremble more with anticipation.

SMACK!

Diana bit her lip and groaned. More smacks came her way and she was finding this beyond erotic.

Kal laid kisses all around her perfect ass. Inching closer and closer to her womanhood but never touching it despite her best efforts to catch his lips on the way by. She jumped and moaned. The contrast between the gentle kisses and the spanking has got to be driving her insane.

SMACK!

Her ass was on fire and she was a mix of hot mess of anger, shock, arousal and... so, SO WET. She was so wet that it was starting to run down her legs now.

SMACK!

Kal landed this blow across both cheeks and Diana almost climaxed right then. He began to caress her ass again now, somewhat soothing the pain, then his hand drops lower, and his fingers find her dripping

THE DARK SPELL

womanhood. He said nothing, but Diana could hear the change in his breathing. He was as turned on as she was.

"I would never hold anything back from you, Di."

"Kal-El..." she groaned looking round at him, her eyes wide with desire and lust. She was in that zone where she was wanting to be pushed to her limits.

He struck her ass cheeks again causing her to yelp out at the shock and pain. He struck again and again, harder each time. She screamed out in a mix of pain and lust, thankful they weren't at the apartment where the neighbors could hear her cries. Although, they've already heard her a many, many times before.

Her cheeks became redder and redder with each strike and more painful yet still she craved more.

Eventually he stopped spanking her ass and looked at his work. Her reddened ass cheeks bent over the bed. He climbed up over her and roughly jabbed a finger in her tight ass.

"Oh Gods!" She gasped and moaned out loud yet again at this intrusion.

Through the fog of lust, she knew what was coming next. He worked his finger in sharply and roughly followed by a second finger. His fingers stretched her tightest hole as he worked them in and out. Suddenly they were out of her ass and she was left there exposed.

His lips kissed down the side of her neck as he whispered to her how much he loved her over and over. Diana was panting beneath him trying to get her mind back on track. Her hips were pressed tight against the bed with Kal's weight on her back.

When Diana turned and tilted her head, Kal kissed her mouth. His hands slid around her waist, one hand sliding down between her thighs sliding over her parted wet nether lips and stroking her clit hard and slow. Diana groaned into his mouth as she tried to suck gently on his tongue.

His other hand slide up her body gripping her breast as he ground his manhood into the crack of her round ass. Kal's hand slid even farther up and wrapped around the front of her throat. Diana moaned into his mouth as he made love to her mouth with his tongue. His hands are holding her ever so tightly against him.

After a few minutes, Kal pulled just enough to break the kiss.

Diana felt his hands again on her ass cheeks making her jolt. His hands roughly and firmly spread them apart. Next she felt the head of his hard member hot against her exposed hole. He pushed and pushed hard forcing his member into her tight hole. She screamed out loudly in a mixture of exquisite pain, pleasure, excitement and desire and braced herself. He pulled back alittle and pushed back in this time farther. She screamed again and continued to do so with every farther push into her ass. Eventually he worked his way as far into her as he could and now settled into a rhythm of thrusting as hard as he could.

"Kal! Beloved, please! Ahhh!" She pleaded through her gaze of desire and lust. "Arrgh!" she screamed out as she then felt his hand smack her ass cheek again.

"You don't know how much I love hearing you scream for me," he growled again followed by another smack on the other cheek.

"Oh...Clark, Kal..." she begged.

He brought his hand back again and spanked the same cheek again but this time harder. And even though the spanking stung combined with him relentlessly thrusting into her ass, it still turned her on and made her even more wet. She grunted everytime he made contact with her ass cheeks and his pace picked up, as she cried.

Kal felt Diana tremble as he leaned down and bit her neck right beneath her jaw. Diana moan deeply. She whimpered beneath him and rubbed her face against his rough jaw like a cat. Kal tongued her ear growling into it.

He pulled back on her hair making her scream again in desire. His other hand reached around and found her clit. She screamed in delight as he rubbed her clit furiously almost in time with the pounding of her ass.

Kal groaned, slamming into her. Diana knew he was heading for his climax. Her legs almost gave way as her long awaited orgasm started to rip through her body. She gripped the lasso as tight as she could as her orgasm built to a crescendo and wave after wave of pleasure rippled through her body.

Kal gasped and instantly shot his load inside her. Diana loved it as her eyes rolled back to her head and she moaned his name over and over.

THE DARK SPELL

He took a moment to recover and then Diana collapsed onto her front. Kal was still on top of her, tenderly kissed her neck, before he whispered in her ear with a raspy breath, "I love you, Di. I want you. Only you. Just like this and more...so much more. We've come too far...I would never jeopardize what we have."

Diana laid there breathing hard. Her body trembling violently. Kal laid on her and reached under her to grab her breasts. Diana lifted slightly to let him have them. After fondling her breasts for several moments, he all of a sudden pulled out of her ass. Diana gasped at the sensation of his member suddenly not being inside of her. He untied the lass and effortlessly flipped her onto her back. Diana gasped looking into his eyes. A mixture of seriousness yet so much intense love and care.

"Kal, I've never seen you like this."

"My Goddess was doubting me. So I need to show her how serious I am."

Diana breathed out slowly and reached to trail her hand down his abs. She gripped his manhood and stroked slowly, looking up at him sympathetically.

"Darling, I know you would never hurt me. I just...I was worried. We are a team, Kal. We shouldn't have to hold anything back from each other no matter what it is."

"I know that, Di. I promise you. It's something very, very good. But that's all I can say right now. You'll see. I promise."

Diana nodded. "Okay, Love. Okay..."

She reached up and wrapped her hand around the back of his neck and pull his 6 foot 4 inch frame down to kiss him. Kal draped his body over hers. Their tongues fight to touch as much of the other as they can.

Diana moaned into Kal's mouth as her body was pressed back into the bed. Kal's hands pinning hers above her head as he kissed her harder and deeper. She whimpered as his tongue thrusts into her mouth again and again, the feel of his teeth bruising her lips.

He growled into her lips as his hands slid down her arms. Diana shivered and opened her eyes to see him watching her intently... his eyes dark and demanding. One hand wrapped around the back of her head, tangling in her long hair as he wrapped it around his fist. Kal pulled her head back slowly while his other hand slid down her body.

Rough fingers caressed her neck and shoulder. He lowered his head and grazed his teeth over the line of her neck as his hand slid lower. Diana gasped as he palmed her breast and bit gently on her neck.

"Mmmmm Gods..."

She loved the feel of him over her body like this. Kal stroked his fingers through her hair as Diana was raking her nails lightly over his bare shoulders to grip her upper arms. Diana reached up and tugged his head back up to her mouth, groaning in excitement as he respond by crushing her with a kiss, his hands tightening on her body, holding her like he was afraid she might try to escape.

Diana nipped at his bottom lip and he growled again deep in his chest... a promise, a warning. That sound that made her heart race and her body tremble. His hand slid even lower, slowly, deliberately. Kal wanted her to know exactly what he had planned for her as he slid his hand over her stomach and push it between his thighs. His hand gripped the inside of her thigh and forced her legs open wider.

Diana was still so incredibly soaked, could barely breathe for wanting his touch so much.

"Mmmmmm..."

Diana parted her thighs and Kal bit her shoulder a bit roughly, making her arch into his hand. He slid his mouth over her skin and sucked her nipple into his mouth, grazing it with his teeth.

Diana cried out then look down to see him sucking on her nipple watching her face intently. As Diana looked at him, his eyes narrow and he slowly slid one thick strong finger between her soaking wet nether lips. Kal made a satisfied rumbling noise around her breast in his mouth and rubbed that finger harder, deeper into her womanhood. Diana's hands gripped his arms. Kal's other hand tightened in her hair, drawing her head back as he slowly slid his fingers between her lips, circling the opening of her womanhood, pressing slightly, but not letting her have more.

Diana parted her legs further, whimpering his name, begging, pleading, "Kal, please, please..."

THE DARK SPELL

She started to hump against his hand. He knew what she wanted, so he raised his head and look her directly in the eyes while he slid his finger in deep.

"Oh Gods... That feels so good..." she moaned low in her throat.

Kal pressed harder than pull out and penetrated her again hard and rough. Diana bit her lower lip and hung on to him. Kal's mouth clamped down on her other breast, sucking hard, demanding more as his fingered her slowly but deeply. Her womanhood tightened on his finger making him grin deviously. Diana drenched his hand and whimpered beneath him.

He immediately pressed another finger in her. Diana bucked beneath him, barely breathing but Kal kept pressing his fingers deeper, enjoying her small whimper. Diana tensed more with Kal being a bit more rough and she continued to drench him, thrusting herself back on his hand. Her nails were digging into his arms.

Kal thrust his fingers harder once, twice, before pulling out suddenly. Diana thrashed beneath him.

"Look at me, Di." His fingers tightening in her hair forcing her face to his. "Diana."

She opened her eyes slowly and gazed up at him. He look at her, her lips red and wet from his kiss, her eyes wide and pleading. He slid his two wet fingers in her mouth. Diana moaned around them and let him watch her suck on them. Kal growled deep and leaned in closer, his lips brushing her ear.

He held her head. His lips inches away from her lips and stare intently at her as his hand pushed between her legs again. Diana gazed into his eyes and gasped as she felt him pressing... pressing. His hand tightened in her hair holding her as he pressed into her womanhood.

Kal rumbled low in his chest. Diana moaned and part her legs wider.

He took that as an invitation and forced his three fingers in stretching her out, she still so tight.

Diana gasped, forgetting to breathe, then cried out beneath him. She groaned as he thrust hard, almost causing her to lift her hips off the bed. Her legs shaking. Diana buried her face in the side of his neck as he whispered roughly in her ear.

Three fingers pushing as deep as they could go while Kal held her down by her hair. Diana whimpered and started to beg him as he just kept thrusting over and over with his fingers.

"Oh GODS!"

Biting his shoulder, nails running down his back, begging him with her lips, her words, her body. Her womanhood milking his fingers.

"Kal!"

He growled and pulled his fingers free. Then he lines his manhood up with her womanhood before slowly pushing inside her. He lifted her legs for deeper access.

"Have me!" she seethed, her lust coming to a head as his head stretched her engorged, deep pink lips.

His gaze roved all over her body, his eyes thick with lust and love. He lifted her legs up higher in the air, almost perpendicular to her body but spread shoulder-width apart to use as leverage as he started his rhythm. Pulling almost all the way out, keeping just the tip of the head inside her warm, wet, snatched womanhood, then violently burying himself in her glorious depths to the hilt.

Repeat.

Savagely speeding up and slowing down, then speeding up again randomly & continually.

Diana kept her legs up, spread eagle as Kal reached up and started groping her breasts. He was driving her over the edge with long strokes in and out of her dripping womanhood.

He asked her again, "do you trust me?"

She nodded as her breasts bounced each time he bottom out in her.

He picked up the pace making sure to grind down on her clit when their hips met each time slowly but surely building her up to another powerful orgasm.

"You...are...my...Moon...Diana. Do...you...hear...me?" He demanded of her; each word punctuated by the slamming of their bodies meeting in carnal bliss.

"Yours..." she practically whispered.

Kal felt her shutter beneath him again, they're both completely lost to their own bodies at the moment. He felt every inch of her sex as it gripped

THE DARK SPELL

his length each time he slid into her again and again. He couldn't imagine a more heavenly feeling than this...

"Kal...my Love...OH GODS! Have me...Take me, Kal! Yes!"

Kal took that as his sign and slowly let his hand slip up around her neck. There was a little bit of surprise there in Diana's eyes, but she relaxed as his fingers pressed to the sides of her neck. This was definitely something she had never thought before but from the looks of it she did trust him to do everything he could to bring her pleasure, and he knew she would lose her mind from this.

She closed her eyes as his grip tightened at the edges of her neck. After a few seconds her eyes shot open again and this time had changed to lightning blue. Diana was closer than he'd thought. Her whole body started to convulse from a massive orgasm. Kal kept pounding into her, faster, harder, and maintained his hold on her neck. Diana came again, and her juices rushed over his member. Her chest and arms were all turning red with orgasmic flush. Kal was careful to be sure she could still breathe albeit with some restriction. She came again, and then her whole body went rigid. He kept thrusting into her as hard as he could then released his grip on her neck as her walls clamped down so hard on his length, he couldn't move.

"OOOOHHH...MY... GOOOOOODDDDDSSSS!" She screamed at the top of her lungs and her whole body locked around Kal's shuddering and milking him for all it was worth, as she gushed all over the two of them.

"C'mere, Di."

Kal suddenly pulled her up, her legs readily wrapped around his strong waist once again as he easily penetrated her even deeper. The way his eyebrows construed in a face of intense pleasure, the way his mouth went agape, the little and sweet murmuring under his breath as he made love to her was insanely euphoric and intimate, it only made the pleasure all that better. Diana knew then, when she was so entranced by the pleasure he was giving her and the way he was adorably loving the feel of her womanhood around his length, the way he was grasping her cheek gently even though he was roughly thrusting his pelvis against hers, they could never be with anyone else. They could never even look at anyone else when they had each other in their arms' reach. It was then when Diana was looking up into his eyes, both their faces contorted in extreme pleasure at each others touch, and her hands raking down his skin, did she climax the hardest she ever had through the night.

Diana was a mess as Kal continued bouncing her up and down on his thick length. It was so much stimulation that she was incoherently whimpering. As Kal chased his own orgasm, he spoke such dirty and raunchy words, she never knew he would say. It made her even more aroused and needy for another orgasm of her own again.

Every filthy word had her whimpering and moaning, clawing at him. Kal moved forward, and ground his pelvis against hers. Diana gasped sharply as he knowingly ground against her clit, and continued just to see her continue to writhe on him.

"Ahh, Clark!" she panted, gripping his shoulders tightly.

He stopped, holding himself inside her and ground upwards into her clit again. Diana moaned, tightly clenching around him as the over-stimulation overcame her. Diana heard him groaning deep in his chest as he started to climax. Kal hissed, and Diana felt the warm pumps of his essence filling her insides. She cried at the sensations, the whole thing being overwhelming. She leaned her forehead against his chest, whimpering and struggling to regain her breath. His hands rubbed her back up and down affectionately, his chin resting on the top of her head as he tried to regain his breath as well.

Softly, Kal laid her back down and made her look up at him. Their eyes slowing going back to normal. Diana was in a daze, both of them were as they looked at each other. Kal bent down, kissing her deeply. Diana moaned into the kiss, feeling spent, yet somehow wanting... more. Gods, she was insatiable when it came to him. He pulled away, leaning downwards and kissing her neck. Diana exhaled somewhat harshly, holding him close by his torso.

They spent what felt like eternity kissing, nuzzling, smiling as they cuddled close in their now messy, sex drenched bed.

At one point, Diana giggled lazily and looked up at him with a raised brow, "I can't believe what we just did...what you just did to me. I had no idea..." She trailed off questioning what she had just enjoyed.

"You bring things out of me I never knew either," He murmured against her cheek.

THE DARK SPELL

Diana bit her lip with a smile. "I like how you were being so...assertive, a little rough around the edges and I still felt a little bit of that gentleness you always have with me."

"You liked that?" He coyly asked. "Well I'm glad you did but I told you I would never hurt you. I just want to show you all the love I have for you, Di."

"Oh, you definitely showed me and more."

Kal chuckled lowly, and Diana giggled again.

Their fingers intertwined on both hands, squeezing and slightly letting go as they spoke, their attention on each other.

"It will be very uncomfortable to sit for a few days," Diana teased raising her brow.

"I admit I got carried away. Enjoyed that maybe a bit too much but that's your fault," he playfully retorted grinning boyishly.

"What?! How?"

"Gorgeous sight watching it move."

"You're so silly!" Diana laughed before leaning up to give him another kiss.

Kal groaned before pulling away, his hand moving to caress her cheek as he suddenly went serious. "You know, I did mean all those things I said. I love you. I don't want you to ever doubt me. Always trust me, Di."

"I know, Darling, I know," she softly said, biting her lip in remembrance of the words.

"When the time is right, which will be soon, you're going to see why it was worth the wait."

"Um...I guess I can have a little fun guessing in the mean time. My birthday is a ways away so no surprise birthday party. Though, I can always be in my birthday suit for you anyway."

Kal raised a brow as Diana grinned up at him, and he roughly kissed her again. He pressed her against him, and bit her bottom lip before pulling away with another groan.

"This is exactly why I can't get enough of you."

"Feeling is very mutual, Beloved!"

They held each other for a good while. Their emotions started to abate, they looked up and she leaned forward and kissed him. Their tongues danced furiously almost as if Diana was desperate to taste him. Kal found his hand working its way down to her still wet and overly sensitive womanhood. He glide his fingers over her ever so gently, which elicited a whiny moan of pleasure and she smiled knowingly.

2 weeks later...9:30 A.M. - Clark and Diana's apartment

Morning Starshine,

Had to leave early. Breakfast and tea already ready for you. I'll talk to you later.

Love you!

-Clark

Diana smiled at the note Clark left her as she sat down at the table with her tea and breakfast.

She was trying to call him but his phone went straight to voicemail. He was probably in a meeting. She glanced at the time, needing to get going for her own meeting.

She quickly got herself ready to head to the Embassy.

2.5 hours later....U.N. Embassy

"I believe it's best we find more ways for school funding instead of taking short cuts with settling for books with missing pages or just barely handing inside the covers. The children are the future of this world. They need all resources to make what needs to be possible possible. I speak this not only as an Ambassador but as an Educator as well."

Senator Herschel cleared his throat. "Well, Ambassador Prince...you've made your stance quite clear."

"I have," she said as a matter of factor raising her brow.

"Um... alright. We will need a draft to send to all boards across the nation. We will also need to make sure this is financially viable."

"Senator, it will be viable if the funds are secure instead of board members selfishly taking from the children. How many scandals has there been within the last few years... even recently within months?"

"You are right. It's a shame how things have been swept under the rug," Counselor Annette Pollard agreed. "Ms. Prince has made quite a lot of valid points that we should take into consideration."

"Thank you, Mrs. Pollard."

THE DARK SPELL

Annette nodded. "Well we are already running over time. We will be having this unnecessary debate all night if we continue. But I think we have addressed everything. Though, we will need to schedule another meeting possibly in a month. So see you all then."

Leaving out of the conference room, Diana checked her phone and there was no missed calls or texts as she usually would've had. She tried calling Clark again but his phone went straight to the voicemail.

"Darling, call me as soon as you can. I hope you didn't forget to charge your phone again. And your other communication device is off as well."

She quickly went to her office.

"Victor? Victor, are you there?" She called from her communicator.

"Sup, Wondy?"

"Have you heard from Kal?"

"Oh...uh...been offline since yesterday."

"Oh, could you tr-"

"Oh...uh...Gotta go."

"Victor? Victor?"

She frowned. "How strange."

She tried calling Dinah, Mari, Arthur, Barry, and Bruce and nothing from them either.

"Bruce, if you hear anything from Clark, call me. I'm about to leave the Embassy heading to Clark's office then the Fortress."

Diana hung up the phone and gathered her things to leave. She closed and locked her office door and was quickly walking to the elevator.

"Diana! Diana, wait!"

She turned around surprised. "What? Donna?"

"Hey, sis! Damn, you walk way too fast in heels."

"Sorry, I'm in a hurry. I haven't heard from Kal all morning and I'm worried."

"He's a grown man. He can take care of himself." Donna waved her hand.

Diana raised her brow. "You know something don't you?"

"Huh? Know what?"

"Donna, don't try to play with my intelligence."

Donna laughed. "Calm down, Diana."

"I'm not laughing, Donna." Diana folded her arms. "Now, where is he? What have you two been up to?"

Donna sighed and rolled her eyes. "Diana, come on..."

"Both of you and the entire league has been keeping something from me and I have the right to know." Diana started looking through her bag. "You have 5 seconds or I'll..."

"You'll what? Use your lasso on me?" Donna smirked.

"Don't be a smart-" Diana was still looking in her bag. "Where is it?!"

"Diana, it's not in there and you don't need it anyway. Now let's stop with the 21 questions. You may get all your answers if we get going now. You are going to make us late for the ceremony."

"Ceremony? What ceremony?"

"Oh, Sis, you really need to get more organized." Donna pushed Diana into the elevator.

"What? I don't know anything about a ceremony."

Donna laughed. "We just need to hurry up to Themyscira."

Location: Themyscira

"Hurry up, Diana. We need to sneak into your room."

"Why?"

"You can't be seen not dressed. Now, come on!"

Diana and Donna snuck into Diana's room through her balcony.

Once in Diana's room, she immediately noticed a note and a dress garment bag. She walked over and picked up the note.

My Diana,

It's time. I'm sorry for all the waiting but this had to be perfect for you...for us.

-Clark

"Donna?" Diana turned around to see her grinning. "What is going on?"

"Just hurry up and get ready, Diana."

45 minutes after...

"Okay...I'm ready..."

Donna gasped standing up from sitting on the edge of the bed.

"Oh wow! Diana that dress is phenomenal!"

THE DARK SPELL

Diana was wearing a sexy charmeuse one shoulder sleeveless high split mermaid/trumpet gown with a court Train and crystals slit embellishment.

"It really is gorgeous!"

Suddenly, the door opened with Hippolyta walking in.

"Oh, my Dear daughter!" Hippolyta embraced her daughter. "I'm so proud of you! Lovely!"

"Mother, I'm sorry for not knowing of this ceremony. There's no excuse to my respons-"

Hippolyta shook her head and smiled. "It is alright. Are you ready now?"

"Yes, I'm ready. I mean as far as being completely dressed. But is there anything I need that you know of?"

"Let's go, Dear."

Diana, Hippolyta, Donna, and two Amazonian guards walked down to the shore.

Diana gasped surprised when she saw all her Amazon sisters and the Justice League.

"What are you all doing here?!"

Dinah was the first to hug her.

"Diana, you are drop dead gorgeous!"

"Thank you!"

"I'm still so surprised all of you are here!"

Mari, Mera and Zatanna hugged her.

"Finally!" They said in unison.

As Diana was walking through, they were smiling and moving aside.

"Diana," Bruce gave a slight nod.

"Wow! That's the most happy emotion Brucie could muster," Hal said sarcastically.

Diana continued walking until she saw the Kents.

"Martha?! Jonathan?!" She gasped. "I- wha?"

They smiled and embraced her.

Diana was so full of emotions. She closed her eyes for a moment embracing them back.

"Diana."

She opened her eyes to see Kal floating above them smiling.

He was dressed in an over the shoulder toga and cape with a golden headband, his insignia engraved in it.

She smiled back. "Kal?"

The Kents stepped aside nodding to their son. Kal held out his hand for Diana to take. When Diana took his hand, she noticed he was trembling a bit.

Kal pulled her close and kissed her softly on the lips. "You're breathtaking."

"Thank you, Love. And I can't get enough of you wearing your toga."

He held her hand tighter. "I'm nervous as hell right now," he laughed.

"What is this, Love?" she smiled wider and titled her head slightly.

Kal took a deep breath. "For months I've been planning this and it's finally happening. I want to thank our family and friends for helping me, being supportive of us and being here right now as our witnesses and sharing this moment. I know keeping this a secret was hard for some of you. Hell, I couldn't even hold it half the time." Kal reached up and caressed Diana's cheek. "Those late nights of being at the Fortress alone, those moments of... changing the subject...that promise I made, Di. Remember that night?"

She blushed. "I could never forget that."

"I meant what I said then and now..." He kneeled down on one knee and revealed her lasso wrapping it around his hand. "Diana, it's been a long journey for us. An unexpected twist we went through together but we caught through it all and it's been all worth it for us to be brought to this moment right here. I love you, Princess Diana of Themyscira, Diana Prince, Wonder Woman. I love all the woman that you are."

Tears welled up in Diana's eyes.

Donna stepped over and handed Kal a ring box. Kal looked back up at Diana opening the box revealing a beautifully crafted engagement ring. A unique white gold vintage floral infinity twist with an oval cut moonstone diamond.

"Oh by Gods!" Diana gasped.

"That is one big shiny rock! It must cost like a bazillion dollars!" Billy whispered to Victor.

THE DARK SPELL

"Definitely more than what Bruce and Oliver has combined," Victor stated.

"No way!"

"Quiet," Bruce said sternly.

"Oh yeah... it's totally true."

"I took my time to make sure this ring was perfect. It combines who we are, creating something new. The gemstones were gifted from your mother, preserved from what my biological Father, Jor-El gave to my mother, Lara, and one of the rings Ma has had that has been past down for generations. I want to continue this journey with you. So will you do me the honour of being my wife?"

Kal looked into her eyes and he was mesmerised by all the love and happiness he found. Diana had a that gorgeous smile on her face that he loved so much and tears were now streaming uncontrollably down her face.

Diana caught her breath, nodding. "Yes! Oh, Gods! Yes, of course, my Beloved!" she answered without a moment hesitation.

He slipped the ring on her finger and as he was standing up, Diana threw her arms around him. Lips intertwined, in a passionate loving kiss, Kal picked her up and spun her around.

They could hear the cheerful claps from everyone.

After a little while they parted, laughing with absolute joy. Diana giggled and held tightly to her now fiancé.

"I can't believe this..." Diana whispered then looked down as she trailed her hands to his chest. "You did this for me...for us and I...for weeks I...I'm sorry, Love."

Kal shook his head and took her hands in his. He lifted their joined hands to his lips.

"I told you, it was all worth it especially with seeing that gorgeous smile and you saying yes is all I need. I love you so much!"

"I love you, too! Gods, I love you!"

Kal caressed her cheek with one hand and kissed her breathless. Diana returned his kiss with everything she had. Sharing a long, tender kiss, basking in the happiness. The engagement ring sparkling as bright as the sun between their entwined finger.

AUTHOR NOTE

Thank you for reading this story, I hope you enjoyed it as much as i did writing it for you. The concluding part of the story will be in the next edition of this book attached to it as a series, hopefully, it would have been released by the time you are reading this. I will really love your feedback so i will have my eyes on my email inbox, so, therefore, please kindly use the comment section of where you purchased this book from to place your reviews, suggestion and ratings for this book for it will help me improve the forth coming stories that are yet to be released. You can contact me the author via my email (viaoptimisticdaily@gmail.com).

Printed in Great Britain
by Amazon